WHEN WE CLOSE OUR EYES

LACI MAE WYLD

Contents

Chapter One

orning light sliced through the dusty blinds of the Preston kitchen, casting thin golden bars across the peeling wallpaper. Casey moved with the quiet efficiency of someone who had learned that noise could shatter more than just silence. Her fingers, red and chapped from too much cleaning with too little lotion, reached for the carton of eggs with the careful precision of a bomb technician. The bruises on her forearms—purple-blue islands against her pale skin—throbbed in time with her heartbeat as she cracked the first egg against the bowl's edge.

The Kitchen bore witness to their dwindling circumstances. Linoleum curled at the corners like dying leaves, revealing the subflooring beneath. Dishes from last night's dinner balanced in a precarious tower in the sink, a monument to exhaustion. Casey had meant to wash them after getting her father to bed, but by then, her body had betrayed her with bone-deep fatigue that no amount of coffee could remedy.

She whisked the eggs, the soft rhythmic sound barely audible over the house's early morning creaks. The refrigerator hummed an off-key note, as if in sympathy. A thin layer of dust coated the tops of cabinets she could no longer reach without feeling dizzy from raising her arms too high. The bruise on her left shoulder blade, hidden beneath her faded t-shirt, testified to yesterday's attempt to retrieve the good mixing bowl from the top shelf. Her father had been having a good day until he wasn't.

The butter sizzled in the pan, releasing a warm, rich scent that momentarily masked the underlying smell of neglect. Casey closed her eyes and inhaled deeply, allowing herself precisely three seconds of pleasure before returning to the task at hand. The toast popped up, slightly burnt around the edges, but she didn't have time to make more. The clock on the microwave blinked an incorrect time – she'd given up resetting it after the last power outage. Another item on a list that grew faster than she could manage.

"Dad?" she called softly, transferring the scrambled eggs to a chipped blue plate that had once been part of a matching set. "Breakfast is ready."

She had already heard him moving about in his bedroom, the shuffle of slippers against hardwood a morning ritual she had learned to listen for. It meant he had managed to dress himself, a good sign for how the day might unfold.

Elliot Preston entered the kitchen like a man wading through invisible currents. His once commanding frame now carried a slight stoop, as though his shoulders bore weights only he could see. His green eyes, still startlingly bright in his weathered face, darted around the room, cataloguing and confused all at once.

"Morning, Dad," Casey said, the corners of her mouth lifting in a smile that cost her more than she would admit. "I made your favourite. Scrambled with cheese, just how you like."

Elliot settled into his chair with a grunt, his gaze falling on the plate before him with a mix of suspicion and hunger. "Is the paper here yet?" he asked, his voice carrying the ghosts of it's former authority.

"Not yet," Casey answered, the lie smooth from repetition. They hadn't been able to afford the newspaper subscription for months now, not to mention it would set him off. "Coffee? Or juice this morning?"

"Juice," he muttered, attention already drifting. "Need to watch the news."

Casey poured the orange juice into a plastic cup—she'd learned that lesson after the third broken glass—and set it carefully beside his plate. The news isn't on yet, Dad. It's still early." She kept her voice light, casual, as if discussing the weather rather than navigating the minefield of his confusion.

"It's only six-fifteen now," Casey explained, sitting down across from him with her own meagre portion. Her stomach knotted with familiar dread. The morning had been going so well.

"Don't lie to me," Elliot snapped, the sudden sharpness in his voice making Casey's fork pause halfway to her mouth. "I know what time my programs are on."

She set her fork down, food forgotten. "You're right, I'm sorry. Let me check again." She made a show of looking at her watch. "My mistake. But we still have a little while before it starts. Why don't you eat while we wait?"

Elliot's eyes narrowed, scepticism etching deeper lines around his mouth. "You think I don't know? You think I am confused?" His voice rose with each question, the tremor in his hands increasing. "I taught history for thirty years. Thirty years! I never missed a class, never showed up unprepared."

"I know, Dad, you were the best teacher at Oakridge

High." Casey reached across the table, her fingers stopping just short of his clenched fist. "Everyone says so."

"Then why are you treating me like I don't know what time it is?" The question emerged as a wounded roar. His arm swept outward in frustration, catching the plastic cup. It toppled, spilling orange juice across the table in a slow-motion flood that Casey watched with resigned familiarity.

The liquid reached the edge and dripped onto Elliot's lap. The shock of cold wetness against his pants triggered something—a connection between action and consequence that dementia had frayed but not completely severed. His expression crumpled from anger to dismay.

"Look what you made me do." He whispered, voice small and bewildered.

Casey was already moving, grabbing the dish towel that perpetually hung from her back pocket. "It's okay, Dad. Just an accident." Her tone was the verbal equivalent of a gentle hand on a fevered brow. "No harm done."

She dabbed at the spill, her movements economical and practised. This dance was so familiar that she could perform it with her eyes closed—identify the crisis, defuse the emotion, clean the mess, reset for the next inevitable spillage of one kind or another.

As she worked, she felt Elliot's gaze on her arms, on the constellation of bruises that told their own story. Something shifted in his expression, a momentary clearing, like clouds parting to reveal a patch of blue sky.

"Did I do that?" he asked, his finger hovering near but not touching the darkest bruise, a plum-coloured bloom just above her wrist.

Casey hesitated, truth and mercy at war in her throat. "It doesn't matter," she said finally, the words soft with forgiveness he couldn't remember needing. "It doesn't hurt."

Elliot's eyes filled with tears, a flash flood of lucidity

and remorse. "I would never hurt you, Casey-girl. You know that, don't you? I would never…"

"I know, Dad." She squeezed his hand, feeling the bones beneath his papery skin, so fragile now. "Why don't you try some of your eggs? They're getting cold."

The moment passed as quickly as it had come. Elliot blinked, confusion settling back over his features like a familiar blanket. "Is the news on yet?" he asked, his voice once again petulant and demanding, all trace of the brief recognition gone.

Casey straightened, tossing the soaked towel into the sink with the rest of the dishes that would wait until later. "Soon," she promised, turning away so he wouldn't see the weariness that threatened to pull her under like a riptide. "Very soon."

CASEY TUCKED THE WORN AFGHAN AROUND HER FATHER'S legs, making sure the remote control rested within easy reach on the arm of his chair. The morning news anchor's voice filled the living room, a professional murmur that seemed to pacify Elliot more effectively than any medication. His eyes fixed on the screen, momentarily anchored to reality by the familiar rhythm of headlines and weather forecasts. Only when she was certain he had settled into the hypnotic blue glow did Casey back away, each step measured and silent, as if retreating from a sleeping predator she didn't wish to wake.

The bathroom door closed behind her with a soft click that felt like thunder in her ears. She leaned against it, eyes closed, lungs expanding with the first full breath she'd taken since waking. This six-by-eight room with its water-stained ceiling and outdated fixtures had become her sanctuary, the only space where she didn't need to maintain constant vigilance. Casey allowed herself thirty seconds of this stillness—she'd learned to count the moments of peace, to parcel them out like precious rations.

When she finally opened her eyes, the mirror above the sink offered no comfort. A stranger stared back, a woman aged beyond recognition. Casey leaned closer, fingertips tracing the contours of her reflection as if trying to find the person she used to be beneath this new cartography of exhaustion. Dark half-moons curved beneath eyes that had once sparkled with ambition and promise. Her brown hair, pulled back in a hasty bun, revealed strands of premature grey at her temples. Twenty-six going on fifty, she thought bitterly.

She peeled off her t-shirt with the careful movements of someone undressing for a medical examination. The cotton fabric caught on her skin, tacky with dried sweat and the orange juice that had splashed her during break-fast. Fresh bruises bloomed alongside yellowing older ones, a grotesque garden spreading across her forearms. The newest addition—a dark purple stain just below her left elbow—throbbed when she pressed it gently. Yesterday's incident had been worse than usual. Her father had mistaken her for an intruder, his confusion rapidly esca-lating to panic and then violence before she could calm him.

Casey turned on the cold water, soaking a washcloth and pressing it against a tender spot. The shock of the cold made her hiss through her clenched teeth, but the relief that followed was immediate, if temporary. As she adjusted the cloth, her gaze fell on the stack of envelopes piled haphazardly on the counter, each one bearing the same ominous red stamp: FINAL NOTICE.

She picked up the top envelope with her free hand, though she already knew its contents by heart. The electric company wasn't interested in explanations about early-onset dementia or the impossibility of balancing caregiving with employment. They wanted their payment, and the threat of darkness loomed larger with each passing day.

Six months ago, Casey had sat in her supervisor's office, resignation letter trembling in her hands. She remembered the concerned furrow between the woman's eyebrows, the sincere offer to consider part-time options, the reluctance to lose a promising young graphic designer. But part-time wouldn't have been enough – not with her father's condition deteriorating so rapidly, not with the incidents becoming more frequent and dangerous. The memory of her desk – the careful arrangement of succulents and colour swatches, the photos of friends pinned to her bulletin board – now seemed like artifacts from someone else's life, preserved in a museum of what might have been.

Her phone buzzed from her pocket, the vibration so unexpected that she nearly dropped the washcloth. Casey extracted it with damp fingers, leaving smudges on the screen as she swiped to unlock it. A text message banner showed briefly — not a personal message, just her phone carrier reminding her that her bill was due. She scrolled through her messages anyway, a masochistic inventory of fading connections.

Three weeks since Megan had asked how she was doing.

Five weeks since her former coworkers had invited her to happy hour.

Two months since anyone had called just to talk.

The conversation threads tapered off like dying breaths—her increasingly delayed responses growing shorter, their check-ins becoming less frequent until silence settled like dust. She couldn't blame them. Who wanted to hear about adult diapers and medication schedules, about the way her father sometimes called her by her mother's name, about how she'd become adept at dodging his flailing fists when the confusion turned to terror?

The small calendar hanging beside the medicine cabinet told a similar story. June was a graveyard of crossed-out events – coffee dates, a concert, her friend Taylor's birthday dinner. Early on, she'd made earnest promises to herself about maintaining some semblance of social life, but reality had eroded those intentions. The spontaneous cancellations when her father refused to be left with the part-time aide she could barely afford had eventually led to fewer invitations. The small X marks were tombstones for the life she'd once had, for the woman who had existed before becoming primarily a caregiver.

Through the thin bathroom wall, she could hear the news transitioning to a commercial, the sudden increase in volume triggering a restless shuffle from her father's chair. The floorboards creaked as he shifted his. Weight, followed by the familiar muttering that signalled growing disorientation. Casey closed her eyes, listening intently for clues about which way his mood might swing. The water continued to run, forgotten until it reached her wrist with its cold shock.

She turned off the faucet and hung the washcloth on the edge of the sink, watching water droplets race each other to the drain. The bathroom smelled of generic soap and the lingering chemical sweetness of cleaning products – antiseptic and impersonal, like a hospital room. Casey wondered when she'd last used her favourite vanilla lotion or spent more than three minutes washing her hair. Self-care had become utilitarian, reduced to the bare minimum required for hygiene.

Her phone buzzed again – a reminder she'd set for her father's medication. In the mirror, Casey watched herself transform, straightening her shoulders and smoothing her features into a mask of capable composure. She pulled her sleeve down to cover the worst of the bruises, a practiced gesture of concealment. No one would see them anyway – there were no visitors, no concerned friends dropping by with casseroles and sympathy. Just her and Elliot, trapped together in this house that was slowly decaying around them, a physical manifestation of their dwindling resources.

"Coming, Dad," she called through the door, hearing his restlessness increase. Her voice emerged stronger than she felt, carrying a reassurance she didn't believe. She gathered up the bills and shoved them into the drawer beneath the sink, burying them beneath a tangle of old hair ties and dried-out tubes of lipstick – remnants of the woman she used to be.

Casey pressed her palms against her eyes for one final moment of privacy, feeling the burning threat of tears she couldn't afford to shed. Then she straightened up, unlocked the bathroom door, and stepped back into her role, the short reprieve already fading like morning dew under a relentless sun.

Chapter Two

*a*fternoon light spilled through the kitchen window like honey, thick and golden as it pooled across the scarred wooden table. Casey sat with her spine pressed against the hard chair back, a battered shoebox open before her like a time capsule unearthed. Outside, the world had softened into the drowsy hush that followed lunch, the neighbourhood settling into its afternoon rhythm. Through the thin walls, Elliot's snores rose and fell in a comforting metronome of deep sleep – the only time his face truly relaxed, years and confusion temporarily smoothed away by unconsciousness.

Casey's fingers hovered over the box, hesitant. These excavations into the past always left her raw, like picking at a wound that never quite healed. Yet she found herself drawn to these photographs with increasing frequency, as if confirming that the man in the other room had once been someone else entirely – someone who existed beyond disease and dependency.

The cardboard box itself was a relic, its corners soft with age, the lid bearing the ghostly outline of where a price sticker had been removed decades ago. Her father had kept their family photos in this same container for as long as she could remember, organising them with the methodical precision he'd applied to lesson plans and lecture notes. Now the careful chronology had been disrupted by Casey's previous forays, the timeline jumbled like her father's memories.

She lifted the top photo gingerly, its edges softened by countless handlings. Elliot Preston stood in front of a blackboard covered with his distinctive handwriting, chalk dust powdering the sleeve of his tweed jacket. His posture was straight, confident, one hand gesturing toward some historical date now erased by time and circumstance. The photographer had captured him mid-sentence, his eyes bright with enthusiasm, mouth curved in the particular smile that emerged only when he discussed history – as if sharing secrets of old friends rather than reciting facts about strangers.

"Mr Preston's class is tough, but worth it," his students used to say, their complaints carrying undertones of respect. Casey remembered walking the halls of Oakridge High during parent-teacher conferences, watching how other teachers deferred to her father, how students straightened their posture when he passed. That authority now existed only in fading Kodak prints and yearbook pages.

Beneath that photo lay another – Elliot standing hip-deep in river water, holding a fishing rod in one hand and guiding Casey's much smaller hands with the other. She couldn't have been more than nine, her face a study in fierce concentration beneath a too large fishing hat. The memory unspooled with cinematic clarity: the cold rush of water against her shins, the earthy perfume of the riverbank mud, her father's patient voice explaining how to feel for the subtle pull that signalled a fish considering the bait.

"Fishing isn't just about catching fish, Casey-girl," he'd told her, using the nickname that had been absent from his vocabulary for months now except during brief moments of clarity. "It's about learning to wait, to pay attention to everything around you. The birds, the insects on the water – they're all telling you something if you know how to listen."

Casey traced the outline of their figures with a fingertip that trembled slightly. Those camping trips had been sacred in their household, three-day excursions where Elliot taught her to read compass directions, to identify edible plants, to build fires that would burn steadily through the night. He'd seemed invincible then – capable of navigating any wilderness, solving any problem, answering any question she could possibly formulate.

The next photograph slid out from beneath a small stack, capturing Casey in cap and gown, clutching her college diploma with one hand while her other arm wrapped around her father's shoulders. Elliot beamed with undisguised pride, his chest puffed out as if he, rather than Casey, had completed the graphic design degree. She remembered his voice booming across the crowded auditorium when her name was called, the mixture of embarrassment and love that had warmed her cheeks. Later that evening, he'd given her the silver pendant she still wore – a small artist's palette that he'd saved up for months to purchase.

"Your mother would have been so proud." He 'd said, voice husky with emotion.

The memory struck Casey with physical force, a sharp pain beneath her ribs. She set the photo down carefully and pressed her palms against the table's surface, anchoring herself against the tide of grief that threatened to pull her under. The musty smell of the old photographs mingled with the lingering scent of the soup she'd made for lunch, creating a strange perfume of past and present colliding.

Beyond the kitchen window, children's voices filtered in – neighbouring kids enjoying the weekend freedom that remained unchanged despite everything else. Their shouts and laughter floated through the glass like visitors from another dimension, reminders of a world that continued to spin while Casey's had narrowed to the four walls containing her father.

The house creaked and settled around her, its aging joints protesting the afternoon heat. The sound had frightened her as a child—ghostly footsteps, she'd thought, until her father explained about wood expanding and contracting, turning fear into fascination with his teacher's knack for making everything a learning opportunity. Now she found comfort in these sounds, their familiar patterns a constant in a life where constants had become precious and rare.

Casey lifted another photograph, this one slightly out of focus—Elliot at the head of their Thanksgiving table three years ago, carving the turkey with ceremonial precision. His hands were steady then, his movements confident. The contrast between those capable hands and his trembling, uncertain ones that now struggled with buttons and silverware made Casey's throat tighten. How quickly it had all changed, a landslide rather than an erosion.

She'd noticed the first signs even then, though she'd attributed them to normal aging – the repeated stories, the misplaced keys, the occasional confusion about dates. By the time the diagnosis came, the disease had already staked its claim, establishing footholds in the geography of Elliot's mind, redrawing boundaries and reclaiming territories once firmly under his control.

Across the hall, the rhythm of Elliot's breathing changed, the deep snores giving way to restless movements. Casey stilled, tuning her senses to the sounds like a mother monitoring a baby's sleep. Not waking yet, just shifting positions. She had perhaps twenty more minutes before he would emerge, disoriented and anxious, needing her steady presence to reorient him to time and place.

Her gaze returned to the scattered photographs, these paper windows into a past that Elliot could no longer access. Sometimes she described the memories to him, using the photos as prompts, but increasingly he responded with blank stares or agitation, unable to recognise himself in these frozen moments. The disconnect between the vibrant, articulate man who had raised her and the confused, sometimes violent stranger who wore his face was a grief that renewed itself daily, an endless cycle of loss.

A tear slipped from Casey's cheek and landed on one of the photos—a perfect, glistening sphere that distorted Elliot's smile beneath its lens. She quickly brushed it away, checking to ensure it hadn't damaged the image. These photographs were more than mementos now; they were evidence of a truth that sometimes seemed impossible to believe: that Elliot Preston had once been whole, that the disease that consumed him was the intruder, not the essence of who he was.

From the living room came the distinctive creak of the recliner's footrest being lowered. Casey began gathering the photographs with careful hands, retuning them to their cardboard home with the reverence of a curator preserving irreplaceable artifacts. Which, in many way, they were – artifacts of a man who existed now only in her memory and these fading images.

From the living room came the distinctive creak of the recliner's footrest being lowered. Casey began gathering the photographs with careful hands, returning them to their cardboard home with the reverence of a curator preserving irreplaceable artifacts. Which, in many ways, they were – artifacts of a man who existed now only in her memory and these fading images.

As she replaced the lid on the shoebox, Casey felt something crystalize within her – not exactly peace, but a strengthening of resolve, like steel being tempered in fire. The exhaustion remained, as did the fear and grief that had become her constant companions. But beneath it all pulsed the certainty that what she did mattered, that preservation of her father's dignity was worth every sacrifice, every bruise, every crossed-out social engagement and unpaid bill.

She slid the box onto its shelf just as Elliot called out – a questioning sound that carried notes of confusion and nascent panic. Casey straightened her shoulders and moved toward the sound, her steps sure despite her weariness. There would be more difficult moments before the day ended, more challenges that would test her endurance and patience. But for now, she carried the images of who her father had been like a talismans against the darkness, bright anchors in a storm that showed no signs of abating.

Chapter Three

*T*he evening descended upon the Preston home like a heavy blanket, muffling the world outside while trapping stale air within. Casey sat on the edge of the sofa, her body angled toward the television but her attention fixed on her father. The blue light from the screen played across Elliots features, casting shadows that deepened the hollows of his cheeks and temples, momentarily disguising the man he had become with the glimpses of the man he had been.

Elliot leaned forward in his recliner, eyes narrowed with the intense concentration he once reserved for grading papers or planning lessons. His fingers curled around the armrests, knuckles white with tension as the news anchor delivered the day's headlines with practiced gravity. These evening broadcasts had become sacred rituals, the familiar faces and voices on screen providing Elliot with anchors to a rapidly dissolving reality.

"They are saying rain tomorrow," Casey offered, her voice carefully modulated—not too loud, not too soft— the way she might approach a skittish animal. "Maybe we could use some. The garden's looking dry."

Elliot grunted, neither agreement nor dismissal, his gaze unwavering from the screen. These moments of absorbed focus were precious, allowing Casey to exhale fully, to release the vigilance that had become as automatic as breathing. She watched him from the corner of her eye as she pretended to read the paperback novel splayed open in her lap, its pages unturned for the past twenty minutes.

The news segment transitioned to a commercial, then to an evening game show—bright colours, enthusiastic applause, a host with too-white teeth and exaggerated gestures. Casey felt her muscles tense instinctively, anticipating the disruption before it came. The change in programming was a hairline fracture in the evening's fragile peace.

Elliot's breathing changed first − deeper, more deliberate − followed by a slight forward tilt of his head, the furrowing of his brow. Casey marked her place in the book she hadn't been reading and set it aside, mentally preparing for what might come.

"Where's the news?" Elliot asked, his voice sharp with confusion.

"It just finished, Dad," Casey answered, the explanation one she had delivered countless times before. "That was the six o'clock broadcast. It's almost seven-thirty now."

Elliot turned toward her, his expression a battlefield of emotions—bewilderment advancing, comprehensions retreating. "No, no. The national news. I always watch the national new at seven."

Casey nodded, acknowledging his certainty without challenging it. "You're right, you usually do, but they changed the schedule recently. The national news comes on at six now." The lie was harmless, a small mercy compared to the truth that his internal clock had slipped its gears, that time no longer moved in orderly progression but jumped erratically, hours and even days collapsing or expanding without warning.

"That's ridiculous." Elliot muttered, reaching for the remote control with trembling fingers. "They've had the same schedule for decades, why would they change it now?"

Casey watched his frustration build as he jabbed at the remote buttons, cycling through channels with increasing agitation. Each press of his thumb seemed more forceful than the last, his breathing growing more laboured with each unfamiliar program that appeared on the screen.

"Maybe we could watch something else tonight," she suggested, keeping her tone light and conversational. "There's that documentary about World War II you liked." Another fabrication – they had never watched such a program together, but history had always been his passion, a potential bridge back to calmer waters.

"I don't want a documentary," Elliot snapped, the remote now clutched in a white-knuckled grip. "I want the news. How am I supposed to know what's happening if I can't watch the news?"

Casey shifted slightly, creating additional distance between them without making the movement obvious. Her sleeve rode up as she adjusted her position, revealing a bracelet of yellowing bruises around her wrist – souvenirs from three days ago when she'd tried to help him out of the bath.

"Let me see if I can find something similar." She offered, extending her hand toward the remote without actually reaching for it. "There might be a local news broadcast on one of the other stations."

"I'm not a child," Elliot growled, his voice deepening with indignation. "I know what I watch and when I watch it. The news comes on at seven. It's always been that way."

The muscles in Casey's jaw tightened, a dull ache

spreading from her temples down her neck. She deliberately unclenched her teeth, forcing her shoulders to lower from where they had crept up toward her ears. "I understand, Dad, you're absolutely right. Let's check the TV guide to see what might have happened to the schedule."

She reached for the TV guide they no longer subscribed to, her hand moving toward the empty space on the coffee table where it used to lie. The gesture, half-theater and half-habit, froze midway as Elliot's face contorted with sudden rage.

"Stop lying to me!" The words exploded from him, his face flushing with blood and anger. "You think I don't know what you're doing? You think I don't see right through you?"

Casey's heart hammered against her ribs, adrenaline flooding her system in a familiar cold rush. "I am not lying Dad; I am trying to help." She kept her voice steady through sheer force of will, though her hands had begun to tremble slightly.

Elliot's fingers drummed an agitated rhythm against the arm of his chair, a warning sign she had learned to heed. His eyes darted around the room, landing briefly on objects before moving on, as if searching for something just beyond his reach. The rapid rise and fall of his chest sent alarm bells ringing through Casey's mind.

"Dad," she said, using the tone that sometimes broke through the fog—authoritative but gentle, an echo of how he used to calm her childhood fears. "Let's take a deep breath together. In through the nose, out through the mouth. Remember how we used to do that when I had bad dreams?"

For a moment, something flickered in his eyes—recognition, perhaps, or the ghost of a memory. Casey leaned forward cautiously, encouraged by that momentary connection. "That's it. Just breath with me. We'll figure this out together."

The moment shattered as quickly as it had formed. Elliot's expression hardened, eyes narrowing to suspicious slits. "You've changed things. You're hiding things from me. Where's the news? What have you done with it?"

"I haven't changed anything Dad I promise." Casey raised both hands in a placating gesture, palms forward to show she meant no harm. The motion pulled her sleeve higher, revealing more bruises—a constellation of hurt mapped across her skin.

Elliot's gaze snagged on those marks, his face twisting with an emotion Casey couldn't decipher. His breathing grew more erratic, chest heaving with exertion though he hadn't moved from his chair. When he spoke again, his voice had dropped to a dangerous whisper.

"Who are you? What have you done with my daughter?"

The question pierced Casey like a physical blow. This wasn't the first time he had failed to recognise her, but the pain never dulled with repetition. "Dad, it's me. It's Casey."

"Liar!" Elliot lurched to his feet with surprising speed, the remote clattering to the floor as he advanced toward her. "My Casey would never keep me from the news. My Casey wouldn't change things without telling me."

Casey backed away, calculating the distance to the door, to the kitchen, to any potential exit or sanctuary. "Dad, please. You're confused right now. It's the disease, not me, I'm Casey, your daughter."

Her words seemed to fuel his anger rather than diminish it. His hands curled into fists at his sides, trembling with rage or fear or both. "Stop saying that! Stop pretending! Where is she? What have you done with my daughter?"

Casey's back met the wall, retreat no longer an option. "Dad," she whispered, "It's me. Please try to remember."

Elliot moved with the sudden, unpredictable violence that had become terrifyingly familiar in recent months. His hands shot out, connecting with Casey's shoulders, driving her hard against the wall. Her head snapped back, colliding with the plaster with a dull thud that sent sparks dancing across her vision. A cry of pain escaped her lips before she could swallow it back.

"Tell me where she is!" Elliot shouted, his face inches from hers, spittle flying from his lips. His fingers dug into her shoulders with bruising force. "What have you done with my daughter?"

His fists colliding with her flesh both body shots and in her head, her head snapping back again struck the wall, a pulse of pain that echoed the rapid hammering of her heart. One of Elliot's hands moved to her throat, not squeezing but resting there – a threat, a question a moment of horrible potential. Casey remained perfectly still, fear and love waging their endless battle within her chest.

Chapter 4

Kirk Manning's boots made no sound on the cracked sidewalk, a habit from years of training that his body remembered even when his mind was elsewhere. His German Shepherd, Max, padded beside him, leash slack between them, a partnership built on mutual understanding rather than restraint. The evening air carried the scent of someone grilling a few blocks over, mixing with the earthier smell of soil from gardens recently watered against the summer heat. Kirk breathed deeply, using the familiar routine of cataloguing sensory details to keep his thoughts anchored in the present rather than drifting to places he worked hard to avoid.

The neighbourhood hummed with the quiet energy of a summer evening—distant laughter from a backyard gathering, the mechanical whir of someone's sprinkler system, the occasional car passing with windows down and music spilling out. Kirk checked his watch. They'd been walking for forty-five minutes, longer than he'd intended, but the air had felt good against his skin after a day spent inside with paperwork and memories.

Max stopped abruptly, ears swivelling forward like

radar dishes, body suddenly alert. The change was instantaneous—from relaxed companion to vigilant guardian. Kirk knew better than to dismiss the dog's signals. He stilled, listening beyond the ambient sounds of the neighbourhood.

The cry came a moment later—a woman's voice, pain-filled and cut short, as if muffled or suppressed. Kirk's body responded before his mind fully processed the sound, muscles tensing, posture straightening, senses heightening to the state of focused alertness that had kept him alive in combat zones. Max looked up at him, waiting for direction, sensing the shift in his handler's energy.

"Where?" Kirk asked quietly, the command familiar between them. Max turned his head toward a modest single-story house with peeling white paint and untrimmed hedges. Light spilled from the windows, casting yellow rectangles into the patchy lawn. As they watched a shadow moved violently across one of those illuminated squares.

Another sound came then – a man's voice, raised in anger, the words indistinct but the tone unmistakeable. Kirk had heard that tone before, had responded to too many domestic disturbance calls during his military police rotations to mistake it for anything else. His throat tightened with the familiar bitter taste of adrenaline.

"Come," he commanded softly, moving toward the house with purpose but without rushing. Max stayed close to his left leg, matching his stride with practiced precision. Kirk noted details automatically—no car in the driveway, mail overflowing from the box by the door, blinds drawn but not completely closed on the front window. The porch light was burnt out, the three steps leading to the front door sagging slightly in the middle from age and wear.

Kirk paused at the bottom step, listening again. A crash from inside, followed by another cry—this one weaker, more resigned. His hand moved instinctively to his hip before he remembered he wasn't armed, wasn't on duty, had no legal authority here. But the memory of Charlotte, of arriving too late, pushed him forward regardless.

He tested the doorknob—unlocked—and made a decision that training told him was reckless but instinct insisted was necessary. "Stay," he told Max, positioning the dog just outside the door where he would be visible but not immediately threatening. Then Kirk pushed the door open, announcing his presence with a firm, "Hello? Is everything okay in here?"

The scene that greeted him seared itself into his mind with brutal clarity. An elderly man stood with his back to the door, one hand pressed against a woman's throat, pinning her to the wall. The woman's face was turned toward Kirk, her expression a complex mixture of fear, pain, and now shock at his appearance. Blood trickled from a small cut on her lip, and her left eye was already beginning to swell. Her chest rose and fell in quick, shallow breaths.

Kirk's training activated like a program running in the background – assess, categorise, respond. The elderly man: likely in his late sixties, showing signs of confusion rather than calculated violence, physically frail despite his aggressive posture. The woman: mid-twenties, injured but conscious, no immediate life-threatening injuries visible, physically capable of defending herself but clearly unwilling to do so.

The relationship dynamic revealed itself in subtle cues – the protective way the woman's hands hovered near but didn't push against the man's arms, the framed photographs on the wall showing earlier versions of them together, the worn care routine evident in the setup of the room. Not an intruder or attacker in the conventional sense, but a loved one in crisis.

"Sir," Kirk said, his voice dropping to the calm, authoritative tone he'd used to talk down armed men in the field. "I need you to step back from her now." He moved into the room slowly, hands visible at his sides, posture non-threatening but ready.

The elderly man whirled around, eyes wild and unfocused. "Who are you? Get out of my house!" His hand fell away from the woman's throat as he faced this new perceived threat.

"My name is Kirk. I'm here to help," Kirk said, maintaining eye contact while assessing the man's body language. Confusion, fear, anger—but not malice. Not cold calculation. The slight tremor in his hands and the disjointed quality of his movements suggested something neurological rather than intoxication. "No one needs to get hurt here."

The woman pressed herself against the wall, one hand moving to her throat, eyes darting between Kirk and the elderly man. "He doesn't understand." She said, voice hoarse but steady. "He has dementia. He doesn't know what he's doing."

"I understand," Kirk replied, still focusing primarily on the agitated man, who was now looking around the room as if searching for something. "Sir, why don't we sit down and talk about what's bothering you?"

"Who is this man, Casey?" the elderly man demanded, turning back to the woman. "Why is he in our house? Did you let him in?"

Kirk caught the name—Casey—filing it away as he continued his careful approach. "I heard sounds of distress from outside," he explained, addressing both of them now. "I was concerned someone might be injured."

The elderly man's face twisted with renewed suspicion. "You're with them, aren't you? The ones who've been changing everything. Moving my things. Hiding the news."

26

His hands curled into fists at his sides, body tensing for another potential outburst.

Kirk recognized the escalation signs immediately. Without taking his eyes off the man, he positioned himself between him and Casey, creating a buffer zone. "I'm not with anyone, sir. I was just walking my dog." He gestured toward the door where Max sat obediently, watching the scene with alert interest. "That's Max. He heard someone in distress and led me here."

The mention of a dog seemed to momentarily derail the man's anger. He looked toward the doorway, brow furrowing as he processed this new information. "A dog?"

"Yes, sir. A German Shepherd. Would you like to meet him?" Kirk kept his voice even, using the distraction to create psychological distance from the confrontation. "He's very well-behaved."

Behind him, Kirk sensed Casey's confusion at this apparent non-sequitur, but he maintained his course. The elderly man's attention had shifted, his breathing beginning to slow from its agitated pace.

"Dad," Casey said carefully, moving slightly away from the wall. "This is a neighbour who heard us…talking. He was just checking to make sure we're okay."

Kirk noted the protective lie without reacting to it, understanding instinctively her need to preserve her father's dignity.

The old man—Casey's father—swayed slightly on his feet, the burst of adrenaline-fueled rage apparently depleting his limited energy reserves. His expression shifted, confusion replacing anger, then a flicker of shame as his gaze fell on Casey's swelling eye.

"Sir, why don't you have a seat?" Kirk suggested, gesturing toward the recliner that showed the distinct compression pattern of regular use. "You look like you could use a rest."

With surprising docility, the man moved toward the chair, his steps uncertain. "I was watching the news," he mumbled, more to himself than to either of them. "It's supposed to be on now. It's always on now."

"Maybe we can find it for you," Kirk offered, moving carefully with him, ready to support if needed but not touching him unless necessary. The military had taught him that people in crisis needed space and respect as much as they needed intervention.

As her father settled into the chair, Casey remained pressed against the wall, watching Kirk with wary amazement, as if he were performing some incomprehensible magic trick. Her fingers probed her swelling eye gingerly, wincing at the contact.

The room fell into an uneasy silence, broken only by the elderly man's increasingly heavy breathing as the adrenaline ebbed from his system. Kirk maintained his position, a calm sentinel between father and daughter, his body language relaxed but prepared. Through the open door, the evening sounds continued unchanged—crickets beginning their nightly chorus, a distant car door slamming, the normal rhythm of life proceeding in stark contrast to the private crisis contained within these walls.

Casey's gaze met Kirk's over her father's bowed head. In her eyes, Kirk saw something that twisted in his chest—gratitude mingled with shame, relief shadowed by embarrassment. He recognized that look. He'd seen it before, in other homes, on other faces. The silent acknowledgment of a secret exposed, a burden momentarily shared, the complex emotion of having a stranger witness your most private pain.

And beneath it all, the unspoken question that always followed such interventions: What happens now?

Elliot's breathing gradually slowed, his gaze fixed on the blank television screen with the distant focus of someone traveling through internal landscapes. The aggression had drained from his body like water from a punctured vessel, leaving behind a frail shell that seemed smaller somehow, diminished by the aftermath of fury. Casey watched the transformation with familiar heartache, the pattern so established she could mark its stages: confusion giving way to exhaustion, followed by the inevitable moment when recognition would flicker across his features like a guttering candle, bringing with it the remorse that was almost harder to bear than the violence.

"Casey?" Elliot's voice emerged thin and uncertain, a child lost in a darkened room. His eyes, when they finally found her, widened with horror at the swelling beneath her left eye. "What happened to you?"

The question—so sincere, so devoid of recollection—struck Casey with its familiar cruelty. She swallowed the bitter truth and offered instead the mercy of an edited reality. "I bumped into something, Dad. It's nothing."

Kirk remained silent during this exchange, his stillness that of an observer rather than a stranger, as if he recognized the delicate choreography playing out before him. Casey felt his presence like a physical weight, an unexpected witness to their private tragedy.

Elliot's head began to droop, chin dipping toward his chest as exhaustion claimed him. These violent episodes always drained him, his compromised brain unable to sustain such intense emotion for long. Casey moved toward him with practiced care.

"He'll fall asleep soon," she said. "After episodes like this, he usually sleeps deeply for hours."

"Let me help you get him to bed," Kirk offered, the words simple but weighted with understanding of what such help meant—not just the physical assistance, but the acknowledgment of her daily reality.

Casey hesitated, the offer of help as foreign to her now

as a language she'd once known but had forgotten through disuse. "You don't have to—"

"I know." His interruption was gentle but firm. "I'd like to."

Together they guided Elliot from the chair, Kirk supporting most of his weight with an efficiency that spoke of experience. Casey led them down the narrow hallway to her father's bedroom, a space that smelled faintly of talcum powder and the peppermint candies Elliot still insisted on keeping in a dish by his bed—one of the few preferences that had survived the disease's erosion.

Elliot allowed himself to be settled onto the edge of the bed, his earlier aggression dissolved completely into confusion and fatigue. "Is it time for school?" he asked Casey, his voice suddenly carrying the tone of the educator he had once been.

"No, Dad. It's time to rest now." Casey slipped his shoes off with practiced movements, set them precisely side by side beneath the nightstand where he would expect to find them in the morning.

Kirk stood back, giving them space for this intimate ritual while remaining close enough to assist if needed. His presence brought an unexpected stability to the room, as if his solid frame and quiet certainty were physical barriers against the chaos that so often threatened to overwhelm Casey's carefully maintained control.

When Elliot finally lay back against the pillows, his eyelids already growing heavy, Casey pulled the lightweight blanket up to his chest—not tucking it in, knowing from experience that feeling constrained could trigger another episode if he woke disoriented.

"There's a storm coming," Elliot murmured, eyes closing as sleep began to claim him. "You should bring the plants in, Charlie."

Casey flinched at the unfamiliar name, but kept her voice steady. "Everything's safe, Dad. You can sleep now."

She watched his breathing deepen, the lines of his face softening as consciousness slipped away. These moments—when he looked once again like the father who had taught her to ride a bike and checked under her bed for monsters—were precious and painful in equal measure, glimpses of a man who existed now only in memory and photographs.

Chapter 5

Kirk waited silently by the door, and when Casey finally turned away from the bed, she found his gaze on her rather than on her father—a small mercy she hadn't expected. He followed her back to the living room without speaking, respecting the fragile quiet that had settled over the house.

Under the harsher overhead light, Casey caught her reflection in the small mirror hung beside the front door— a stranger with a swelling eye and blood dried at the corner of her mouth. She touched her face gingerly, the pain registering as if from a distance, dulled by a numbness that extended beyond the physical.

"You should put ice on that eye," Kirk said, his voice pitched low out of deference to the sleeping man down the hall.

Casey nodded automatically, but made no move toward the kitchen. Her body felt suddenly leaden, the adrenaline that had sustained her through the confrontation draining away and leaving exhaustion in its wake.

Kirk seemed to understand without explanation. "Sit

down," he suggested, nodding toward the sofa. "I can get the ice if you tell me where to look."

"I can do it." The words emerged with a defensiveness that surprised even Casey. Independence had become her armor, self-reliance her religion. Accepting help felt like a dangerous admission of inadequacy.

Kirk met her gaze steadily. "I know you can. But you don't have to."

Something in his tone—not pity, but a simple acknowledgment of fact—loosened a knot in Casey's chest. "Freezer," she conceded. "There's a blue ice pack on the door."

While Kirk moved into the kitchen, Casey sank onto the sofa, suddenly aware of every ache in her body—not just the fresh injuries from tonight, but the accumulated toll of months spent in a state of constant vigilance. The springs of the worn sofa creaked beneath her weight, the sound oddly comforting in its familiarity.

Kirk returned with not only the ice pack.

"May I?" he asked, waiting for her nod before gently pressing the ice pack against her swelling eye.

His movements were precise and methodical, the careful ministrations of someone trained to treat injuries under far worse conditions than a quiet living room. Casey hissed when the cold connected with tender skin, but held the pack in place when he released it.

"Military?" she asked, the question unnecessary given his bearing and efficiency, but easier than acknowledging the strange intimacy of this moment.

A shadow crossed Kirk's features, there and gone so quickly she might have imagined it. "Partly. I also spent some time with the military police. You learn to patch people up in that line of work."

He examined the bruises on her arms with professional detachment, testing the edges with careful fingers to ensure nothing was broken beneath the mottled skin. There was no judgment in his assessment, no horror at the evidence of repeated injuries. Just practical attention to immediate needs.

Chapter 6

The house had settled into an uneasy quiet, broken only by the distant sound of Elliot's breathing from down the hall. Casey sat on the edge of the sofa, ice pack pressed against her swelling eye, while Kirk stood by the mantel, his posture too disciplined to be casual yet too careful to be imposing. Between them hung the unspoken acknowledgment of what he had witnessed – a family's private tragedy exposed to a stranger's gaze.

"He wasn't always like this," Casey said, her voice barely above a whisper, as if afraid to disturb the fragile peace they'd achieved. "Two years ago, he was still teaching part-time at the community college. History. He could recite dates and battles that most people had forgotten existed."

Kirk's eyes moved over the living room, taking in details with the practiced observation of someone trained to assess environments quickly. The furniture bore the hallmarks of another era – a floral-patterned sofa with worn arms, a recliner with the imprint of Elliot's body permanently molded into its cushions. A bookshelf sagged beneath the weight of history volumes and teaching materials that hadn't been touched in months, their spines dusty except for one section where finger marks showed someone's attempt to maintain order in a disordered world.

"Frontotemporal dementia is what they called it," Casey continued, wincing as she shifted the ice pack to a different angle. "The behavioural variant. It affects the frontal lobe first. Impulse control. Recognition. Emotional regulation." She recited the medical terminology with the detached precision of someone who'd repeated these phrases to herself so many times they'd lost their sting, become merely syllables rather than sentences that had shattered her life.

On the wall behind her hung a collection of framed photographs – Elliot in academic regalia, arm around a much younger Casey at what appeared to be her high school graduation; father and daughter on a fishing trip, holding up identical catches with identical grins; Elliot at a lectern, mouth open mid-lecture, eyes bright with passion for his subject. The progression of images told its own story – of a vibrant man gradually fading from the frames, his posture stooping, his smile becoming uncertain, his eyes increasingly confused.

"How long have you been managing alone?" Kirk asked, his voice carrying the even tone of someone asking for tactical information rather than pursuing emotional disclosure.

"Since the diagnosis, more or less. There was a part-time aide at first, but..." Casey glanced toward a stack of mail on the side table, their edges visible beneath an outdated phone book – bills, most likely, their corners peeking out like red flags. "Dad's insurance covers some things, but not enough. Not nearly enough."

As she spoke, Kirk's mind filled with overlapping images – Casey's bruised arms superimposed over another set of arms he'd once examined across a kitchen table in the small hours of the morning, offering arnica and excuses in equal measure. Charlotte had worn long sleeves even in summer, had developed an expertise in covering marks with makeup and covering pain with smiles. The resemblance wasn't physical – Charlotte with her blonde hair and blue eyes had looked nothing like Casey's dark waves and deeper colouring – but in the stubborn set of their jaws, the determined way they carried burdens too heavy for single pairs of shoulders.

"The violent episodes," Kirk said carefully, "how frequent are they?"

Casey looked away, her gaze falling on a crack in the plaster wall – recent damage, he guessed, though it was merely the newest addition to a collection of household wounds that mapped the progression of Elliot's decline.

"They were rare at first. Maybe once a month, and mostly just shouting." Her fingers traced the edge of the ice pack, skin pale against the blue plastic. "Now? Three, sometimes four times a week. When he's tired. When routines change. When he loses track of time, which is..." She gestured vaguely around them, the motion encompassing not just the room but their entire situation. "Most of the time now."

Kirk nodded, understanding more than she realized. He'd seen the patterns before – the increasing frequency, the escalating intensity, the growing risk that one day the damage would be more than bruises and split lips. He'd arrived too late once. The guilt from that failure had carved itself into his bones, become part of his structural integrity. He shifted his weight, feeling the familiar ache of that old emotional injury.

"I'm sorry about the disturbance," Casey said suddenly, straightening her spine with visible effort. "You didn't sign up for this when you took your dog for a walk. We'll be fine now, really. He'll sleep through the night after episodes like this."

The practiced reassurance rang hollow in the quiet room, a script she'd recited so many times she might have believed it herself if the evidence of its untruth wasn't still throbbing beneath her eye, still visible in the dried blood at the corner of her mouth.

"I've had some experience with this," Kirk said, the admission coming more easily than he'd expected. He moved closer, not sitting yet, but reducing the distance between them with deliberate care. "Not dementia specifically, but volatile situations. De-escalation techniques."

Casey's eyebrow raised slightly; the question unspoken but clear.

"Marine Corps, then military police." He offered the information like identification, necessary credentials before proceeding. "I worked with veterans in crisis, among other things."

Her expression softened with understanding. "That explains how you knew what to do with him. How to talk him down without making things worse." She lowered the ice pack, revealing the full extent of the swelling that would become a spectacular bruise by morning. "Most people either get confrontational, which escalates everything, or they get scared and back away completely."

"Your approach was good," Kirk said, recognizing the competence in how she'd handled the situation despite her injuries. "The way you kept your voice steady, gave him space to process. You've learned adaptation techniques on your own that took me formal training to master."

A ghost of a smile touched Casey's lips, there and gone like a brief glimmer of sunlight on a clouded day. "Trial and error. Mostly error at first."

Kirk crossed to the recliner and sat, the movement deliberate – not just reducing his height advantage but also claiming space in the room, sending a subtle signal that he wasn't leaving yet, wasn't going to be deflected by her practiced self-sufficiency. Max settled at his feet, the dog's calm presence adding another layer of steadiness to the scene.

"Would it help if I showed you a few techniques?" he offered. "For redirecting attention during escalation? Military training has some advantages when it comes to crisis management."

The question hung between them – not just an offer of practical assistance but a tentative bridge extending across the chasm of their unfamiliarity. Casey's fingers tightened around the ice pack, her knuckles whitening briefly before she exhaled, shoulders dropping a fraction of an inch in what might have been surrender or simply exhaustion.

"Why would you do that?" she asked, the question genuine rather than defensive.

Kirk's gaze drifted to the photographs on the wall, to the evidence of the man Elliot had been before disease rewrote his neural pathways, stole his self-control, turned him against the daughter he clearly adored. His chest tightened with a familiar pressure – not quite pain, not exactly guilt, but something adjacent to both, something that had driven him out walking at night for years now, restless with the need to prevent what he'd once failed to stop.

"Because I know what it's like," he said finally, "to watch someone you love disappear by degrees. To try to protect them when they can't protect themselves." He met her eyes directly. "And because sometimes the people who most need backup are the last ones to call for it."

In the quiet that followed his words, something shifted in the space between them – not trust exactly, not yet, but the possibility of it, fragile as a first spring bud pushing through frozen ground after a long winter.

"I should check on him once more before you go," Casey said, rising from the sofa with the careful movements of someone cataloguing each new pain. The ice pack had numbed the worst of the swelling, but other aches announced themselves as she straightened—a twinge in her lower back where she'd hit the wall, a burning sensation along her shoulder blade where Elliot's grip had left its mark. She moved toward the hallway with the automatic navigation of someone who could traverse these spaces blindfolded, her body remembering the path even as her mind wandered elsewhere.

Kirk followed a step behind, his footfalls deliberately audible – a courtesy Casey recognized. Nighttime visitors in her house were rare enough that even this small consideration stood out, a reminder of how long it had been since someone else had occupied these spaces with her.

The door to Elliot's bedroom stood partially open, a soft night light casting amorphous shadows across the threshold. Casey paused before entering, her hand resting on the doorframe as she listened to the rhythm of her father's breathing – deep and even now, the storm of his earlier rage reduced to gentle surf upon distant shores.

"I always check the oxygen," she explained in a whisper as she slipped inside. "His levels drop sometimes when he sleeps."

The bedroom revealed a stark contrast between the personal and the medical, the past and present versions of Elliot Preston colliding in physical space. A hospital-style bed dominated the center of the room, its railings raised and locked, the mechanical controls for elevation discreetly tucked beneath the mattress edge. But the quilt covering Elliot was handmade, its pattern faded with years of use – a personal touch amid institutional practicality.

The nightstand beside the bed had been transformed into a pharmacy outpost – amber prescription bottles arranged in neat rows, each labeled with time and dosage in Casey's careful handwriting. A blood pressure monitor sat beside them, its digital display dark now but ready for the morning's readings. An oxygen concentrator hummed quietly in the corner, its clear tubing snaking across the floor to where Elliot lay, the nasal cannula resting against his face with the impersonal intimacy of medical necessity.

Yet amid these clinical intrusions, evidence of Elliot's former life persisted. Bookshelves lined one wall, the volumes organized with academic precision – historical biographies, analysis of ancient civilizations, dog-eared teaching texts with colored tabs still marking important passages. A framed diploma hung above them, the university seal catching the dim light as if winking in recognition of all that had been lost.

"The oxygen helps with the sundowning," Casey murmured as she checked the flow meter, adjusting it with practiced fingers. "His neurologist thinks the cognitive confusion gets worse when his blood oxygen drops, especially at night."

Elliot stirred at the sound of her voice, eyelids fluttering without fully opening. "Margaret?" he called, the name emerging slurred with sleep and confusion. "Is that you?"

Casey's hand froze on the meter, her spine stiffening almost imperceptibly before she leaned closer to her father. "It's Casey, Dad. Everything's fine. Go back to sleep."

"The garden needs watering, Margaret," Elliot continued, his voice drifting through decades, addressing a woman who had left them so long ago that Casey sometimes struggled to recall her face without photographs. "The roses will wilt in this heat."

"I'll take care of it," Casey assured him softly, her hand smoothing the quilt across his chest with a tenderness that made Kirk look away, suddenly conscious of witnessing something deeply private. "The roses are fine. Everything's fine."

Elliot's face relaxed, the worry lines smoothing as he

slipped back into deeper sleep. Casey remained beside him for a moment longer, her fingers lingering on his shoulder, before she straightened and turned toward the door.

Kirk caught the slight wince as she moved, the involuntary tightening around her eyes that betrayed pain she was trying to conceal. Her movements, so fluid and practiced while tending to her father, became stiffer as she focused on herself, as if her body only remembered its injuries when not occupied with caregiving.

They retreated to the hallway, Casey pulling the door mostly closed behind them. "He'll sleep through now," she said with the weary confidence of someone who had mapped every predictable aspect of an unpredictable condition. "The confusion is always worse after an episode, but the exhaustion usually guarantees at least six hours of solid rest."

"And what about you?" Kirk asked, his voice low but direct. "How do you rest with injuries like that?"

Casey's fingers moved automatically to her swollen eye, a defensive gesture that answered more honestly than her words. "I've had worse." She attempted a smile that failed to reach her eyes. "Not exactly the accessory I'd choose, but it'll fade."

Rather than responding immediately, Kirk gestured toward the kitchen at the end of the hall. "Do you have a proper first aid kit? That cut needs cleaning, and the bruising would benefit from proper treatment."

Casey hesitated, that familiar resistance to help rising in her expression. "It's late. You've already done more than—"

"I was a field medic," Kirk interrupted gently. "Let me help with what I know. Then I'll go."

The kitchen's fluorescent light clicked on with an electrical sputter, harsh and unforgiving compared to the living room's softer lamps. Casey blinked against the sudden brightness, her injuries thrown into stark relief – the swelling beneath her eye more pronounced, the cut at her temple deeper than it had appeared in dimmer lighting. A collar of reddened skin around her throat revealed where Elliot's hand had pressed, the marks already darkening toward bruises that would bloom by morning.

Kirk swept his gaze around the kitchen, noting its similar state of functional neglect – clean but dated, maintained through necessity rather than choice. The appliances were aging relics, the linoleum floor pattern faded to ghostly outlines near the sink where someone had stood for countless hours. A calendar on the refrigerator showed a month's worth of medical appointments, each one carefully noted in the same neat handwriting that had labeled Elliot's medications.

"First aid kit?" he prompted again, bringing her attention back from wherever it had wandered.

Casey pointed to a cabinet above the refrigerator. "Up there. I haven't restocked it in a while, though."

Kirk reached up and retrieved the kit – a battered metal box with a red cross painted on its lid, the kind that belonged in another era. As he set it on the kitchen table and opened it, the contents revealed a haphazard collection – bandages of various sizes, half-empty tubes of antibiotic ointment, a bottle of hydrogen peroxide with a faded label.

"Sit," he said, pulling out a chair at the small kitchen table. It wasn't an order, but it carried the quiet authority of someone accustomed to being obeyed in emergency situations.

Casey sat, her movements betraying more fatigue than she likely intended to reveal. Under the merciless kitchen light, she looked not just injured but exhausted in a bone-deep way that no single night's sleep could remedy. Her hair fell from its hasty bun in dark tendrils around her face, framing features drawn tight with pain she refused to acknowledge.

Kirk washed his hands at the sink with methodical thoroughness, the ritual so ingrained that he didn't need to think about it. The familiar sequence of movements centred him, pushed back the memories that threatened to surface – Charlotte sitting at a different kitchen table, making similar excuses, hiding similar pain.

"This might sting," he warned as he prepared a gauze pad with antiseptic. "The cut near your temple needs cleaning before it can be properly assessed."

"I'm familiar with stinging," Casey replied, a wry note entering her voice for the first time that evening. "Dad was a science teacher before switching to history. Our first aid kit was always better stocked than our pantry."

Kirk's hands were surprisingly gentle for their size as he began cleaning the cut, his movements precise and efficient. He worked in silence for a moment, maintaining a clinical distance that seemed to help Casey relax incrementally, her shoulders lowering from their defensive hunch.

"Your technique is good," she observed, watching his face rather than his hands. "Did you treat a lot of injuries like this overseas?"

"More than I'd care to remember," Kirk answered, his focus remaining on the wound rather than the memories her question evoked. "But field medicine teaches you to work with what you have. To improvise when necessary. To prioritize."

He discarded the used gauze and prepared a fresh piece, his movements economical. "This cut isn't as deep as it looked at first. No stitches needed. The bruising will be more problematic."

Casey flinched slightly as he touched a particularly tender spot, her hand rising automatically to push his away.

Kirk paused, waiting for her to lower it again before continuing.

"Charlotte would never let anyone help her either," he said quietly, the words emerging before he'd fully decided to speak them. "She'd patch herself up in the bathroom with the door locked. Wouldn't even let me see, and I was the one with medical training in the family."

The mention of his sister hung in the air between them, an offering of shared vulnerability, a context for his presence in her kitchen at this late hour tending wounds inflicted by someone she loved.

"Your sister," Casey said carefully, "she was..."

"Stubborn. Independent. Convinced she could handle everything herself." Kirk placed a butterfly bandage across the cut with gentle pressure. "Sound familiar?"

Casey's expression softened slightly, recognition flickering beneath the wariness. "It's not the same situation."

"No," Kirk agreed, preparing an arnica cream for the bruising. "Your father isn't responsible for his actions in the way that—" He stopped himself, jaw tightening briefly. "But the physical reality is similar. And the isolation that comes with it."

His hands moved with careful precision, applying the cream to the edges of the bruise forming beneath her eye. The kitchen light cast harsh shadows across both their faces, creating a strange intimacy in its unforgiving illumination – two people with nowhere to hide their scars or secrets beneath flattering shadows.

"You don't have to do this," Casey said, though she remained still under his ministrations, her body contradicting her words.

"I know." Kirk met her gaze directly. "But sometimes we need to let people do what they're good at. For me, it's this – fixing what can be fixed." His voice carried a weight of things left unsaid, of other situations where his skills had proven insufficient, where damage had progressed beyond repair.

Casey studied his face, perhaps recognizing in his expression the same determination that propelled her through each day – the need to be useful, to apply whatever skills one possessed against problems that defied simple solutions. She nodded once, a small but significant surrender.

"Okay," she said simply, and closed her eyes, allowing him to continue his careful work in the harsh kitchen light that revealed everything and forgave nothing.

The kettle's whistle pierced the kitchen's silence, a shrill note cutting through layers of unspoken thoughts. Casey rose to silence it, her movements slower now as fatigue settled into her muscles like sediment in still water. Outside, the neighborhood had surrendered to the deep quiet of midnight, the occasional distant car passing like a memory of daylight hours. She poured hot water over teabags in two mismatched mugs – one bearing the faded logo of Oakridge High School, the other a Christmas gift with snowmen whose painted faces had partially worn away from years of washing. The mundane ritual of preparing tea felt strangely significant, as if by offering this simple hospitality she was acknowledging something neither of them had directly named.

"Sugar?" she asked, the single word hanging in the air between them.

Kirk shook his head. "Black is fine." He had repacked the first aid kit with military precision, each item returned to its proper place, the surface of the table wiped clean of any evidence of treatment. His hands, so capable while tending her injuries, now rested flat against the worn Formica surface, large and still and somehow patient.

Casey placed the mugs on the table and lowered herself into the chair opposite him. The kitchen clock ticked above the refrigerator, marking the passage of hours that had transformed them from strangers to something undefined but no longer unfamiliar. Through the small window above the sink, the night pressed against the glass, a darkness made more absolute by the kitchen's harsh fluorescent glare.

"I haven't had anyone to talk to this late in a long time," Casey admitted, wrapping her fingers around the warmth of her mug. "It's strange how nights feel different when you're always the only one awake."

Kirk nodded, understanding evident in the slight softening around his eyes. "Charlotte used to call me at odd hours," he said, the name emerging more easily now that it had been spoken once. "She knew the time difference between wherever I was stationed and home. She'd calculate exactly when I'd be awake but not on duty."

He sipped his tea, gaze focused on some middle distance beyond the kitchen walls. "She was the stubborn one in the family. Four years younger than me, but always acted like she was the older sibling. Always protecting, always taking care, never accepting help." A ghost of a smile touched his lips. "She could make me laugh even after the worst days in the field. Had this way of telling stories that made you feel like you were right there with her."

The kitchen light buzzed faintly overhead, a subliminal soundtrack to their quiet voices. Casey watched Kirk's face as he spoke about his sister, noting how animation entered his features, how his hands began to move slightly with his words – not grand gestures, but small, controlled movements that suggested deeper emotions carefully contained.

"She sounds wonderful," Casey said, the simple acknowledgment opening a door for him to continue.

"She was." Kirk's expression shifted, the past tense landing between them with palpable weight. "She was an elementary school art teacher. Used to send me pictures her students had drawn for 'Miss Manning's brother the Marine.' Had them in my footlocker, taped up in every barracks I stayed in." He paused, his fingers tightening almost imperceptibly around his mug. "She could see the good in anyone. Sometimes in people who didn't deserve that kind of vision."

Casey sensed the approaching shadow in his narrative, the turn toward darkness that she recognized from her own life – that moment when the story changed irrevocably. She remained silent, offering the rare gift of attentive listening.

"Her boyfriend seemed fine at first," Kirk continued, his voice dropping to a lower register. "Charming, attentive. By the time the control issues started, she was already isolated. Classic pattern – I should have recognized it sooner." His jaw tightened briefly. "She kept making excuses for the bruises, for the canceled plans, for why she couldn't talk on the phone anymore unless he was at work."

The tea cooled in their mugs, steam no longer rising between them. Beyond the kitchen, the house's old pipes creaked and settled, a counterpoint to the heavy silence that followed Kirk's words.

"I was overseas when it happened," he said finally. "My third tour. She'd been planning to leave him, had packed a bag, contacted a shelter. She called to tell me she was going to be okay, that she'd call again when she was safe." His voice roughened, fingers now completely still around his mug. "She was trying to escape when her car went off the road. They said it was an accident, but the investigation showed evidence of tampering with the brakes."

Casey reached across the table without thinking, her fingers briefly touching the back of his hand – a fleeting connection, there and gone, but the imprint of warmth lingered between them. "I'm so sorry," she said simply, the words inadequate but sincere.

Kirk nodded once, accepting both the touch and the sympathy with equal solemnity. "By the time I got back for the funeral, there wasn't enough evidence to charge him. He'd moved away within a month." His expression hardened momentarily before deliberately relaxing. "That's why I walk at night. Why Max and I take the same routes through neighborhoods. Some patterns are hard to miss when you know what to look for."

The revelation settled between them − not just the tragedy itself, but the purpose it had given him, the vigilance it had instilled. Casey understood suddenly that her situation had triggered something primal in him, some need to prevent what he couldn't change in his own past.

"I never meant to become isolated," Casey said after a moment, offering her own vulnerability in exchange for his. "When Dad's diagnosis came, I thought I could handle both − my job, my friends, and caring for him. I had spreadsheets, care schedules, everything organized." A rueful smile touched her lips. "I was so naïve about what it would really mean."

She rotated her mug slowly, watching the dark liquid inside swirl with the movement. "My friends tried at first. They'd visit, offer to sit with Dad so I could get out for an hour or two. But after the third or fourth time he didn't recognize them, or got agitated by their presence..." She shrugged, the gesture encompassing all the faded connections and abandoned plans of the past two years. "It's easier for people to drift away when there's a built-in excuse. Nobody has to feel guilty about abandoning the woman with the sick father. It's understandable, right? Who wants to be around illness all the time?"

"It's not you they're uncomfortable with," Kirk observed quietly. "It's their own helplessness."

Casey nodded, surprise flickering across her face at his perception. "Exactly. They want to fix things, and when they can't, it's easier to just... not see them." She absently touched the bandage on her temple. "I gave up my graphic design position at the marketing firm. I'd just been promoted, too. Had my own small team." The memory tasted bittersweet on her tongue. "Sometimes I sketch when Dad's having a good day, but mostly I just maintain. Survive. Keep us both going."

"And the episodes?" Kirk asked gently.

Casey exhaled slowly. "The hardest part isn't the physical stuff. It's looking into his eyes and seeing a stranger looking back. Someone who's afraid of me, who thinks I'm an impostor." Her voice wavered slightly. "Sometimes I don't recognize him either. The man who raised me, who taught me to change a tire and appreciate history and stand up for myself – he appears in flashes, then disappears again. We're strangers to each other more often than not now."

The kitchen clock ticked past one in the morning, the sound drawing both their attention. Kirk straightened slightly, recognition of the late hour registering in his posture.

"I should let you rest," he said, though he made no immediate move to leave. "You'll need to check those bandages tomorrow. Apply more arnica to the bruising. I can stop by to—" He paused, perhaps hearing the presumption in his own words. "If you'd like help with that."

Casey found herself nodding before she'd consciously decided to accept his offer. "Dad usually sleeps late after episodes like this. Morning would be... morning would be good."

They moved toward the front door with the awkward courtesy of people unsure of the protocol for ending an encounter that had ventured far beyond conventional boundaries. Max rose from where he'd been waiting patiently by the door, tail sweeping in a gentle arc as Casey approached.

"He's beautiful," she said, carefully extending her hand for the dog to sniff before lightly stroking his head. "How long have you had him?"

"Four years," Kirk answered, watching the interaction with quiet approval. "He was a military working dog. Retired after an injury. We understood each other." The simple explanation contained volumes beneath its surface – shared trauma, mutual healing, companionship forged through recognition of similar wounds.

Casey opened the front door, the night air rushing in – cooler now, carrying the scent of dew-dampened grass and distant rain. The porch light remained unlit, plunging them into a darkness relieved only by distant streetlamps and the faint glow spilling from the house behind them. Their silhouettes merged briefly in the doorway, two shadows connecting and separating as Kirk stepped onto the porch.

"Thank you," Casey said, the words encompassing more than the medical attention, more than the listening ear, perhaps even more than she herself recognized. "For stopping. For not looking away."

Kirk turned back to face her, his features half-illuminated, half-hidden in shadow. "I'll come by tomorrow," he said, the statement both a promise and a question. "Around nine?"

"Nine," Casey confirmed, her hand resting on the doorframe as if needing its support. "I'll make real coffee instead of tea."

Something passed between them then, in that liminal space between night and morning, between strangers and whatever they were becoming – not quite a spark, but the potential for one, the necessary elements aligning. Max's tail thumped against the porch boards, an approving punctuation to the moment.

As Kirk and Max descended the steps and moved into the deeper darkness beyond the yard, Casey remained in the doorway, watching until they disappeared around the corner. The night seemed less empty somehow, less absolute in its isolation. She closed the door slowly, listening to the familiar sounds of her home – the refrigerator's hum, her father's distant breathing, the settling of old wood. But for the first time in longer than she could remember, she also heard something else beneath those familiar notes – the faint but unmistakable rhythm of possibility.

Chapter 7

The first time Kirk returned with groceries, Casey stared at the paper bags in his arms as if they were foreign objects she couldn't quite identify. Sunlight filtered through the dusty blinds, striping the worn entryway with golden lines that caught the uncertainty in her eyes. She stood with one hand braced against the doorframe, her body angled slightly, a posture of protection rather than welcome. The bruise beneath her eye had faded to a watercolor smudge of yellow and green, but the wariness in her gaze remained vibrant and undiluted.

"I noticed you were running low on some basics," Kirk explained, his voice neutral, neither apologetic nor expectant. Max sat obediently at his feet, tail sweeping a gentle arc across the porch boards.

Casey's fingers tightened around the doorframe, then consciously relaxed. "You didn't have to do that," she said, the words automatic, a reflex built from years of declining assistance.

"I know." Kirk remained still, the paper bags cradled in his steady arms, waiting for her decision rather than assuming it.

The house exhaled around them, the old wooden floors creaking slightly as Casey shifted her weight. From the living room came the familiar drone of a news anchor's voice, Elliot's anchor to reality for another day. After a moment that stretched like taffy between them, Casey stepped back, the invitation implicit in the movement.

By the third visit, Kirk knew where the flour belonged and which cabinet housed the drinking glasses. Casey watched from the kitchen doorway as he unloaded a fresh set of groceries with the efficient movements of someone accustomed to organizing supplies. Her arms were crossed over her chest, sleeves pulled down despite the summer heat, concealing the constellation of bruises that had evolved from violent purples to sickly greens and fading yellows.

"The bread goes in the drawer," she said, stepping forward to redirect a loaf he'd placed on the counter. Their fingers didn't touch during the exchange, but the space between them had narrowed since that first visit – proximity measured not just in physical distance but in the diminishing hesitation that preceded her corrections.

Elliot appeared in the kitchen doorway, his movements sluggish with medication, eyes narrowed at Kirk's presence. "Are you the repairman?" he asked, the question emerging with genuine confusion rather than hostility. "The sink's still dripping. I can hear it at night. Tick, tick, tick..." His fingers mimicked the rhythm against his thigh.

"Dad, this is Kirk," Casey reminded gently, drawing closer to her father with the automatic vigilance of someone accustomed to unpredictable reactions. "He's helping with some groceries today. Remember? He's been here before."

Elliot's gaze traveled from Kirk to the groceries to Casey's face, searching for connections his mind could no longer reliably forge. "Is he staying for dinner? Your mother should know if we're having company."

Kirk continued unpacking, his movements deliberately unhurried, giving father and daughter space for this familiar navigation. His presence in their home had already begun to acquire its own rhythm – appearing at predictable hours, occupying himself with practical tasks, maintaining a careful distance from the emotional cross-currents that swirled through the Preston household.

"I can take a look at that sink before I go," he offered once Elliot had wandered back to his armchair, the television reclaiming his fractured attention.

The sink's persistent drip had formed a rust-colored ring in the stainless steel, a perfect circle of neglect born from prioritizing human needs over household mainte-nance. Kirk knelt before the cabinet beneath, tools arranged with military precision on an old towel beside him. Casey hovered nearby, filling a glass with water she didn't drink, wiping an already clean counter, manufac-turing reasons to remain in the kitchen while maintaining the pretense of independent activity.

"Hand me the adjustable wrench?" Kirk asked, extending a hand without looking up from the exposed pipes.

Casey selected it from the lineup of tools, her fingers brushing his briefly during the transfer. The contact lasted less than a second, but Kirk noted how she no longer flinched from accidental touches, how the automatic tension in her shoulders eased a fraction more quickly each time.

Water stains mottled the inside of the cabinet, telling the story of a leak that had begun long before Casey had more pressing concerns than household repairs. Kirk worked methodically, tightening connections, replacing a worn washer, movements precise and focused. The physical problem offered a straightforward solution – identify the failure point, apply the correct tool, test the result. So unlike the human complications that surrounded him in this house, with their absence of clear guidelines and guaranteed outcomes.

Dust motes danced in the sunbeams that angled through the kitchen window, catching in the humid air above the sink. The refrigerator hummed its off-key note, a counterpoint to the wall clock's metronomic ticking. These sounds had faded into background noise for Casey, but Kirk cataloged them with fresh attention – the auditory fingerprints of a home both sustained and neglected, maintained just enough to remain functional.

By the fifth visit, Casey's bruises had faded, though she still favored long sleeves as if the habit of concealment had outlived its necessity. Kirk arrived to find her at the kitchen table, sketching in a notebook that she closed at his approach, not quickly enough to hide the flowing lines of what appeared to be a garden design. This glimpse of creativity, of forward thinking beyond immediate survival, registered with Kirk as significant – a small green shoot pushing through frost-hardened ground.

"I brought lightbulbs for the porch," he said, setting down his offerings – groceries again, but also household supplies, small tools, practical items selected with careful attention to actual needs rather than imagined ones.

"How did you know about the porch light?" Casey asked, her head tilting slightly, the movement freer than when they'd first met, her neck no longer held rigid with constant vigilance.

"You mentioned it last time." Kirk began organizing items on the counter, each one finding its designated place through repetition and careful observation. "Said you kept meaning to replace it but hadn't gotten around to it."

From the living room came a sudden increase in

volume – Elliot had turned up the news, his agitation triggered by some headline or image. Casey's body tensed automatically, her attention diverted like a compass needle swinging toward magnetic north, but the response was tempered now, less immediate panic and more measured assessment.

"I've got it," she said, rising from the table. "He just needs the remote adjusted. The buttons confuse him."

While she calmed her father, Kirk continued his work – a rhythm they had established without discussion. He existed in parallel to their dynamics rather than intersecting directly, available but not intrusive, present but not presumptuous. He unpacked the remaining groceries, replaced the burned-out bulb in the refrigerator, wiped down the counters with methodical thoroughness.

When Casey returned, she found him studying the ceiling above the stove, where water stains suggested another problem requiring attention. "It's the upstairs bathroom," she explained, following his gaze. "There's a leak in the tile grout. I've been meaning to—"

"I could take a look next time," Kirk suggested, the words offered without presumption, a possible future rather than a definite commitment.

Casey's reflexive denial remained unspoken this time, caught somewhere between habit and a new willingness to accept that some burdens could be shared without surrendering autonomy. "Next time," she echoed instead, the phrase an acknowledgment of continuation, of something taking root between them – not friendship exactly, not yet, but perhaps its quiet precursor.

As Kirk prepared to leave, Casey walked him to the door with steps that no longer suggested she was escorting an intruder from her territory. She stood with her weight evenly distributed, arms loose at her sides rather than wrapped protectively around herself. The change was subtle but unmistakable – a body gradually recalibrating to a presence that had proven itself consistent rather than threatening.

"Thursday?" Kirk asked, Max already at attention beside him, anticipating their departure.

Casey nodded, her face catching the light from the newly functioning porch lamp. "Thursday works." The words emerged with less effort than they once had, acceptance no longer fighting quite so hard against the instinct for self-reliance.

Kirk descended the steps, feeling the weight of her gaze follow him to the sidewalk. Neither of them acknowledged the shifting ground beneath their interactions, the tentative bridges being constructed over weeks of practical assistance and careful distance. Behind her, the house stood with its mixture of decay and resilience – peeling paint and sturdy bones, broken fixtures and enduring foundation. Not unlike its inhabitants, Kirk thought, who continued to stand despite the forces that threatened to collapse them.

Chapter 8

Midmorning light streamed through the kitchen window, turning ordinary dust particles into miniature constellations that drifted between Kirk and Casey as they worked. Their movements had acquired a natural synchronicity over the weeks – Kirk chopping vegetables while Casey assembled sandwiches, the space between them no longer charged with the awkward electricity of strangers but settled into something approaching comfortable familiarity. The radio hummed softly from its perch atop the refrigerator, filling the silences with gentle background noise that required no response from either of them.

"Dad prefers the crusts cut off," Casey said, her knife poised above the sandwich. "It's a texture thing now. The medications make his mouth dry."

Kirk nodded, sliding the cutting board of sliced cucumbers closer to her. Their hands had learned to navigate the same spaces without collision, a choreography built on repetition and unspoken accommodation. From the living room came the measured cadence of the news anchor's voice, punctuated occasionally by Elliot's soft muttering – his running commentary on events he only partially comprehended but still felt compelled to address.

"Is tomato soup still okay?" Kirk asked, gesturing toward the pot he'd been stirring. The soup had become something of a routine – one of the few dishes Elliot consistently recognized and accepted without question. Casey had explained once that it reminded him of his teaching days, of thermoses carried to school during winter months, memories that somehow remained intact while more recent ones crumbled.

"Perfect," Casey answered, her shoulders looser than they had been weeks ago, her movements less sharp-edged with constant anticipation. She arranged the sandwich quarters on a plate, her fingers lingering over the presentation as if this small act of care might compensate for all the larger ones that went unnoticed or unremembered. "I'll take his plate in. He likes to eat while watching the news."

Kirk ladled soup into a bowl with careful precision, the steam rising between them, carrying the scent of comfort and simplicity. Casey took both dishes, balancing them with the practiced ease of someone who had turned basic caregiving tasks into muscle memory. Kirk followed a step behind, carrying his own plate and a glass of water, their lunchtime routine established through wordless agreement rather than explicit planning.

The living room glowed with filtered sunlight, dust motes dancing in the beams that cut across Elliot's armchair. He sat with the rigid posture of someone fighting gravity's constant pull, his attention fixed on the television where stock market figures scrolled across the bottom of the screen. His fingers drummed against the armrest, an irregular tapping that might have been anxiety or simply the misfiring of neural connections that no longer followed predictable pathways.

"Lunch, Dad," Casey announced, using the bright, clear voice she reserved for these interactions – neither patronizing nor overly cautious, but distinct from her natural tone. She set the plate and bowl on the TV tray beside him, adjusting its height with automatic precision.

Elliot's gaze remained fixed on the screen for several seconds before sliding reluctantly toward the food. "Is it time already?" he asked, the question genuine rather than rhetorical. Time had become elastic for him, stretching and compressing without warning or pattern.

"Just about noon," Casey confirmed, settling on the edge of the sofa closest to his chair, her own plate balanced on her knees. Kirk took the opposite end, maintaining the careful distance that had become their unspoken agreement – close enough for conversation, far enough for comfort.

The news transitioned from financial reports to international coverage, images of distant cities flashing across the screen. Elliot's attention drifted between his food and the television, fork occasionally pausing midway to his mouth as something captured his fragmented focus. Casey watched him from the corner of her eye, the vigilance so habitual now that it seemed less a conscious choice than an extension of her nervous system.

And then, between one moment and the next, something shifted. Elliot's posture changed – a straightening of the spine, a lifting of the chin, a focusing of the gaze that had been absent minutes before. The transformation was subtle but unmistakable, like a radio suddenly finding clear signal after hours of static. He set his fork down with deliberate care and turned toward Casey, really seeing her for what might have been the first time in weeks.

"Casey," he said, his voice different – clearer, more present, carrying the resonance that had once commanded classrooms of reluctant students. The drumming fingers stilled, then lifted, reaching across the small space between them to touch her wrist with trembling hesitation.

Casey froze, sandwich halfway to her mouth, body suddenly rigid with recognition of the change. Her eyes widened, pupils dilating with something between hope and terror. Kirk felt the shift in atmosphere like a drop in barometric pressure, the air in the room suddenly heavy with potential.

"Dad?" she whispered, the word barely audible, as if speaking too loudly might shatter the moment.

Elliot's fingers circled her wrist, his touch feather-light but purposeful. His eyes – clear now, focused with painful intensity – searched her face, lingering on the faded remnants of bruises that makeup couldn't completely conceal. "I'm sorry for how I've been," he said, his voice cracking with emotion, each word emerging distinct and deliberate. "You've always been such a good daughter. I'm so proud of you."

The plate on Casey's lap tilted dangerously as her body went completely still, a prey animal sensing something too significant to flee from or fight against. Her throat worked, swallowing repeatedly, but no words emerged. Her eyes filled with sudden moisture that she seemed unable to blink away or release, tears suspended in a moment of perfect, painful clarity.

"I know what's happening to me," Elliot continued, each word appearing to cost him tremendous effort, as if he were fighting through fog to deliver them. "I know what I've done. What I've become." His fingers tightened slightly around her wrist, the pressure gentle but insistent. "You shouldn't have to bear this. You should be living your life, not watching mine disappear."

Something broke in Casey's expression – a crack in the careful composure she'd maintained through countless difficult days. Her lips parted, but whatever response she might have formed dissolved into a small, wounded sound. The plate slid from her knees as she abruptly stood, catching it with reflexive dexterity that belied her emotional state.

"I need to check on the soup," she said, the words emerging strangled and dissonant, a transparent excuse that fooled no one. She set the plate on the coffee table with hands that had begun to visibly tremble, avoiding both men's eyes. "Just... I'll be right back."

She moved toward the kitchen with careful control, her steps measured to the point of stillness, as if she feared that normal movement might fracture her completely.

Kirk saw the rigid set of her shoulders, the way her fingers curled into fists at her sides, the slight tremor that ran through her frame with each controlled breath.

As Casey disappeared from view, Kirk turned back to Elliot, whose eyes had followed his daughter with a clarity that was already beginning to cloud over. The moment was receding like tide pulling away from shore, leaving only scattered evidence of its brief presence. Elliot blinked once, twice, his gaze drifting back to the television screen where news anchors continued their dispassionate reporting of world events.

"The market's down again," Elliot observed, his voice sliding back into its familiar distant quality, the words emerging without the weight of personal significance they had carried moments before.

His hand, which had reached for Casey with such purpose, now returned to its restless drumming against the chair arm. "They always say it'll bounce back, but I'm not so sure this time."

The transition was complete – lucidity retreating like a visitor who had stayed only long enough to deliver an urgent message before departing without farewell.

Elliot picked up his fork again, attention recaptured by the television, the moment of connection already fading from his consciousness. But in the hallway beyond the living room, Kirk heard the first soft, broken sound of Casey's control finally shattering, a dam giving way after withstanding pressure far beyond its intended capacity.

Chapter 9

Kirk found Casey pressed against the hallway wall, her body rigid as though the peeling floral wallpaper alone kept her upright. Her hands were splayed flat against the surface behind her, fingers spread wide as if trying to anchor herself to something solid while the floor beneath her threatened to give way. The narrow passage trapped the afternoon light in amber bands that illuminated her face in strips—revealing the struggle playing across her features as she fought to maintain the composure that had sustained her for months, perhaps years, but was now crumbling like a dam pushed beyond its capacity.

She didn't look at him when he approached, her gaze fixed on some middle distance, seeing neither the worn carpet beneath her feet nor the family photographs that lined the opposite wall. Her breathing came in measured counts—inhale for four, hold for four, exhale for four—the deliberate rhythm of someone who had taught herself to manage crisis through controlled respiration. But the technique was failing her now; each exhale caught slightly, hitching with the effort of containing what threatened to spill over.

"I'm fine," she said without prompting, the words emerging strangled and unconvincing. A tear escaped despite her rigid control, tracking a solitary path down her cheek before she roughly wiped it away with the heel of her hand. "I just needed a minute. I'll be back in there in a second."

Kirk remained several feet away, close enough to offer presence without crowding her space. He recognized the particular agony etched in the lines of her face—the specific pain of witnessing someone you love surface briefly from the disease consuming them, only to slip away again before you could fully respond. That cruel gift of clarity that offered no resolution, only a sharper awareness of what was being lost.

"It's alright if you're not fine," he said, his voice low enough that it wouldn't carry back to the living room where Elliot had already returned to his news program, the moment of recognition faded like morning mist burned off by harsh sun. "No one could be."

Another tear fell, then another, Casey's blinks becoming more rapid as she tried to contain the flood. Her shoulders rose toward her ears, body curling inward as if bracing for impact. "I can't do this right now," she whispered, the words directed at herself rather than at Kirk. "I have to finish lunch. I have to give him his medication at one. I have to—"

Her voice broke on the final word, fracturing into a sound so raw it seemed to scrape against the walls of the narrow hallway. She pressed her fist against her mouth, trying to physically contain the sob that followed, but it escaped around her knuckles—a wounded animal sound that had been caged for too long.

"Casey," Kirk said gently, taking one step closer but still maintaining a respectful distance. "It's okay to grieve. Even when they're still here."

Something in his words—perhaps their simple permission, perhaps their recognition of her impossible position —unlocked what remained of her restraint. Her face crumpled, composure deserting her completely as tears spilled freely now, no longer solitary tracers but steady streams that carved glistening paths down her cheeks. Her chest heaved with the effort of drawing breath between sobs that seemed to rise from the soles of her feet, tremors running through her entire body.

"I can't," she gasped, the words barely comprehensible through tears. "I can't fall apart. There's no one else. If I start, I don't know if I can stop."

Her legs gave way then, strength deserting her as grief claimed territory long denied to it. She slid down the wall in a controlled collapse, landing on the hallway floor with her knees drawn up, arms wrapped tightly around them as if physically holding herself together. The sobs came harder now, her entire frame shaking with their force, each one torn from somewhere deep and long-buried.

Kirk lowered himself to the floor as well, settling beside her with enough space between them to allow her this private unraveling. The afternoon light shifted through the hallway window, casting elongated shadows across their seated forms as time passed unmarked except by the changing angle of sunbeams.

"After Charlotte died," he said quietly, when Casey's sobs had softened enough that she might hear him, "I kept finding things of hers I'd forgotten she'd left at my place. A hairbrush. A sweater. Shopping lists in her handwriting." He rested his forearms on his bent knees, gaze directed forward rather than at Casey, giving her privacy even in this shared space. "But with your dad, you're losing him while he's still here. Grieving someone who's sitting across from you at breakfast. That's a special kind of hell."

Casey's breathing gradually steadied, though tears

continued to fall. She uncurled slightly, her posture soft-ening from its protective hunch. "Sometimes I catch glimpses of him," she admitted, voice hoarse from crying. "The real him. Like today. And it's worse, somehow, than if he were gone completely." She wiped ineffectually at her face with her sleeve. "Is that terrible to say?"

"It's honest," Kirk replied simply. "And a hell of a lot braver than pretending it's not happening."

A fresh wave of tears followed his words, but these were different—less the violent breaking of a dam and more the steady release of a pressure valve finally allowed to function. Casey's shoulders shook with quieter sobs as years of accumulated grief found expression, each tear carrying some small fraction of the weight she had carried alone for so long.

"I miss him," she whispered. "He's right there in the next room, and I miss him so much I can't breathe with it sometimes." The confession emerged raw and unfiltered, words she had likely never spoken aloud. "I keep thinking if I just try harder, if I'm more patient, if I find the right combination of things, I'll get more moments like today. More glimpses of my dad."

Kirk nodded, understanding the bargaining stage of grief all too well—the desperate search for formulas and conditions that might temporarily reverse the irreversible. "You're doing everything humanly possible," he said, the simple truth offered without platitude or false comfort. "And it's still not enough. It can't be. That's not failure, Casey. It's just the nature of what you're up against."

As they sat in the narrow hallway, the distance between them gradually decreased—not through dramatic move-ment but through the subtle shifting that happens when bodies release their rigid self-containment. Casey's shoulder came to rest lightly against Kirk's arm, the contact so gentle it might have been accidental if not for the way she remained there, accepting the simple comfort of human touch.

Kirk's hand moved then, coming to rest on her shoulder with careful pressure—not pulling her closer, not demanding response, simply offering connection. Beneath his palm, he felt the slight tremor that still ran through her, the physical aftermath of emotional release.

The sunlight continued its slow journey across the hallway, stretching their shadows into elongated versions of themselves against the opposite wall. Through the thin walls came the muffled sounds of the television, of Elliot's occasional comments to anchors who couldn't hear him, the ordinary soundtrack of their days continuing despite the extraordinary moment unfolding in this liminal space between rooms.

Neither spoke for several minutes, existing together in the strange intimacy that comes from witnessing another person's raw vulnerability. Casey's tears gradually subsided, her breathing settling into a more natural rhythm, though she made no move to rise or to pull away from the slight contact between them. In this moment of shared stillness, something shifted—not dramatic enough to name, but significant enough to feel, like tectonic plates adjusting far below the surface, changing the landscape in ways that wouldn't be visible for some time to come.

Chapter 10

The fork slid from Elliot's grasp for the third time that morning, clattering against the plate with a sound that seemed to physically pain him. Casey watched her father's face crumple in frustration, his fingers trembling as they reached again for the utensil, determined despite their betrayal. She resisted the urge to help him, knowing that his remaining dignity hung by threads she dared not sever, though each failed attempt squeezed her heart like a vise.

"Stupid thing," Elliot muttered, his voice carrying none of the professor's authority that had once commanded lecture halls. "They make these handles too small now. Not like they used to be."

Casey nodded, the lie between them so familiar it had become a third presence at their meals. "Would you like me to cut the pancake smaller?" she offered, careful to frame the assistance as a preference rather than a necessity.

Elliot's eyes narrowed, suspicious flickers darting across his face like minnows in shallow water. "Who told you I can't cut my own food?" he demanded, volume rising with each word. "Have you been talking about me to strangers again?"

The accusation hung in the air between them, absurd yet painful in its implications. Three weeks had passed since the afternoon Kirk had held her while she cried in the hallway, and Elliot's paranoia had bloomed like a poisonous flower in that time, unfurling new and more troubling petals each day.

"No one's talking about you, Dad," Casey assured him, the words worn smooth from repetition. "It was just a suggestion."

His gaze settled on a point beyond her left shoulder, focused on something — or someone — only he could see. "There's a man watching the house again," he whispered, leaning forward with conspiratorial urgency. "Been there since dawn. Military type. Taking notes on everything we do."

Casey didn't turn to look at the empty driveway she knew lay beyond the kitchen window. These phantom observers had populated Elliot's world with increasing frequency, their imagined surveillance extending from occasional comments to elaborate theories that consumed hours of his diminishing lucidity.

"Would you like more coffee?" she asked instead, rising to refill his mug whether he wanted it or not, desperate for the momentary reprieve of turning her back, of not having to school her features into neutral acceptance of his slipping reality.

Her hands braced against the kitchen counter, Casey drew a deep breath. The muscles between her shoulder blades ached from sleeping upright in the hallway chair for the third night that week, positioned to intercept her father during his midnight wanderings. The bruises on her forearms — concentric ovals in varying shades of purple and yellow where his fingers had gripped her during yesterday's confusion — throbbed beneath her long sleeves, a physical manifestation of pain that seemed almost welcome compared to the emotional wounds that left no visible marks.

When she turned back, Elliot was staring at her with complete bewilderment, his eyes traveling her face as if encountering a stranger. "Have we met?" he asked politely, his head tilting in gentle confusion. "Are you from the department?"

Casey's throat tightened, air suddenly too thick to draw properly into her lungs. These periods of complete disorientation had been happening with increasing frequency – minutes stretching into hours where she ceased to exist in his fractured memory, where their shared history dissolved like sugar in hot liquid, leaving nothing solid to grasp.

"It's Casey, Dad," she said, muscle memory forming the words her conscious mind was too exhausted to assemble. "Your daughter. I live here with you."

He studied her with the careful attention he'd once given to historical artifacts, searching for context clues, for anything that might anchor him to this piece of information. "Casey," he repeated, the name a question rather than a confirmation. His gaze dropped to his plate, to the half-eaten pancake and abandoned fork. "I don't seem to be very hungry today."

The doorbell rang before Casey could respond, its cheerful chime incongruous in the heavy atmosphere of the kitchen. Elliot's head snapped up, eyes wild with sudden fear.

"They're here," he hissed, pushing back from the table with surprising strength, his chair scraping against the linoleum. "I told you they were watching. Don't let them take me. Don't—"

"It's just Kirk, Dad," Casey assured him, though the familiar panic was already blooming across her father's features, the tightening of his jaw that preceded agitation she might not be able to contain. "Remember Kirk? He's been helping us with groceries. The tall man with the dog."

Elliot's breathing accelerated, shallow pants that never seemed to deliver enough oxygen. "I don't know any Kirk," he insisted, the tremor in his hands intensifying. "Don't open that door. They'll take me away. They'll lock me up."

Casey hesitated, torn between answering the door and staying with her increasingly agitated father. The decision was made for her when Elliot suddenly lurched from his chair, making a clumsy dash toward the hallway, presumably to hide or to secure some imagined vulnerable entry point to their home. She managed to intercept him, hands gentle but firm on his shoulders.

"Dad, it's okay. You're safe here. No one's going to take you anywhere," she promised, the lie burning her tongue even as she spoke it. Because wasn't that exactly what she'd been considering these past weeks, as his deterioration accelerated beyond what she could manage? Wasn't that precisely what Kirk had gently suggested during his last three visits, his eyes taking in her increasing exhaustion, the new bruises she failed to hide? "Why don't you go to the living room while I see who's at the door?"

The doorbell rang again, followed by a gentle knock – Kirk's particular rhythm that he'd established as his signature, a courtesy to prevent startling either of them. Elliot allowed himself to be guided toward his armchair, muttering about intruders and conspiracies, his gait unsteady. Casey waited until he was seated before rushing to answer the door, her movements those of someone jumping between emergencies with no time to fully address any of them.

Kirk stood on the porch, a paper bag of groceries cradled in one arm, his expression shifting from greeting to concern as he registered the strain etched into her features.

"Bad morning?" he asked, voice lowered as he stepped inside.

"Bad week," Casey corrected, closing the door behind him and leaning against it momentarily, allowing herself three seconds of supported weight before straightening. "He's having more episodes. Longer ones. Sometimes he doesn't know who I am for hours at a stretch."

Kirk's gaze dropped to where her sleeve had ridden up, exposing the bracelet of fresh bruises circling her wrist. His jaw tightened, though his voice remained measured. "Those are new."

Casey tugged her sleeve down in an automatic gesture of concealment. "He thought I was an intruder last night. Grabbed me when I tried to lead him back to bed." The explanation emerged flat, factual, stripped of emotion she couldn't afford to indulge. "It's fine. I've had worse."

Kirk set the groceries on the hall table, his attention fully focused on her now. "Casey," he said, her name carrying weight beyond its single syllable. "We need to talk about this. About what comes next."

She shook her head, an instinctive rejection. "Not now. He's already agitated. He thinks people are watching the house, that they're coming to take him away." Her laugh held no humor, only bitter irony. "Turns out his paranoia isn't entirely unfounded, is it?"

They moved to the living room, where Elliot sat rigidly in his armchair, eyes fixed on the blank television screen. His fingers worked at the arm of the chair, picking at a loose thread with single-minded focus. Casey settled on the sofa opposite him, while Kirk remained standing, his tall frame positioned where he could observe both father and daughter.

"He's getting worse," Kirk said quietly, stating what Casey had been avoiding acknowledging aloud. "You can't keep doing this alone. Not safely, for either of you."

"I promised him," Casey replied, her voice barely above a whisper. "I promised I'd take care of him at home. That I wouldn't—" She broke off, pressing her fingers against her eyes as if physically holding back tears she couldn't afford to shed. "He was so afraid of ending up warehoused somewhere, forgotten. Before the diagnosis, he made me swear I wouldn't let that happen."

"That was before," Kirk countered gently. "Before the violence. Before he stopped recognizing you more often than he remembers you."

As if summoned by their hushed conversation, Elliot stirred, his gaze focusing on the two of them with sudden sharpness. "Margaret?" he called, looking directly at Casey. "Margaret, who is this man? Why is he in our house?"

Casey's breath caught painfully in her chest. Margaret – her mother's name, unused in their household for decades, now emerging with increasing frequency from Elliot's confused mind. "Dad, it's Casey," she corrected, rising to move toward him. "Mom's not here. Remember? It's just you and me."

Elliot's confusion visibly deepened, brow furrowing with the effort of processing information that didn't align with his internal reality. "But you can't be Casey," he insisted, voice rising. "Casey's just a little girl. My little girl. Where is she? What have you done with her?"

His agitation escalated quickly, body struggling to rise from the chair as panic overtook him. "They're trying to take me away," he accused, gaze darting wildly between Casey and Kirk. "You're working with them, aren't you? Pretending to be my wife. Where's my daughter? I want my daughter!"

Casey moved toward him, hands outstretched in the calming gesture she'd developed through painful trial and error. "Dad, please. It's me. It's Casey. I'm right here."

Elliot recoiled from her touch, his expression twisted

with fear and anger. "Don't touch me! Imposter! Where's my Casey?" His voice broke on her name, raw with emotion that cut through the confusion. For a terrible moment, his eyes cleared, recognition dawning like a brief break in storm clouds. "Casey? Is that really you?"

"Yes, Dad," she whispered, hope flaring briefly. "It's me."

The moment of clarity vanished as quickly as it had appeared. Elliot's face contorted with renewed confusion, his body suddenly sagging as the adrenaline of agitation drained away, leaving exhaustion in its wake. He collapsed back into his armchair, breathing heavily, gaze once again unfocused and distant.

In the terrible silence that followed, Kirk approached Casey, who stood frozen before her father's chair. He took her hands in his – carefully, mindful of the bruises – and waited until she met his eyes.

"You've done everything humanly possible," he said, his voice firm but kind, each word weighted with under-standing of what it cost her to hear them. "It's time to get him the help you can't provide alone."

Casey's shoulders slumped, the rigid posture that had carried her through weeks of increasing crisis finally collapsing. Her resistance crumbled like a sandcastle against an inevitable tide, leaving only the bare truth exposed. She looked at her father – this shell that contained fragments of the man who had raised her – and nodded once, the motion almost imperceptible.

"I know," she whispered, the admission rising from some deep place of painful clarity. "I know."

Chapter 11

Casey stood in the doorway of her father's bedroom, the empty duffel bag hanging from her fingertips like a pronouncement. Afternoon light filtered through the faded curtains, illuminating the space where Elliot Preston had spent his recent years – part museum to his former self, part medical station, the dual nature of his existence captured in the contradictions of the room. Medical alert buttons and prescription bottles shared space with leather-bound history books and the antique clock he'd inherited from his own father. Casey inhaled deeply, willing strength into her limbs before stepping across the threshold to begin the dismantling of their shared life.

The doctor's sedative had taken effect shortly after Kirk's arrival, transforming Elliot from the agitated, confused man who'd called Casey by her mother's name into a quieter version of himself, docile and heavy-lidded in his armchair. This pharmacological calm had given Casey the window she needed to prepare, though each movement felt like betrayal as she began collecting the necessities for his transition to institutional care.

She began with the medications – the constellation of

pills that marked the hours of their days like secular prayers. Her fingers moved with the precision of long practice, gathering orange bottles from the nightstand, checking labels, counting remaining doses, and arranging them in the specialized organizer she'd purchased months ago. The plastic compartments clicked shut with finality as she sorted morning doses from evening ones, weekday from weekend, creating order from the chemical chaos that regulated her father's failing mind.

"Do you need help with anything specific?" Kirk asked from the doorway, his frame filling the space without entering it, respecting the invisible boundary between support and intrusion.

Casey shook her head, unable to look away from the task at hand. "There's a list on the refrigerator," she said, her voice distant even to her own ears. "Things he'll need. I've been adding to it for weeks." The admission hung between them – evidence that part of her had known this day was coming, had been preparing even while consciously resisting it.

She moved to the dresser next, pulling open drawers that stuck slightly from age and humidity. The scent of cedar and the faint traces of the sandalwood aftershave Elliot had used for decades wafted upward, triggering a memory so visceral it momentarily stopped her breath – sitting on his lap as a child while he graded papers, that same scent enveloping her in safety and certainty. Her fingers tightened on the edge of the drawer until her knuckles whitened, the physical effort of maintaining composure manifesting in her grip.

Kirk moved quietly around the periphery of the room, gathering items from the bathroom – toothbrush, electric razor, the special soft-bristled hairbrush that didn't irritate Elliot's increasingly sensitive scalp. His movements were deliberate and unobtrusive, filling gaps in Casey's focus without drawing attention to her momentary lapses.

From the dresser, Casey selected underwear, soft cotton pajamas worn to perfect thinness, loose-fitting shirts that accommodated the blood pressure cuff without requiring Elliot to undress completely. Each item represented a concession to his condition, modifications made incrementally as his independence receded like a tide that would never return. She folded each piece with ritualistic care, as if the precision of her creases could somehow compensate for the disorder of their circumstances.

Her hands paused as they reached the cardigan hanging on the back of the bedroom door – oatmeal-colored wool with leather buttons and elbow patches worn to a shine from decades of lecture hall podiums and grading papers. The sweater that had been as much a part of Professor Preston as his precise diction and encyclopedic memory for historical dates. Casey lifted it from its hook, the weight of it in her hands carrying emotional heft beyond its physical substance.

"He wore this to every parent-teacher conference," she said softly, not really speaking to Kirk but needing to externalize the memory. "Said it made him look approachable while maintaining professional authority." Her smile was brittle as she carefully folded the cardigan, placing it atop the growing stack of clothing. "The students called him 'Professor Patches' behind his back. He pretended not to know, but he was secretly proud of the nickname."

Kirk nodded, acknowledging both the story and the pain beneath it. "It's good to bring familiar things," he said. "They help with the transition."

Casey moved to the nightstand, where a silver-framed photograph stood guard beside the lamp – a woman with Casey's eyes and a wider smile, her hair styled in the distinctive waves of three decades past.

Margaret Preston's image had acquired a patina of reverence over the years, the photograph one of the few items Elliot could still reliably identify even on his worst days.

"He needs this," Casey murmured, wrapping the frame carefully in a soft t-shirt before placing it in the bag. "It's the only thing that still consistently grounds him sometimes."

She continued through the room, selecting slippers, a robe, the digital watch with the oversized numbers that sometimes helped Elliot orient to time. Each item carried its own weight of memory, its own silent testimony to the man who had existed before disease began erasing him stroke by relentless stroke.

In the closet, Casey found herself suddenly unable to move, her hand frozen on the doorknob, a wave of vertigo washing over her without warning. She gripped the wooden frame with both hands, knuckles white with the effort of remaining upright as reality pressed down on her with crushing force. This was happening. After years of promises and determination, of adjustments and accommodations, of telling herself she could manage one more day, one more incident, one more decline – she was surrendering.

Kirk was beside her instantly, not touching but present, his stability an offering rather than an imposition. "Breathe," he reminded her simply. "Just breathe."

Casey nodded, focusing on the mechanical process of drawing air into her lungs, holding it, releasing it. The dizziness receded gradually, leaving in its wake a hollow clarity. "I never thought I'd be the one to break my promise to him," she whispered, the words emerging from some deep well of shame.

"You're not breaking a promise," Kirk countered gently. "You're fulfilling the deeper one – to take care of him, to keep him safe. Sometimes that means recognizing when you can't do it alone anymore."

Casey straightened, her spine realigning with the truth of his words. She opened the closet and selected the final items – comfortable shoes for hospital hallways, the soft flannel pajamas Elliot preferred for what he still sometimes called "sick days," as if his condition were temporary, a mere pause in ordinary life rather than its redefinition.

With the duffel bag full, Casey attempted to close it, but found her hands suddenly uncooperative, trembling too severely to align the zipper's teeth. The failure seemed disproportionately devastating – one final betrayal of her body when control mattered most. Kirk stepped forward without comment, his hands closing the bag with efficient, gentle movements. The absence of pity in his assistance made it possible to accept.

They carried the bag to the living room, where Elliot sat in his armchair, the sedative having created an artificial calm that softened the edges of his earlier agitation. His gaze tracked their entrance, settling on the duffel with the focused attention he could still occasionally summon.

"We're going somewhere, aren't we, Casey?" he asked, his voice carrying an unexpected lucidity, as if the medication had temporarily cleared away some of the neural static that typically interfered with his thought processes.

Casey set the bag down and knelt before her father's chair, taking his hands in hers. They felt smaller somehow, the bones more prominent beneath papery skin that had once been callused from years of woodworking and chalk dust. "Yes, Dad," she confirmed, striving for a steadiness she didn't feel. "You need some special care now. The kind I can't give you here at home."

Elliot's gaze traveled her face, something like understanding flickering in his eyes. "The hospital," he said, not a question but a recognition. "Because of the episodes."

Casey nodded, surprised and grateful for this temporary window of comprehension. "They have specialists there who can help with the confusion. With the... with the times when you get frightened or angry."

"When I hurt you," Elliot clarified, his gaze dropping to the bruises visible beneath her sleeve. His fingers traced the outline of the marks with feather-light pressure, his weathered face crumpling with grief. "I see these sometimes, and I can't remember how they happened. But I know... I know I'm the one who put them there."

"It's not your fault," Casey insisted, the automatic response she'd given so many times before. "It's the disease, Dad. Not you."

Elliot shook his head slightly, a professor gently correcting a flawed premise. "The disease is part of me now," he said, the words emerging with careful precision, as if he'd been saving his clarity for this moment. "I can feel it, Casey. Feel myself disappearing a little more each day." His fingers tightened around hers with surprising strength. "You're a good daughter. Better than I deserve. Too good to have your life stopped by my ending."

The stark truth of his assessment – this flash of the man he had been, perceptive and unflinching – broke something in Casey that had been holding her together. Tears welled in her eyes, spilling over before she could contain them. "I don't want to let you go," she whispered, the admission torn from some deep, selfish place she rarely acknowledged. "I'm scared of what comes next."

Elliot's hand moved to cup her cheek, the gesture achingly familiar from childhood comforts. "You've already let me go," he said, his voice gentle with a terrible wisdom. "Piece by piece. Day by day. This is just... making it official." His thumb brushed away a tear with the tender precision he'd once used to bandage her skinned knees. "Maybe in that place, without you getting hurt, I can just be your dad again for whatever time I have left. Not your patient. Not your burden."

Kirk stood silently at the periphery of this exchange, witness to a moment of connection so profound it felt almost intrusive to observe. The afternoon light slanted through the living room windows, casting long shadows across the worn carpet, illuminating father and daughter in a tableau of goodbye that had been happening incrementally for years, now crystallized into this single, deliberate moment of recognition.

"I love you, Dad," Casey said, the simple declaration containing all she couldn't articulate – gratitude, grief, guilt, and the bottomless ache of anticipated loss.

"I know, Casey-girl," Elliot replied, using the childhood endearment that had become increasingly rare as his vocabulary contracted. "I know."

His gaze drifted then, the lucidity beginning to recede like a tide pulling away from shore, leaving behind only scattered shells of awareness. Casey remained kneeling before him, hands still holding his, watching as the father she'd just reclaimed began once more to slip beyond her reach.

Chapter 12

The hospital corridor stretched before them like a fluorescent-lit purgatory, its antiseptic scent burning Casey's nostrils with each breath. The squeaking of the wheelchair's left front wheel marked their procession in metronomic rhythm – a tiny imperfection in the otherwise ruthlessly efficient machinery of institutional care. Casey's hand rested on her father's shoulder, feeling the unfamiliar contours of his bones through the fabric of his cardigan, his body somehow diminished since they'd left home just thirty minutes earlier, as if the very act of crossing the hospital threshold had accelerated his reduction.

The walls were painted a shade that couldn't commit to being either beige or green, a color designed to offend no one while comforting absolutely no one. Framed prints of abstract watercolors hung at precise intervals, their bland swirls selected for their complete absence of provocation. Even the lighting seemed deliberate in its neutrality – bright enough for medical assessment but diffuse enough to blur the harsher edges of decline, of surrender, of endings disguised as transitions.

A nurse with practical shoes and an expression of

professional compassion guided the wheelchair, her steady pace suggesting hundreds of similar journeys down these identical hallways. "The geriatric neurology wing is just ahead," she explained, her voice pitched to the particular cadence of someone communicating simultaneously with the confused and the grieving. "Dr. Winters will examine your father once we've completed the intake process."

Elliot's head swiveled as they passed doorways revealing glimpses of other lives paused in similar circumstances – an elderly woman staring out a window, a man connected to monitors that beeped in electronic approximation of his continuing existence. Elliot's hand reached up to grasp Casey's where it rested on his shoulder, his fingers cold against her skin.

"Where are we?" he asked, voice small and bewildered, the lucidity of his earlier moment at home already receded like a dream upon waking. "Are we going to your school concert? I ironed my good shirt."

The confusion – this slippage between decades – was familiar territory that nonetheless stabbed Casey freshly each time. "We're at the hospital, Dad," she explained, squeezing his hand gently. "Remember? We talked about this at home. The doctors here are going to help you feel better."

Elliot's grip tightened, then abruptly released as his attention scattered, drawn to something only he could perceive. "There's water coming through the ceiling," he announced with sudden urgency, pointing toward the unblemished white tiles above them. "We need to get buckets. The manuscripts will be ruined."

Casey's eyes met Kirk's over her father's head, the silent exchange communicating volumes – concern, resignation, shared recognition of how rapidly Elliot could slide from connection to confusion. Kirk had remained a step behind them throughout this processional, a silent support whose presence allowed Casey to focus entirely on her father rather than the practicalities of admission.

The nurse showed no reaction to Elliot's non-sequitur, her composed features suggesting she'd heard far stranger pronouncements in these hallways. "Here we are," she announced, guiding the wheelchair into a small office where a desk was stacked with forms and a computer hummed with quiet efficiency. "If you could start on these while I get Professor Preston's vitals, we'll have him settled into his room shortly."

The stack of papers slid across the desk toward Casey – liability releases, medical history forms, insurance verifications, advance directives. The words swam before her eyes, legal and medical terminology blurring into an incomprehensible mass that seemed designed to transform her father from person to patient, from individual to case number. Her hand hovered over the top form, pen poised but immobile, suddenly unable to complete even this simple mechanical task.

Kirk moved beside her, his presence solid and grounding. "Why don't I help with these," he suggested quietly, not really a question. "You can stay with your dad while they take his vitals."

Gratitude washed through Casey, though she managed only a nod in response. She turned back to Elliot, who was now allowing the nurse to wrap a blood pressure cuff around his arm, his expression one of polite confusion, as if he were participating in some social ritual whose purpose he couldn't quite recall but didn't wish to offend by questioning.

"The systolic is a bit elevated, but that's to be expected with the transition," the nurse commented, making a note on her tablet. "Temperature normal, pulse steady." Her assessment continued with brisk efficiency, reducing Elliot to a collection of measurements and readings, data points on a medical chart that couldn't possibly capture the man who had once filled lecture halls with his resonant voice and encyclopedic knowledge of ancient civilizations.

Casey knelt beside the wheelchair, trying to position herself within Elliot's increasingly narrow field of focus. "They're just checking that you're okay, Dad," she explained, keeping her voice even despite the tremor that threatened to overtake it. "Like when Dr. Simons comes to the house, remember?"

Elliot's gaze fixed on her momentarily, recognition flickering across his features. "Casey," he said, her name a momentary anchor in his drifting consciousness. "Did you finish your history project? Is that why we're here? The museum exhibit?"

"No, Dad," she corrected gently, the familiar ache of these corrections never dulling with repetition. "We're at the hospital. You're going to stay here for a while so the doctors can help with your medication."

The nurse continued her assessment, checking pupil response, asking orientation questions that Elliot answered with increasing agitation as the reality of their location began to penetrate his confusion. "Name?" the nurse asked.

"Elliot Preston," he replied, a flash of his former precision.

"Current year?"

A hesitation, brow furrowing. "1997?" The question in his voice revealing his uncertainty.

"Current president?"

Longer pause, frustration building visibly. "How is that relevant to my treatment?" he snapped, the professor momentarily resurfacing with indignation at irrelevant inquiries.

The nurse made another note without reaction. "Just standard questions, Professor Preston. Thank you for your cooperation." She turned to Casey, lowering her voice slightly. "The doctor will be in shortly to complete the neurological assessment. In the meantime, let's get him settled in his room."

Kirk had been steadily working through the forms, his neat, precise handwriting filling in blanks with information he'd learned during his weeks of helping Casey – insurance details, medication lists, emergency contacts. He'd become her backup memory, holding pieces of practical information she'd begun to drop as exhaustion and stress corroded her capacity for detail management.

They followed the nurse down another corridor to a room with two beds, one empty and one occupied by an elderly man who appeared to be sleeping, monitors tracking his vital signs in silent vigilance. The space was divided by a thin curtain, offering the illusion rather than the reality of privacy. A window provided a view of the parking lot, cars gleaming under the midday sun like exotic insects trapped in amber.

"This will be Professor Preston's bed," the nurse explained, gesturing to the one nearest the window. "You can help him get settled if you'd like. Dr. Winters should be by within the hour."

The process of transferring Elliot from wheelchair to bed went smoothly until the nurse began explaining the call button, the meal schedule, the visiting hours. It was this last item that penetrated Elliot's confusion, clarifying his situation with sudden, devastating precision.

"Visiting hours?" he repeated, looking from the nurse to Casey with dawning comprehension. "You're not staying?"

Casey felt the floor tilt beneath her feet, the moment she'd been dreading now unavoidable. "Dad, this is a hospital. I can't stay overnight. But I'll come visit every day, I promise."

Elliot's face transformed, panic replacing confusion as his hand shot out to grasp Casey's wrist with surprising strength. "No," he said, the single syllable loaded with desperation. "You can't leave me here with strangers. Casey, please. I don't know these people. I don't know where I am."

The nurse stepped forward, her expression compassionate but resolute. "Professor Preston, your daughter will be back tomorrow. For now, we need to help you get comfortable and settled."

"I don't want to get comfortable!" Elliot's voice rose, his grip on Casey's wrist tightening to the point of pain. "I want to go home. Casey, take me home. Don't leave me here. Please don't leave me."

Casey tried to maintain her composure, though something was shattering inside her chest with each plea. "Dad, please. This is to help you get better. The doctors here can do things for you that I can't do at home."

Elliot's eyes – suddenly clear with terror – locked onto hers with perfect recognition. "You promised," he whispered, the accusation slicing through her defenses. "You promised you wouldn't send me away."

A second nurse appeared, apparently summoned by some silent signal from the first. Together they began to gently but firmly disengage Elliot's fingers from Casey's wrist, murmuring reassurances that seemed to have no effect on his escalating distress.

"It's often easier for everyone if family members exit quickly during the transition," the first nurse advised, her tone suggesting this was standard protocol rather than a specific judgment. "The initial separation anxiety usually subsides within a day or two."

Separation anxiety. The clinical term for her father's desperation stripped it of its humanity, rendered it a textbook symptom rather than the primal fear of a man watching his last connection to familiar life being severed. Casey stood frozen, torn between the rational understanding that these professionals knew best and the visceral need to respond to her father's pleas.

"Casey!" Elliot called as the nurses positioned themselves between father and daughter, creating a human barrier that was both physical and symbolic. "Don't go! Please don't go!"

Kirk's hand pressed gently against the small of Casey's back, a silent reminder of reality beyond this awful moment. "They need to get him settled," he said quietly. "And you need a moment to breathe."

Casey allowed herself to be guided toward the door, her body moving while her mind remained locked on her father's face – the betrayal and terror in his eyes as he realized she was actually leaving. She maintained a rigid posture through sheer force of will, spine straight and shoulders back as if proper alignment could somehow prevent the collapse she felt building within her.

The last image before the door closed behind them was Elliot straining against the gentle restraint of the nurses' hands, his voice calling her name with diminishing volume as sedation was likely being administered. The sound of the latch clicking shut felt terminal, a period at the end of a chapter she hadn't been prepared to finish.

In the corridor, away from her father's gaze, Casey's knees finally buckled. Kirk's hand moved from her back to her elbow, supporting her weight without comment or judgment, his steady presence the only thing preventing her complete surrender to gravity's insistent pull.

Chapter 13

Morning light sliced through the venetian blinds, laying stripes of gold across Elliot's sleeping form. Casey paused in the doorway, fresh daisies cradled in the crook of her arm, taking in the tableau of her father's diminishing presence in the world. Two weeks of hospital routine had established its own rhythm – this early moment of observation had become as much a part of her daily ritual as the coffee she carried in her other hand, black and cooling, forgotten in the act of watching her father breathe. In sleep, his face retained echoes of the man he had been, the furrows of confusion smoothed temporarily into a peace that vanished the moment consciousness returned.

She moved quietly into the room, not wanting to disturb this rare interval of tranquility. Elliot's roommate had been discharged three days prior, leaving the second bed empty, its pristine sheets and untouched pillow a clinical still life. Casey placed her coffee on the rolling bedside table and began removing the previous day's wilting carnations from their vase. The daisies – bright yellow with white tips – took their place with cheerful indifference to the gravity of their surroundings.

"Good morning, Dad," she said softly, not expecting a response but maintaining the convention of greeting. The monitors beside his bed continued their steady electronic vigilance – heart rate, oxygen levels, blood pressure translated into digital certainties while the mysteries of his mind remained beyond quantification.

Elliot's eyelids fluttered but didn't open, his consciousness hovering somewhere between sleep and waking. His hands lay perfectly still atop the blanket, the tremors that had plagued him at home now subdued by medication carefully calibrated by white-coated strangers. Casey took one of those hands in hers, noting how the skin had grown looser around the knuckles, how the veins stood out in stark blue relief against pallor that deepened with each passing day.

"The daisies are from Mrs. Abernathy's garden," she continued, her one-sided conversation another established ritual. "She said to tell you she's keeping an eye on the house. Making sure the newspapers don't pile up." The fiction was kind – Mrs. Abernathy had said no such thing, had in fact stopped acknowledging Casey's existence months ago when Elliot's evening wanderings had become disruptive to the neighborhood's placid routines. But the imagined connection to their former life seemed important somehow, a thread of continuity in the unraveling of their shared narrative.

Casey settled into the visitor's chair that had become her second home, its vinyl upholstery bearing the impressions of her body after countless hours of vigil. From her tote bag, she withdrew the book they'd been working through – a biography of Theodore Roosevelt that Elliot had once assigned to his students, its margins filled with his precise handwriting, observations and arguments with the author's conclusions preserved in fading ink.

"Where did we leave off yesterday?" she asked,

thumbing through to find the bookmark. "Ah, here we are. The Rough Riders were about to charge San Juan Hill."

She began to read, her voice carefully modulated to the same cadence she'd used for bedtime stories throughout her childhood. The words flowed around Elliot's still form, creating an atmosphere that existed alongside but separate from the antiseptic reality of the hospital room. Outside in the corridor, a meal cart rattled past, the squeak of its wheels a counterpoint to the steady beeping of monitors and the distant chime of the nurses' station phone.

The morning stretched, sunlight shifting angles as it filtered through the blinds. Casey read until her throat grew dry, pausing occasionally to sip her cold coffee or to watch for any sign that her father was absorbing the words. Sometimes – less frequently now than during the first days of his admission – Elliot would stir during these readings, would murmur corrections to historical details or nod in agreement with particularly astute observations. Today he remained still, his breathing the only movement beneath the thin hospital blanket.

Nurses came and went with practiced efficiency, checking vitals, adjusting medication, helping with the basic bodily functions that Elliot could no longer manage independently. They moved around Casey as if she were part of the room's furniture, their gentle acknowledgments – a smile, a pat on the shoulder, an update murmured in passing – integrated into the flow of their duties. They had become characters in this new chapter of her life, their names and faces blending together as days accumulated into weeks.

By midday, the light through the windows had lost its golden morning quality, turning white and direct. Casey replaced the Roosevelt biography with a volume of poetry – Whitman, whose Leaves of Grass had stood on her father's nightstand throughout her childhood, a literary touchstone he returned to in moments of contemplation or distress. The familiar verses filled the sterile air with images of open roads and vast possibilities, a cruel contrast to the confines of this room with its limited horizon.

"'O Captain! my Captain!'" she read, the elegy's opening lines catching in her throat as their relevance struck her anew. "'Our fearful trip is done...'" Her voice faltered, the parallel too painful to navigate. She closed the book, marking their place with a hospital cafeteria receipt.

The days had begun to blend together, differentiated only by the changing flowers she brought – Monday's daisies giving way to Tuesday's chrysanthemums, Wednesday's carnations, Thursday's modest roses purchased from the grocery store display. Sometimes she brought objects from home instead – Elliot's pipe that he hadn't smoked in years but used to hold while grading papers, the paperweight shaped like the Roman Colosseum that had sat on his desk throughout her childhood, photographs of places they'd traveled together when she was younger. These talismans of memory seemed to reach him in ways words increasingly failed to do, his fingers sometimes tracing their contours with the reverent attention of an archaeologist examining artifacts from a lost civilization.

The afternoon sun shifted again, shadows lengthening across the linoleum floor as Casey read from the local newspaper, filtering out stories that might agitate or confuse. She created a curated version of reality for her father – a world where confusion and violence were minimized, where order prevailed and the bewildering complexities of modern life were rendered in simple, digestible fragments. It was, she realized, not so different from what he had once done for her as a child, protecting her from harsh truths until she was ready to bear them.

The rhythmic cadence of her reading was interrupted by a familiar presence in the doorway – Kirk, arriving at the same time he had every evening for the past two weeks, a paper cup of coffee in each hand and a brown paper bag tucked under his arm. The sight of him – solid, steady, precisely on schedule – loosened something in Casey's chest that had been wound tight all day.

"They had turkey sandwiches in the cafeteria today," he said by way of greeting, setting the coffees on the rolling table and extracting wrapped packages from the bag. "And I smuggled in some cookies from that bakery on Maple. The ones with the cranberries you mentioned liking."

His thoughtfulness – remembering a casual comment about cookies from a conversation days earlier – struck Casey with unexpected force. This awareness of her preferences, this attention to small comforts, had been absent from her life for so long that its reappearance felt almost disorienting.

"Thank you," she said, accepting the coffee he offered. Their fingers brushed during the exchange, a momentary warmth that lingered after the contact ended. "Any change in the weather?"

It was their established opening, this exchange of meteorological updates – a neutral topic that connected her to the world beyond these walls, to the continuing cycle of days and seasons that proceeded without regard for the suspended animation of hospital time.

"Cooler today. Might rain tomorrow," Kirk replied, settling into the second visitor's chair that had become unofficially his. "The maple trees on Fourth Street are starting to turn. Just the edges of the leaves, hints of orange."

These small observations – delivered without sentiment but with careful attention to detail – were gifts that Casey had come to treasure. Kirk's eyes moved to Elliot, assessing the day's changes with the same precision he brought to everything. "How has he been today?"

Casey unwrapped the sandwich, suddenly aware of hunger she had been ignoring. "Quiet. He hasn't spoken at all. But he squeezed my hand when I showed him the photograph of the fishing trip to Green Lake." She took a bite, the simple act of eating requiring more concentration than it should. "The doctor adjusted his medication again this morning. Said the new combination should help with the agitation without causing as much sedation."

Kirk nodded, his gaze moving between father and daughter, noting the similarities in their profiles that persisted despite Elliot's diminishment. Casey caught him watching her, his expression bearing a concern he tried to mask but which emerged despite his control. It wasn't pity – she had grown sensitive to that particular look from nurses and doctors – but something more complex, a recognition of suffering twinned with respect for the strength with which she bore it.

"You should go home earlier tomorrow," he suggested, his tone carefully neutral. "Get some real sleep. I could sit with him in the afternoon if you wanted."

Casey's automatic refusal rose to her lips, then receded. The bone-deep exhaustion she'd been ignoring pressed more insistently against her consciousness. "Maybe," she conceded, the single word representing a surrender previously unthinkable.

They ate in comfortable silence, the hospital's evening sounds forming a backdrop to their unspoken communication. When Kirk reached across to straighten Elliot's blanket where it had bunched beneath his arm, the gesture carried a tenderness that caught in Casey's throat. This man had somehow become part of their story, integrated into the fabric of her daily existence with a seamlessness that defied the brevity of their acquaintance.

As twilight gathered beyond the windows, Elliot stirred, his first significant movement in hours. His eyelids flickered open, gaze unfocused but seeking. Casey leaned forward, hope rising despite her efforts to contain it. "Dad? Are you with us?"

Elliot's lips moved, forming words without sound. Casey moved closer, ear nearly touching his mouth to catch the whispered sounds. "The books," he murmured, voice paper-thin, "need to be cataloged... by subject... not author."

The non-sequitur – some fragment of his professional life surfacing through the layers of confusion – was nonetheless precious for its coherence, for the brief connection to the organized mind that had once inhabited his body. Casey squeezed his hand, not correcting or questioning, simply acknowledging.

"I'll make sure of it, Dad," she promised, the fiction a kindness they both deserved.

Elliot's eyes drifted closed again, his momentary engagement receding like a wave pulling back from shore. Casey remained bent over him for several seconds, watching the subtle shifts in his expression as consciousness retreated. When she straightened, she found Kirk holding out a napkin, the gesture made without comment or explanation. Only when she felt the dampness on her cheeks did she realize she was crying.

The evening nurse arrived to check vitals and administer the night's medications. She moved with practiced efficiency, her scrubs rustling softly as she worked. "His heart rate's a little slower today," she observed, reading the monitor's display. "Blood pressure's holding steady though."

Casey nodded, absorbing this information without reaction. Numbers and measurements had become another language she'd had to learn, a clinical dialect that translated her father's decline into quantifiable data points. The nurse adjusted Elliot's position with gentle hands, relieving pressure points, checking for the early signs of bedsores that could complicate his already complex condition.

"He's comfortable," the nurse assured her, the standard reassurance offered when medical intervention had reached its limits. "The new medication seems to be helping with the restlessness."

After she left, silence settled over the room again, broken only by the soft electronic beeping of monitors and the distant sounds of the hospital's evening routines. Kirk's hand found Casey's where it rested on the chair's arm, his fingers covering hers in a gesture that asked nothing, demanded nothing, simply offered connection in a moment where words would have been insufficient.

The day's final light filtered through the blinds, painting stripes of gold and shadow across Elliot's sleeping form. His body seemed to have sunk deeper into the mattress since morning, as if gravity were exerting a stronger pull, drawing him incrementally downward. Casey watched him breathe, each inhale a little shallower than she remembered from the day before, each exhale a little more prolonged.

Time stretched and compressed in the quiet room, minutes bleeding into hours as darkness claimed the windows completely. Kirk remained beside her, their hands still connected, a tether to reality as her thoughts drifted through memories and regrets and the curious emptiness that accompanied prolonged grief. Tomorrow would bring more flowers, more one-sided readings, more careful monitoring of incremental changes. But for now, in this suspended moment between one difficult day and the next, there was only breathing, and waiting, and the surprising comfort of not being alone in either.

Chapter 14

A gentle pressure on Casey's shoulder pulled her from dreamless exhaustion, the boundary between sleep and waking as thin as hospital blankets. The night nurse – Marianne, with the silver-streaked braid and quiet efficiency – stood above her, face softened by the dim lighting and something else Casey recognized immediately. Twenty-one days of hospital rhythms had taught her to read the subtle language of medical staff, the minute shifts in expression that conveyed what professional distance often prevented them from saying directly. This look, this particular gentleness, carried its own diagnosis.

"Ms. Preston," Marianne whispered, her hand lingering on Casey's shoulder like an anchor, "I think it won't be long now. His vitals have been gradually decreasing throughout my shift."

Casey straightened in the visitor's chair, her neck protesting the awkward angle it had held during her impromptu sleep. The clock on the wall read 2:17 AM, its red digital numbers the only harsh element in the otherwise subdued room. The overhead lights had been dimmed to their lowest setting, and the machines monitoring Elliot's condition seemed muted, their electronic vigilance continuing with subdued respect.

"I've called Dr. Levin," Marianne continued, her voice maintaining its gentle hush. "And I took the liberty of calling your emergency contact as well. Mr. Manning said he'd be here shortly."

Casey nodded, gratitude mixing with the leaden weight spreading through her chest. She'd listed Kirk as her emergency contact three days earlier, when the doctor had first mentioned that Elliot was entering what they termed "the transitional phase" – a clinical euphemism for active dying that somehow managed to be both vague and precise simultaneously.

"Thank you," Casey said, her voice rough with sleep and the emotion she was already working to contain. "Could I have a moment alone with him before everyone arrives?"

Marianne nodded, adjusting the IV drip with practiced fingers before retreating. "I'll be at the nurses' station if you need anything. Just press the call button."

The door closed with a barely audible click, leaving Casey in the cocoon of near-silence that surrounded her father's bed. The usual mechanical sounds continued – the soft hiss of oxygen, the rhythmic beeping of the heart monitor, now slower than it had been when she'd fallen asleep – but they seemed to exist at a distance, as if the universe had created a small pocket of stillness around this moment.

Casey moved from the chair to the edge of Elliot's bed, careful not to disturb the arrangement of tubes and wires that had become extensions of his body. She took his hand between both of hers, noting how the skin felt different now – cooler, the texture changing in some subtle way she couldn't articulate but instinctively recognized. His breathing was shallow, each inhale a visible effort, each exhale lingering as if reluctant to complete the cycle.

"Dad," she said softly, not expecting a response but needing to break the silence. "It's Casey. I'm here."

Elliot's face had acquired a translucent quality over the past few days, the skin stretched taut over cheekbones that seemed more prominent with each passing hour. In the soft glow of the bedside lamp, the hollows beneath his eyes appeared deeper, more defined, as if his features were being gradually distilled to their essential elements. His hair – thinner now and completely white – lay against the pillow in disarray, one stubborn cowlick still standing up at the crown as it had throughout his life.

Casey smoothed it down with gentle fingers, the familiar gesture opening a flood of memories – her father bent over student papers at the kitchen table, absently trying to tame that same unruly tuft; Elliot dressed in his academic regalia for graduation ceremonies, checking his reflection in the hall mirror; even as a child, watching him prepare for parent-teacher conferences, his nervous habit of running his hand through his hair creating the very cowlick he was trying to eliminate.

"Do you remember," she whispered, "when you taught me to iron? I must have been about nine. You said a professor's daughter should know how to press a proper collar." Her thumb traced small circles against the paper-thin skin of his hand. "You were so patient, even when I scorched your second-best shirt. You wore it anyway, told everyone it was the latest academic fashion."

The memory warmed her despite the chill that seemed to emanate from the hospital walls. These past weeks had been filled with such one-sided reminiscences, as if by reciting their shared history she could preserve what disease was determined to erase. She continued this oral history now, voice low and steady, recounting fishing trips and school projects, the Christmas he'd built her a doll-house perfectly scaled to match their own home, the way he'd taught her to change a tire in the pouring rain when she was sixteen.

The door opened with such careful quietness that Casey didn't notice Kirk's entrance until he was standing at the foot of the bed. He wore the clothes he'd had on earlier that day – jeans and a navy sweater with a small tear near the cuff – suggesting he hadn't been asleep when Marianne's call came. His hair was slightly damp, perhaps from the mist that had been falling when Casey had looked out the window before falling asleep hours earlier.

"The nurse called," he said, the unnecessary explanation offered in deference to the moment's gravity. "How is he?"

Casey glanced at the monitors, their digital readouts telling a story of gradual diminishment. "Slipping away, I think." Her voice caught slightly on the final word. "The doctor's on his way."

Kirk moved to stand on the opposite side of the bed, his presence creating a balance to the scene – Elliot centered between them, Casey still holding his father's hand, Kirk watching with the steady compassion that had become an essential element of her daily existence. The bedside lamp cast a golden circle that encompassed the three of them, holding back the deeper shadows of the room's corners.

"I was just telling him about the time he taught me to iron," Casey said, needing to fill the silence with something other than the sound of her father's labored breathing. "And about the fishing trip to Lake Morgan when I was eleven."

Kirk nodded, his gaze moving from Casey to Elliot with gentle attention. "Tell me," he encouraged, offering her the gift of audience, of witness to these final narratives.

So Casey continued, her voice gaining strength as she recounted stories that Kirk had never heard – Elliot's disastrous attempt to bake her birthday cake when she turned eight, the time he'd accidentally set fire to his tweed jacket while demonstrating proper Roman candle technique for her high school Latin club, the way he'd stayed up all night helping her finish a science project after she'd procrastinated until the last minute.

The stories flowed, creating a current of memory that seemed to carry them all through the long hours that followed. Dr. Levin arrived, performed a brief examination, and confirmed what they already knew – Elliot was actively dying, comfortable with the medication they'd provided, unlikely to linger more than a few hours. He offered additional sedation, which Casey declined after studying her father's peaceful expression. The doctor nodded, made a note in the chart, and quietly withdrew, leaving them to their vigil.

Time stretched and compressed in the dimly lit room. Casey continued talking until her voice grew hoarse, then fell silent, the physical connection of her hand around her father's becoming the primary channel of communication. Kirk occasionally offered water, a tissue, quiet support when her composure threatened to break, but mostly he maintained a reverent silence, understanding instinctively that this space belonged primarily to Casey and Elliot.

The sky beyond the window gradually lightened from black to deep blue, suggesting approaching dawn. Elliot's breathing had become increasingly irregular, with long pauses that caused Casey to hold her own breath until the next shallow inhale finally came. His skin had taken on a waxy pallor, the blueish tint at his fingertips spreading slowly upward.

It was during one of these extended pauses, as Casey was bracing herself for the breath that might not come, that Elliot's eyelids suddenly fluttered open. Casey froze, startled by this unexpected development after so many hours of stillness. His gaze, which had been unfocused or confused during his increasingly rare moments of consciousness over the past weeks, now appeared startlingly clear, the cloudiness of dementia temporarily lifted.

"Dad?" Casey whispered, leaning closer, hardly daring to believe this moment of lucidity.

Elliot's eyes found hers with a precision that had been absent for months. His lips moved, initially without sound, but on the second attempt, words emerged – faint but distinct. "There you are."

The simple phrase – not confused, not disoriented, but a clear recognition – struck Casey with the force of revelation. Her father was seeing her – truly seeing her – perhaps for the last time. His fingers tightened around hers with surprising strength, a final physical communication that conveyed everything words could not.

"I'm here, Dad," Casey assured him, her own grip equally firm. "I'm right here."

Elliot's gaze held hers for a moment that seemed to stretch beyond normal dimensions of time, containing within it all the love and recognition that disease had stolen in fragments over the past years. Then his eyes drifted closed again, his expression peaceful as he exhaled a breath that lacked the force to draw in its counterpart.

The silence that followed was absolute, a complete stillness that even the machines seemed to acknowledge, the heart monitor flatlined into a continuous tone that Marianne quickly silenced upon reentering the room. The cessation of Elliot's breathing created a vacuum in the small space, as if all oxygen had briefly evacuated with his final exhale.

Casey remained perfectly still, her hands still wrapped around her father's. The tears that had threatened throughout the night now fell silently, tracking warm paths down her cheeks and dropping onto their joined hands, creating small dark circles on the hospital blanket. She made no sound, no movement beyond the slight trembling of her shoulders, as if any disruption might somehow fracture this moment of transition.

Kirk moved around the bed to stand behind her, his presence solid and grounding. He placed a hand lightly on her shoulder, the weight and warmth of it an anchor to the physical world when everything else seemed suddenly insubstantial. He said nothing, understanding that words were insufficient vessels for this moment's contents.

Dawn broke fully beyond the window, the first direct rays of sunlight finding their way through the venetian blinds to lay stripes of gold across Elliot's face – peaceful now beyond confusion, beyond fear, beyond the disease that had stolen him piece by piece. In that gentle morning light, the resemblance between father and daughter reasserted itself, as if his features had briefly reclaimed their original clarity, returning to the essence of the man he had been before illness began its slow erasure.

Casey watched that light move across her father's face, marking the final illumination of a life that had shaped hers in every conceivable way. Her tears continued to fall, but something else was emerging beneath the grief – a recognition that in this final moment of clarity, of connection, her father had given her one last gift: the certainty that somewhere beneath the confusion and fear of his final months, he had remained himself, had recognized her, had never truly been lost.

Chapter 15

Death, Casey discovered, arrived with paperwork. Forms materialized in triplicate – cause of death certificates, body release authorizations, organ donation declinations, personal effects inventories – each requiring signatures that Casey provided with handwriting grown increasingly foreign to her own eyes. The doctor's official pronouncement had come with practiced solemnity, professional sympathy calibrated to acknowledge loss without becoming entangled in it. Casey had nodded at appropriate intervals, her responses automatic, as if her body had developed its own autopilot for grief while her mind drifted somewhere beyond the institutional beige walls of the hospital room where her father no longer existed.

"Would you like some time alone with him before we take him downstairs?" a new nurse asked, her voice gentle but practical. Casey couldn't recall seeing this woman before – a different shift, perhaps, or a specialized staff member who appeared only for these specific transitions. "Some families prefer a private goodbye."

Casey glanced at the bed where Elliot lay, his features settled into unfamiliar stillness. She had already said her goodbye in the moment that mattered, when his eyes had found hers with that final clarity. This empty vessel, already beginning to look unlike her father, required no further farewells.

"No," she heard herself say. "We've said goodbye."

Time compressed and expanded unpredictably. Minutes stretched into eternities as she watched attendants prepare her father's body, disconnecting tubes and monitors, removing the hospital gown and replacing it with a simple white garment whose purpose she recognized but couldn't name. Then suddenly hours seemed to have vanished when she found herself in a small office, a sympathetic administrator explaining cremation options versus burial choices, payment plans, death certificate procedures – information that entered her ears but failed to fully register in her brain.

Throughout this processional of logistics, Kirk remained beside her, a steady presence that occasionally materialized in her peripheral awareness. He spoke when she couldn't, handled details when her focus scattered, steered her gently through the labyrinth of post-death protocols with quiet efficiency. His voice reached her as if through water, the words less important than their tone – calm, respectful, occasionally protective when questions became too intrusive or options were presented with insufficient sensitivity.

"Ms. Preston needs a moment," he said at one point, his hand gentle on her elbow as he guided her from some office whose purpose she had already forgotten. "We'll continue this discussion after a short break."

He led her to a small courtyard tucked between hospital wings, where morning light illuminated a modest garden of hardy plants selected for minimal maintenance rather than beauty. Casey stood beneath a young maple tree, its leaves just beginning to turn at their edges, and drew the first breath that seemed to fully inflate her lungs since Elliot's last exhale.

"Thank you," she said, the words emerging stiff from disuse. How long had she been silent? Minutes? Hours? "For handling... all of that." She gestured vaguely back toward the building, encompassing the bureaucratic machinery of death that continued to operate regardless of personal devastation.

Kirk nodded, his expression neither pitying nor falsely cheerful, but attentive and present in a way that required no response from her. This undemanding companionship felt like the only bearable form of human contact in a world suddenly reconfigured around absence.

Eventually they returned to complete what needed completion – collecting Elliot's meager hospital possessions (the watch with oversized numbers, the photograph of Margaret, the paperback novel Casey had been reading to him), signing the final authorizations, arranging for the hospital chaplain to contact the funeral home they had preliminarily selected.

When every signature had been provided, every form filed, every condolence accepted with automatic thanks, they walked through the hospital's main entrance into daylight that seemed offensive in its ordinary brilliance. The parking lot stretched before them, cars gleaming with indifferent normalcy, people coming and going with the rhythms of regular life that seemed suddenly alien to Casey, as if she had returned from some distant dimension where time operated by different principles.

She stopped abruptly at the edge of the visitor parking section, keys halfway from her pocket, struck by a realization that paralyzed her mid-motion. "I can't go back there," she said, the words escaping before she could contain them. "To the house. Not yet. It's too—" She couldn't complete the thought, couldn't articulate the hollowness that awaited her in rooms still haunted by her father's diminishing presence, the accumulated evidence of his decline now transformed into relics of absence.

Kirk's hand settled lightly on her shoulder, steadying her without restraint. "My place isn't far," he said, the offer made without pressure or expectation. "You shouldn't be alone right now."

The suggestion should have triggered her instinctive resistance to help, the reflexive insistence on self-sufficiency that had characterized her life these past years. Instead, Casey felt only gratitude as Kirk guided her toward his car instead of hers, the decision made without discussion that she was in no condition to drive and in no state to face an empty house still bearing the imprints of her father's illness.

Kirk's home revealed itself as an unexpected sanctuary – a modest craftsman bungalow with simple, solid furniture and walls painted in muted earth tones. Max greeted them at the door with subdued enthusiasm, apparently sensing the gravity of the situation, his usual exuberance tempered to gentle nudges against Casey's hand and attentive presence at her side as Kirk led her to the kitchen.

Sunlight spilled through windows framed by simple wooden blinds, illuminating a space that felt both masculine and welcoming – practical without being austere, functional without being cold. A wooden table that looked handcrafted anchored the room, its surface bearing the honorable scars of actual use rather than decorative distressing.

"Sit," Kirk said, pulling out a chair that somehow received her collapsing weight at the precise moment her legs decided to surrender. "I'll make coffee."

The ordinary domesticity of the scene – coffee grounds measured into a filter, water poured, the quiet gurgle of the machine beginning its work – created a strange counterpoint to the extraordinary weight of the morning's events. Casey watched Kirk move with efficient grace around his kitchen, retrieving mugs, setting out cream though she'd never specified her preference, his back a solid presence that allowed her the privacy to compose herself without feeling abandoned.

When steaming coffee sat before her in a blue ceramic mug, its warmth seeping into her palms, Kirk placed a slim folder on the table between them. "The hospital gave me some information about arrangements," he said, his voice matter-of-fact without being detached. "Whenever you're ready."

Ready. The word seemed to contain impossible expectations. How could anyone be ready for this? Yet decisions awaited, choices that would define how Elliot Preston was committed to memory and earth. Casey opened the folder with reluctant fingers, confronting glossy brochures featuring caskets photographed like luxury furniture, burial plots presented like real estate opportunities, services packaged like vacation options.

"He would hate all of this," she said, a ghost of a smile touching her lips for the first time in days. "Dad was always suspicious of anything that tried to sell itself too aggressively."

Kirk's answering smile held understanding rather than mere agreement. "What would he want instead?"

The question opened something in Casey, a channel to considerations beyond immediate grief. She turned pages slowly, rejecting ornate metal caskets and plush interiors until she found a simple design in oak, its clean lines and natural grain reminiscent of the workbench where Elliot had spent countless hours, crafting small treasures from wood with the same patience he'd applied to shaping young minds.

"This one," she said, tapping the image. "It looks like

something he would have made himself, if he could have." Her throat tightened around the irony – her practical father would have considered building his own casket perfectly reasonable, would have approached it as an engineering problem with his characteristic blend of precision and wry humor.

Kirk made notes in his precise handwriting, creating order from the chaos of options and decisions. Together they navigated the necessities – cemetery plot selection (a quiet corner beneath a maple tree), service arrangements (small, secular, focused on celebration rather than mourning), obituary wording that would capture Elliot before his illness without denying the courage with which he'd faced his decline.

"Should we mention the dementia?" Casey asked, pen hovering over the draft they'd created. "It seems wrong to erase it completely, like we're ashamed, but I don't want it to define him either."

"What about something acknowledging his strength?" Kirk suggested. "'Professor Preston faced frontotemporal dementia with the same courage and dignity that characterized his life.' It honors the struggle without making it the centerpiece."

Casey nodded, adding the sentence, recognizing in Kirk's suggestion the perfect balance between honesty and respect. They continued working through the afternoon, the process oddly healing despite its inherent pain – each decision a small act of love, a final caregiving for a man who could no longer speak for himself.

The sun had begun its westward slide when they reached the most personal question, one Casey had been unconsciously avoiding. "We'll need to select clothing for the burial," Kirk said gently. "Is there something specific you'd like him to wear?"

The question struck with unexpected force, breaking

through the fragile composure Casey had maintained throughout the day's decisions. "His tweed," she said, voice suddenly thick. "The one with the leather patches. And his blue tie with the tiny books printed on it. Students gave it to him when he retired."

The mention of these specific items – these tangible pieces of her father's identity – cracked something fundamental in Casey's carefully maintained facade. "We need to go to the house," she managed, the prospect suddenly overwhelming. "His clothes are there. His—" Her voice broke, the simple logistics of retrieving burial clothing suddenly expanding into the immensity of confronting her father's personal effects, his entire material existence now reduced to objects requiring disposition.

Kirk's hand covered hers where it rested on the table, steadying her without restraint. "We can go together," he said. "Whenever you're ready. There's no rush."

But there was, Casey realized – a rushing inside her, a tide of grief finally breaking through the numb efficiency that had carried her through the morning. Her breath caught, then emerged as a sound too raw to be called a sob, too fundamental to be named anything but anguish. She pressed her fist against her mouth, trying to contain what could not be contained.

Kirk moved without hesitation, crossing to her side of the table and gently drawing her up and against him, his arms encircling her with steady pressure. "Let it come," he murmured, one hand moving to cradle the back of her head as she collapsed against his chest. "You don't have to be strong right now."

The permission undid her completely. Casey's grief poured out in violent, wracking sobs that bent her double, would have taken her to her knees if not for Kirk's supporting embrace. She clutched at his shirt, fingers digging into the fabric as if it were the only solid thing in a world suddenly liquid with loss. The dam that had held back her tears through weeks of hospital visits, through the relentless decline, through the final hours of vigil, now collapsed completely, releasing a flood that seemed without end.

Kirk held her through the storm, his shirt growing damp beneath her face, his steady heartbeat providing counterpoint to her jagged breathing. He made no attempt to quiet her, offered no platitudes or false assurances, simply provided the solid presence necessary for her to finally release what she had been carrying alone for too long. His hand moved in slow circles against her back, the motion neither demanding nor dismissive, simply present and steady as she broke apart in the safety of his arms.

"He knew," Kirk said quietly, when her sobs had begun to subside into hiccuping breaths. "At the end, he knew you. He saw you. He was himself again, just for that moment."

The truth of this observation – the recognition of the gift contained in Elliot's final lucidity – brought fresh tears, but of a different quality. Casey nodded against Kirk's chest, unable yet to form words but acknowledging the profound comfort in his understanding of what that final exchange had meant.

Outside the kitchen window, afternoon light slanted through tree branches, casting dappled shadows across the wooden table where they had begun the practical business of honoring Elliot Preston's life. Casey remained in the circle of Kirk's arms, gradually becoming aware of the steady rise and fall of his chest, the subtle scent of his laundry detergent, the gentle pressure of his hand against her back – small, concrete details anchoring her to the physical world when grief threatened to sweep her into formless darkness.

The first step toward whatever came next would

require returning to the house, confronting the closet where her father's tweed jacket hung with its worn elbow patches, selecting the tie with tiny books that represented his life's work. But for now, in this moment of sanctuary, Casey allowed herself to be held, to be witnessed in her grief, to accept the support she had denied herself for so long. Tomorrow would bring more decisions, more arrangements, more steps toward a life reconfigured around absence. But in this kitchen, as afternoon light softened toward evening, there was only the simple human comfort of being held while the world realigned itself around loss.

Chapter 16

Autumn had painted the cemetery overnight, transforming green into tapestries of amber, crimson, and burnished gold. Leaves crunched beneath somber shoes as the small procession made its way along the narrow path toward the grave site, the sound oddly cheerful against the day's solemnity, nature refusing to align with human grief. Casey walked at the front, the simple black dress hanging loosely on her frame, her father's absence having carved itself into her physical form over the weeks of hospital vigil. The oak casket gleamed with subtle warmth in the morning light, carried by six men – Kirk among them, his face set with respectful concentration, his shoulders bearing their portion of the weight with the same steady reliability he had offered Casey throughout these impossible days.

The chapel service had been brief, attended by a modest gathering that surprised Casey with its size – former colleagues from Oakridge High and the community college, students whose lives Elliot had touched decades earlier, neighbors who had overlooked his declining years to remember the man who had once organized block parties and community lectures. They filled only the first few rows of the small chapel, but their presence formed a testament to a life whose influence had rippled outward in ways Casey hadn't fully appreciated until seeing them assembled in shared remembrance.

Now they stood in a loose semicircle around the open grave, autumn wind occasionally lifting the edges of coats and scarves, tugging at carefully arranged hair, reminding everyone of life's continued movement even in this moment of stillness. Casey stood at the head of the grave, her hands clasped before her, fingernails pressing half-moons into her palms. Kirk remained beside her, close enough that their shoulders occasionally touched when the wind pushed them together, these brief contacts anchoring her to the physical world when grief threatened to dissolve her boundaries.

The minister's words washed over Casey like gentle waves, familiar phrases about life and death, beginning and ending, resurrection and remembrance. She hadn't been raised with formal religion, but the traditional service had seemed appropriate for her father, who had appreciated ritual without requiring dogma. The words themselves mattered less than their rhythm, their ancient cadence providing structure to a moment that might otherwise have collapsed under its own emotional weight.

"And now," the minister said, "Elliot's daughter Casey would like to say a few words."

A hush fell over the gathering, attention shifting toward Casey with that particular combination of sympathy and curiosity that accompanies personal testimony at funerals. She stepped forward, unfolding the paper she'd tucked into her pocket, though the words she'd written were now embedded in her mind, having been revised and refined throughout a sleepless night.

"My father was a builder," she began, her voice steadier

than she had expected, carrying clearly on the autumn air. "Not by profession – as many of you know, he was a dedicated teacher and historian. But in his heart, in his hands, he was always a craftsman."

The paper trembled slightly between her fingers, but her voice remained clear, gaining strength with each sentence. "He built bookshelves that could withstand earthquakes, tree houses that outlasted the childhood they were created for, and furniture that will likely outlive us all. He approached every project with the same precision and patience he brought to his teaching – measuring twice, cutting once, standing back to evaluate before proceeding."

Casey paused, looking up from her notes to scan the faces surrounding her father's grave – former colleagues nodding in recognition, students whose features had matured beyond their classroom days but who still carried the imprint of her father's influence. "When I was nine, he let me help with a dollhouse he was building for my birthday. I was impatient, wanted to skip ahead to the decorating part. But Dad wouldn't let me rush. 'Good craftsmanship can't be hurried,' he told me. 'The quality of what you build depends on the care you take with the foundation.'"

A soft murmur of recognition passed through the older faculty members, who had heard Elliot apply similar wisdom to curriculum development and student guidance. Casey continued, her gaze returning to the polished oak of the casket, its grain catching the morning light. "When I was sixteen and thought I knew everything, he taught me how to change a tire in the pouring rain, standing beside me getting soaked, refusing to take over even when I struggled. 'You need to know how to do this yourself,' he insisted, 'because I won't always be here to help.'"

Casey's voice caught briefly on these words, their prophetic truth striking her anew. She took a breath, finding her composure again in the solid presence of Kirk beside her, in the rustling leaves overhead that suggested continuity beyond individual ending.

"As many of you know, my father's final years were difficult. The disease that took him piece by piece was cruel in its precision, dismantling first his impulse control, then his recognition, finally his connection to his own history. But even as these parts of himself were being stripped away, the core of who he was – his kindness, his patience, his fundamental decency – remained, visible in moments of clarity that became increasingly precious as they grew more rare."

She looked up again, meeting the eyes of those gathered around the grave. "My father built everything that mattered in my life – not just physical objects, but the foundation of who I am. He constructed my understanding of integrity, crafted my capacity for wonder, assembled my belief in the value of knowledge and the importance of compassion. These are his true legacy, more lasting than any wooden creation, more significant than any academic achievement."

Casey refolded her notes, no longer needing them for the conclusion she had rehearsed in her mind throughout the darkest hours of the previous night. "In woodworking, there's a technique called 'revealing the grain,' where the craftsman applies finish not to hide the wood's nature but to bring out its inherent beauty, to highlight what was always present beneath the surface. My father did that for his students, for his friends, and most of all for me – he saw what was possible, what was already present but not yet revealed, and helped bring it into the light."

She placed her hand briefly on the casket, the wood warm beneath her palm despite the autumn chill. "Thank you, Dad, for everything you built, especially the parts of myself I'm still discovering."

As she stepped back, a collective exhale seemed to pass through the gathering, as if they had been holding their breath throughout her words. The minister stepped forward again, continuing the service with the traditional committal phrases, but Casey heard them only distantly, her focus narrowing to the immediate sensory details of the moment – the crisp scent of autumn leaves, the gentle pressure of Kirk's shoulder against hers, the unexpected warmth of sunlight breaking through clouds to illuminate the scene.

When the time came, Casey stepped forward with the single white rose she had selected, its petals still beaded with morning dew. She held it briefly to her face, inhaling its subtle fragrance, before dropping it onto the casket. The soft thud of its landing echoed in her chest, a physical sensation of finality that no words or ceremonies had fully conveyed.

The mechanical lowering of the casket began, a process both gentle and inexorable. Casey watched as the polished oak descended gradually into the earth, diminishing from view inch by measured inch. Without conscious thought, her hand reached sideways, seeking anchor in this moment of ultimate separation. Kirk's fingers met hers, interlacing with a gentle pressure that asked nothing, demanded nothing, simply offered connection when it was most needed.

They stood like that, hands joined, as the first ceremonial shovelfuls of earth were cast into the grave – the minister first, then Casey, then others in turn, each handful of soil landing with soft finality on the casket below. The sound was both terrible and strangely comforting, concrete and undeniable, marking an ending that had been occurring in increments for years but was only now being formally acknowledged.

Gradually, the gathering began to disperse – colleagues

patting Casey's arm as they passed, former students offering awkward but sincere condolences, neighbors mentioning casseroles and practical assistance with the quiet earnestness of those who understand that life continues in mundane details even after profound loss. Casey nodded, thanked, accepted business cards and telephone numbers she suspected she would never use, all while maintaining her grip on Kirk's hand as if it were a lifeline to reality.

Finally, they stood alone beside the partially filled grave, the cemetery workers tactfully withdrawn to a respectful distance, waiting to complete their practical duties once the ritual of farewell had concluded. The autumn breeze had strengthened, carrying the scent of distant woodsmoke and the promise of colder days ahead. Overhead, a formation of geese passed in perfect V-formation, their distant honking carrying across the cemetery's peaceful expanse.

Casey stared at the dark earth, at the white rose now partially covered with soil, at the tangible evidence of an ending she had been anticipating and dreading in equal measure for months. The weight of funeral arrangements, of hospital procedures, of immediate necessities had carried her through the days since Elliot's death. Now, standing in the aftermath of ceremony, she faced the vastness of what came next – a life reconfigured around absence, days no longer structured by caregiving, a house filled with memories but emptied of purpose.

"What do I do now?" she whispered, not looking at Kirk but gripping his hand tighter, the question emerging from some deep place beyond conscious thought.

Kirk's fingers returned her pressure, warm and solid against the autumn chill. "Whatever comes next," he answered simply, his voice carrying neither false cheer nor heavy solemnity, but the steady certainty that had become essential to her equilibrium. "But not alone."

Casey turned to face him fully then, studying the features that had become so familiar over these past months – the precise line of his jaw, the quiet strength in his eyes, the slight asymmetry of his smile that emerged now, gentle but unflinching in the face of her grief. In that smile she saw no empty reassurance that the pain would soon fade, no impatience for her to move forward before she was ready, only the steady promise of presence through whatever lay ahead.

The cemetery stretched around them, autumn-painted trees standing sentinel over generations of endings and beginnings, of losses absorbed and lives continued. Casey looked once more at her father's grave, at the evidence of a story completed but not erased, then turned toward the path that would lead them back to the waiting cars, to the gathering at Kirk's house where food and conversation awaited, to the first steps of whatever came next.

Her hand remained in Kirk's as they walked, leaves crunching beneath their feet, creating percussion for the wind's melody in the branches overhead. The path curved gently through stands of maple and oak, their leaves burning bright against the deepening blue of the October sky, nature's reminder that endings and beginnings were merely human constructs, arbitrary divisions in a continuous cycle of transformation that required no names or ceremonies, only participation.

Autumn had painted the cemetery overnight, transforming green into tapestries of amber, crimson, and burnished gold. Leaves crunched beneath somber shoes as the small procession made its way along the narrow path toward the grave site, the sound oddly cheerful against the day's solemnity, nature refusing to align with human grief.

Casey walked at the front, the simple black dress hanging loosely on her frame, her father's absence having carved itself into her physical form over the weeks of hospital vigil. The oak casket gleamed with subtle warmth in the morning light, carried by six men – Kirk among them, his face set with respectful concentration, his shoulders bearing their portion of the weight with the same steady reliability he had offered Casey throughout these impossible days.

The chapel service had been brief, attended by a modest gathering that surprised Casey with its size – former colleagues from Oakridge High and the community college, students whose lives Elliot had touched decades earlier, neighbors who had overlooked his declining years to remember the man who had once organized block parties and community lectures. They filled only the first few rows of the small chapel, but their presence formed a testament to a life whose influence had rippled outward in ways Casey hadn't fully appreciated until seeing them assembled in shared remembrance.

Now they stood in a loose semicircle around the open grave, autumn wind occasionally lifting the edges of coats and scarves, tugging at carefully arranged hair, reminding everyone of life's continued movement even in this moment of stillness. Casey stood at the head of the grave, her hands clasped before her, fingernails pressing half-moons into her palms. Kirk remained beside her, close enough that their shoulders occasionally touched when the wind pushed them together, these brief contacts anchoring her to the physical world when grief threatened to dissolve her boundaries.

The minister's words washed over Casey like gentle waves, familiar phrases about life and death, beginning and ending, resurrection and remembrance. She hadn't been raised with formal religion, but the traditional service had seemed appropriate for her father, who had appreciated ritual without requiring dogma. The words themselves mattered less than their rhythm, their ancient cadence providing structure to a moment that might otherwise have collapsed under its own emotional weight.

"And now," the minister said, "Elliot's daughter Casey would like to say a few words."

A hush fell over the gathering, attention shifting toward Casey with that particular combination of sympathy and curiosity that accompanies personal testimony at funerals. She stepped forward, unfolding the paper she'd tucked into her pocket, though the words she'd written were now embedded in her mind, having been revised and refined throughout a sleepless night.

"My father was a builder," she began, her voice steadier than she had expected, carrying clearly on the autumn air. "Not by profession – as many of you know, he was a dedicated teacher and historian. But in his heart, in his hands, he was always a craftsman."

The paper trembled slightly between her fingers, but her voice remained clear, gaining strength with each sentence. "He built bookshelves that could withstand earthquakes, tree houses that outlasted the childhood they were created for, and furniture that will likely outlive us all. He approached every project with the same precision and patience he brought to his teaching – measuring twice, cutting once, standing back to evaluate before proceeding."

Casey paused, looking up from her notes to scan the faces surrounding her father's grave – former colleagues nodding in recognition, students whose features had matured beyond their classroom days but who still carried the imprint of her father's influence. "When I was nine, he let me help with a dollhouse he was building for my birthday. I was impatient, wanted to skip ahead to the decorating part. But Dad wouldn't let me rush. 'Good craftsmanship can't be hurried,' he told me. 'The quality of what you build depends on the care you take with the foundation.'"

A soft murmur of recognition passed through the older faculty members, who had heard Elliot apply similar wisdom to curriculum development and student guidance. Casey continued, her gaze returning to the polished oak of the casket, its grain catching the morning light. "When I was sixteen and thought I knew everything, he taught me how to change a tire in the pouring rain, standing beside me getting soaked, refusing to take over even when I struggled. 'You need to know how to do this yourself,' he insisted, 'because I won't always be here to help.'"

Casey's voice caught briefly on these words, their prophetic truth striking her anew. She took a breath, finding her composure again in the solid presence of Kirk beside her, in the rustling leaves overhead that suggested continuity beyond individual ending.

"As many of you know, my father's final years were difficult. The disease that took him piece by piece was cruel in its precision, dismantling first his impulse control, then his recognition, finally his connection to his own history. But even as these parts of himself were being stripped away, the core of who he was – his kindness, his patience, his fundamental decency – remained, visible in moments of clarity that became increasingly precious as they grew more rare."

She looked up again, meeting the eyes of those gathered around the grave. "My father built everything that mattered in my life – not just physical objects, but the foundation of who I am. He constructed my understanding of integrity, crafted my capacity for wonder, assembled my belief in the value of knowledge and the importance of compassion. These are his true legacy, more lasting than any wooden creation, more significant than any academic achievement."

Casey refolded her notes, no longer needing them for the conclusion she had rehearsed in her mind throughout the darkest hours of the previous night. "In woodworking, there's a technique called 'revealing the grain,' where the craftsman applies finish not to hide the wood's nature but to bring out its inherent beauty, to highlight what was always present beneath the surface. My father did that for his students, for his friends, and most of all for me – he saw what was possible, what was already present but not yet revealed, and helped bring it into the light."

She placed her hand briefly on the casket, the wood warm beneath her palm despite the autumn chill. "Thank you, Dad, for everything you built, especially the parts of myself I'm still discovering."

As she stepped back, a collective exhale seemed to pass through the gathering, as if they had been holding their breath throughout her words. The minister stepped forward again, continuing the service with the traditional committal phrases, but Casey heard them only distantly, her focus narrowing to the immediate sensory details of the moment – the crisp scent of autumn leaves, the gentle pressure of Kirk's shoulder against hers, the unexpected warmth of sunlight breaking through clouds to illuminate the scene.

When the time came, Casey stepped forward with the single white rose she had selected, its petals still beaded with morning dew. She held it briefly to her face, inhaling its subtle fragrance, before dropping it onto the casket. The soft thud of its landing echoed in her chest, a physical sensation of finality that no words or ceremonies had fully conveyed.

The mechanical lowering of the casket began, a process both gentle and inexorable. Casey watched as the polished oak descended gradually into the earth, diminishing from view inch by measured inch. Without conscious thought, her hand reached sideways, seeking anchor in this moment of ultimate separation. Kirk's fingers met hers, interlacing with a gentle pressure that asked nothing, demanded nothing, simply offered connection when it was most needed.

They stood like that, hands joined, as the first ceremonial shovelfuls of earth were cast into the grave – the minister first, then Casey, then others in turn, each handful of soil landing with soft finality on the casket below. The sound was both terrible and strangely comforting, concrete and undeniable, marking an ending that had been occurring in increments for years but was only now being formally acknowledged.

Gradually, the gathering began to disperse – colleagues patting Casey's arm as they passed, former students offering awkward but sincere condolences, neighbors mentioning casseroles and practical assistance with the quiet earnestness of those who understand that life continues in mundane details even after profound loss. Casey nodded, thanked, accepted business cards and telephone numbers she suspected she would never use, all while maintaining her grip on Kirk's hand as if it were a lifeline to reality.

Finally, they stood alone beside the partially filled grave, the cemetery workers tactfully withdrawn to a respectful distance, waiting to complete their practical duties once the ritual of farewell had concluded. The autumn breeze had strengthened, carrying the scent of distant woodsmoke and the promise of colder days ahead. Overhead, a formation of geese passed in perfect V-formation, their distant honking carrying across the cemetery's peaceful expanse.

Casey stared at the dark earth, at the white rose now partially covered with soil, at the tangible evidence of an ending she had been anticipating and dreading in equal measure for months. The weight of funeral arrangements, of hospital procedures, of immediate necessities had carried her through the days since Elliot's death. Now, standing in the aftermath of ceremony, she faced the vastness of what came next – a life reconfigured around absence, days no longer structured by caregiving, a house filled with memories but emptied of purpose.

"What do I do now?" she whispered, not looking at Kirk but gripping his hand tighter, the question emerging from some deep place beyond conscious thought.

Kirk's fingers returned her pressure, warm and solid against the autumn chill. "Whatever comes next," he answered simply, his voice carrying neither false cheer nor heavy solemnity, but the steady certainty that had become essential to her equilibrium. "But not alone."

Casey turned to face him fully then, studying the features that had become so familiar over these past months – the precise line of his jaw, the quiet strength in his eyes, the slight asymmetry of his smile that emerged now, gentle but unflinching in the face of her grief. In that smile she saw no empty reassurance that the pain would soon fade, no impatience for her to move forward before she was ready, only the steady promise of presence through whatever lay ahead.

The cemetery stretched around them, autumn-painted trees standing sentinel over generations of endings and beginnings, of losses absorbed and lives continued. Casey looked once more at her father's grave, at the evidence of a story completed but not erased, then turned toward the path that would lead them back to the waiting cars, to the gathering at Kirk's house where food and conversation awaited, to the first steps of whatever came next.

Her hand remained in Kirk's as they walked, leaves crunching beneath their feet, creating percussion for the wind's melody in the branches overhead. The path curved gently through stands of maple and oak, their leaves burning bright against the deepening blue of the October sky, nature's reminder that endings and beginnings were merely human constructs, arbitrary divisions in a continuous cycle of transformation that required no names or ceremonies, only participation.

Chapter 17

The emptiness of the house had a weight to it, a physical presence that pressed against Casey's skin as she moved from room to room. Three days after the funeral, the silence felt wrong—artificial, like the pause between heartbeats stretched beyond endurance. She traced her fingers along the hallway wall, leaving no mark but needing the tactile confirmation that something in this hollow shell still existed, still remained solid while everything else had turned to vapor and memory.

She paced the perimeter of the living room for what must have been the twentieth time that morning, her steps creating a worn path that served no purpose except motion for its own sake. The television remained dark, the absence of its background drone highlighting smaller sounds that now seemed intrusive—the refrigerator's mechanical sigh, the occasional settling of old wood, the distant ticking of her father's study clock that she couldn't bring herself to stop winding.

Casey paused at Elliot's armchair, the indentation in its cushion still visible, as if his body had just vacated the spot and might return at any moment. Without conscious thought, her hand reached out, hovering above the fabric before dropping to brush against the worn armrest where his fingers had drummed countless rhythms—grading papers, watching baseball games, during his more recent confused states when the tapping served as his only method of self-soothing.

She closed her eyes and inhaled. Beneath the funeral flowers' lingering sweetness and the faint mustiness of a house closed too long against fresh air, she caught it—the whisper of sandalwood and cedarwood, her father's after-shave that had been as much a part of him as his voice or his handwriting. The scent triggered a cascade of memories so vivid they stole her breath: sitting on his lap while he read history books aloud, the scratchy texture of his sweater against her cheek; standing beside him at the kitchen sink, learning to properly wash dishes as he explained the historical significance of soap; the last moment of clarity in the hospital room, his eyes finding hers with perfect recognition.

The sound that escaped her wasn't quite a sob—she'd exhausted those in the days immediately following his death—but something more fundamental, a raw exhala-tion that contained no words but communicated every-thing about the hollow space now occupying her chest. Her knees gave way, and she sank into his chair, curling her body into the depression his had left behind.

Time slipped through her fingers like water. The shadows shifted across the hardwood floor, the light changing quality as morning stretched toward afternoon. Casey remained in the chair, unwashed hair hanging limply around her face, yesterday's clothes rumpled from sleep she couldn't remember getting. Somewhere in the kitchen, a glass and plate from a meal she might have eaten sat unwashed, evidence of basic functions continuing despite their seeming pointlessness.

The doorbell's sudden chime was jarring, an intrusion from a world that continued operating on normal schedules and expectations. Casey flinched at the sound but didn't immediately rise. Another ring followed, then a gentle knocking with a distinctive rhythm she recognized despite her mental fog. Kirk. The third time he'd come by since the funeral. She should probably answer.

Her body felt impossibly heavy as she pulled herself up, limbs moving with the stiff reluctance of someone underwater. She opened the door without checking her appearance, beyond caring about the impression she might make.

Kirk stood on the porch, Max sitting attentively beside him, afternoon light catching in the German Shepherd's glossy coat. Kirk's eyes tracked over her quickly—taking in the unwashed hair, the same sweater and jeans she'd worn when he'd dropped her off after the funeral reception, the hollow shadows beneath her eyes that suggested sleep remained elusive.

"Hey," he said simply, no judgment in his tone, just quiet acknowledgment.

Casey nodded, unable to summon words that felt adequate or necessary. She stepped back, the implicit invitation requiring no verbalization after weeks of his presence in her life. Max waited for Kirk's permission before entering, then padded inside with the careful awareness of a creature sensing emotional fragility in his surroundings.

Kirk followed, closing the door against the autumn chill. He didn't comment on the state of the house—dishes in the sink, mail piling on the entry table, curtains drawn against daylight—but his eyes took in each detail, assessing without criticizing.

"How long since you've been outside?" he asked, the question gentle but direct.

Casey shrugged, the motion requiring more energy than she wanted to expend. "Yesterday. Maybe." She couldn't actually remember if she'd stepped onto the porch to collect the newspaper or if that had been the day before. The days had begun bleeding together, unmarked by the routines that had structured her life during her father's illness.

Kirk nodded, absorbing this information without visible reaction. "Fresh air won't fix everything," he said, "but it beats staring at these walls." It wasn't quite a suggestion, but not fully a command either—something in between, an extended hand rather than a push.

"I'm not really up for company," Casey replied, the words automatic, a defensive barrier erected without conscious thought.

"Not asking you to be," Kirk countered, his voice matter-of-fact rather than cajoling. "Just suggesting we walk Max. He needs the exercise, and I could use the company." The slight rewording of the situation—presenting it as a favor to him rather than an intervention for her—was transparent but oddly effective.

Casey looked down at Max, who returned her gaze with the uncomplicated attention of a creature who existed fully in the present moment, unburdened by past grief or future anxiety. His steady presence offered something her father's empty chair couldn't—life continuing, breath and warmth and movement in a house that had become a mausoleum to absence.

"Let me get a sweater," she conceded, the decision feeling monumental despite its simplicity.

In her bedroom, Casey pulled a oversized cardigan from her closet, the sleeves long enough to cover her arms completely. The habit of concealment persisted though the bruises her father had left during his confused episodes had faded weeks ago. Some protective instincts remained embedded in muscle memory long after their necessity had passed. She caught her reflection in the mirror—pale face, shadows beneath her eyes, hair that needed washing—but couldn't summon the energy to care or correct any of it.

When she returned to the living room, Kirk was standing by the front window, a sliver of sunlight cutting through the partially opened curtains, illuminating dust motes that danced in the beam. He turned at her approach, offering a nod of approval that asked nothing more of her than this small step outside her grief.

The first breath of outside air hit Casey with unexpected force—clean, sharp with the scent of fallen leaves and distant woodsmoke, utterly different from the closed, stale atmosphere of the house where her father's scent was both comfort and torment. She inhaled deeply despite herself, her lungs expanding more fully than they had in days.

Leaves crunched beneath their feet as they made their way down the front walk, the sound crisp and satisfying in its concrete reality. Max moved slightly ahead, his leash loose in Kirk's hand, his pace deliberate as if understanding the humans behind him needed a slower rhythm today. The neighborhood spread around them in autumnal splendor, trees shedding their summer green for amber and crimson, nature's reminder that transformation continued regardless of individual human grief.

They walked without speaking, the silence between them different from the suffocating quiet of the empty house—this was a living silence, filled with birdsong, distant traffic, the whisper of breeze through branches overhead. Kirk maintained a respectful distance beside her, close enough for support if needed but never crowding her physical space, understanding instinctively that grief required both presence and room to breathe.

Casey kept her eyes on the sidewalk at first, focused on the simple mechanical process of placing one foot before the other. Gradually, her awareness expanded outward—to the brilliant red of a maple at the corner, to a child's abandoned tricycle in a neighboring yard, to the weight of afternoon sunlight against her skin. Her shoulders, which had been held rigid with tension, began to release incrementally with each block they traveled, the physical distance from her father's house correlating directly with her ability to draw fuller breaths.

They turned at the corner, following Max's gentle guidance toward the small community park three blocks over. Casey glanced sideways at Kirk, studying his profile in the autumn light—the straight line of his nose, the set of his jaw that suggested strength without brutality, the careful attention he paid to their surroundings. She noticed for the first time that day that his presence didn't demand response from her, didn't require her to perform wellness or progress. He simply walked beside her, offering companionship without expectation, his steady stride matching hers without deliberate effort.

The weight on her chest hadn't disappeared—nothing so simple or immediate—but as they continued their slow procession through the neighborhood, Casey felt something shift slightly, like a door cracked open to allow the first tentative circulation of fresh air through a long-closed room. She maintained her careful distance from Kirk, emotional boundaries still firmly in place, but found herself lifting her gaze more frequently from the sidewalk to the world around her, registering colors and movements and life continuing beyond the perimeter of her grief.

By the third week of October, the walks had become ritual. Each afternoon, Kirk would appear at her door with Max's leash in hand, no longer requiring pretext or persuasion. Casey would be waiting, dressed in layers against the deepening autumn chill, her hair pulled back in a simple ponytail that spoke of function rather than vanity but at least suggested basic self-care had resumed. They followed the same route to Winston Park, where crimson and gold leaves carpeted the winding paths like scattered jewels, the canopy overhead thinning daily to reveal more sky. Neither commented on this routine they had constructed – to acknowledge it might somehow break the fragile structure they had built around her grief.

Today marked their third visit to the park this week. Casey had counted twenty-one walks in total since the funeral, each one stretching longer than the last as her stamina gradually rebuilt itself. Some days they spoke little, content to move through the shifting autumn landscape in companionable silence. Other times, conversation flowed more easily – Kirk sharing anecdotes about his work or Max's latest training achievements, Casey occasionally offering memories of her father that now carried bitter-sweet warmth rather than solely pain.

Max trotted ahead as they approached the small pond at the park's center, his movements more animated as they neared his favorite spot for investigating water birds and interesting scents. The afternoon sun hung low in the sky, casting long shadows across the water's surface and turning the remaining leaves overhead into stained glass through which light filtered in dappled patterns. They followed the gravel path to their usual bench – a simple wooden structure positioned to overlook the water, its surface worn smooth by years of visitors.

Casey settled onto the weathered wood, pulling her scarf tighter against the breeze that skimmed across the pond's surface, rippling the water into delicate waves. Kirk sat beside her, leaving the customary few inches between them that had become their unspoken boundary. Max, released from his leash to explore, immediately began investigating a cluster of bushes at the water's edge, his nose working with concentrated purpose.

Across the pond, a family of four scattered bread

crumbs for an eager assembly of ducks. The children – perhaps five and seven – squealed with delight each time a bird approached to claim their offerings. The mother laughed, capturing photographs with her phone while the father stooped to help his younger child toss crumbs without falling into the water. The scene played out like a silent film from Casey's distance, their joy visible but their voices merely contributing to the ambient sounds of the park.

Casey's fingers found the edge of her sleeve, tugging and twisting the fabric in an unconscious gesture that had become familiar to Kirk over their weeks together. Her eyes remained fixed on the family, something in their ordinary happiness both painful and magnetic to witness.

"I feel guilty," she said finally, her voice barely audible above the rustle of leaves overhead and the distant calls of the children. The words emerged without preamble, as if continuing a conversation they'd been having silently all along.

Kirk didn't turn to look at her, giving her the privacy of his gaze while she gathered her thoughts. He simply nodded, acknowledging her words without demanding elaboration.

"Part of me feels..." she continued, each word emerging with the reluctance of a confession, "relieved he's gone." Her fingers twisted more frantically at her sleeve now, knuckles whitening with the effort of forcing out truth she had barely admitted to herself. "How terrible is that? After everything I did to keep him at home, to keep us together, there was this moment when he died where I just... exhaled. Like I'd been holding my breath for years."

The ducks across the pond erupted in a flurry of activity as the younger child enthusiastically flung an entire handful of bread at once. Casey watched their chaotic movement, finding it easier than turning to see judgment she feared might cross Kirk's face.

"My sister died five years ago," Kirk said after a long pause, his voice deliberately steady. "Charlotte. Charlie, she preferred. She was twenty-seven."

Casey turned to him then, surprise momentarily overriding her self-absorption. In all their conversations, he had mentioned his sister only in passing, never with details or emotion. Now his profile was etched against the afternoon light, jaw tight with controlled remembrance.

"I knew the signs. We'd had training about domestic violence. I tried to talk to her, but she shut me down completely, said I was overreacting."

A squirrel darted across their path, causing Max to temporarily abandon his investigation to give half-hearted chase before returning to his previous position. The brief interruption seemed to help Kirk gather himself.

Casey's hand moved without conscious thought, coming to rest lightly on the bench between them, not quite touching him but closing the distance that had been their standard. "I'm so sorry," she said, the words inadequate but sincere.

Kirk nodded, accepting both the sympathy and its limitations. "Sometimes the hardest part isn't losing someone," he said, his voice softening as he finally turned to meet her eyes directly. "It's living with the complicated feelings afterward. For me, it's knowing I saw the danger and didn't do enough. For you, it's feeling relief after suffering alongside him for so long. Neither makes us terrible people – just human ones."

The simple absolution in his words – the permission to contain multitudes of seemingly contradictory emotions – loosened something that had been wound tight in Casey's chest since the moment of her father's death. Her eyes burned with unexpected tears, not the overwhelming grief of previous weeks but something cleaner, like rain washing away built-up grime.

"There were moments," she admitted, "in the worst times when he didn't recognize me, when he was frightened and lashing out, that I wished it would just...end. Then I'd hate myself for thinking it." She took a shuddering breath. "I loved him so much, but watching him disappear piece by piece was its own kind of torture."

"Loving someone doesn't mean you have to love what their illness does to them," Kirk said. "Or what it does to you."

Their hands rested inches apart on the bench between them, close enough that Casey could feel the warmth radiating from Kirk's body against the afternoon chill. She became suddenly, acutely aware of his physical presence beside her – not just the emotional support he'd provided these past weeks, but the actual solidity of him. The breadth of his shoulders beneath his jacket, the clean scent of his soap mingling with the autumn air, the way his fingers curled slightly against the wooden bench as if consciously preventing themselves from bridging the final distance to hers.

A gust of wind blew across the pond, sending a shower of golden leaves spiraling down around them. Casey shivered, drawing her jacket tighter, and in the motion, her shoulder accidentally brushed against Kirk's. The contact was brief, inconsequential, and yet she felt a flush creep up her neck that had nothing to do with the afternoon chill. She shifted slightly, creating space again, but the awareness remained – an electric current humming beneath her skin where they had touched.

Kirk seemed not to notice, his attention drawn to Max, who had returned to sit patiently at his feet, mission of exploration apparently complete. But something had altered in Casey's perception, as if a filter had been removed from her vision. She found herself noticing details she had overlooked or deliberately ignored during their previous encounters – the way Kirk's hair curled slightly at his collar, the fine lines at the corners of his eyes that deepened when he smiled, the careful grace with which his hands moved as he reached down to ruffle Max's fur.

"We should probably head back," Kirk said, glancing at the lowering sun. "It'll be dark earlier today with those clouds moving in."

Casey nodded, grateful for the practical suggestion that diverted her from this new and disorienting awareness. She stood quickly, brushing invisible debris from her jeans, avoiding his eyes as if they might somehow reveal the shift in her thoughts. Kirk clipped Max's leash back on, movements efficient and familiar, utterly unaware of the tumult his proximity was suddenly causing.

As they began walking back along the leaf-strewn path, Casey maintained a slightly greater distance between them than during their arrival. Her mind raced, cataloging and dismissing this newfound awareness as merely a natural progression from grief to normalcy, a return to basic human responses after weeks of emotional numbness. Yet she couldn't quite convince herself that the quickening of her pulse when Kirk's hand accidentally brushed hers while adjusting Max's leash was entirely within the boundaries of friendly gratitude.

The realization was unsettling in its implications – not just for what it might mean about her feelings for Kirk, but for what it suggested about her capacity to move forward when her father's absence still carved such a prominent hollow in her days. The guilt that had begun to ease minutes earlier returned in a different form, compounded by confusion and an unexpected vulnerability that left her feeling exposed despite her layers of autumn clothing.

She tucked her hands firmly into her pockets as they

walked, turning the conversation toward safer territory – the weather forecast for the coming week, the Halloween decorations appearing on houses along their route, anything to restore the comfortable dynamic that had sustained her through these difficult weeks. If Kirk noticed her withdrawal, he gave no indication, responding with his usual thoughtful attention to her deliberately mundane observations.

Yet beneath the resumed normalcy of their interaction, something had undeniably shifted, like tectonic plates moving imperceptibly beneath the earth's surface – nothing visible had changed, but the foundation had altered in ways that would eventually reshape the land-scape above.

Chapter 18

Morning frost etched delicate patterns across the café window, nature's lace work transforming the ordinary glass into something ethereal and fleeting. Casey traced one crystalline whorl with her fingertip from inside, the cold seeping through despite the barrier, a reminder of the November chill that had driven them indoors after forty minutes of walking. Their breath had formed visible clouds as they'd made their way through the park, autumn's gold and crimson now faded to more subdued browns and ambers, the season advancing toward winter with the same relentless patience that had carried her through the weeks since her father's funeral.

The Little Spoon Café hummed with quiet morning activity – the hiss of the espresso machine, murmured conversations, the occasional chime of the door announcing new customers seeking warmth and caffeine. Casey and Kirk had claimed a small table by the window, where Max could sprawl beneath it without obstructing the narrow walkway between tables. The German Shepherd had settled with a contented sigh, his body a comforting weight against Casey's feet.

They had never discussed when or how their morning walks had extended to include these café stops, just as they had never formally acknowledged how the distance between them while walking had gradually diminished over the past weeks. Changes accumulated in small increments – Kirk's hand occasionally brushing hers when they navigated narrow paths, Casey no longer flinching at the contact; conversations that stretched deeper into personal territory; silences that had evolved from careful politeness to comfortable shared quiet.

Steam rose from their coffee cups in lazy spirals, dissipating into the warmer air of the café. Casey wrapped her hands around her mug – a substantial ceramic vessel glazed in deep blue – and let the heat seep into her fingers, still chilled from their walk despite her gloves. Kirk added a splash of cream to his black coffee, the white liquid blooming and curling through the darkness until it disappeared completely, absorbed into the whole.

"I called the school district yesterday," Casey said, her eyes fixed on the swirling surface of her coffee rather than Kirk's face. "They have an opening for a long-term substitute in the art department starting next week." She took a sip, the liquid still hot enough to burn slightly, the discomfort providing an anchor for the nervousness that accompanied her announcement. "I told them I'd take it."

Kirk's hands stilled around his own mug, his expression carefully neutral though something flickered in his eyes – surprise, perhaps, or another emotion she couldn't quite identify. "That's at Westridge High?" he asked, his voice level.

Casey nodded. "The same school where I was teaching before..." She didn't need to finish the sentence. Before her father's diagnosis. Before she'd put her career on indefinite hold to become his caregiver. Before her life had narrowed to the dimensions of their shared house and his increasing needs.

"That's great," Kirk said, and she could hear the genuine support in his voice despite something else coloring the edges – a hint of reservation or perhaps disappointment that she might have missed weeks ago, before she'd learned to read the subtle shifts in his tone. "You mentioned you missed teaching. Art, right?"

"Mixed media, mainly. Some photography." She attempted a smile that felt rusty but sincere. "I need something normal again," she explained, her eyes not quite meeting his. "Something that existed before... everything. A piece of who I was that I can reclaim."

Kirk nodded, taking a slow sip of his coffee. His gaze tracked the movement of a barista behind the counter, focusing there rather than on Casey as he asked, "When do you start?"

"Monday," she replied, watching his profile for reaction. "It's only part-time to begin with. Three days a week." She detected a subtle relaxation in his shoulders at this clarification, confirming her suspicion that he had been calculating how her return to work would affect their daily routine – these walks that had become the structural framework of her gradual healing and, she now realized, an important part of his life as well.

"That's perfect," he said, turning back to her with a smile that reached his eyes. "Easing back in instead of diving headfirst."

Casey watched his hands wrap around his coffee mug – strong, capable hands that had steadied her at her father's funeral, had fixed leaking pipes in her house, had gently restrained Max when the dog grew too enthusiastic around children in the park. Hands that had never pushed or demanded, only offered and supported. She noticed how his fingers had developed a slight tremor since they'd entered the café, a barely perceptible vibration that suggested he wasn't as composed as his voice indicated.

"I'd still like to keep our walks," she said quickly, the words tumbling out before she could reconsider them. "If that's okay. Maybe later in the afternoons on the days I'm teaching. Or weekends." She focused intently on stirring her coffee though it needed no further mixing, avoiding his eyes as heat crept up her neck that had nothing to do with the steam rising from her cup.

"I'd like that," Kirk replied, his voice carrying a warmth that drew her gaze back to his face. The smile he offered was different from his usual careful encouragement – less guarded, reaching his eyes and creating faint creases at their corners that she found herself wanting to trace with her fingertips.

Beneath the table, Max shifted, his heavy head coming to rest on Casey's foot. Without thinking, she reached down to scratch behind his ears, her fingers finding the spot that always made his tail thump contentedly against the floor. The dog had become her ally in these weeks of gradual recovery, his uncomplicated affection providing comfort when human interaction felt too demanding, his need for consistent care and exercise giving structure to days that might otherwise have dissolved into formless grief.

"He'll miss you on the mornings you're teaching," Kirk said, watching her hand disappear beneath the table to pet Max. "He's gotten used to having two humans fussing over him every day."

Casey smiled, genuine and unguarded. "I'll miss him too." She hesitated, then added, "Both of you."

The admission hung between them, simple yet weighted with implications neither had addressed directly during these weeks of cautious companionship. Casey focused on the window again, where the morning frost was beginning to melt in patterns that resembled teardrops, tracking down the glass as the café's warmth gradually overcame the cold outside.

When she looked back, she found Kirk watching her with an expression that made her breath catch in her throat. His eyes held a depth of feeling he usually kept carefully banked, a warmth that spoke of more than friendship or caretaking. It lasted only a moment before he blinked and reached for his coffee, but the impression remained, like the afterimage of light against closed eyelids.

Something unfurled in Casey's chest – a sensation both terrifying and exhilarating, like standing at a great height and feeling simultaneously the fear of falling and the wild urge to fly. She recognized it with a clarity that startled her – attraction, yes, but something deeper too, more substantial, built not on fleeting physical awareness but on weeks of shared silence and careful support, on walks through falling leaves and conversations that had gradually carved new channels through the landscape of her grief.

The realization must have shown on her face because Kirk's expression shifted, a question forming in his eyes that she wasn't ready to answer. Casey dropped her gaze to her coffee, her fingers tightening around the mug as if it might anchor her against the sudden vertigo of possibility.

"I should pick up some supplies before Monday," she said, steering them abruptly back to practical matters, using the concrete details of returning to work as a shield against the vulnerability of new emotions. "The principal mentioned their budget for art materials was approved last month. I'll need to inventory what they have and what I'll want to order."

Kirk allowed the diversion, responding with questions about her teaching plans that required no emotional exposure. Yet something had altered in the air between them, a current that hummed beneath their resumed conversation about class schedules and curriculum requirements. Max seemed to sense it too, his head lifting from Casey's foot to look between them with canine curiosity before settling back down with a sigh that sounded almost human in its knowing resignation.

Outside, the morning frost continued its gradual retreat, water droplets gathering and falling from the windowsill in a silent percussion that marked time's passing. Casey found herself speaking more rapidly than usual, filling potential silences with details about art projects and classroom management, as if the accumulation of practical considerations might form a barrier against the recognition that had passed between them moments earlier.

Yet beneath her practical chatter, her mind circled back repeatedly to that unguarded look, to the warmth she had glimpsed in Kirk's eyes before he had masked it with his usual careful restraint. She had spent so many months focused solely on her father, then on her grief, that this awareness of another person – not as caregiver or support but as someone who stirred dormant emotions – felt both foreign and vaguely transgressive, as if moving forward somehow dishonored what she had lost.

But as their conversation continued, as Kirk leaned forward slightly to better hear her when the espresso machine's hiss momentarily drowned her words, as his hand briefly covered hers when emphasizing a point of agreement, Casey felt something shifting within her – not an erasure of grief but its gradual repositioning, making space for new possibilities that could exist alongside the sorrow rather than replacing it.

The café had grown busier around them, the morning crowd swelling as the hour advanced, yet they remained in their small bubble of shared space, coffee growing cold as conversation flowed more naturally. Casey found herself laughing at Kirk's dry observation about the school district's bureaucracy, the sound surprising her with its authenticity. His answering smile – unguarded and warm – sent a flutter through her chest that was both alarming and exhilarating in its ordinariness, in its suggestion that perhaps the landscape of her life was not permanently altered into barren terrain, but simply entering a different season, one where new growth might eventually emerge from dormant soil.

Chapter 19

Casey stood in the center of her father's living room, watching dust motes dance in the shafts of November light that cut through the partially open curtains. Six weeks after the funeral, the house had acquired the forlorn air of abandonment – peeling wallpaper curling at the seams, a fine layer of dust settling over surfaces that had once been fastidiously maintained, the subtle must of disuse overtaking her father's lingering scent. She ran her finger along the edge of the mantelpiece, leaving a clean trail in the dust like a timeline dividing before and after.

The decision not to sell had come gradually, crystallizing over morning walks with Kirk and late nights staring at real estate websites without clicking a single listing. She wasn't ready. The thought of strangers occupying these rooms, erasing the imprints of her father's life without knowledge of their significance, felt like a second death she couldn't yet bear. But staying meant confronting the house's deterioration – the water stain spreading its tendrils across the dining room ceiling, the bathroom tiles loosening in their grout, the wallpaper that had begun peeling years before her father's illness had made such concerns seem trivial.

Her fingertips traced the edge of Elliot's reading chair, the fabric worn smooth at the armrests where his hands had rested through countless evenings of history books and pipe tobacco. The house whispered with memories – her father's voice calling her for dinner, the creak of specific floorboards that had formed a map of his nighttime wanderings during the worst periods of his dementia, the wall beside the kitchen doorway where pencil marks tracked her growth through childhood.

The sound of car tires on gravel pulled her from her reverie. Through the front window, she watched Kirk's truck pulling into the driveway, its bed loaded with supplies covered in a blue tarp. For a moment, she felt a reflexive tightening in her chest – the old impulse to handle everything alone, to reject help as if accepting it might diminish her competence. But she had begun to recognize this reaction as one of the many defensive patterns she'd developed during her father's decline, a protective shell that no longer served her.

The doorbell rang – a courtesy, since they both knew she was expecting him. When she opened the door, Kirk stood on the porch with a red toolbox in one hand and rolled drop cloths tucked under his arm. His navy work shirt with pushed-up sleeves revealed forearms corded with lean muscle, a light dusting of sawdust already clinging to the fabric.

"Ready to transform this place?" he asked, without the forced cheerfulness others might have adopted. His practical tone acknowledged the weight of the task without dragging it into unnecessary sentimentality.

Casey stepped back to let him enter. "I'm not sure if I'm being practical or making a huge mistake," she admitted, closing the door against the November chill. "The rational part of me knows selling would make more sense."

Kirk set the toolbox on the floor, surveying the living room with the assessing eye of someone who understood buildings in their bones. "Depends on what you're measuring with," he said. "Financially, maybe. Emotionally..." He let the sentence hang, giving her space to fill it.

"Emotionally I'm not ready," Casey finished, appreciating his directness. "But I don't know the first thing about renovation. The most I've ever done is hang pictures."

Kirk smiled, the expression warming his usually reserved features. "Marine Corps," he said by way of explanation. "Four years of building, rebuilding, and jury-rigging everything from barracks to field hospitals. After that, I helped renovate my parents' place when Dad's arthritis got bad." He unrolled one of the drop cloths across the hardwood floor with practiced efficiency. "Besides, you've got the harder job. I'm just handling the physical stuff. You're sorting through memories."

The simple acknowledgment of what she was really facing – not just peeling wallpaper and worn floors but the archaeological layers of a shared life – loosened something in Casey's chest. She felt her shoulders relax marginally, the persistent tension of the past months easing by increments.

"Thank you," she said, the words carrying more weight than their simplicity suggested. "For understanding. For showing up."

Kirk nodded once, accepting her gratitude without minimizing it. "Let's start with the wallpaper," he suggested, gesturing to the faded floral pattern that had once been fashionable when Casey was in elementary school. "Strip it down to plaster, assess what we're working with. The house will tell us what it needs."

They spread the remaining drop cloths across the floor

and furniture. Kirk produced plastic scrapers from his tool-box, demonstrating the technique for removing the old paper without gouging the plaster beneath. The work was immediately engaging – physical enough to demand attention but not so challenging that conversation became impossible. With the first strip removed, Casey found herself oddly satisfied by the clean line of exposed wall, as if she'd uncovered something essential beneath decorative layers.

"My dad hung this wallpaper himself," she said, working on a stubborn section near the window. "I was about nine. He let me help choose the pattern – hence the overwhelming florals. I thought it looked like a garden that would never die." She smiled at the memory. "He spent an entire weekend on this room, cursing under his breath when he thought I couldn't hear, but never once complaining when I 'helped' in ways that probably doubled his work."

Kirk listened as he worked, his attention a tangible thing even with his back turned. "Sounds like he had infinite patience," he observed, carefully peeling a long section away from the wall.

"With me, always," Casey confirmed, pausing to wipe dust from her forehead with the back of her wrist. "This is where he taught me to read. We'd sit in that chair by the window, and he'd help me sound out words, acting out different voices for each character." Her throat tightened unexpectedly. "Even after I could read perfectly well on my own, we kept it up. Right through high school, he'd sometimes read passages from whatever he was teaching, testing them on me before inflicting them on his students."

Kirk turned, watching her with quiet attention. "My dad was more the outdoor type," he offered after a moment. "Taught me to fish before I could tie my shoes. We'd go to this little creek behind our house, sit for hours without catching anything worth keeping. Took me years to realize the fishing was just his excuse to talk with me."

The shared confidence − a small piece of his history exchanged for hers − felt significant. Casey found herself visualizing a young Kirk, serious-eyed even then, absorbing life lessons along with fishing techniques from a father whose arthritis now prevented him from casting a line.

They continued working side by side, strips of old paper accumulating on the drop cloths like shedding skin. The physical labor felt cleansing, purposeful in a way Casey hadn't experienced since before her father's illness. Beneath the floral pattern, they discovered an earlier layer − faded blue stripes that must have predated her birth.

"Look," she said, tracing a line where childish crayon marks had somehow transferred through to the surface layer. "That's my doing. Dad was furious − or pretended to be − until Mom pointed out that Picasso probably started the same way."

They uncovered other secrets as the afternoon progressed − a patched section of wall where Elliot had apparently fixed some long-forgotten damage, initials carved into a baseboard that might have been from previous owners, water stains telling stories of winters past when ice had backed up in the gutters. The house revealed itself as a palimpsest of lives lived, her father's and her own just the most recent layers.

As sunlight shifted through the windows, casting longer shadows across the increasingly bare walls, Casey found herself growing more comfortable with Kirk's presence in this space that had been exclusively family territory. There was something steadying about his methodical approach, his respect for both the physical structure and the memories it contained. He asked questions about her father that focused on who Elliot had been rather than how he had declined − what he'd taught, books he'd loved, projects he'd tackled around the house. In answering, Casey found herself remembering aspects of her father she'd almost forgotten beneath the weight of his illness.

By late afternoon, they had stripped one wall completely and made significant progress on another. Dust hung in the air despite the open windows, the smell of aged paper and plaster creating a curious blend with the house's inherent scents. Standing back to survey their work, Casey felt a curious lightness – not happiness exactly, but something adjacent to it, a sense of movement where she had been static for so long.

"It looks worse before it looks better," Kirk said, correctly reading her expression as she took in the partially demolished room. "But there's good bones here. Solid plaster, nothing a little patching won't fix."

Casey nodded, understanding he was talking about more than walls. "One room at a time," she agreed, the phrase feeling like a philosophy that might apply beyond home renovation.

The back porch steps creaked beneath their weight as Casey and Kirk lowered themselves onto the weathered wood, their bodies releasing identical sighs of exhaustion. Dust clung to Casey's hair and smudged Kirk's forearms, evidence of hours spent wrangling ancient wallpaper into submission. The November air carried a sharp edge that felt cleansing after the cloistered stuffiness of the house, though not cold enough yet to drive them back inside. Before them stretched the backyard, once meticulously maintained but now a tangle of overgrown grass and fallen leaves, nature reclaiming territory during the months when Casey's attention had been focused entirely on her father's care.

"I found this in the refrigerator," Casey said, holding up a pitcher of lemonade she'd discovered during their search for water. "Dad always kept some made. It was his one culinary specialty." She poured the pale yellow liquid into two mismatched glasses, the ice long since melted but the chill still present. "Probably not as good as when he made it, but..."

Kirk accepted the glass, his fingers briefly brushing hers in the exchange. "Thanks," he said, taking a sip with appreciative slowness. "Perfect level of tartness. My mother always made hers too sweet."

They sat in comfortable silence for several minutes, the physical labor of the day settling into their muscles with the particular satisfaction of earned fatigue. Casey stretched her legs before her, noting the dust covering her once-clean jeans, the small tear at the knee from kneeling on a hidden staple. Kirk sat with forearms resting on his thighs, glass dangling between his knees, his profile etched against the afternoon light as he surveyed the yard.

"There used to be a garden," Casey said, gesturing toward an area now overtaken by weeds. "Dad grew tomatoes every summer. Said store-bought ones tasted like disappointment with skin." Her gaze drifted to the far corner of the yard, where massive oak branches stretched over the fence. "And that was my domain," she added, pointing to weathered boards still visible among the branches. "The finest treehouse in the neighborhood, according to its architect."

Kirk followed her gesture, squinting to make out the structure nearly hidden by the tree's canopy. "Your dad built that?"

"When I was eight. It took him all summer." Casey smiled at the memory, the expression softening the weariness of her features. "He had no carpentry experience but refused to admit defeat. The first iteration collapsed under my weight—terrifying him more than me. He went to the library the next day and checked out three books on basic construction."

Kirk's answering smile contained genuine warmth. "Sounds like the kind of dad who'd rather learn something new than admit he couldn't do it."

"Exactly," Casey confirmed, her voice warm with remembered affection. "That treehouse became more elaborate with each passing year. By the time I was twelve, it had a trap door, a pulley system for hauling up supplies, and actual glass windows we salvaged from someone's renovation down the street." She took another sip of lemonade, her eyes distant with memory. "I practically lived up there during summers. Dad would call me for dinner, and I'd pretend not to hear until the third or fourth attempt."

Kirk's gaze remained on the distant treehouse, its weathered boards a testament to craftsmanship that had withstood decades of seasons. "Charlie was like that," he said, the name emerging with careful casualness that didn't quite mask its weight. "My sister. Could never get her to come inside once the street lights came on. Had to physically drag her home most nights."

Casey watched his profile, noting how he mentioned his sister with deliberate normalcy, as if practicing her name in casual conversation. She'd learned fragments about Charlotte over their weeks together—her death in what Kirk had described as a car accident with darker undertones, his lingering guilt over failing to protect her.

"She sounds like she was fearless," Casey offered, opening the space for him to continue if he wanted.

Kirk nodded, a brief smile touching his lips. "Too fearless sometimes. When she was about nine, she decided she could fly if she just believed hard enough. Made these cardboard wings, covered them in aluminum foil, and was seconds away from jumping off our garage roof when I caught her." He shook his head, the memory both amusing and painful in retrospect. "I was supposed to be watching her while our parents were out. Lost track of her for maybe fifteen minutes, and there she was, about to launch herself into thin air."

"Did she ever try again?" Casey asked.

"The next weekend," Kirk confirmed with a soft laugh. "But that time she'd 'improved' her design with an umbrella. Mary Poppins-style. And I was her designated safety spotter."

Casey laughed, the sound warming the cool afternoon air. "I did something similar," she admitted. "Though I used a bedsheet as a parachute. Dad nearly had a heart attack when he came out to check the mail and saw me standing on the roof ridge."

"How old were you?"

"Ten. Old enough to know better, according to my very upset father." She traced a small scar on her forearm. "Didn't break anything in the landing, but scraped myself up pretty good on the rosebushes."

Kirk's eyes followed her finger on the scar, his expression shifting subtly. "Charlie broke her arm the summer she was eleven. Trying to set a neighborhood record for highest swing jump." His voice carried a note of something darker as he added, "She was always charging into danger without seeing it. Even as an adult."

The unspoken reference to Charlotte's death hung in the air between them. Casey watched as Kirk's expression clouded, his eyes still fixed on the distant treehouse but clearly seeing something else entirely—perhaps his sister in her final days, perhaps the warning signs he believed he should have recognized sooner.

Without conscious thought, Casey's hand moved to rest on his forearm, her touch light but deliberate. "She was lucky to have you," she said quietly. "Someone who saw her clearly, who tried to protect her."

Kirk's gaze dropped to her hand on his arm, the unexpected contact seeming to anchor him to the present moment. His skin was warm beneath her fingers despite the afternoon chill, the light dusting of hair on his forearm soft against her palm. Something electric passed between them—not merely physical attraction but deeper recognition, the understanding that flowed between two people who had both loved and lost, who had both carried weights that others couldn't fully comprehend.

"Sometimes seeing clearly isn't enough," he said, his voice low but without the edge of bitterness that might have colored it weeks earlier.

Casey's fingers remained on his arm, neither withdrawing nor increasing their pressure. "No," she agreed. "But it matters that you tried. That you saw her."

Their eyes met, and Casey felt a curious sensation of falling while remaining perfectly still. The moment stretched between them, weighted with unspoken possibilities. Kirk's hand moved to cover hers, his thumb brushing once across her knuckles in a gesture so brief she might have imagined it, yet its impact resonated through her with unmistakable clarity.

The spell broke when Max appeared around the corner of the house, having completed his exploration of the yard's perimeter. The dog trotted toward them, tail wagging with the satisfaction of territory thoroughly investigated. Kirk withdrew his hand as Casey pulled hers back, both movements unhurried yet deliberate, acknowledging rather than denying the moment's significance.

"Successful patrol?" Kirk asked the dog, his voice slightly rougher than usual.

Casey stood, brushing dust from her jeans with hands that weren't quite steady. "We should probably get back to it," she said, gesturing toward the house. "At least finish the second wall before it gets dark."

Kirk nodded, rising in a single fluid movement that

spoke of physical discipline maintained despite the day's exertion. He gathered their empty glasses, following Casey up the porch steps and back into the house. The air inside felt different somehow—still dusty and worn, but charged with something new that hadn't been present earlier in the day.

Chapter 20

They resumed their work with synchronized efficiency, falling into the rhythm they'd established before the break. Yet something had shifted between them, evident in the new awareness that pulsed beneath their practical conversation about plaster repair and paint selections. Their hands never brushed accidentally as they worked side by side, yet each remained acutely conscious of the other's proximity, of the deliberate space maintained between them that now felt less like boundary and more like anticipation.

As afternoon light faded toward evening, they worked in companionable silence punctuated by occasional questions or observations. The practical business of renovation continued, but beneath it ran a current of mutual recognition—of grief shared and understood, of possibilities neither was quite ready to name but both had begun to acknowledge. The house around them, half-dismantled and in transition, seemed a fitting backdrop for whatever was slowly taking form between them: neither completely new nor fully realized, but unmistakably in the process of becoming.

Days bled into one another, marked by the evolving state of the house rather than the calendar. Morning light would find them already at work—Kirk sanding woodwork while Casey applied primer to newly repaired walls, their bodies developing an instinctive choreography that required minimal conversation. Afternoons brought different tasks—sorting through Elliot's clothing, cataloguing books to keep or donate, Kirk on a ladder installing new light fixtures while Casey passed tools up with increasing familiarity with their names and purposes. Dust settled on new surfaces, paint fumes replaced the smell of old paper and plaster, and gradually, imperceptibly, the house began to shed its abandonment like an outgrown skin.

The living room emerged first from its chrysalis—walls painted a soft sage that caught the light differently throughout the day, the original hardwood floors revealed and refinished to a honeyed glow beneath Kirk's patient labor. The kitchen followed, its dated cabinets transformed with paint and new hardware that Casey had selected after hours deliberating between seemingly identical nickel finishes. Each completed room felt like a victory, not just over the house's decay but over the inertia that had gripped Casey since her father's death.

Kirk moved through the spaces with quiet competence, repairing leaks, replacing rotted window frames, rewiring ancient electrical fixtures with careful precision. He arrived early each morning with coffee and departing each evening with the satisfied exhaustion of physical work, leaving the imprint of his presence in more than just the repairs he completed. Casey found herself looking for his truck each morning with an anticipation that had nothing to do with renovation progress.

While Kirk handled the structural work, Casey undertook the more emotionally fraught task of sorting through her father's possessions. Each drawer and closet presented a new archaeological layer of Elliot's life—teaching notes from decades earlier, carefully preserved letters from students expressing gratitude, the collection of pocket watches he'd inherited from his own father and meticulously maintained. Some items were easy to categorize— clothes to donate, kitchen implements to keep or discard— but others carried emotional weight that stopped her mid-task, frozen between past and future.

On the tenth day of their shared project, Casey found herself in Elliot's study, the one room they had yet to begin renovating. Unlike the rest of the house, here the air still held traces of her father's presence—the lingering notes of pipe tobacco though he hadn't smoked in years, the subtle leather scent of book bindings, the indefinable essence that her mind categorized simply as "Dad." She stood before his desk, a solid oak piece that had dominated the room throughout her childhood, its surface bearing the honorable scars of decades of use—rings from coffee cups, shallow scratches from pencils pressed too hard, the darkened spot where his right hand had rested while grading countless papers.

Casey's fingers traced these imperfections with the reverence of a scholar examining ancient text. This desk had been the center of her father's intellectual life, the place where he'd prepared lessons that shaped generations of students, where he'd patiently explained complex concepts when she'd come to him struggling with homework. The wood felt warm beneath her touch despite the room's chill, as if it retained some essential energy of the man who had spent so many hours seated before it.

She didn't hear Kirk enter, wasn't aware of his presence until she caught his reflection in the window she'd been staring through. He stood in the doorway, a respectful distance maintained, watching her with the quiet attentiveness that had become his hallmark. Casey turned, unsurprised to find her cheeks damp with tears she hadn't realized she'd been shedding.

"This is the hardest room," she said, not bothering to wipe away the moisture. With Kirk, such pretenses had fallen away over their days working side by side. "It's still so much him."

Kirk nodded, his gaze taking in the desk, the bookshelves lining the walls, the reading lamp positioned precisely at the angle Elliot had preferred. "We can leave this for later," he offered. "Or not touch it at all."

Casey shook her head, one hand still resting on the desk's scarred surface. "No, I want to...honor it, I guess. Not leave it as a shrine." She managed a smile that wobbled but held. "I used to sit right here," she said, indicating the corner of the desk closest to the window. "Dad would give me paper and colored pencils while he worked. Said having me drawing quietly beside him helped him think more clearly."

Kirk crossed the room then, his footsteps deliberately audible on the hardwood floor. He ran his hand along the desk's edge with the assessing touch of someone who understood wood and its possibilities. "It's beautiful construction," he said. "Solid oak. They don't make furniture like this anymore."

"He bought it at an estate sale when I was four," Casey said. "Spent an entire Saturday wrestling it through doorways that were almost too narrow. Mom was furious until she saw how perfect it looked in here."

Kirk circled the desk slowly, examining its structure with professional appreciation. "It needs refinishing, but the integrity is intact," he said, dropping to one knee to check the joints. "We could move it to the center of the room, make it the focal point instead of having it against the wall."

The suggestion—so practical yet reflecting such under-standing of the desk's importance—touched Casey deeply. "You'd help me refinish it?" she asked, the question encom-passing more than just the task itself.

"Of course," Kirk replied, straightening to meet her eyes. "It's a two-person job anyway. One of us can work on the drawers while the other handles the surface."

The following morning they began, carefully removing the drawers and hardware, laying out drop cloths to protect the floor. Kirk demonstrated the proper technique for applying stripper to remove the aged varnish without damaging the wood beneath, his hands moving with confident precision as Casey watched atten-tively. When he passed her the sanding block, their fingers brushed in a contact that had become increas-ingly frequent over the days of working together— touches that lingered just a beat longer than necessary, creating currents of awareness that neither acknowledged directly.

They worked on the desk for three days, stripping away layers of old finish to reveal the true grain beneath, then carefully applying new stain that deepened the wood's natural beauty. The process became a metaphor neither needed to articulate—the gentle restoration of something valuable that had been obscured by time and wear, the patience required to reveal essential beauty rather than impose artificial improvement.

Throughout the house, similar transformations contin-ued. The upstairs bathroom emerged from decades of outdated fixtures and cracked tiles into a space of simple elegance. The guest bedroom that had become a storage area during Elliot's illness returned to its intended purpose, freshly painted in soothing blue. Even the basement, with its perpetual dampness and mysterious collections of preserved household items, received Kirk's attention—

waterproofing applied, shelving installed, order imposed on chaos.

But it was in the small moments between tasks that the more significant changes occurred. Casey finding herself laughing at Kirk's dry observations about home improvement television shows. Kirk bringing specific types of coffee he'd noticed she preferred in the mornings. The gradual dissolution of the careful personal space they'd maintained in early days, replaced by an easy physical proximity that felt increasingly natural. Their fingers brushing when passing tools or paint cans, shoulders touching as they worked side by side, the unconscious synchronization of their movements suggesting a deeper harmony developing beneath conscious awareness.

By the third week, the house had transformed from a hollow memorial to a space of possibility. New paint colors Casey had selected replaced the faded choices of decades past. Updated fixtures brought light into previously shadowed corners. Furniture arrangements shifted to accommodate contemporary living rather than preserving the patterns of Elliot's final years. Throughout it all, Casey found herself breathing more easily, the weight of grief not vanishing but shifting, becoming portable rather than immobilizing.

Chapter 21

The afternoon light slanted through the half-draped windows, painting golden rectangles across the drop cloths that protected the newly refinished hardwood floors. Casey dipped her brush into the paint can, the soft sage green rich and velvety against the stark white of the plastic tray. Each methodical stroke against the wall felt like a reclamation - not just of the house but of herself, piece by piece, room by room. Behind her, she could hear Kirk's steady breathing, the whisper of his brush against plaster creating a rhythm that had become as familiar to her as her own heartbeat over these weeks of shared labor.

They worked in companionable silence, the kind that forms only after bodies and minds have learned each other's patterns. The quiet between them wasn't empty but filled with small sounds that had become their private language – the gentle tap of a brush against a can's edge to remove excess paint, the soft scuff of sock-covered feet shifting position on the drop cloth, the almost imperceptible sigh of satisfaction when a difficult corner came out just right. Casey found herself attuned to Kirk's movements even with her back turned, aware of his presence as if her skin had developed a new sense specifically calibrated to his proximity.

The living room had transformed under their hands. What had once been a shrine to her father's decline was now a space reborn – the built-in bookshelves freed from decades of dusty volumes and restored to honey-colored warmth, the crown molding Kirk had installed framing the ceiling with crisp definition, the hardwood floors glowing with renewed vitality beneath the protective cloths. Only the walls remained unfinished, their sage green coverage nearly complete except for the final section they now addressed with meticulous care.

Casey reached to reload her brush, turning slightly to find Kirk had moved closer than she'd realized. They'd been unconsciously gravitating toward each other as they worked inward from opposite corners, the remaining unpainted wall section shrinking between them like a physical manifestation of the distance they'd been maintaining. Now barely two feet separated them, both focused on adjacent areas of wall, their brushes moving in unintentional tandem – up, across, down, reload.

"Almost there," Kirk said, his voice low and warm in the quiet room. "The color looks even better than I expected in this light."

Casey nodded, allowing herself a moment to study his profile while his attention remained on the wall. The weeks of physical labor had left their mark on him – his forearms more defined beneath rolled-up sleeves, a faint tan on his neck from days spent repairing exterior window frames, a new relaxation in his shoulders that hadn't been there when they'd begun. She'd been cataloguing these changes unconsciously, each one filed away in a growing archive of observations she wasn't ready to name.

"It reminds me of the forest behind my grandparents' cabin," she said, returning to her section before he could catch her watching. "Early summer, when everything's still fresh but settled into itself."

Kirk smiled, the expression visible in her peripheral vision. "That's exactly it. Not too bright, not too muted. Alive but peaceful."

The words hung between them, carrying more meaning than their simple syllables suggested. Alive but peaceful. It described the color perfectly, but also something else that had been growing in the spaces between their shared labors – this new awareness that felt both vital and serene, urgent yet unhurried.

They continued painting, gradually working toward the final unpainted section. Casey reached up to tackle a spot near the ceiling, stretching to her full height as Kirk simultaneously bent to reload his brush. When he straightened, he was close enough that she could feel the heat radiating from his body, smell the clean scent of his soap beneath the sharper notes of paint and wood stain. She lowered her arm, turning to find him watching her with an expression that made her breath catch – focused intensity softened by something that looked remarkably like tenderness.

"You've got paint," he said, his voice rougher than it had been moments before. His hand rose toward her face, hovering just short of contact. "May I?"

Casey nodded, unable to form words as his thumb gently brushed her cheekbone, removing the fleck of sage green she hadn't felt land. His touch was light but deliberate, and when the paint was gone, his hand didn't retreat. Instead, his palm settled against her cheek in a gesture that crossed the boundary from practical assistance into unmistakable caress. His skin was warm against hers, slightly calloused from weeks of renovation work, yet impossibly gentle.

Time seemed to suspend itself around them – the motes of dust hanging motionless in the slanting afternoon light, the half-painted wall forgotten, their breathing gradually synchronizing until Casey couldn't distinguish her inhales from his. Kirk's eyes never left hers, dark amber in the golden hour illumination, asking questions she'd been avoiding since the day they'd sat together on her father's back porch steps and shared lemonade and memories.

Casey felt herself leaning into his touch, the slightest movement but unambiguous in its meaning. Something shifted in Kirk's expression – surprise yielding to recognition, caution transforming into certainty. His thumb traced an arc along her cheekbone, the touch exploratory and reverent.

Their paintbrushes hung forgotten from slack fingers, dripping occasional green droplets onto the protective cloth below. Neither seemed to notice or care. The work that had brought them together, that had provided structure and purpose and plausible deniability for their growing connection, suddenly receded into insignificance compared to the current flowing between them.

Casey's free hand rose to cover Kirk's where it rested against her face, not to remove it but to confirm its welcome presence, to keep it there as if she feared he might withdraw. Her pulse hammered in her throat, visible in the delicate skin below her jaw. Kirk's gaze dropped to track that flutter of life before returning to her eyes, his own breathing noticeably deeper.

The house settled around them with a barely audible creak of old timber, the sound like a sigh or perhaps permission. In the slanting afternoon light, surrounded by the tangible evidence of what they'd rebuilt together, they stood perfectly still yet moving toward each other in all the ways that mattered – their shared work on her father's house having silently constructed something else entirely, something neither had planned but both now recognized was inevitable.

Kirk's hand remained against her cheek, its warmth radiating through her skin and into places far deeper than mere flesh. Casey heard her own voice saying his name, the single syllable carrying the weight of weeks of unspoken longing. Time seemed to suspend itself in the golden afternoon light that spilled across the half-finished room, catching dust motes that danced between them like silent witnesses to whatever might happen next.

His thumb traced a delicate path along her cheekbone, no longer concerned with removing paint but exploring the contours of her face with deliberate slowness. Casey felt herself leaning into his touch, her body making a decision her mind hadn't yet fully articulated. Kirk's eyes held hers, searching, questioning.

"Casey," he whispered, her name a question and an answer simultaneously.

She responded by lifting her hand to the back of his neck, fingers threading through the short hairs there. The slight pressure was all the invitation Kirk needed. He leaned forward as she tilted her face upward, their lips meeting with the hesitant wonder of explorers discovering territory both foreign and somehow familiar.

The first kiss was feather-soft, a trembling question pressed against warm lips. Casey's heart thundered as Kirk's mouth tilted on hers, lips brushing once…twice… each delicate contact testing the boundary of their simmering desire. He hesitated, as though afraid she might vanish, his restraint palpable in the gentle hold of his hand on her jaw. She leaned into him, parted her lips beneath his in wordless invitation.

Something inside them gave way—a sluice of caution crashed into a torrent of need. Kirk's fingers curled into the nape of her neck, weaving through her hair, while his other arm circled her waist, pulling her flush against him. Casey arched back, a soft moan slipping free as his mouth deepened the kiss, tongue tracing the seam of her lips in a slow, hungry exploration. Heat bloomed through her belly, spreading to the tips of her toes, as she clung to him.

The paintbrush tumbled from her fingers onto the tarp with a muted thump, forgotten. Kirk's dropped brush clattered beside it as his hands slid lower, mapping the curve of her spine, the swell of her hip beneath paint-spattered jeans. Casey pressed back, fingers clawing into his broad shoulders. A guttural sigh rumbled from her throat when his lips trailed from hers to the hollow at her collarbone, sucking a bright bead of skin into his mouth.

Beneath the scent of fresh acrylic and warm flesh, his rasped whisper vibrated against her ear: "I've wanted this…for so long."

She tilted her head, exposing the curve of her throat. "How long?" she managed, breath hitching.

His laughter was a soft exhale. "Since that afternoon in the park—when you told me about your dad's tomatoes. Maybe, before then even."

A rush of tenderness coursed through Casey—she melted into him at being so vividly remembered. Fingers tracing his jawline, she drew him back for a kiss that tasted of paint and promise.

Kirk's hand hovered at the hem of her t-shirt, thumb brushing her skin in a silent question. Casey responded by fumbling at his buttons, yanking them free with eager fumbling fingers. Her shirt rose over her head in a slick flick of wet paint against the half-finished wall; Kirk's faded plaid fell open, revealing the taut planes of his chest and the dark trail of hair leading south.

Golden light streamed through the studio windows, carving bright stripes across his skin. Casey's palms slid from his shoulders over the ridges of muscle, skimming calloused fingertips across old scars. He bent to kiss the underside of her ear, teeth grazing her lobe until a shiver rocked her spine.

"Here?" he murmured, lips brushing hers.

She glanced at the tarp beneath her, slick with splotches of color. "Yes. Here." Her grin was wicked, lighting a spark behind her eyes.

He lowered them onto the drop cloth, the coarse fabric rustling under their weight. Casey's breath hitched as denim rode down her thighs and he slipped the clasp of her bra, letting the straps slip away. Her breasts fell free, nipples already pebbling beneath his reverent touch.

"God, you're beautiful," he breathed, voice thick with awe. Casey felt tears prick her eyes at the raw sincerity in his tone. Instead of words, she drew him down to her again, kissing him until he groaned deep in his chest.

Their last clothes fell away—jeans and knickers discarded in a messy heap—until only the sheen of sweat bound them together. Kirk's hands roamed with worshipful precision: arching along her ribs, curling beneath her hips, thumbs brushing wetness that pooled between her thighs. Casey arched into each touch, coaxing him, guiding his fingers where she ached most.

Casey mirrored him, trailing her tongue over the taut belly of his abs, tasting paint flecks and salt. She found the ridge of muscle above his hip, traced it with her teeth, and he hissed her name like a benediction.

When Kirk slid upward, pausing to brush a fingertip over her glistening navel, his eyes burned with hunger. "Casey," he murmured—her name a prayer on his lips. She wrapped her legs around his hips, pulling him closer, moisture glistening on her folds.

He positioned himself at her opening, pressing in with infinite slowness. Casey's breath caught in a ragged gasp as he filled her, inch by inch, until she was stretched perfectly around him. Foreheads pressed together, they paused in shared stillness—two souls entwined.

With a soft sigh that echoed through the quiet room, Kirk began to move. His hips rocked in gentle thrusts, building rhythm as Casey gripped his shoulders. Outside, the sun sank lower, slanting amber through the windows and gilding their bodies.

Each pulse of his pelvis sent a thrill of fire coiling in her core. Casey's nails raked down his back, sweat beading at his temples. He bent his head to capture her mouth, tongues dancing as he drove deeper, faster, matching her moans with ragged groans.

When her body tensed around him, shuddering in the ascent of her climax, Casey cried out—a raw, beautiful sound he caught on his lips. She clamped down around him, drawing him closer, igniting him toward his own release. With one final, shuddering thrust, Kirk spilled into her, his voice a strangled prayer of her name against her neck.

They clung to each other as the waves of aftershocks subsided, hearts hammering in unison. Casey's cheek rested against his chest, lulled by the steady beat of his ribs. The paintbrushes lay abandoned on the floor, their work forgotten—because in that moment, nothing mattered but the heat of their skin and the echo of desire finally given free rein.

The room fell silent except for their gradually slowing breaths, the distant sounds of the neighborhood filtering through the windows – a dog barking, a car passing, ordinary life continuing while something extraordinary had transformed the space between them forever. Afternoon light stretched in longer beams across their entwined bodies, the angle suggesting late afternoon had arrived while they'd been lost in each other.

Kirk's weight pressed Casey into the drop cloth, not

uncomfortable but grounding, real. She traced lazy patterns on his back, feeling the subtle shift of muscle beneath warm skin, cataloging this new intimacy with the same attention she'd given to every other aspect of their evolving relationship. Neither spoke immediately, both recognizing that words might diminish what had just passed between them – this crossing of a threshold that could never be uncrossed, this transformation of friendship into something far more complex and potentially precious.

Gradually, their breathing slowed, bodies cooling in the still air of the half-finished room. Casey stared up at the ceiling, watching how the late afternoon light painted elongated rectangles across the newly plastered surface. Beside her, Kirk's presence felt simultaneously strange and utterly familiar – the contradiction creating a curious floating sensation in her chest, as if something essential had been untethered and now drifted free of its moorings.

The drop cloth beneath them crinkled with each subtle movement, its surface a canvas of accidental art – splatters of sage green wall paint, smudges of white primer, even the faint outlines of their bodies now immortalized in unintentional impressions. Casey became aware of every point of contact between them – her shoulder against his, the brush of his thigh alongside hers, the subtle expansion of his ribcage with each breath. These ordinary touches now carried extraordinary weight, transformed by what had passed between them.

Neither spoke. The silence wasn't uncomfortable but expectant, as if the room itself held its breath, waiting for whatever might come next. Words seemed inadequate, too blunt an instrument for the delicate architecture of this moment. Casey listened to the house settling around them – the subtle creaks and sighs of old timber, the distant drip of the bathroom faucet they hadn't quite fixed, the occasional car passing on the street outside. These ordinary sounds anchored her to reality when everything else felt dreamlike and surreal.

Kirk's hand moved first, fingers seeking hers across the small expanse of drop cloth between them. The gesture was tentative, questioning, his fingertips brushing against her knuckles before his palm turned upward in silent invitation. Casey's hand responded before conscious thought could intervene, her fingers interlacing with his as naturally as breathing. Their joined hands rested between them – a bridge spanning the narrow physical distance that represented the far greater emotional territory they had just crossed.

The ceiling above them bore witness to their stillness, its newly repaired surface a blank canvas for the shifting patterns of light as afternoon edged toward evening. A bird landed briefly on the windowsill outside, its silhouette casting a fleeting shadow across the wall before it took flight again, continuing its journey to some distant destination. Casey found herself envying its certainty of purpose, its instinctive knowledge of where it belonged.

She turned her head, allowing herself to study Kirk's profile with the new privilege of intimacy. The strong line of his jaw carried a slight shadow of stubble that had emerged throughout the day's work. His eyelashes – surprisingly long for a man so solidly masculine in other aspects – cast delicate shadows on his cheekbones. A small scar near his temple that she'd never noticed before caught the fading light, its origin a story she suddenly wanted to know. His lips, which had traced such exquisite patterns across her skin minutes earlier, now held a slight curve that wasn't quite a smile but suggested contentment. Seen this way, in unguarded repose, his features revealed a vulnerability she'd rarely glimpsed beneath his careful self-control.

As if sensing her observation, Kirk turned his head, meeting her gaze directly. The honesty in his eyes –

unshielded by his usual measured composure – caught at something deep in Casey's chest. She saw questions there that mirrored her own, uncertainties balanced against wonder, the complex calculation of risk and reward that accompanied any profound shift between two people. His thumb moved across her knuckles in a slow caress that seemed to ask what words could not yet articulate.

"Hey," he said finally, the simple greeting carrying layers of meaning in its soft delivery.

"Hey yourself," Casey replied, her voice slightly hoarse from sounds she'd made during their lovemaking.

Kirk's eyes searched hers, his expression open in a way that made her heart constrict with sudden tenderness. "I didn't come here today expecting..." he began, then paused, seemingly unable to reduce what had happened between them to simple language.

"I know," Casey said, saving him from the necessity of finding words that didn't exist. "Neither did I."

A shadow of concern crossed his features. "Do you regret it?"

The question hung between them, honest and unadorned. Casey considered it with the same seriousness with which it had been asked, turning inward to examine her feelings beyond the lingering physical pleasure, beyond the comfortable weight of his hand in hers. She found many emotions – wonder, vulnerability, a hint of fear about what might come next – but regret was notably absent.

"No," she answered with quiet certainty. "Do you?"

"God, no," Kirk replied, the words emerging with such evident sincerity that Casey felt something unclench in her chest. His free hand reached across to brush a strand of hair from her forehead, the gesture achingly tender. "I just don't want to complicate things for you. After everything with your father, and the house..."

Casey understood what he couldn't quite articulate — his concern that their crossing this line might disrupt the foundation of support and friendship that had sustained her through grief's darkest passages. The consideration was so essentially Kirk — placing her wellbeing above his desires, weighing consequences before pleasure — that she felt tears prick unexpectedly behind her eyelids.

"You've been my anchor," she said softly, turning more fully toward him, their joined hands pressed between them. "Through everything. This doesn't change that. It just..." She searched for words that could convey the complexity of her feelings. "It adds another dimension. A good one."

Kirk's smile deepened at her words, reaching his eyes and creating the creases at their corners that she had come to cherish. His body shifted slightly closer to hers, their legs tangling comfortably beneath the spare corner of drop cloth he'd pulled over them earlier. The light in the room had changed while they talked, the golden afternoon glow deepening toward the amber hues of approaching evening.

Casey glanced around the half-finished space — at the wall they'd been painting when everything changed, at their discarded clothes creating unintentional sculpture on the floor, at the tools and buckets now serving as silent witnesses to this transformation. The room itself seemed different somehow, charged with new significance. These walls that had once contained only her father's memories now held this new moment as well — passion and tenderness layered over grief and healing like fresh paint covering old marks without erasing their underlying texture.

"We should probably finish that wall," Kirk observed, following her gaze to the partially completed painting, though his tone suggested this was the furthest thing from his actual concerns.

Casey laughed softly, the sound breaking the remaining

tension between them. "Probably," she agreed, making no move to disentangle herself from him. "But not yet."

His answering smile contained both relief and something deeper – a recognition that neither was ready to return to ordinary actions and interactions, to practical considerations that would inevitably reassert themselves. For now, this suspended moment between what had been and what might be seemed too precious to abbreviate, too delicate to rush.

They lay together in comfortable silence as the room gradually dimmed around them, shadows lengthening across the floor, across their entwined bodies. Questions about tomorrow and all the days that might follow hovered at the edges of Casey's consciousness – practical concerns about definitions and boundaries, about how this new intimacy would fit into the friendship they had so carefully constructed. But she deliberately set these thoughts aside, choosing instead to inhabit this perfect, liminal present where nothing existed beyond the warmth of Kirk's body beside hers and the gentle rhythm of his breathing.

The house creaked softly around them, settling into evening's cooler temperatures. Through the window, the first stars appeared in the darkening sky, pinpricks of light emerging one by one like possibilities being born. Casey's thumb traced small circles against Kirk's palm, a wordless communication of contentment and presence. Whatever came next would emerge in its own time, shaped by the solid foundation they had built together long before their bodies had found each other. For now, that certainty was enough.

Chapter 22

The last remnants of daylight clung to the corners of the room, casting elongated shadows across their entwined bodies. Casey's hair spilled across Kirk's chest in dark waves, her cheek pressed against the steady rhythm of his heart. The drop cloth beneath them crinkled with each subtle movement, its surface a chaotic canvas of paint splatters and primer smudges now joined by the faint impressions of their bodies. In the growing dimness, the half-finished wall seemed to watch them with patient indifference, as if it had all the time in the world to wait for their hands to return to their interrupted work.

Kirk's fingers traced lazy patterns along Casey's spine, each touch a whispered promise against her skin. She shivered slightly, not from cold but from the newness of this intimacy, the strange vulnerability that accompanied such complete exposure. A corner of the drop cloth had become a makeshift blanket, draped haphazardly across their lower bodies, the plastic backing cool against overheated skin.

"Your heart's still racing," Casey murmured, her lips brushing against his chest as she spoke.

Kirk's laugh was a gentle rumble beneath her ear. "Might have something to do with you," he said, his voice carrying that particular roughness that made her stomach flutter. His hand continued its gentle exploration, trailing upward to tangle in her hair, cradling the base of her skull with careful pressure.

Casey raised herself slightly, propping her chin on her hand to study his face. In the fading light, his features had softened, the usual vigilance around his eyes replaced by something more open, more vulnerable. A smudge of sage green paint traced his jawline like an artist's afterthought.

"Did you ever think," she asked, "when you first showed up with Max and practically dragged me out of the house, that we'd end up here?"

Kirk's eyes held hers, his expression thoughtful. "Not exactly here," he admitted, gesturing vaguely to their current state of undress and the abandoned painting project. "But somewhere... significant. From that first walk, there was something about you, Casey. Even wrapped in grief, you had this... light."

His fingers found a strand of her hair, twirling it gently before tucking it behind her ear. The gesture was so tender it made her throat tighten unexpectedly.

"I was such a mess," she said, remembering those early days after her father's death, the hollowness that had seemed permanent, immovable. "I could barely function."

"You were surviving," Kirk corrected gently. "There's strength in that. I saw it, even when you couldn't."

Casey let her head rest against his chest again, listening to the steady thump of his heart. Around them, the house settled into evening with its familiar creaks and sighs, a symphony they'd both learned to read over the weeks of shared renovation. The half-painted wall stood as testament to their interrupted work, brushes abandoned in trays where paint was now developing a thin skin.

"You rebuilt me while we rebuilt this house," Casey said softly, the realization crystallizing as she spoke it aloud. "Piece by piece, room by room."

Kirk's hand stilled in her hair. "You rebuilt yourself," he said, his voice low but firm. "I just handed you tools when you needed them."

The metaphor made her smile against his skin. She traced the line of an old scar that crossed his ribs, a thin white mark with a story she hadn't yet learned. There would be time for that now—time to discover each mark, each story, each piece of Kirk she hadn't yet uncovered. The thought was both exhilarating and terrifying in its potential.

"So what happens now?" she asked, the question emerging before she could reconsider its weight.

Kirk's chest expanded with a deep breath, his arm tightening slightly around her shoulders. "Now," he said carefully, "we finish painting the living room. Eventually."

Casey lifted her head again to find him watching her with that small half-smile that always made her heart beat faster. "Very practical," she teased, though she was grateful for the lightness he brought to a question that could have felt too heavy, too soon.

"And after the paint dries," he continued, his voice dropping to a register that sent pleasant shivers across her skin, "I'd like to take you to dinner. Somewhere that requires actual clothes."

"Are you asking me on a date, Kirk Manning?" Casey felt her lips curve into a smile that matched his own. "After all this time?"

"Seems like the right order of things," he replied, his thumb tracing the line of her jaw. "I've never been conventional, but I do believe in foundations."

Casey turned her face to press a kiss into his palm. "You would have made a terrible architect, then," she said, deliberate lightness in her tone. "Foundations come first, not after the walls are up."

Kirk laughed, the sound filling the room with unexpected warmth. "Fair point." His expression sobered slightly, though his eyes remained soft. "But I mean it, Casey. This isn't... casual for me. You're not."

The words hung between them, simple yet weighted with significance. Casey felt something unfurl in her chest, a cautious bloom of happiness she'd nearly forgotten was possible.

"You're not casual for me either," she whispered, the admission both freeing and frightening in its honesty.

Kirk's hand cupped her cheek, drawing her face toward his. Their lips met in a kiss that felt different from the urgent heat of earlier—this was slower, deeper, a careful exploration rather than a desperate claiming. Casey melted into him, her body remembering with startling precision how perfectly they fit together.

The growing darkness had nearly consumed the room, their bodies now shadow-forms against the lighter backdrop of the drop cloth. Kirk's hands slid lower, retracing paths discovered earlier with renewed purpose. Casey gasped softly against his mouth as his fingers found sensitive skin, her body arching into his touch.

"We should probably turn on a light," she murmured, though she made no move to separate from him. "Or get dressed. Or both."

"Mmm," Kirk agreed without conviction, his lips finding the sensitive spot beneath her ear that he'd discovered earlier. "Probably."

The knock, when it came, was so unexpected that both of them froze in perfect stillness. Three sharp raps against the front door echoed through the house like gunshots, shattering the intimate silence they'd been cultivating.

"Are you expecting someone?" Kirk whispered, his body suddenly tense beneath hers.

Casey shook her head, already disentangling herself from his embrace. "No one knows I'm here except..." She trailed off, unease creeping along her spine. "Maybe a neighbor? Or a delivery I forgot about?"

Kirk sat up, reaching for his jeans that lay crumpled at the edge of the drop cloth. Casey cast about for her own discarded clothing, but found only her T-shirt, still damp with paint where it had brushed the wall. The knock came again, more insistent this time.

"Just a minute!" she called, her voice sounding strained even to her own ears. She grabbed the cleanest section of drop cloth, wrapping it around her body like a makeshift toga. The plastic backing was cool against her still-warm skin, a physical reminder of the abrupt shift from intimacy to intrusion.

"Want me to get it?" Kirk offered, fastening his jeans but still shirtless, his chest bare in the dim light.

Casey shook her head. "No, I've got it. Probably just someone selling something." She adjusted the sheet more securely around her body, tucking the corner between her breasts to hold it in place. "I'll get rid of them quickly."

She padded barefoot across the hardwood, the floor cool beneath her feet. Behind her, she heard Kirk moving quietly, probably gathering their scattered clothing. The intimacy they'd built over the afternoon suddenly felt fragile in the face of this mundane intrusion. Casey paused at the door, taking a deep breath to center herself before reaching for the handle, bracing for the embarrassment of facing a stranger while wrapped in nothing but a paint-spattered sheet.

The door swung open, and Casey found herself facing a woman who seemed to materialize from another universe entirely – one of gleaming surfaces and sharp edges.

Expensive perfume billowed into the house, a cloying cloud that battled against the honest scent of paint and sweat. The woman stood perfectly poised on the threshold, her blonde hair arranged in an immaculate updo that framed features too precisely symmetrical to be entirely trusted. Diamond studs winked from her earlobes, catching the last glimmers of daylight like predatory eyes.

"Hi there," the woman said, her voice carrying a practiced warmth that never reached her calculating green eyes. Those eyes took in Casey's sheet-wrapped form with swift assessment, lingering on the exposed skin of her shoulders and the paint smudges on her collarbone. "I'm Layla. Kirk's wife."

The words hit Casey like a physical blow, stealing the air from her lungs and turning her skin to ice despite the evening's warmth. She clutched the sheet tighter around her body, suddenly acutely aware of her nakedness beneath the thin fabric, her bare feet vulnerable against the hardwood floor. The ground seemed to tilt beneath her as the afternoon's tender moments recalibrated themselves into something unrecognizable, toxic.

"Wife?" The word emerged as barely more than a whisper, her throat constricting around it as if rejecting a poison.

"Yes," Layla confirmed, her smile widening to reveal teeth too white, too perfect. "I've been trying to reach him all day. When he wasn't answering his phone, I thought I'd swing by his latest... project." Her gaze flicked meaningfully to Casey's state of undress, the implication hanging in the air between them.

Casey's mind reeled, fragments of the past weeks flashing through her consciousness – Kirk's careful attention during her father's funeral, his steady presence through her grief, his hands guiding hers as they restored the house, his body moving against hers just hours earlier.

None of it aligned with the woman standing before her, claiming him with casual ownership.

"Kirk?" Casey called, her voice catching on his name, the sound barely carrying through the house. Then, louder, with an edge that surprised even her: "Kirk!"

She heard movement behind her – the rustle of fabric, the soft pad of feet across hardwood – and then he was there, appearing at her shoulder like a summoned ghost. Casey didn't turn to look at him, couldn't bear to see his face, but she felt the sudden tension radiating from his body, felt the subtle shift in the air as he registered who stood at the door.

"Layla." His voice emerged flat, drained of the warmth that had colored it when he'd whispered Casey's name against her skin. "What are you doing here?"

"Looking for my husband," Layla replied smoothly, her smile never faltering. "You've been difficult to reach lately, darling."

Casey finally turned to look at Kirk, her eyes searching his face for confirmation or denial. What she found there sent ice spreading through her veins – his complexion had drained to ashen gray, his jaw clenched so tight a muscle jumped beneath the skin. He'd managed to pull on his jeans but remained shirtless, the evidence of their afternoon visible in the faint scratch marks Casey had left along his shoulders.

"Casey," he said, his eyes finding hers with desperate intensity, "she's my ex-wife. The divorce has been final for years."

Before Casey could process this, Layla laughed – a practiced, musical sound that scraped against Casey's raw nerves like fingernails on glass. "Oh, Kirk, are we still playing that game? The divorce might be final on paper, but we both know it's just a temporary... adjustment." She shifted her weight, the movement causing light to catch on a large diamond ring adorning her left hand. "Why else would you still be wearing your wedding band when you visited last month?"

Casey's gaze dropped instinctively to Kirk's left hand, now conspicuously bare of any ring. The absence seemed suddenly significant, a void where evidence should be. Her mind struggled to reconcile the man she thought she knew with this new narrative unfolding before her.

"That's not true," Kirk said, his voice low and tight. He moved forward slightly, positioning himself partially between Casey and Layla, though whether to protect or to hide, Casey wasn't certain anymore. "Casey, listen to me. Layla and I have been divorced for years. She's lying."

"Am I?" Layla countered, her perfectly manicured hand reaching into her designer purse to extract a phone. "Should we call your mother and ask her? I'm sure she'd love to hear about your... renovation project." Her gaze slid to Casey, assessing and dismissive in a single sweep. "She was just telling me last Sunday at dinner how much she misses seeing you regularly."

Casey felt each word like individual blows, the specific details lending credibility to Layla's version that Kirk's blanket denials couldn't match. Her body had gone numb, the sheet suddenly insufficient protection against the chill spreading through her. She took a step back, creating distance from both of them, the drop cloth trailing behind her like discarded illusions.

"Casey—" Kirk began, reaching toward her, his eyes pleading.

She recoiled from his touch, her back hitting the wall. The contact with the solid surface steadied her, anger finally burning through the initial shock, warming her blood enough to find her voice.

"Were you married when we met?" she asked, the question cutting through the tension between them. "When you showed up at my father's funeral? When you held my hand through all of it?"

"No," Kirk insisted, his hands opening in supplication. "The divorce was final long before that. Layla is trying to—"

"I'm trying to understand why my husband has been avoiding my calls while apparently playing house renovation with you," Layla interrupted, her voice perfectly calibrated between hurt and indignation. "I've been patient, Kirk. I've given you the space you said you needed. But disappearing completely is—"

"Stop it," Kirk snapped, turning to face Layla fully for the first time. Something dangerous flashed in his eyes, a glimpse of a hardness Casey had never seen before. "You know exactly what you're doing, Layla. This isn't going to work this time."

Layla's expression shifted subtly, a momentary crack in her perfect façade revealing something cold and calculating beneath. She recovered quickly, her eyes welling with tears that seemed to materialize on command. "See what I've been dealing with, honey?" she said to Casey, as if they were conspirators rather than strangers. "The anger issues, the denial. It's been so difficult trying to work through our problems when he just shuts down."

Casey stood rooted to the spot, her mind racing to process the conflicting narratives. The sheet had slipped slightly from her shoulder, and she hitched it higher, trying to reclaim some dignity in a situation that had stripped her of everything else. Her eyes moved between Kirk's desperate face and Layla's practiced performance, seeking truth in a situation suddenly composed entirely of quicksand.

"I think you should both leave," she said finally, her voice emerging steadier than she felt.

"Casey, please," Kirk began, taking a step toward her. "Let me explain without her—"

"No." The word came out sharper than she'd intended, but she couldn't soften it now. "I can't do this. Not like this." She gestured vaguely at her sheet-wrapped body, at the half-finished room behind them that had witnessed their intimacy just moments before. "Just go, Kirk. Please."

Layla's smile held subtle triumph as she reached for Kirk's arm with practiced familiarity. "Come on, darling. Let's give her some space. We can talk about this like adults later." Her fingers curled around his bicep, red nails stark against his skin like warning signs Casey had somehow missed.

Kirk stood frozen, caught between them, his expression a battlefield of emotions Casey couldn't begin to decipher. For a moment, she thought he might refuse to leave, might insist on explaining. Part of her wanted him to. But then his shoulders slumped slightly, defeat etching new lines around his eyes.

"This isn't what it looks like," he said quietly, his eyes never leaving Casey's face. "I swear to you."

Casey turned away, unable to bear the intensity of his gaze or the hollow feeling expanding in her chest. She stared at the half-painted wall instead, its unfinished state a perfect mirror for everything that had just shattered between them.

"Goodbye, Kirk," she said to the wall, her voice barely audible.

The silence that followed stretched into unbearable tension, broken only when Layla spoke again, her voice honeyed with false sympathy. "We'll let ourselves out. Take care now."

Casey didn't turn as their footsteps receded, didn't look as the door opened and closed with a finality that echoed through the empty house. She remained perfectly still, wrapped in nothing but a paint-stained sheet and the cooling ashes of what she'd believed was something real.

The sound of the closing door echoed through the house like the final note of a requiem, reverberating through Casey's bones long after silence had reclaimed the space. She remained perfectly still, lungs burning with breath held too long, fingers white-knuckled around the edge of the sheet that now seemed like mockery rather than covering. Behind her, the half-painted wall watched with indifferent witness, sage green streaks abandoned mid-stroke when passion had overtaken purpose just hours before. Hours that now seemed to belong to someone else's life, some other woman who hadn't yet learned that foundations could crack beneath your feet without warning.

The first breath she managed was shallow, insufficient, a mere ripple across the surface of the ocean building inside her chest. The second came with a sound—not quite a sob, not quite a gasp, but something primal that scraped her throat raw on its way out. Her legs, which had held her upright through her father's funeral, through weeks of grief and renovation and rebirth, finally surrendered. Casey sank to the floor, the sheet pooling around her like spilled paint, her bare skin meeting the cool hardwood with shocking intimacy.

"Wife," she whispered to the empty room, the word tasting of ash and betrayal. "His wife."

Memory assaulted her with cruel precision—Kirk's hands cupping her face with reverent care, his voice rough with desire against her ear, his body moving with hers in perfect synchronicity. Each recollection, so precious moments ago, now twisted into something poisonous. Had he touched Layla with that same tenderness? Whispered the same words? Created the same illusions of honesty and connection?

Casey's fingers dug into the drop cloth beneath her, the

plastic backing cool against her overheated skin. She'd been so careful since her father's death, so determined to protect herself from further pain. She'd built walls around her grief, allowing Kirk access only in measured increments, trusting him to handle each piece of herself with the same care he brought to restoring her father's house. And all that time—what? Had he been returning to Layla? Making promises to both of them? Living a double life with the same calm competence he brought to everything else?

"Divorced for years," she echoed his words, the sound hollow in the empty room. But Layla had been so specific —his mother, Sunday dinner, a wedding band worn last month. Details that lent weight to her claims in ways Kirk's denials couldn't match. Casey's legal mind, dormant beneath grief and desire, stirred reluctantly to life. Evidence. Credibility. The scales of judgment tipping inexorably away from the man she'd thought she knew.

A sob tore through her then, unleashing the dam she'd been desperately maintaining. Casey curled forward, arms wrapping around her middle as if to hold herself together physically while she came apart emotionally. The tears came hot and fast, tracking down her cheeks to drip onto the drop cloth, creating tiny dark circles alongside the paint splatters and primer smudges—evidence of earlier creation now joined by proof of destruction.

Around her, the house stood in various states of renovation—some rooms complete and renewed, others gutted to the studs, still more waiting for transformation to begin. The parallels weren't lost on her, even through the haze of pain. She'd been rebuilding herself alongside these walls, finding new purpose in the restoration. And Kirk had been central to that process, his steady hands guiding hers, his quiet strength providing foundation when her own faltered.

"I trusted you," she whispered to the absent Kirk, her

voice breaking on the final word. The betrayal cut deeper than simple deception—it sliced through the careful reconstruction of her life after loss, undermining everything she'd begun to believe about possibility and future.

Casey's gaze fell on Kirk's abandoned toolbox, sitting open beside the wall they'd been painting. Inside lay the careful organization of his personality—screwdrivers arranged by size, measuring tape precisely coiled, sandpaper sheets stacked in descending grits. She'd teased him about his methodical nature, finding comfort in his attention to detail. Now she wondered what else that precision had concealed, what compartments in his life had remained closed to her scrutiny.

Anger flared suddenly through the hurt, a welcome heat against the cold shock of betrayal. Casey pushed herself upright, the sheet falling from one shoulder as she wiped roughly at her tears. She'd been here before—not this specific pain, but pain itself. Her father's long decline had taught her that grief doesn't kill, that betrayal by one's own body and mind can be endured. This new wound, however deep, would not destroy her.

She staggered to her feet, wrapping the sheet more securely around her body, its inadequacy as armor painfully evident. The abandoned paint brushes stood in their tray like accusing fingers, the sage green now drying to a dull finish that no longer held any promise of renewal. Casey turned away from them, her bare feet silent on the hardwood as she moved toward the stairs, toward clothes and cover and some semblance of dignity.

Halfway across the room, her foot connected with something soft—Kirk's shirt, discarded in their earlier passion, now a crumpled reminder on the floor. Casey stared down at it, the familiar blue fabric that had been warm with his body heat when she'd pulled it over his head. Her fingers reached for it automatically, lifting it from the floor with a gentleness that contradicted the storm raging inside her.

The scent hit her immediately—pine and clean sweat and something indefinably Kirk, a combination that had become synonymous with safety in her mind. She clutched the fabric to her chest for one suspended moment, pressing it against her heart as if it might answer the questions burning inside her. Then, with deliberate slowness, she set it aside on the arm of a nearby chair, refusing the indulgence of further contact.

Fresh tears welled, blurring her vision as she continued toward the stairs. Each step felt like moving through water, the air too thick to navigate with normal ease. The realization that had been building beneath her conscious awareness finally crystallized, its clarity devastating in its simplicity: she loved him. Somewhere between grief and healing, between demolition and reconstruction, she had fallen in love with Kirk Manning—his careful consideration, his steady presence, his hands that rebuilt both her house and her faith in possibility.

The knowledge settled in her chest like a stone, heavy and irrefutable. Casey paused at the foot of the stairs, one hand gripping the banister her father had installed decades earlier. The wood was smooth beneath her palm, worn by years of touch and care, solid despite the house's other transformations. She leaned into its support, allowing herself one moment of complete vulnerability before the necessary work of rebuilding began again.

"Stupid," she whispered, though whether to herself or to the universe that seemed determined to take everything she loved, she couldn't say. "So stupid."

Upstairs, her clothes waited. Hot water to wash away the evidence of the afternoon. Practical tasks to occupy hands that still remembered the feel of Kirk's skin. Beyond that lay harder work—dismantling the tender feelings that had been growing inside her, excising the hope that had begun to take root. Casey drew a deep breath, feeling the air fill lungs that continued to function despite the weight pressing against them. She'd survived her father's long decline and final absence. She would survive this too.

The first step upward required conscious effort, the second slightly less. By the third, her body had remembered its purpose if not its ease. Casey climbed toward temporary sanctuary, leaving behind the half-finished wall and the abandoned brushes, the evidence of interrupted possibility. The sheet trailed behind her like a tattered wedding train, its edges dragging against the stairs with soft whispers of fabric against wood.

At the landing, she paused, looking back at the living room below. From this vantage point, the chaos was more evident—the displaced furniture, the tools scattered in mid-use, the impression of their bodies still visible in the rumpled drop cloth. Evidence of passion and care, of work abandoned in favor of connection. All of it, she now understood, built on shifting sand rather than the solid foundation Kirk had claimed to value.

Casey turned away, continuing up the stairs toward the bathroom where she could finally shed the sheet that had become both shield and shackle. Hot water would wash away the physical evidence of the afternoon, though she knew with grim certainty that the internal marks would remain far longer. The betrayal would leave scars, joining those left by her father's death, creating a roadmap of loss across her heart.

But as she reached the top of the stairs, a curious calm began to settle alongside the pain—not replacing it, but existing in parallel. Whatever Kirk's truth might be, whether Layla's claims were accurate or manufactured, one fact remained irrefutable: Casey had opened herself to love again after believing that capacity had died with her father. That knowledge, however painful in this moment, carried its own significance. She had rebuilt enough of herself to risk connection, to allow vulnerability, to believe in possibility.

The revelation offered cold comfort against the immediate ache of betrayal, but Casey recognized its importance nonetheless. She had survived greater losses. She would survive this one too, carrying forward both the pain of Kirk's deception and the proof that her heart remained capable of love despite everything. In that complex duality lay a truth more enduring than the afternoon's pleasure or its aftermath of pain: she was still herself, still standing, still capable of feeling everything—even when what she felt threatened to bring her to her knees.

Chapter 23

Casey sat motionless in the darkness, her father's reading chair cradling her body like a hollow embrace. The half-finished living room stretched around her in shadowed accusation – primer showing through partially painted walls, drop cloths still rumpled from where their bodies had pressed against them hours earlier, abandoned paint-brushes hardening in their trays. She hadn't bothered with lights. The darkness suited her mood, matched the hollow space that had opened inside her chest where something warm and hopeful had been growing only this afternoon.

Rain tapped against the windows, a persistent rhythm that had begun an hour ago, washing the November day into premature evening. Casey had showered, scrubbing her skin until it reddened beneath the spray, as if she could wash away the memory of Kirk's touch along with the evidence. She'd dressed in layers – thick socks, sweatpants, an oversized sweater that had belonged to her father – armor against vulnerability that couldn't protect her from the thoughts cycling through her mind like hungry ghosts.

Layla's words played on endless loop, each repetition carving deeper grooves into Casey's consciousness. "Kirk's wife." The diamond glinting on her finger. "Sunday dinner with his mother." Specific details that lent weight to her claims in ways Kirk's desperate denials couldn't combat. Casey's fingers twisted in the loose threads of her sweater's cuff, picking, pulling, needing something tangible to focus on while her mind unraveled every moment she'd shared with Kirk, searching for signs she should have recognized.

The sage green wall – their unfinished project – loomed before her like a monument to deception. They'd chosen the color together, spent hours debating the precise shade, their heads bent close over paint chips spread across the coffee table. Had he been lying even then? Planning his exit strategy while pretending to care about the undertones in Gentle Forest versus Meadow Mist?

Her eyes burned, swollen from hours of crying that had finally exhausted itself into hollow emptiness. She'd thought herself familiar with grief after her father's long decline, believed she understood its contours and dimensions. But this was different – not the clean pain of death's finality but the jagged edges of betrayal, cutting anew with each remembered touch, each shared confidence, each moment she'd allowed herself to believe in possibility again.

The house creaked around her, settling into night with familiar sounds that now felt like mockery. This space they'd transformed together from a mausoleum of her father's decline into something living and hopeful. Casey's gaze drifted to the oak desk – the first piece they'd restored together, its surface now gleaming in the dim light filtering through the curtains. Kirk's hands had moved across that wood with such care, such patience, showing her how to reveal the grain's true beauty beneath years of neglect. The same hands that had traced her body with equal reverence just hours ago.

"Who were you?" she whispered to the empty room, her voice strange in the silence. "Which version was real?"

No answer came except the persistent patter of rain against the windows, water tracking down the glass like tears on a face. Casey pulled her knees to her chest, making herself smaller in the large chair, as if physical compression might ease the expanding ache behind her ribs. Outside, the storm intensified, wind driving the rain in sheets against the house. The sound carried a strange comfort – nature's violence matching her internal turmoil, external chaos reflecting her inner landscape.

She'd been sitting in darkness so long that her eyes had adjusted, familiar objects taking shape in the gloom – the bookshelf they'd reinforced together, the coffee table they'd refinished over a weekend of laughter and shared sandwiches, the doorframe where Kirk had measured her height against his own in a moment of playful intimacy that now twisted in her memory like a knife. Each piece of the room held evidence of him, of them, impossible to excise without dismantling everything they'd built.

The knock, when it came, was so unexpected that Casey's entire body flinched, a small sound escaping her throat before she could swallow it back. Three sharp raps against wood, distinct from the storm's ambient chaos. For a moment, she sat frozen, wondering if she'd imagined it – her mind playing tricks, manufacturing his return the way a phantom limb creates sensation where nothing exists.

But it came again – more insistent this time, unmistakable. Something tightened in Casey's chest, a simultaneous surge of hope and dread that left her lightheaded. She uncurled from the chair slowly, each movement deliberate, as if sudden motion might shatter something fragile within her. Her sock-covered feet made no sound against the hardwood as she approached the door, every step an argument between longing and self-preservation.

At the door, she hesitated, hand suspended above the knob. The rational part of her brain – the part that had protected her through her father's long illness, that had managed his finances and medical care when emotion threatened to overwhelm her – whispered warnings. Don't open it. Don't let him explain. Don't risk believing again.

But beneath that voice lay another, quieter one that remembered Kirk's steadiness through her grief, his hands gentle on her father's casket as he'd served as pallbearer, his patience as he'd taught her to use a sander on ancient baseboards. Could all of that have been false? The question hung unanswered as Casey leaned forward to peer through the peephole.

The distorted fish-eye view revealed Kirk standing on her porch, head bowed against the rain that had soaked through his jacket, plastering his dark hair to his forehead. Even through the small lens, she could see the haggard lines of his face, the defeated slump of his shoulders. He looked like a man who had been standing in the rain far longer than it would take to walk from car to door, as if punishment by elements might somehow cleanse whatever had transpired between them.

As she watched, he raised his hand to knock again, then paused, dropping his arm back to his side in a gesture of such profound weariness that something twisted painfully in Casey's chest. She rested her forehead against the door, eyes closing briefly against the surge of emotion his mere presence evoked. After everything, after Layla's revelations and the hours of anguish that followed, how could her body still respond to him with such persistent yearning?

Before she could reconsider, Casey turned the dead-bolt, the metallic click sounding final in the quiet entryway. She opened the door just enough to see him directly, her body positioned to block entrance, one hand maintaining firm grip on the edge as if it might shield her from whatever came next. Rain misted through the narrow opening, cool against her face, carrying the scent of wet earth and fallen leaves.

Kirk's eyes met hers, amber darkened to near-black in the porch light's unforgiving glare. She saw the moment he registered her swollen eyes, the defensive set of her shoulders, his expression shifting from desperate hope to guarded caution.

"Please," he said, his voice breaking on the single syllable. "Just five minutes. Let me explain." Water dripped from his hair onto his face, tracking like tears along the stubbled line of his jaw. "Please, Casey."

She said nothing, her fingers tightening on the door's edge until her knuckles whitened, her body a battleground where anger warred with longing, betrayal with the stubborn, persistent hope that somehow, impossibly, there might be an explanation that could rebuild what had shattered between them.

Casey stepped back, allowing just enough space for Kirk to enter without their bodies coming into contact. He hesitated at the threshold, as if crossing it might trigger some invisible alarm, then moved past her with the careful deliberation of someone navigating a minefield. Water dripped from his soaked jacket onto the entryway rug, creating dark circles that spread and connected like the complications of their shared history. Casey closed the door against the rain but left it unlocked – a small detail that spoke volumes about her uncertainty, her need for an escape route if his explanations proved insufficient.

"Thank you," Kirk said, his voice hoarse either from emotion or from standing in the rain. He made no move to remove his jacket, as if understanding that claiming any comfort in this space would be presumptuous. The overhead light in the entryway cast harsh shadows across his face, highlighting the hollows beneath his cheekbones, the exhaustion etched around his eyes.

Casey crossed her arms over her chest, creating a physical barrier between them. She hadn't bothered turning on lights in the living room behind her, its half-finished state hidden in merciful shadow. "Five minutes," she said, the words emerging with more steadiness than she felt. "That's what you asked for."

Kirk ran a hand through his wet hair, water tracking down his wrist and disappearing beneath his jacket sleeve. He looked like a man struggling to determine where to begin dismantling a bomb – which wire to cut first, which approach might prevent complete destruction.

"I should have told you about Layla from the beginning," he said finally, his eyes finding hers with painful directness. "I have no excuse for that. But what she told you – what she implied – it wasn't true."

Casey kept her expression carefully neutral, though something inside her chest loosened infinitesimally at the raw honesty in his voice. "Then tell me what is true," she said. "All of it."

Kirk nodded, accepting the directive with the same respect he'd shown her grief, her boundaries, her healing. "I met Layla eight years ago when we were both Marines. She worked in administration at Camp Pendleton; I was preparing for my second deployment." A muscle twitched in his jaw, memory tightening his features. "She was... incandescent. That's the only word I can think of. Beautiful, charming, the kind of person who makes everyone else in the room feel special just by noticing them."

He laughed, a harsh sound devoid of humor. "I was twenty-four and thought I understood people. Prided myself on reading situations, assessing threats. But with her..." He shook his head, water droplets flying from his hair. "I missed every red flag. The way she isolated me from friends. How she always had dramatic stories about ex-boyfriends who'd mistreated her. The love-bombing followed by cold withdrawal when I didn't respond exactly as she wanted."

Casey's arms remained crossed, but her weight shifted slightly, her posture no longer quite so rigidly defensive. She recognized the pattern he described – had seen it with friends who'd found themselves trapped in similar relationships, the gradual erosion of self beneath a manipulator's skilled hand.

"We got married three weeks before my deployment," Kirk continued, his voice dropping lower, weighted with regret. "Everyone said it was too fast, but I thought they just didn't understand what we had. Thought I was being romantic, decisive. In reality, I was being manipulated by someone who saw me as a military benefit package and a reliable source of income while I was overseas."

Rain drummed against the windows, filling the silence as Kirk gathered himself. Casey noticed his hands – always so steady, so capable with tools and renovation work – trembling slightly before he clenched them at his sides.

"Six months into my deployment, the care packages stopped coming. Her video calls became less frequent, always with excuses about her schedule, her family obligations. I was in combat zones, living with constant adrenaline and fear, desperately holding onto the idea of home and the person waiting there." His eyes closed briefly, pain flashing across his features. "When I finally got emergency leave because my father had a heart attack, I came home to find our apartment empty of my belongings, our joint accounts drained, and Layla living with someone else – her 'cousin' who'd 'needed a place to stay' according to her earlier explanations."

Casey uncrossed her arms, one hand unconsciously rising to her throat as if to ease the tight feeling gathering there. The specific details of Kirk's story carried the unmistakable weight of lived experience, nothing like Layla's carefully calibrated performance on the doorstep.

"The divorce was ugly," Kirk said, his expression hardening. "She contested everything, claimed PTSD had made me violent, unstable. Told mutual friends I'd threatened her. It took nearly two years to finalize, even with evidence of her infidelity, because she kept finding ways to delay proceedings, to drag things out."

He took a halting step forward, then stopped himself when Casey tensed. "The divorce has been final for three years, Casey. Three years. But Layla has never accepted it. She tracks me down every few months, creates scenes, tries to insert herself back into my life. Sometimes she pretends she wants reconciliation; other times she plays victim to mutual acquaintances. The things she said about dinner with my mother, about me wearing a wedding band – all lies designed to cause maximum damage."

Casey's mind flashed to the calculated precision of Layla's appearance, the practiced vulnerability in her voice, the specific details she'd woven into her narrative. Manipulation required research, preparation, an understanding of which buttons to push for maximum effect. Nothing about Layla had felt spontaneous or genuine; everything had been performance crafted for specific impact.

"Why didn't you tell me?" Casey asked, the question holding all the hurt of the afternoon, the betrayal of discovering such a significant piece of his history through its sudden, destructive arrival at her door.

Kirk's shoulders sagged, the movement releasing water from his jacket to patter against the floor. "At first, it felt too heavy to lay on someone already carrying so much grief. You were dealing with your father's death, with rebuilding your life. I didn't want to burden you with my baggage." His expression twisted with self-recrimination. "Then, as we grew closer, I was afraid. Afraid that telling you about Layla would change how you saw me, would make you question whether I was worth the risk."

He met her eyes directly, vulnerability raw in his gaze. "I was a coward, Casey. I convinced myself I was protecting you, but really, I was protecting myself. I couldn't bear the thought of losing what was growing between us."

Casey studied him – the water dripping from his hair onto his shoulders, the genuine distress in his eyes, the rigidity of his posture that spoke of a man expecting judgment and prepared to accept it. Nothing in his demeanor suggested calculation or performance. There was only open pain, regret, and something else beneath it all that looked remarkably like fear – fear of losing her, of having destroyed through omission what they had been building together.

She remained silent, arms now hanging loosely at her sides, her expression thoughtful rather than closed. The rage that had fueled her earlier tears had receded, leaving behind a hollow space where certainty had been. In that emptiness, doubt bloomed – not doubt about Kirk's words, which rang with painful truth, but doubt about her own reaction, about the walls she'd instantly erected when Layla appeared. About how quickly she'd allowed another woman's performance to overwrite months of evidence of Kirk's steadiness, his integrity, his genuine care.

"I should have trusted you enough to tell you everything," Kirk said into the silence, his voice barely audible above the rain. "Instead, I left the door open for Layla to weaponize my past against both of us. I'll never forgive myself for that."

Kirk took a tentative step forward, his sodden boots leaving damp impressions on the hardwood. He stopped when Casey's body tensed, respecting the invisible boundary she'd erected between them, though the yearning to cross it showed plainly in his eyes. Rain continued its persistent drumming against the windows, the sound filling the silence that stretched between them like a living thing. Outside, water washed away dirt and debris; inside, truth slowly dissolved the calcified layers of misunderstanding that had formed in a single devastating afternoon.

"I should have told you about her from the beginning," Kirk said, his voice carrying the weight of hard-won insight. "I've spent years compartmentalizing – keeping the different parts of my life separate, contained. It became instinct after Layla, after Charlotte." He swallowed, Adam's apple bobbing in his throat. "After everything."

Casey's expression softened at the mention of his sister. She knew the outline of that loss – Charlotte's death in what Kirk had described as a car accident with darker implications, his lingering guilt over failing to protect her from an abusive relationship. It was a confidence he'd shared during their weeks of renovation, a rare glimpse beneath his composed exterior that had felt significant in its trust.

"After Charlotte died, I closed myself off from everyone," Kirk continued, his eyes fixed on some middle distance between them, seeing not the half-finished living room but ghosts of his past. "My marriage was already over, but losing her... it confirmed everything I'd started to believe – that connection meant vulnerability, and vulnerability inevitably led to pain. I convinced myself I was better off alone."

Water dripped steadily from his jacket onto the floor, the soft patter creating a counterpoint to his words. Casey found herself watching the growing puddle, focusing on this tangible evidence of his presence when his words threatened to overwhelm her defenses.

"Then I heard you that night," Kirk said, his voice softening with the memory. "Three days after your father's funeral. I'd dropped off that casserole my mother insisted on making, and I was halfway down your front walk when I heard it – this raw sound, not quite crying. More like..."

"Keening," Casey supplied, remembering the night with sudden clarity. She'd found her father's reading glasses between sofa cushions, the discovery ambushing her with grief she'd thought was temporarily exhausted. "I didn't know anyone could hear."

Kirk nodded, a sad smile touching his lips. "I almost kept walking. Told myself it wasn't my business, that you needed privacy. But something made me turn around, knock on your door again." His eyes found hers, naked emotion in their depths. "When you opened it, trying so hard to pretend you hadn't been falling apart moments earlier, something changed in me. I recognized that kind of pain – putting yourself back together for other people's benefit, hiding the broken places."

Casey remembered his unexpected return that night, his quiet offer to sit with her awhile, no pressure to talk or explain. They'd ended up on the back porch, drinking her father's lemonade in silence as darkness gathered around them. It had been the first moment since her father's death that the solitude had felt bearable, the grief slightly less crushing.

"You helped me heal, Casey," Kirk said, his voice breaking slightly on her name. "Not just with your own pain, which somehow gave me permission to acknowledge mine. But with how you approached rebuilding this house – methodically, patiently, accepting that some cracks would always show but could become part of its character rather than flaws to be hidden."

He took another step closer, stopping just outside her personal space, close enough that she could smell the rain on him, see the individual droplets clinging to his eyelashes. "You showed me I could care about someone again, that I could trust again. That the risk might be worth the reward."

Casey felt something shift in her chest – the tight knot of betrayal that had formed when Layla appeared on her doorstep beginning to loosen, strands of pain and doubt unraveling as Kirk's honesty washed over her. She saw no calculation in his eyes, no practiced performance like Layla's carefully orchestrated appearance. Only raw vulnerability and something deeper that made her breath catch.

"I love you," Kirk said simply, the words falling between them like stones into still water, creating ripples that changed everything in their expanding circles. His eyes filled with tears that didn't fall, held in check by the same discipline that had carried him through combat and loss and rebuilding. "I've been falling in love with you since that first night. And I was so afraid of losing that, of losing you, that I convinced myself my past could stay buried. That Layla couldn't touch what we were building."

The confession hung in the air between them, unadorned by elaborate declarations or dramatic gestures. Just three words offered with the same straightforward honesty Kirk brought to everything – setting tile, hanging drywall, now exposing his heart.

Casey's carefully maintained composure finally cracked, tears spilling down cheeks already raw from earlier crying. The emotional whiplash of the day – from intimacy to betrayal to this unexpected declaration – left her feeling scraped hollow, every nerve ending exposed and humming with dangerous awareness. She took a shaky breath that seemed to catch in her throat, releasing it on a sound that was part laugh, part sob.

"I thought I was protecting myself," she whispered, her voice unsteady. "All those weeks of keeping careful distance, telling myself we were just friends, just renovation partners. Then today, when everything happened at once – being with you, then Layla showing up – I realized I'd been lying to myself. That somewhere between grief and healing, I'd fallen in love with you too."

She took a step toward him, closing the careful distance they'd maintained since he'd entered the house. Her hand rose to his chest, coming to rest over his heart, feeling its strong, rapid beat beneath the damp fabric of his shirt. The contact was electric after hours of believing she would never touch him again, never allow herself such vulnerability.

"I love you," she said, the words simultaneously terrifying and liberating in their truth. Her fingers curled slightly against his chest, feeling the solid reality of him. "But I'm scared, Kirk. I'm scared of building something with you and watching it collapse. I've already lost so much."

Kirk's hand came up to cover hers where it rested against his heart, his palm warm despite his rain-soaked clothes. His other hand gently cupped her face, thumb brushing away tears with infinite tenderness. "I'm scared too," he admitted, the confession carrying profound intimacy in its honesty. "But whatever comes next, we face it together. No more hiding pieces of ourselves, no more pretending we're invulnerable."

His eyes searched hers, seeking permission before he leaned forward. Their lips met in a kiss unlike their earlier passion – this was tender, tentative, a covenant rather than a claiming. Casey tasted the rain on his lips, felt the subtle tremor in his hand where it cradled her face. Her fingers curled into the damp fabric of his shirt, anchoring herself against the tide of emotion threatening to sweep her away.

When they parted, Kirk rested his forehead against hers, eyes closed as if memorizing the moment through touch alone. "I'm sorry," he whispered against her lips. "For not trusting you with all of me from the beginning."

"I'm sorry too," Casey replied, understanding blooming that forgiveness wasn't a single moment but a process they would both participate in. "For believing the worst so quickly."

They stood entwined in the entryway, water pooling around Kirk's boots, neither making any move to increase their comfort or change their surroundings. The house settled around them, creaking softly as if acknowledging this new configuration within its walls. Outside, rain continued to fall, the sound gradually shifting from violent downpour to steady patter, nature's rhythms slowing toward eventual calm.

Casey's hand slid from Kirk's chest to circle his waist, her body finally relaxing fully against his as the last defensive barriers dissolved between them. His arms tightened around her, solid and secure without constraining, offering support without demanding surrender. They had weathered the storm – this one, at least – and though both understood that others might come, they had built something stronger than before: a foundation based not on illusion or omission, but on the complete truth of who they were, broken places included.

Through the small window beside the door, the rain-washed world glistened in the porch light, droplets hanging from leaves and eaves like suspended possibilities. Tomorrow would bring practical concerns – more explanations, boundaries to establish against Layla's future intrusions, trust to rebuild stone by careful stone. But tonight, in this moment of reconnection, the rain continued its gentle cleansing, washing away the day's pain and offering, if not absolution, at least a clean slate for whatever came next.

Chapter 24

Morning light spilled through the curtains Casey had forgotten to close, painting warm stripes across her bedsheets. She stirred slowly, consciousness returning in gentle waves rather than the jarring alertness that had characterized her mornings since her father's death. For the first time in weeks, perhaps months, she felt something close to peace—a fragile equilibrium born from truth finally spoken, from barriers dismantled between herself and Kirk. She stretched beneath the covers, allowing herself the luxury of remembrance: his rain-damp hair against her fingers, the solid warmth of his chest beneath her palm, words of love exchanged in the entryway while water pooled around his boots and the storm outside gradually surrendered to calm.

Birds chirped enthusiastically outside her window, the November morning surprising in its clarity after yesterday's deluge. Casey glanced at the bedside clock—6:42 AM. Kirk would arrive around eight for the breakfast they'd planned, a deliberate attempt at normalcy after the emotional earthquake of the previous day. The thought of seeing him again so soon sent a pleasant flutter through her stomach, a sensation so foreign after months of grief that she almost didn't recognize it as happiness.

Her feet found the cool hardwood as she slipped from bed, toes curling against the chill. The house felt different somehow—not just because of the renovations they'd completed but because of what had transpired within these walls. Confession. Forgiveness. The tentative first steps toward something neither had planned but both now embraced with cautious hope.

In the bathroom, Casey caught her reflection in the mirror—cheeks flushed with life rather than pallid with grief, eyes brighter despite lingering redness from yesterday's tears. She touched her lips, remembering the gentle pressure of Kirk's mouth against hers, the restraint in his kiss that spoke of reverence rather than mere desire.

The kitchen greeted her with morning stillness, countertops gleaming in the early light. Kirk had installed the backsplash three weeks ago, his hands steady as he'd demonstrated how to apply grout between the subway tiles. The memory brought a smile as Casey filled the coffee maker, measuring grounds with practiced precision. The familiar ritual anchored her to the ordinary world after yesterday's emotional tempest.

While the coffee brewed, filling the kitchen with its comforting aroma, Casey leaned against the counter and gazed out the window. The rain had washed everything clean, giving the world that peculiar post-storm luminosity where colors seem impossibly vivid. Her backyard—still overgrown but less neglected since she and Kirk had begun tackling the worst of it—looked almost hopeful in the morning light, dead leaves beaten down by rain, revealing the promise of soil beneath.

Her eyes drifted to the driveway where her car sat—

The coffee mug slipped from her suddenly nerveless

fingers, shattering against the tile with a crash that seemed distant, unimportant compared to what confronted her through the window glass. For a moment, Casey's mind refused to process what she was seeing, as if rejecting a reality too jagged to incorporate into the peaceful morning she'd been enjoying.

Her car—the reliable sedan that had carried her through her father's countless medical appointments, that had been her sanctuary during the worst days of his decline—sat defiled in her driveway. Across the blue hood, stark black letters dripped like wounds: "WHORE."

Casey's breath caught painfully in her chest, her lungs seemingly forgetting their function. Her hands began to tremble, first subtly then with increasing violence until she had to grip the counter's edge to steady herself. The kitchen tilted alarmingly around her; the cheerful bird song outside her window transformed into something mocking and sinister.

She stepped back from the window, as if distance might transform what she'd seen into something benign, something explainable. Her heel crunched on ceramic shards from the dropped mug, the sharp pain barely regis-tering through the numbness spreading from her core to her extremities. Coffee spread across the tile in a dark pool, steam rising like gossamer spirits into the morning air.

Layla. The name formed in Casey's mind with terrible certainty. Not a random act of vandalism but a deliberate strike, precisely calculated to violate the sanctuary she'd been rebuilding with Kirk's help. Her stomach heaved, bile rising in her throat as she imagined Layla's hands moving across the hood of her car in the darkness, painting that single vicious word while Casey slept unaware inside.

The doorbell's chime sliced through her frozen horror, causing her to flinch violently. Kirk. She'd forgotten he was coming for breakfast. Casey looked down at herself—

pajama pants and an old t-shirt, bare feet now surrounded by broken ceramic and spilled coffee. The doorbell rang again, followed by a gentle knock.

"Casey?" Kirk's voice carried through the door, concern already evident in the single word.

She moved toward the entryway with leaden steps, each one requiring conscious effort. Her hand trembled visibly as she reached for the doorknob, hesitating before turning it. What would Kirk think? Would he blame himself for bringing this chaos into her life? Would he—

The door opened before she could complete the thought, revealing Kirk on her porch, his expression immediately shifting from anticipation to alarm as he took in her pale face, her shaking hands.

"What's wrong?" he asked, crossing the threshold without waiting for invitation, his body already angling protectively toward her. "Casey, what happened?"

"My car," she managed, the words emerging rough-edged and broken. She gestured vaguely toward the driveway, unable to articulate the violation more specifically.

Kirk moved to the window in three quick strides, his entire body tensing as he registered the black letters defacing the blue hood. "Layla," he muttered, jaw clenching, the single word carrying the weight of understanding and fury in equal measure.

Casey hugged herself tightly, gaze darting to the neighboring houses, imagining curious eyes behind curtains, whispered speculation about the kind of woman who would warrant such public shaming. Shame burned through her despite her innocence, despite the irrationality of feeling responsible for being targeted.

"I'm calling the police," Kirk said, already pulling his phone from his pocket, his movements precise and controlled in a way that suggested military training reasserting itself in crisis.

"No," Casey protested weakly, then more firmly, "No police." The thought of official reports, of explaining Layla to strangers, of having her private life documented in clinical language, sent fresh waves of nausea through her. "It's just paint. It'll wash off."

Kirk's expression darkened. "This is criminal vandalism, Casey. And it's targeted harassment. If we don't document it now, establish a pattern of behavior..." He left the sentence unfinished, the implications hanging heavy between them.

"The neighbors will see," she whispered, voicing only one of the many fears swirling through her mind. "Everyone will know."

Kirk's expression softened marginally, understanding flickering across his features. He crossed to where she stood, his hands gentle on her shoulders, thumbs moving in small, comforting circles against her collarbone. "I know this is humiliating," he said quietly. "And I know you want it to just go away. But ignoring Layla only emboldens her. Trust me on this."

Casey closed her eyes briefly, drawing strength from his steady presence before nodding once. "Okay," she whispered. "Call them."

While Kirk made the call, his voice low and controlled as he explained the situation to the dispatcher, Casey watched through the window as he circled her car, examining it for additional damage or anything that might serve as evidence. His protective stance, the careful way he documented the scene with his phone's camera, the controlled anger evident in every line of his body—all of it should have reassured her. Instead, a new fear took root alongside her shock and embarrassment: that Layla's vendetta would eventually force Kirk to choose between his own peace and his relationship with Casey.

The thought left her cold despite the morning sunlight

streaming through the windows, turning the spilled coffee on her kitchen floor into a gleaming dark mirror that reflected nothing but uncertainty.

The police station assaulted Casey's senses with its particular blend of institutional efficiency and human disorder—fluorescent lights that rendered everyone slightly jaundiced, the background symphony of ringing phones and measured conversations, the faint undercurrent of industrial cleaner failing to completely mask the scent of too many bodies in too little space. She sat rigidly in the molded plastic chair beside Officer Rodriguez's desk, her hands clasped so tightly in her lap that her knuckles had gone white. The drive here had been silent, Kirk focused on the road with the hypervigilance of someone expecting threats from every quarter, Casey lost in the suffocating realization that her private life had now become a matter of public record.

Officer Rodriguez's desk presented a geography of organized chaos: case files stacked in precarious towers, sticky notes affixed to every available surface, a half-empty coffee cup leaving concentric rings on an outdated blotter. The officer himself matched his workspace—methodical yet slightly rumpled, his uniform crisp but his eyes carrying the weary patience of someone who had seen too many human dramas played out before him.

"So, Ms. Preston," Rodriguez said, fingers poised over his keyboard, "let's go through this again from the beginning. You discovered the vandalism at approximately what time this morning?"

Casey cleared her throat, her voice emerging smaller than she intended. "Around seven, I think. I was making coffee and looked out the window and..." She trailed off, the words sticking in her throat as the image of her defaced car flashed behind her eyes again. Instinctively, she glanced at Kirk, drawing strength from his steady presence beside her.

Kirk sat unnaturally still, only the subtle flexing of his jaw muscles betraying the tension coiled within him. His eyes remained fixed on Rodriguez, watchful and assessing in a way that reminded Casey of Max when the dog sensed potential threats.

"And you believe you know who might have done this?" Rodriguez prompted, his tone professionally neutral despite the hateful word that had been painted across her car.

Casey inhaled slowly, forcing herself to maintain eye contact with the officer rather than shrinking into herself as she desperately wanted to do. "Yes. My... Kirk's ex-wife." The term felt inadequate to describe the calculating woman who had appeared on her doorstep, whose diamond-bright smile had concealed such malice.

"Layla Manning," Kirk supplied, his voice clipped and precise. "We've been divorced for three years, but she has a history of harassment and unwanted contact."

Rodriguez's fingers clicked efficiently across the keyboard, transcribing their statements into the sterile language of police reports. "And Ms. Manning came to your residence yesterday afternoon, correct? Can you describe that interaction?"

Casey felt heat rising to her face, remembering how Layla had found her wrapped in nothing but a paint-splattered drop cloth, the aftermath of intimacy with Kirk still evident in her flushed skin and tangled hair. "She showed up unannounced. Made insinuations that she and Kirk were still... involved." The clinical description felt inadequate against the emotional devastation Layla had caused, the momentary fracturing of trust between herself and Kirk.

"She deliberately created confusion and conflict," Kirk

added, leaning forward slightly in his chair. "It's a pattern with her. She finds where I am, who I'm with, and inserts herself to cause maximum damage."

Rodriguez nodded without looking up from his screen. "Do you have any previous reports filed against Ms. Manning? Restraining orders? Documentation of other incidents?"

Kirk's hand tightened on the armrest of his chair. "Not here. When I lived in San Diego, yes. But nothing since moving back."

"And you have no direct evidence that Ms. Manning was responsible for the vandalism? No witnesses who saw her? No surveillance footage?"

"It was her," Kirk said flatly, certainty hardening his voice. "This is exactly how she operates."

Rodriguez's hands stilled on the keyboard as he finally looked up, his expression sympathetic but tinged with the practiced caution of someone who had delivered unwelcome news many times before. "I understand your conviction, Mr. Manning. But without concrete evidence linking this to Ms. Manning specifically, there's not much we can do beyond filing a report." He gestured to the screen where their statement was being processed. "We'll have patrol cars make extra passes by Ms. Preston's address for the next few days, but legally..."

"So we just wait until she does something worse?" Kirk interrupted, each word precisely enunciated through clenched teeth. "Until she escalates from property damage to something more direct?"

Casey placed her hand on Kirk's forearm, feeling the tension vibrating through him like a taut wire about to snap. His skin was warm beneath the fabric of his jacket, the subtle shift of muscle as he registered her touch a reminder of their still-new physical language. "Kirk," she murmured, the single word carrying layers of meaning—caution, support, a request for restraint.

Kirk exhaled slowly, some of the rigidity leaving his posture as he nodded once, acknowledging both her concern and the futility of antagonizing the officer who was simply explaining procedural realities.

Rodriguez watched their interaction with the assessing eye of someone who had witnessed countless relationship dynamics played out in his cramped office. "Look," he said, his tone softening slightly, "I get your frustration. But there are things you can do to protect yourselves and build a case if this continues." He pulled a form from one of the stacks on his desk. "Document everything. Times, dates, any contact or suspected contact. Install security cameras—the doorbell ones are pretty affordable now. Keep all text messages, emails, voicemails."

He slid the form across the desk toward Casey—a restraining order application, the paper worn at the edges from being handled by countless others in similar situations. "This is an option if there are further incidents. It won't physically stop someone determined to cause trouble, but it creates legal consequences if they violate it."

Casey took the form, the official language swimming before her eyes—"credible threat," "reasonable fear," "pattern of harassment." Words that attempted to contain the messy reality of human malice within bureaucratic boundaries.

"Thank you," she said quietly, folding the paper and slipping it into her purse. "We'll document everything moving forward."

Rodriguez nodded, his attention already drifting toward the stack of other cases awaiting his attention. He printed their report, the pages emerging from the ancient printer with a mechanical wheeze. "Sign here," he indicated, sliding the document and a pen toward them. "The report number is at the top. Reference that if there are any further incidents."

Casey signed her name, the familiar motion of pen across paper feeling strangely formal against the chaotic emotions churning inside her. Kirk's signature followed, his normally controlled handwriting betraying his tension in slightly harder strokes.

As they rose to leave, Rodriguez offered a final piece of advice. "Don't engage with her if she makes contact. That's what she wants. Document and report, that's it."

Kirk nodded stiffly, his hand coming to rest at the small of Casey's back as they navigated between desks toward the exit. The gentle pressure of his palm against her spine carried reassurance, protection, a silent promise that she wouldn't face this alone.

At the station entrance, Kirk paused, his body subtly shifting to position himself between Casey and the door before he pushed it open. Outside, November sunlight had given way to thickening clouds, the air carrying the metallic promise of more rain. Casey watched as Kirk's eyes methodically scanned the parking lot—sweeping from vehicle to vehicle, noting occupants, assessing potential threats with the practiced efficiency of his military training.

"She's not here," Casey said softly, though she found herself following his gaze, newly aware of how quickly security could be shattered, how vulnerable ordinary life really was.

Kirk didn't respond immediately, his attention still moving across the lot with careful precision. Finally, he nodded, though the tension remained in his shoulders as he guided her toward his truck. "Probably not," he agreed, his voice low. "But underestimating Layla has always been a mistake."

The words hung between them as they walked across

the asphalt, Casey suddenly conscious of the exposed openness of the lot, the countless windows overlooking it, the spaces between parked cars where someone might wait unseen. For the first time since her father's death, she felt genuinely afraid—not of grief's hollowing absence but of malice's deliberate presence, of someone actively seeking to harm what fragile happiness she had begun to rebuild.

Chapter 25

Evening gathered at the windows of Casey's house, shadows lengthening across the yard where earlier police officers had taken photographs and collected samples from her vandalized car. Kirk moved through the living room with methodical precision, testing each window lock with careful hands, the soft click of securing mechanisms punctuating the weighted silence between them. Casey leaned against the kitchen doorframe, watching his deliberate progress around the perimeter, a complex emotion settling in her chest—gratitude for his protection tangled with an uneasy awareness of how quickly their relationship had been forced to evolve, skipping the gentle unfolding of normal courtship and plunging instead into crisis management.

The day had exhausted her in ways physical labor never could. After returning from the police station, they'd spent hours scrubbing the black paint from her car's hood, the hateful word gradually dissolving beneath their combined efforts though a faint shadow remained, visible if you knew where to look. Like the aftermath of Layla's appearance yesterday, Casey thought—superficially removed but leaving traces that altered how you perceived what had once been untarnished.

Kirk paused at the front window, drawing the curtains closed after a final survey of the darkening street. His profile was etched against the remaining light, shoulders set with a tension that hadn't fully released since morning. Casey studied the unfamiliar vigilance in his posture—so different from the relaxed competence he'd displayed during their renovation work, yet somehow equally intrinsic to who he was.

"I think that's everything," he said, turning toward her. "All windows and doors are secure. I've got the motion sensor lights installed on both sides of the house." He patted his pocket where his phone rested. "They'll alert if anything triggers them."

Casey nodded, arms folded across her chest in unconscious self-protection. "You don't have to stay," she offered, the words emerging with a casualness that felt fabricated even to her own ears. Her body betrayed her with subtle tells—the tightness in her shoulders, the way her fingers gripped her upper arms, the careful control she maintained over her breathing to prevent it from quickening with unacknowledged anxiety.

Kirk crossed to where she stood, stopping just short of touching her. In the dim light of the entryway, his eyes were serious, searching hers with an intensity that made her want to look away. "I'm not leaving you alone tonight," he said, his voice gentle but firm. "Not with Layla in this state."

Relief flooded through Casey, though she worked to keep it from showing too plainly on her face. Pride and independence had been her armor throughout her father's illness, traits that had sustained her through grief's darkest passages. Admitting vulnerability, accepting protection—these were muscles she'd allowed to atrophy, and their reawakening brought its own discomfort.

"We should talk about practical things, then," she said, retreating to the safer territory of logistics. "What's the plan if she does show up?"

Kirk followed her into the kitchen, where the overhead light created a pool of brightness against the gathering darkness outside. He leaned against the counter, close enough that Casey could feel the subtle warmth radiating from his body but not so near as to crowd her when she needed space to process.

"If anything triggers the sensors, we don't investigate ourselves," he said, the military precision in his words evidence of a mind accustomed to threat assessment. "We call the police immediately. Document everything—time, what we observe, any interaction. No engagement if we can avoid it."

Casey nodded, filling two glasses with water more for the familiar motion than from actual thirst. "And you'll sleep where? The spare room is still full of boxes from Dad's study that I haven't sorted."

"The couch is fine," Kirk replied. "I've slept in far worse places." A small smile softened his features, easing some of the vigilant tension that had defined him throughout the day. "During my second deployment, I spent three weeks sleeping on what was basically a glorified shelf. Your couch is luxury by comparison."

Casey returned his smile tentatively, the expression feeling unfamiliar after hours of stress and procedural discussions. "I'll get you some blankets. And there's a spare toothbrush in the bathroom cabinet."

They moved through the practical arrangements with careful coordination, establishing the parameters of this unexpected domestic arrangement without acknowledging the deeper currents flowing beneath ordinary actions. Casey gathered linens from the hallway closet while Kirk brought in his overnight bag from the truck, the simple tasks creating a rhythm that gradually eased the day's sharp edges.

Later, with darkness fully claimed the world outside, they sat on the couch in the living room's dim lamplight, the television providing background noise neither of them actually watched. Casey had changed into comfortable clothes—soft leggings and an oversized sweater that enveloped her like armor—while Kirk wore faded jeans and a simple gray t-shirt that revealed the lean strength of his arms. The casual intimacy of seeing him this way, relaxed in her space despite the circumstances that had brought him there, stirred something warm beneath Casey's lingering anxiety.

"Are you okay?" Kirk asked softly, his gaze steady on her profile. "Really, I mean. Not the version you'd tell the police or the neighbors."

Casey considered the question, appreciating that he hadn't offered empty reassurances or dismissed her feelings. "I'm angry," she admitted, the emotion surfacing more clearly now that the initial shock had receded. "And violated. And I hate that she's managed to insert herself into our lives so effectively." She turned to face him fully. "But I'm not scared of her, not really. I'm more afraid of what she represents—this chaotic force that could disrupt everything we've been building."

Kirk nodded, understanding darkening his eyes. "She's always been good at finding vulnerabilities and exploiting them." His hand moved to rest lightly on the couch between them, not quite touching her but offering connection if she wanted it. "But we're not as vulnerable as she thinks. Not if we're facing this together."

Casey looked at his outstretched hand, the same hand that had carefully restored her father's desk, that had held hers through the funeral, that had traced her body with such reverence. Without conscious thought, her fingers moved to cover his, the contact sending a current of warmth up her arm despite the simplicity of the touch.

"Together," she repeated, the word both acknowledgment and promise.

Kirk's free hand rose to her face, fingertips tracing the delicate line of her cheekbone with a gentleness that contrasted sharply with the protective vigilance he'd displayed throughout the day. His eyes reflected the lamp's soft glow and something deeper—concern, yes, but also a certainty that made Casey's breath catch in her throat.

"I meant what I said yesterday," he murmured, thumb brushing the corner of her mouth with exquisite care. "I love you, Casey. Layla can't change that, can't touch that unless we let her."

The declaration hung between them, simple yet profound in its defiance of the chaos Layla had tried to sow. Casey leaned into his touch, her body making the decision her mind might have hesitated over—choosing connection over caution, intimacy over isolation.

"I love you too," she whispered, the words emerging easier this time, strengthened by repetition and conviction.

His lips met hers in a kiss that began tentatively, a careful reclaiming of the territory they'd briefly lost to doubt. Casey's hand rose to the nape of his neck, fingers threading through the short hairs there as the kiss deepened, transformed from reassurance to something more urgent. Kirk's arm circled her waist, drawing her closer until she was practically in his lap, the heat of his body a shield against the November chill and the colder fear that had shadowed her since morning.

The subtle scent of his cologne—cedar and something

darker, more complex—filled her senses as his mouth moved from her lips to her jaw, tracing a path that sent shivers racing across her skin. Casey heard herself make a small sound, half sigh and half plea, as her body remembered the pleasure they'd discovered together before Layla's intrusion. The memory, instead of being tainted by what followed, now fueled a determination to reclaim what was theirs, to refuse the poison of Layla's interference.

Kirk's hands trembled with anticipation as they slid beneath her sweater, his fingers tracing the warm, smooth skin of her back. Casey responded with a soft moan, shifting to straddle his lap, their bodies pressing together in a dance of desperation and longing. The house hushed its usual nightly symphony of creaks and sighs, as if holding its breath to listen to theirs—a rapid, urgent rhythm that betrayed the depth of their need. Outside, motion-sensor lights flickered futilely against the darkness, but within the sanctuary of Kirk's embrace, Casey found an impenetrable fortress—a place where she was seen, known, and loved without bounds or barriers.

Her lips found his, their tongues entwining in a fierce, explosive passion that could no longer be contained. Kirk's hands roamed her body, committing every curve, every line to memory. Casey ground against him, her breath hitching as she felt his arousal pressing insistently against her. With a growl, Kirk flipped her onto her back, his body covering hers as he began to explore her with a hungry, almost wild intensity.

Their clothing became an unnecessary barrier, each piece shed hastily and thrown aside until there was nothing but skin on skin. Kirk's mouth blazed a trail down her neck, across her collarbone, and captured one taut nipple, drawing a sharp gasp from Casey. She arched against him, her nails raking down his back, urging him on.

He moved lower, his tongue circling her navel before hooking her legs over his shoulders and burying his face between her thighs. Casey cried out, her hips bucking as he devoured her, his tongue and fingers working in tandem to drive her towards the edge. The room spun, her vision blurring as wave after wave of pleasure crashed over her, leaving her boneless and gasping.

Kirk kissed his way back up her body, his eyes locked onto hers as he positioned himself at her entrance. With one powerful thrust, he buried himself deep inside her, a groan tearing from his throat at the exquisite sensation. Casey wrapped her legs around his waist, meeting each of his thrusts with her own, their bodies moving in sync as they climbed higher and higher.

In a flurry of urgency, Kirk swept Casey into his arms, carrying her to the bedroom without breaking their connection. He lowered her onto the bed, his body covering hers once more as he began to move with a primal, relentless rhythm. The room filled with the sound of their lovemaking—the slick slide of skin against skin, the symphony of their moans and whispered endearments.

Casey's orgasm hit her like a freight train, her body convulsing beneath him as she screamed his name. Kirk followed her over the edge, his release pulsing deep within her as he whispered her name like a prayer.

As they lay entwined in the aftermath, their hearts slowly returning to a normal rhythm, Casey looked into Kirk's eyes and saw her future. "You should only ever sleep in this bed with me," she declared, her voice fierce with conviction. Kirk smiled, his heart swelling with love and contentment as he pulled her close, knowing that he had finally found his home.

They would face whatever came next—Layla's machinations, legal proceedings, the careful reconstruction of boundaries she'd tried to demolish. But tonight, in the dim glow of the living room lamp, they reclaimed something Layla couldn't touch unless they allowed it: the tender, insistent promise of a future they would build together, stronger for having weathered the first of what might be many storms.

Chapter 26

Casey awoke to the gentle percussion of rain against her bedroom window, a steady rhythm that would have been soothing if not for the lingering unease that had settled beneath her skin since Layla's appearance. The digital clock's red numbers glowed 6:17 in the pre-dawn dimness. Too early to be awake, yet too late to reclaim the scattered fragments of sleep. She lay still, listening to the house's familiar sounds beneath the rain's patter, cataloging each creak and settling groan as either normal or potentially something else—something deliberate, calculating, waiting.

Kirk's breathing beside her remained deep and even, his arm a warm weight across her waist. They'd finally abandoned the pretense of him sleeping on the couch three nights ago, his protective presence more necessary than propriety. Casey slid carefully from beneath the sheets, padding silently to the window. The motion-sensor lights Kirk had installed remained dark, suggesting nothing had triggered them overnight. A small victory.

She peered through the gap in the curtains at her car parked in the driveway. The rain blurred its outline, washing away the last faint shadows of Layla's vandalism from the hood. Something about the car's silhouette seemed wrong, though—a subtle alteration in its stance that registered in Casey's mind before she could identify the specific difference.

"No," she whispered, dressing quickly in jeans and one of Kirk's sweatshirts that she'd claimed as her own. She moved silently through the darkened house, slipping out the front door into the misty dawn.

The truth revealed itself with brutal clarity as she approached the car. All four tires lay flattened against the wet pavement, the car's weight settling it unnaturally low to the ground. Casey crouched beside the front passenger tire, rain immediately soaking through her jeans at the knees. Her fingers traced the gash in the rubber—not a random puncture or the result of running over something sharp, but a deliberate, precise slice.

She examined each tire in turn, the methodical destruction telling its own story. These weren't rage-filled stabbings but calculated cuts, made with a sharp blade by steady hands. The precision chilled her more than random violence would have. This wasn't impulsive; this was planned, executed with cold determination. Just like Layla's earlier appearance on her doorstep, just like the "WHORE" painted across her hood—each action carefully choreographed for maximum impact.

Rain traced cold fingers down her spine as Casey stood, water dripping from her hair into her eyes, mingling with the tears she refused to acknowledge. She glanced around the silent street, the houses dark except for occasional kitchen lights where early risers prepared for their day, oblivious to the quiet violence that had occurred outside her home. The rain would wash away footprints, fingerprints, any evidence that might have connected these cuts to Layla's manicured hands.

Inside, Casey's fingers trembled as she dialed the police

station. Officer Rodriguez's voice on the other end of the line carried professional sympathy that did little to ease the cold dread pooling in her stomach.

"I'll send someone out to document it, Ms. Preston," he said after listening to her description. "But I should warn you, without witnesses or surveillance footage..."

"It was her," Casey interrupted, her voice tight with frustration. "First my car hood, now the tires. This is exactly the pattern of escalation you talked about."

"I understand your conviction," Rodriguez replied, the words familiar from their previous conversation. "And I agree it fits the pattern. But the district attorney needs evidence that will stand up in court. Do you have those security cameras installed yet?"

"They're being delivered today," Casey admitted, the delay now seeming like a critical error in judgment. "We were waiting for the weekend to install them."

Rodriguez's sigh carried through the phone, not impatient but resigned. "Document everything. Take photos before the tow service arrives. We'll add it to the existing report."

After hanging up, Casey stood at the kitchen window, watching rain transform her driveway into a network of puddles that reflected the gradually lightening sky. The sensation of being observed prickled across her skin—an awareness that extended beyond rational thought into something more primal. She scanned the street again, eyes lingering on parked cars, shadows between houses, the dense foliage of rhododendrons across the way where someone could easily conceal themselves.

Kirk appeared in the kitchen doorway, his hair mussed from sleep but his eyes instantly alert as he registered her posture. "What happened?" he asked, crossing to her in three quick strides.

"All four tires," Casey said, gesturing toward the driveway. "Slashed."

Kirk's expression hardened, jaw clenching as he processed this escalation. Without speaking, he moved past her to the front door, returning minutes later with rain dampening his t-shirt, darkening it in patches across his shoulders and chest.

"I've called for a tow," he said, voice tight with controlled anger. "And took photos for the police report."

"Rodriguez is sending someone, but he basically said the same thing as before. Without concrete evidence linking her to this—"

"I know," Kirk cut her off, the frustration in his voice directed not at Casey but at the situation, at the legal system's limitations, at his own inability to shield her from Layla's calculated malice.

They waited for the tow truck in strained silence, the kitchen filling with gray morning light that did nothing to dispel the shadows beneath Kirk's eyes, the tension in Casey's shoulders. When blue lights flickered through the window, announcing the police officer's arrival, Kirk placed his hand gently on the small of her back—a gesture of support as they stepped out into the drizzle.

On the driveway, Kirk positioned himself between Casey and the street as they spoke with the officer, his body angled subtly to shield her while maintaining casual appearance. Casey found herself drawing strength from his solid presence, his unwavering attention as she once again described discovering the damage, the precise nature of the cuts, the escalating pattern of harassment.

While the officer photographed the tires from multiple angles, Kirk turned to Casey, his expression grave. "I think I should stay here," he said quietly. "Not just overnight anymore. Move in temporarily."

Casey's immediate instinct was to resist—to maintain

what remnants of independence and normalcy she could cling to in the face of Layla's intrusions. The thought of admitting that she needed this level of protection felt like conceding something important, like letting Layla dictate the terms of her own life.

Kirk seemed to read her hesitation. "She knows where you live," he said, his voice gentle but firm. "And she's clearly willing to cross boundaries, to come onto your property. This isn't random anymore, Casey. It's calculated."

Casey's gaze drifted to her car, its wounded posture an accusation against her previous optimism that Layla would lose interest, move on, find another target for her fixation. The methodical precision of those cuts told a different story—one of patient malice, of someone willing to wait in rain and darkness to inflict damage, to instill fear.

"Okay," she said finally, the word emerging as barely more than a breath. "You're right."

Relief flickered across Kirk's features, his hand finding hers and squeezing gently. "I'll get some things from my place after we deal with your car," he said. "And we'll install those cameras as soon as they arrive, not wait for the weekend."

As they watched the tow truck operator maneuver her car onto the flatbed, Casey felt a curious lightness beneath the morning's heavy reality. Kirk's arm around her shoulders anchored her against both the literal and figurative chill, his body radiating warmth that reached beyond physical comfort. There was something oddly freeing in acknowledging that she couldn't face this alone—that accepting help, accepting protection, wasn't weakness but wisdom.

She leaned into Kirk's side, her arm circling his waist as the tow truck pulled away with her damaged car. Around them, the neighborhood stirred to life—garage doors rising, cars backing from driveways, people rushing to beat the morning traffic, oblivious to the small war being waged on this quiet street. Casey glanced once more at the rhododendrons across the way, half-expecting to glimpse a figure withdrawing into deeper shadows.

Nothing moved except rain-heavy leaves shuddering in the morning breeze. But the sensation of being watched lingered like a phantom touch against her skin, raising goosebumps that had nothing to do with the damp November chill.

The rental car's unfamiliar engine cut off with a hesitant sputter, leaving Casey sitting in sudden silence in her driveway. Late afternoon shadows stretched across the lawn, transforming familiar shapes into elongated specters that seemed to reach toward the house with grasping fingers. She gathered her work bag and the groceries she'd picked up—ordinary actions that now required deliberate focus, her mind constantly divided between immediate tasks and vigilant awareness of her surroundings. The weight of being constantly on guard had settled into her muscles over the past days, a persistent ache that no amount of hot showers or nighttime stretches could ease.

The rental car was too new, too clean, too obviously not hers—another reminder of what Layla had taken from her. The repair shop had called that morning: four new tires plus labor would cost nearly eight hundred dollars. Casey had authorized the work without complaint, refusing to give Layla the satisfaction of financial distress on top of everything else.

She approached her front door with the careful attention that had become second nature, keys already positioned between her fingers—a small defensive measure Kirk had taught her, inadequate against real danger but providing the illusion of preparedness. The porch light hadn't yet activated in the fading daylight, leaving the front steps draped in blue-gray shadows. Something dark lay on the welcome mat—a package perhaps, though she wasn't expecting any deliveries besides the security cameras.

Three steps from the door, Casey froze. What she had taken for a package resolved itself into a grotesque tableau —three small birds arranged in a perfect triangle, their delicate bodies positioned with unnatural precision. Their wings had been splayed outward, tiny feathered limbs extending from their bodies like broken spokes. Glass-black eyes stared upward, reflecting nothing.

The grocery bag slipped from Casey's suddenly nerve-less fingers, sending apples tumbling across the porch with hollow thuds. She took an instinctive step backward, then another, bile rising hot and bitter in her throat. The birds —sparrows, she thought distantly—hadn't been simply killed. They'd been arranged, positioned, transformed from innocent creatures into a message laid at her doorstep like a perverse offering.

Casey's back hit the porch railing as her knees threatened to buckle. The birds' glassy eyes seemed to follow her retreat, their tiny heads angled just enough to create the unsettling impression of attention. Breath came in short, shallow gasps that failed to provide sufficient oxygen, dark spots dancing at the edges of her vision.

The sound of tires on pavement barely registered through the rushing in her ears. Only when the familiar profile of Kirk's truck appeared at the end of her driveway did reality re-establish itself around her. His duffel bag was visible in the passenger seat, containing the belongings they'd discussed that morning—the physical evidence of their decision for him to move in temporarily.

Kirk's expression shifted from neutral to alert the moment he spotted her frozen against the railing. He was out of the truck in one fluid motion, moving toward her with controlled urgency, eyes quickly scanning for immediate threats before landing on the macabre arrangement at her door.

"Don't touch anything," he said, voice calm but authoritative as he climbed the porch steps. The transformation was subtle but unmistakable—the easygoing contractor giving way to the marine trained to assess and neutralize threats. He set his duffel down carefully, pulling his phone from his pocket with a practiced motion. "I need to document this before we disturb it."

Casey watched as Kirk photographed the arrangement from multiple angles, his movements efficient and precise. His face remained expressionless except for a muscle jumping along his jawline—the only visible evidence of the anger she knew was building beneath his careful control.

"Birds don't just die in perfect triangles," Casey whispered, her voice sounding foreign to her own ears.

"No, they don't," Kirk agreed, his tone deliberately neutral as he finished documenting the scene. He pocketed his phone and retrieved a pair of work gloves from his truck, returning to gather the birds with careful detachment. "I'll dispose of these away from the house. Wait inside."

Casey fumbled with her keys, the metal scraping against the lock as her hands shook. Inside, the familiar scent of her home—old books and the faint lingering notes of the morning's coffee—provided momentary comfort before her mind replayed the image of those splayed wings, those empty eyes. She moved mechanically to the kitchen, gathering the scattered groceries she'd retrieved from the porch, placing apples in the fruit bowl with trembling fingers.

The coffee maker's familiar gurgle provided acoustic normalcy as she filled the carafe with water, measured grounds with shaking hands. Ordinary actions as defense against the extraordinary, routine as shield against horror.

Behind her, the back door opened and closed as Kirk returned from disposing of the birds.

"I've checked the perimeter," he said, removing his gloves and washing his hands thoroughly at the kitchen sink. "No signs of anyone still around, though the rain would have washed away footprints." He dried his hands on a dish towel, movements deliberate and controlled. "I moved my truck into the garage. Less visible target."

Casey nodded, grateful for his practical approach when her own thoughts scattered like startled birds at each small sound—the house settling, a car passing outside, the refrigerator's compressor cycling on. "Coffee?" she offered, holding up the pot with a hand she forced to remain steady.

Kirk accepted the mug she poured, his fingers brushing hers in a brief contact that anchored her more effectively than any words could have. He disappeared upstairs with his duffel bag, footsteps moving directly to the guest room they had cleared of her father's boxes just days earlier. The sounds of drawers opening and closing, familiar domestic noises, filtered down to where Casey leaned against the kitchen counter, clutching her coffee mug as if it might protect her from the images still flickering behind her eyes.

They both knew Kirk wouldn't actually sleep in the guest room, she didn't want to admit it even to herself but she didn't like the idea of not being in the same bed as him. The guest room was merely a place for his belongings, a pretense of normalcy in a situation that had long since abandoned normal parameters.

Evening settled around the house, drawing darkness against the windows like a shroud. They sat together on the couch, laptops open as they researched security systems, comparing features and installation requirements. Kirk's shoulder pressed against Casey's, the contact simultaneously casual and deliberate—comfort disguised as practicality, intimacy offering security.

"This one has motion-activated recording and infrared capability," Kirk said, pointing to a system on his screen. "We could have full coverage of all entry points, plus alerts sent directly to our phones."

Casey nodded, appreciative of the way he framed it as a joint decision, a shared problem with a technical solution. As if the right combination of cameras and sensors could neutralize the malice that had arranged dead birds on her doorstep with meticulous care. "The reviews mention false alarms triggered by neighborhood cats," she noted, trying to match his practical tone.

"We can adjust the sensitivity," Kirk replied, scrolling through additional specifications. "And add backup power so it can't be disabled by cutting electricity."

As he spoke, a sharp scraping sound came from the window—branch against glass, harmless but startling in the quiet room. Casey flinched violently, coffee sloshing over the edge of her mug onto her fingers. The hot liquid barely registered against the sudden cold rush of adrenaline.

Kirk's hand immediately covered hers, warm and steady against her sudden trembling. "Just the oak tree," he said, his voice gentle but firm, grounding her in reality. "The wind's picked up."

Casey nodded, embarrassed by her reaction yet unable to control it. Fear had become a constant companion, lurking at the edges of consciousness, ready to surge forward at the slightest provocation. "I hate this," she admitted, setting down her mug before she could spill more. "I hate that she's made me afraid in my own home."

Kirk's arm encircled her shoulders, drawing her against his side. His heartbeat was steady beneath her ear, a rhythmic counterpoint to her own rapid pulse. "We'll get through this," he promised, the words vibrating in his chest. "The security system will be here tomorrow. We'll have evidence next time."

Casey heard what he didn't say—that there would almost certainly be a next time, that Layla's campaign was unlikely to end with dead birds and slashed tires. The knowledge settled like ice in her stomach, even as Kirk's warmth seeped into her side, a living barrier against the fears circling like shadows beyond the windows.

"We'll get through this," he repeated, pressing a kiss to her temple, his lips lingering against her skin. "Together."

Casey closed her eyes, focusing on the solid reality of Kirk's presence, allowing it to temporarily override the memory of glassy bird eyes and meticulously arranged wings. Outside, the branch scraped against glass again— innocent movement transformed by circumstance into something that set her nerves jangling like overwound piano strings. But Kirk's hand remained steady against hers, his breathing deep and even, offering a rhythm she could follow back toward something resembling calm.

Chapter 27

The legal office hummed with Tuesday morning efficiency —phones ringing at measured intervals, the gentle click of keyboards, occasional laughter from the break room where someone had brought in birthday cupcakes. Casey sat at her desk, reviewing a contract that should have taken her thirty minutes but had consumed nearly two hours of fragmented attention. Words blurred on the page, legal terminology dissolving into meaningless patterns as her mind cycled through the now-familiar loop of hypervigilance: scanning for threats, cataloging normal sounds versus potential warnings, maintaining the exhausting façade of professional composure while internally mapping escape routes from every room.

Two weeks ago, she had been offered a admin position at a mutual friends legal office and it had felt like a step toward normalcy. Now, the office felt exposed—too many entrances, too many strangers passing through, too many opportunities for Layla to insert herself into yet another aspect of Casey's life. Three times during her morning coffee, Casey had jerked to attention at the sound of high heels clicking across the reception area's marble floor, certain she would look up to find Layla's perfect smile and calculating eyes approaching her desk.

Her desk phone rang, the ordinary sound causing her hand to jerk, spilling coffee onto the contract she'd been attempting to review. Casey blotted the liquid with a tissue, cursing under her breath as she lifted the receiver.

"Casey Preston," she answered, her professional voice remarkably steady despite the adrenaline already coursing through her system.

Silence greeted her—or not quite silence. A soft, rhythmic breathing on the other end of the line, punctuated by an odd clicking sound, like fingernails tapping against a hard surface. Casey's mouth went dry.

"Hello?" she tried again, her voice dropping lower, losing its professional edge.

The breathing continued for three more seconds before the line went dead, leaving Casey clutching the receiver against her ear, pulse hammering in her throat. She slowly replaced the handset in its cradle, her fingertips lingering against the plastic as if it might offer some explanation, some evidence beyond the memory of those measured breaths.

"You okay, Casey?" Jen from the neighboring cubicle peered over the partition, concern evident in her furrowed brow. "You look like you've seen a ghost."

Casey manufactured a smile that felt like stretching plastic. "Just a weird call. Probably a wrong number."

Jen nodded, though her expression remained doubtful. "You've been jumping at shadows all morning. Everything alright at home?"

The question, meant kindly, struck Casey as darkly amusing. Nothing had been "alright at home" since Layla had painted that single vicious word across her car, had arranged dead birds on her doorstep, had transformed her sanctuary into contested territory. But she couldn't explain this to Jen, couldn't describe how it felt to be systematically targeted by someone who viewed her existence as an offense.

"Just readjusting to the workload," Casey offered instead, the lie bitter on her tongue.

When her phone rang again an hour later, Casey stared at it for three full rings before answering. The same breathing, the same clicking, this time lasting nearly fifteen seconds before disconnection. By the third call—identical to the first two—Casey's hands had developed a persistent tremor, fine shivers running through her fingers as she tried to type, to organize files, to maintain the appearance of productivity.

Lunchtime arrived with a relief that bordered on desperation. Casey declined Jen's invitation to the deli across the street, needing the refuge of solitude to collect herself, to rebuild the façade of normalcy that the anonymous calls had systematically dismantled. She waited until her colleagues had cleared out before retrieving her lunch bag from the break room refrigerator, planning to eat at her desk while catching up on the work her distraction had delayed.

The stack of photographs on her keyboard stopped her cold, one foot still lifted mid-step, as if approaching too closely might detonate some invisible explosive. Perfectly squared edges bound with a thick rubber band, the glossy finish reflecting overhead fluorescents in sickly white rectangles. Casey's half-extended hand hovered above them, trembling visibly in the empty office.

With a deliberate effort that felt like moving through water, she picked up the stack, slipping off the rubber band with clumsy fingers. The first image showed Kirk and Casey on her front porch—him arriving with coffee, her smiling up at him with unguarded affection. A perfectly ordinary moment from three days earlier, now transformed into something sinister by its unauthorized documentation. Both their faces had been crossed out with thick red marker, violent strokes that suggested rage barely contained.

The second photo showed them through Casey's kitchen window, standing close together at the sink. The third captured them loading groceries into the rental car. Image after image revealed moments they had believed private, angles suggesting Layla had circled the house like a predator, documenting their movements with obsessive thoroughness. The final photo, taken just yesterday, showed Kirk installing motion sensor lights along the side of the house—his face crossed out with the same angry red slashes, the image itself bent at the corners as if handled with particular violence.

Casey's breath came in short, sharp gasps that failed to provide sufficient oxygen. The photographs slipped from her nerveless fingers, scattering across her desk like fallen leaves. She backed away, colliding with a filing cabinet, the metal edge digging into her spine barely registering through the panic flooding her system.

The women's restroom provided temporary sanctuary, the handicap stall large enough for Casey to press her back against the cool tile wall, sliding down to crouch on the floor as she struggled to control her breathing. She wrapped her arms around her knees, making herself smaller as if physical compression might contain the terror threatening to burst from her chest. The bathroom's institutional lighting hummed overhead, the sound merging with the rushing in her ears as black spots danced at the edges of her vision.

Later, she wouldn't remember driving home—only disconnected impressions of traffic lights, other vehicles moving in slow motion around her, her white-knuckled grip on the rental car's unfamiliar steering wheel. Kirk's truck in the driveway provided the first real anchor since discovering the photographs, its solid presence promising safety, however temporary.

She found him on a ladder against the side of the house, methodically mounting a security camera beneath the eaves. Additional cameras and mounting brackets lay on a tarp spread across the lawn, along with tools arranged in precise rows—the ordered implements of Kirk's trade repurposed for their protection. He descended immediately upon seeing her, concern evident in the line between his brows.

"What happened?" he asked, closing the distance between them in five long strides.

Casey described the calls, the photographs, her voice remarkably steady despite the tremors still running through her hands. Kirk's expression darkened as she spoke, the muscle in his jaw working beneath stubble that had grown heavier since he'd moved in, his normal grooming routine disrupted by constant vigilance.

"She was here," he said when Casey finished, gesturing toward the house. "While we were both gone. The basement window has new scratches around the lock—someone tested it, seeing if it would give."

Fresh fear coursed through Casey's system, the thought of Layla attempting entry while they were away sending ice through her veins. "Did she get in?"

Kirk shook his head. "The window didn't yield. And I've installed sensors on all ground-floor access points now." He ran a hand through his hair, a rare gesture of frustration breaking through his controlled exterior. "We need to establish new routines. Vary our schedules, check in with each other more frequently, double-check all locks."

That evening, they moved through the house like inhabitants of a fortress under siege—testing window latches, establishing a text system for arrivals and departures, Kirk walking Casey through the new security app on her phone that would alert them to any breaches. The practical tasks provided temporary distraction from the surveillance photos still burning in Casey's memory, the evidence of how thoroughly Layla had been documenting their movements.

As darkness settled around the house, Kirk made a final check of the security cameras he'd installed throughout the day. Casey followed him outside, unwilling to be alone inside even for the few minutes this would require. They circled the house together, Kirk confirming each camera's position and field of view on his phone's screen.

At the northeast corner, Kirk stopped abruptly, his body tensing in the beam of their flashlight. The camera he'd mounted that morning now pointed uselessly at the sky, its orientation completely altered. As they drew closer, the reason became clear—the lens had been spray-painted black, a single clean stroke that had eliminated its protective gaze.

"When did you install this one?" Casey asked, her voice barely audible above the evening insects.

"Around ten this morning," Kirk replied, already retrieving tools from his belt to remove the damaged camera. "It was functioning when I checked at noon."

The implication hung in the cool evening air between them—Layla had been here while they were both at work, had deliberately disabled the camera, had stood in this very spot knowing they would discover her handiwork. Kirk's expression hardened as he unbolted the camera, his movements precise despite the anger evident in the set of his shoulders.

"I'll mount the replacement higher," he said, voice controlled but tight. "Add a protective cage. Make it harder to reach."

Casey stared at the spray-painted lens, its surface dully

reflecting their flashlight beam. "She's watching us," she whispered, the words emerging unbidden from the darkest corner of her thoughts.

Kirk nodded grimly, his free hand finding hers and squeezing gently—reassurance offered even as they both acknowledged the truth. Layla wasn't merely harassing them; she was studying them, learning their patterns, testing their defenses with the methodical patience of a predator assessing its prey.

The darkness beyond their flashlight's beam suddenly seemed alive with malevolent possibility, the shadows between trees taking on dimensions that suggested a human form, the rustle of leaves carrying whispers just below the threshold of comprehension. Casey pressed closer to Kirk's side, drawing what comfort she could from his solid presence while knowing that even his protection had limits against someone so determined to cause harm.

Chapter 28

The week unfolded like a fever dream—each day bringing new violations, each night shorter than the last as sleep retreated before the advancing army of anxieties. Dead sparrows gave way to a mutilated rabbit left on the back step, its body arranged with the same meticulous care as the birds had been. Their mail appeared one morning slashed to confetti, the mailbox itself daubed with red paint that dried the color of old blood. Anonymous deliveries arrived—a funeral wreath with Casey's name spelled out in withered carnations, a child's doll with its eyes gouged out, ordinary items transformed into menace through context and intention. Through it all, Casey maintained a brittle composure that fooled no one, least of all herself, her body moving through necessary routines while her mind cataloged each new transgression with diminishing capacity for shock.

Police reports accumulated, photographs were taken, evidence bags filled—all with the same result. "Without direct proof linking these incidents to Ms. Manning..." The phrase had become a refrain, a bureaucratic wall against which their fear and frustration broke like waves, receding without impact. Their security measures expanded with each new incursion—motion sensors, cameras with night vision, doors reinforced with additional locks—each addition tacit acknowledgment that the previous barriers had been insufficient.

Casey had believed herself prepared for whatever might come next. She'd survived her father's long decline, had weathered grief's brutal aftermath, had rebuilt herself alongside the house she now shared with Kirk. She had reserves of strength she'd never known existed until circumstances demanded them.

Or so she'd thought.

Returning home Thursday evening, she knew immediately that something was wrong. Nothing obvious—the house appeared undisturbed from the outside, security system reported no breaches, cameras showed no unexpected movement. But some primitive instinct raised the hairs on her neck as she entered, Kirk close behind her with groceries balanced against his hip.

The living room looked exactly as they'd left it that morning. Same arrangement of furniture, same books on shelves, same throw pillows arranged on the couch. Yet Casey halted three steps inside, her breath catching as her eyes registered what her unconscious mind had already detected.

The family photographs had been rearranged.

Not dramatically—nothing so obvious that casual observation would notice. But the silver-framed photo of Casey with her father that normally sat on the end table now occupied the center of the mantel. The graduation picture usually displayed in the hallway had migrated to the bookshelf. Each framed memory had been moved to a different location in the room, the displacement subtle enough to create disorientation rather than immediate alarm.

"She was in here," Casey whispered, frozen in place as if sudden movement might trigger some unseen trap. "While we were at work. She touched our things."

Kirk set the groceries down carefully, his body already scanning the room with military precision, noting exits, potential weapons, signs of continuing threat. "Stay here," he said, voice low and controlled as he moved toward the hallway, intent on clearing the rest of the house.

Casey remained motionless, eyes fixed on the photographs—tangible evidence that Layla had invaded their most private space, had handled their memories, had imposed her presence on objects imbued with deep personal significance. The silver frame on the mantel caught the evening light, reflecting it back in a sharp glint that seemed to mock her illusion of security.

She didn't follow Kirk's progress through the house, didn't register his careful room-by-room assessment. Her focus had narrowed to those displaced photographs, each one representing a boundary crossed, a sanctuary violated. Beneath her sternum, something essential began to fracture—the careful scaffolding of courage and composure that had supported her through each escalating incident finally buckling under accumulative strain.

When Kirk returned to report the house clear, he found Casey still standing where he'd left her, her expression frozen in a peculiar blankness that alarmed him more than tears would have. He approached slowly, hands visible at his sides, movements telegraphed to avoid startling her.

"Casey," he said gently, "we should check the security footage. See if we can—"

"She touched my father's picture," Casey interrupted, her voice eerily calm despite the storm gathering behind her eyes. "She held it in her hands. She—" The words stopped abruptly, severed by something breaking loose inside her chest.

Casey moved then, not toward Kirk but toward the kitchen where boxes of additional security equipment awaited installation—door sensors, glass-break detectors, panic buttons for each room. Items they'd ordered with urgent desperation after each new violation, accumulating protective technology as if sufficient gadgetry could finally create the barrier Layla seemed determined to breach.

The box cutter lay where Kirk had left it that morning, its blade extended for the day's work. Casey picked it up, the weight of it cold and certain in her palm. With a single, fluid motion more instinct than decision, she slashed through the nearest box, cardboard yielding with a satisfying rip that matched the tearing sensation inside her ribcage.

"Casey—" Kirk started, concern evident in his voice.

But Casey was beyond hearing, beyond rational response. The box cutter sliced through another package, then another, her movements becoming increasingly frantic as boards and wires and plastic components spilled across the kitchen floor. Tears she'd refused to shed for days now streamed unchecked down her face, her breathing coming in ragged gasps that bordered on hyperventilation.

"I can't—" she managed between sobs, the box cutter falling from her hand to clatter against the tile. Her legs folded beneath her, depositing her amid the scattered security equipment—physical evidence of their futile attempts to create safety in a world suddenly devoid of it. "I can't live like this anymore."

Her body curled forward, arms wrapping around her middle as if physically holding herself together while everything inside threatened to fly apart. The sobs that tore from her throat carried weeks of accumulated terror, exhaustion, and helpless rage, the sound raw and primal in the kitchen's clinical brightness.

Kirk knelt beside her, heedless of the debris

surrounding them. For a moment he seemed uncertain, hands hovering near her shoulders without making contact, as if afraid his touch might shatter her completely. Then, with infinite gentleness, he gathered her into his arms, one hand cradling the back of her head as he pulled her against his chest.

"I'm here," he murmured, the words vibrating against her ear as she collapsed into him, fingers clutching at his shirt with desperate strength. "I've got you. Let it out."

Casey's tears soaked through the fabric covering his chest, her body shaking with the force of emotion finally given full release. Kirk held her through the storm, his arms creating a fortress around her trembling form, his heartbeat a steady counterpoint to her ragged breathing. He murmured soothing nonsense against her hair, one hand making slow circles between her shoulder blades, the other keeping her securely anchored against him.

Gradually, the violent sobs quieted to hiccupping breaths, then to the occasional shudder as Casey's system exhausted its reserves of adrenaline and fear. She remained within the circle of Kirk's arms, face pressed against his chest, unwilling to move from this temporary sanctuary even as awareness of their surroundings slowly returned— the hard kitchen tile beneath them, the scattered security components, the evening light fading through the windows.

"I can't do this anymore," she whispered, the words muffled against his now-damp shirt. "Living like prisoners in my own house. Jumping at every sound. Wondering what she'll do next, how much worse it can get."

Kirk's arms tightened fractionally around her, his chin resting gently atop her head. "I know," he acknowledged, his voice rough with emotion he'd been carefully control-ling for her benefit. "I know, sweetheart."

When Casey finally lifted her face, Kirk's expression caught at something in her chest—guilt and determination warring across features she'd come to know as intimately as her own. He reached to cup her face between his palms, thumbs gently wiping away the tear tracks on her cheeks. The tenderness in the gesture nearly undid her composure again, fresh tears threatening.

"I brought this into your life," he said, voice rough with self-recrimination. "Layla, the harassment, all of it. You were already dealing with so much with your father, with the house. And then I—" His voice broke, the crack in his composure revealing the depth of guilt he'd been carrying beneath his protective exterior.

Casey's hands rose to cover his where they framed her face, fingers curling around his wrists, feeling the steady pulse beneath warm skin. "You didn't create Layla," she corrected softly. "You didn't make her do these things."

Kirk's thumbs traced gentle arcs along her cheekbones, his eyes never leaving hers. "But I brought her into your orbit. If we hadn't met, if I hadn't—"

"If we hadn't met, I'd still be drowning in grief," Casey interrupted, strength returning to her voice despite the hoarseness left by prolonged crying. "Alone in a house full of ghosts."

Something shifted in Kirk's expression—determination crystallizing into resolution, protectiveness hardening into something more potent. He leaned forward until their foreheads touched, his breath warm against her lips.

"I brought this into your life," he repeated, each word deliberate and weighted with promise. "But I swear to you, Casey, I will end it." His hands remained gentle against her face, the contrast between his touch and the steel in his voice sending a shiver along her spine. "We'll get through this together. I love you too much to let her win."

The declaration hung between them, simple yet profound in its certainty. Casey's fingers tightened around his wrists, feeling the subtle proof of life in his steady pulse.

"Together," she echoed, the word both acknowledgment and promise.

Kirk's lips brushed hers—not a passionate kiss but a covenant, a sealing of the vow just spoken. Casey's fingers curled into the fabric of his shirt, anchoring herself to his solid presence amid the chaos their lives had become. The fear hadn't vanished—it still lurked at the edges of her consciousness, ready to surge forward at the next strange sound or unexpected shadow. But now it was met with something equally powerful, equally primal: the determination reflected in Kirk's eyes, the love evident in his gentle hands, the promise contained in that single word. Together.

Outside, evening shadows lengthened across the yard where the security lights would soon activate, where cameras maintained their vigilant watch, where somewhere beyond their vision Layla might be waiting, watching, planning her next intrusion. But here, in the circle of Kirk's arms amid scattered equipment that had failed to provide the security his presence offered, Casey drew breath that felt less constricted than it had in days. They would face whatever came next—not because they were unafraid, but because they refused to allow fear to dictate the terms of their lives any longer.

Chapter 29

The cemetery gates stood half-open in welcome or warning – Casey couldn't decide which – as Kirk guided the truck down the narrow gravel path that wound between ancient oaks and newer plantings. Two days had passed since she'd collapsed in their kitchen, since she'd finally surrendered to the weight of Layla's campaign against them. Today was supposed to be about reclaiming normalcy – a simple visit to her father's grave, bringing fresh flowers to replace those that would have wilted in the November chill. Such an ordinary ritual of grief, now laden with the hypervigilance that had become their constant companion.

Kirk parked near the eastern boundary, the truck's engine ticking into silence as he turned to Casey. "You sure you're up for this?" His voice was gentle, a contrast to the vigilant sweep of his eyes across the cemetery's rolling expanse.

Casey nodded, fingers tightening around the bundle of white chrysanthemums resting in her lap. Her father had always preferred practical plants – vegetables that produced food, trees that offered shade – but these had been the exception. He'd planted them faithfully each fall around the house's foundation, their sturdy blooms defying early frosts. "I need to do this," she said. "For Dad. For me."

The afternoon hung heavy with approaching rain, clouds stretched low across the sky in bands of charcoal and pewter. Their footsteps crunched against gravel, then softened as they transitioned to the grass path that would lead to her father's section. Kirk's hand found the small of her back, a gentle pressure that anchored her against the memories threatening to surface – her father's casket disappearing into the ground, Kirk's solid presence beside her even then, before they'd understood what was growing between them.

Distant traffic hummed beyond the cemetery's boundaries, the occasional horn or engine acceleration punctuating the otherwise pastoral quiet. Leaves skittered across their path, brittle and copper-colored, dancing away on gusts that smelled of woodsmoke and impending rain. Casey drew her jacket tighter, less against the chill than against the vulnerability of this place – a landscape dedicated to acknowledging loss, to making physical the absences that shaped lives.

"His stone is just over that rise," Casey said, pointing toward a gentle slope crowned with a solitary maple. Its few remaining leaves fluttered like crimson flags in the shifting breeze, markers guiding their approach. Her father had chosen this spot himself during one of his last lucid periods, appreciating the tree's seasonal transformations and the eastern exposure that would bathe his headstone in morning light.

They crested the small hill together, Casey already rehearsing the introduction she would make – Dad, this is Kirk, really Kirk this time, not just the helpful neighbor I've mentioned but the man who... The thought dissolved as her eyes registered the scene before them, her brain struggling to process what couldn't possibly be real.

The neat rectangle of recently settled earth before her father's granite headstone had been violated, gouged with crude channels that collected rainwater in muddy pools. But worse – infinitely worse – was the stone itself. Bright red paint dripped down its polished surface like blood from an open wound, forming garish puddles against the dark granite. Jagged letters screamed their message across her father's name, the carefully chosen dates of his birth and death now obscured beneath a crimson threat: "HE'S NEXT."

Casey heard a sound – animal, wounded – before recognizing it had emerged from her own throat. Her body moved without conscious direction, legs folding beneath her as she collapsed to her knees on the damp grass. The chrysanthemums fell from her nerveless fingers, white petals instantly muddied against the disturbed earth.

"No," she whispered, the word insufficient against such deliberate cruelty. Her hand reached toward the stone as if she might wipe away the hideous letters, restore her father's memorial to its dignified simplicity. Her fingers hovered inches from the paint, still tacky and glistening in the gray afternoon light. "No, no, no."

Behind her, Kirk's voice emerged clipped and controlled as he spoke into his phone. "Yes, vandalism at Oakridge Cemetery, section fourteen east. A grave has been desecrated with threatening language... No, the paint appears fresh. We need officers here immediately." The professional cadence of his words belied the fury Casey could feel radiating from him like heat from banked coals.

A drop of rain struck her cheek, then another, indistinguishable from the tears now streaming unchecked down her face. Her shoulders shook with silent sobs that seemed wrenched from the deepest part of her chest, grief tangled with rage and beneath it all, a terrible, consuming fear. Not for herself — something had burned away inside her at the sight of her father's desecrated grave, some final barrier between endurance and something darker, more primitive.

"Casey." Kirk crouched beside her, one hand hovering above her shoulder as if uncertain whether touch would comfort or shatter her. "Don't touch the paint. It's evidence."

She nodded mechanically, hand still extended toward the stone, toward the father who had raised her alone, who had slipped away piece by piece through the long cruelty of his disease, whose final dignity was now sullied by this obscene message. The iron-tang smell of the paint mingled with wet earth and the sweet decay of offerings left at neighboring graves — flowers, pinwheels, small stones arranged in patterns of remembrance.

"She was here," Casey said, her voice strangely calm despite the tremors running through her body. "She touched my father's grave. She—" Words failed as another wave of sobbing overtook her.

Kirk's arm finally encircled her shoulders, drawing her against the solid warmth of his chest. Rain fell more steadily now, darkening his jacket in expanding circles, plastering Casey's hair against her cheeks in damp tendrils. He tilted his head back, rain striking his face as he surveyed the surrounding area, eyes narrowed against both weather and rage.

"Police are on their way," he said, lips close to her ear so she could hear him over the increasing patter of raindrops against leaves. "Five minutes. Can you stand?"

Casey shook her head, not in negation but in disbelief that her body would respond to normal commands in this moment of absolute violation. Her father's stone watched her through its mask of dripping paint, the granite eyes of his name obscured by crimson threat. "He's next," she repeated, the words bitter on her tongue. "You. She means you're next."

Kirk's body tensed against hers, the only acknowledgment that he'd reached the same conclusion. His arm tightened fractionally around her shoulders, protection offered even as they both recognized its limitations against someone willing to violate the sanctity of the dead.

"She won't touch you," Casey whispered, her voice finding strength despite her trembling limbs. "I won't let her."

The rain fell steadily now, beginning to dilute the brightest edges of the paint, sending thin rivulets of pink down the stone's polished surface. Casey watched, transfixed, as her father's name emerged in fragments through the streaming crimson – letters appearing and disappearing like his lucidity had during those final months. Present, then absent. Recognizable, then foreign.

In the distance, sirens wailed their approach, the sound distorted by rain and wind into something mournful rather than urgent. Too late, Casey thought, watching red paint mingle with rainwater at the base of her father's stone. Too late for peace, for normalcy, for the quiet visit she'd imagined. Layla had been here first, had marked this most sacred ground with her malice, had transformed even grief into a battlefield.

The crunch of tires on wet gravel announced Officer Rodriguez's arrival, his patrol car moving with deliberate slowness through the cemetery paths. Rain beaded on the vehicle's surface, gathering in rivulets that swept across the windshield despite wipers working at half-speed. Casey watched from her place on a stone bench where Kirk had guided her, her body still trembling with aftershocks of rage and grief. Rodriguez emerged from the car with the careful economy of movement she recognized from their previous encounters – procedural, measured, a man stepping through the choreography of his profession with practiced ease.

His eyes found them immediately, a brief nod acknowledging their presence before his gaze shifted to the desecrated headstone. Something flickered across his features then – a tightening around the eyes, a subtle hardening of his jaw – as professional detachment gave way to genuine concern. The rain had begun to dilute the paint, sending watery crimson streaks down the granite face, but the message remained starkly legible: "HE'S NEXT."

"Ms. Preston. Mr. Manning." Rodriguez approached, his regulation shoes sinking slightly into the rain-softened earth. Water darkened the shoulders of his uniform, collecting along the brim of his cap before dripping in measured tempo. "I'm sorry you're dealing with this escalation."

It wasn't the standard police phrasing – "sorry for your trouble" or "we'll look into this incident" – and the deviation registered with Casey through her numbed consciousness. Rodriguez had dropped, momentarily, the bureaucratic shield that had characterized their previous interactions.

"How long ago did you discover this?" Rodriguez directed the question to Kirk, his eyes still tracking the desecration with professional assessment that couldn't quite mask personal disgust.

"Twenty minutes, maybe thirty." Kirk stood behind Casey, one hand resting lightly on her shoulder, a gesture both protective and grounding. "The paint was still tacky when we arrived."

Rodriguez nodded, pulling latex gloves from his pocket with practiced efficiency. "I need to document everything before the rain washes away evidence." He crouched before the headstone, removing his department phone to take photographs from multiple angles. The camera's flash punctuated the gray afternoon with stark bursts of light, briefly illuminating the obscene message like lightning revealing a nightmare landscape.

Casey watched through a strange emotional distance, as if the scene were unfolding on a screen rather than before her eyes. The chrysanthemums she'd brought lay forgotten in the mud, their white petals gradually darkening with rainwater and cemetery soil. A terrible symmetry, she thought distantly – flowers intended to honor her father's memory now mirroring her own collapse onto the damp earth.

"The message," Rodriguez said, glancing back at them as he photographed close-ups of the painted letters. "You believe it's directed at Mr. Manning?"

"Yes." Casey's voice emerged rougher than expected, scraping her throat raw. "Layla's trying to tell us she'll target Kirk next."

Rodriguez's expression remained neutral, though his eyes tracked briefly to Kirk's face, assessing. "Has Ms. Manning made similar threats previously? Anything specific about harming you physically?"

Kirk's hand tightened fractionally on Casey's shoulder. "Not explicitly. Her pattern has been escalating property damage, psychological tactics. This—" he gestured toward the desecrated grave, "—is the first direct threat."

Rodriguez nodded, rising to his feet with a slight grimace that betrayed knees accustomed to desk work rather than field investigation. He pulled a small notebook from his breast pocket, the pages already damp at the edges from the persistent rain. "I'll need statements from both of you. Details about recent incidents, communications, anything that might establish pattern and intent."

Casey closed her eyes briefly, fatigue washing over her in a wave that threatened to pull her under. How many times had they cataloged Layla's transgressions? How many reports had been filed, evidence collected, statements given? All while the violations continued, each more intrusive, more personal than the last.

"Ms. Preston." Rodriguez's voice had softened, drawing her attention back to his face. He had moved closer, crouching now to meet her eyes directly, his notebook momentarily forgotten in his hand. "I know this process must feel frustratingly slow. But this—" he gestured toward the headstone, "—crosses a line that changes how we approach your case."

Casey felt Kirk shift behind her, his body tensing slightly at Rodriguez's words.

"What do you mean?" Kirk asked, the question edged with the first hint of hope they'd felt in weeks.

Rodriguez straightened, tucking his notebook away and removing his cap to run a hand through rain-dampened hair. "Desecration of a grave is a felony. Combined with the explicit threat, we have grounds for immediate action on the restraining order you filed." He replaced his cap, adjusting it with a practiced motion. "I'll push the paperwork through tonight personally. And I'll have patrol cars increase frequency in your neighborhood starting immediately."

He pressed his pen hard into his notebook as he wrote, leaving deep indentations that would show on the reverse side, permanent evidence of his determined documentation. The small detail registered with Casey – the physical pressure matching Rodriguez's newfound intensity, his investment in their case suddenly personal rather than procedural.

"We appreciate that, Officer," Kirk said, his voice carrying a weight of gratitude that belied the skepticism Casey knew they both still harbored about official protection.

Rodriguez nodded, his gaze shifting once more to the

headstone where rain continued its slow cleansing, diluting but not erasing Layla's message. "Cemetery management has been notified. They'll have workers here shortly to begin cleaning the stone." He hesitated, something unspoken hovering behind his professional demeanor. "If you have somewhere else you can stay tonight – a friend's house, a hotel – I'd recommend it. Just until we can establish more comprehensive protection."

The suggestion hung between them, its implications settling cold against Casey's skin despite her rain-soaked clothes. Abandoning her home – her father's home – felt like another victory handed to Layla, another piece of normal life surrendered to fear.

"We have security measures in place," Kirk answered before Casey could formulate a response. "And I'm not leaving her alone."

Rodriguez studied Kirk's face, something like respect flickering briefly across his features. "Call dispatch immediately if you notice anything suspicious. Anything at all. I've flagged your address for priority response."

As if summoned by his words, a cemetery maintenance truck appeared on the winding path, wipers struggling against the steadily falling rain. Two workers emerged, carrying buckets and cloths, their expressions carefully neutral as they approached the vandalized grave.

"We'll get your statements at the car," Rodriguez said, offering a small nod toward the maintenance workers. "Give them space to work."

Casey rose from the bench, her legs unsteady beneath her. Kirk's arm encircled her waist, supporting without controlling, his warmth penetrating the damp chill of her jacket. Together they watched as the workers began their careful ministrations, specialized solvents applied with gentle precision to remove Layla's threat without damaging the stone beneath.

"He would have hated this," Casey whispered, thinking of her father's lifelong aversion to being the center of attention, his embarrassment at any fuss made over him. "All these people, all this... spectacle."

Kirk's arm tightened around her waist, drawing her closer against his side. "He would be proud of you," he murmured, his lips close to her hair. "Your strength. Your refusal to be broken by this."

Casey leaned into him, drawing what comfort she could from his solid presence while the workers scrubbed at her father's headstone, gradually revealing the name and dates that defined a life now reduced to granite and memory. The chrysanthemums lay forgotten in the mud, their intended purpose rendered meaningless by this new ritual of violation and restoration.

Chapter 30

Rain tapped against the windows of Casey's living room, the sound transformed from earlier threat to evening lullaby by the warm glow of lamps and the distance from the cemetery's raw wounds. They had returned home in weighted silence, stripping off wet clothes and moving through the rituals of recovery with mechanical precision – hot showers, dry clothes, hair toweled into damp submission. Casey had suggested tea, a small domestic comfort against the day's horror, and Kirk had nodded his agreement while checking the security system for the third time in an hour, his movements betraying the vigilance that never fully receded.

The security panel's green light cast an eerie glow across Kirk's features as he studied the system's status, the regular pulse of "Armed" offering cold comfort against the day's revelations. His phone sat on the side table, screen dark but presence looming like a sentinel awaiting bad news. Casey watched him from the kitchen doorway, noting the rigid line of his shoulders, the controlled deliberation of each movement – warning signs she'd learned to read like approaching weather.

"Earl Grey or chamomile?" she called, trying to inject normalcy into the evening's heavy silence.

Kirk turned, his attempt at a smile not quite reaching his eyes. "Chamomile might help you sleep," he answered, though they both knew sleep would be elusive tonight, chased away by images of red paint dripping down granite.

Casey nodded, returning to the kitchen where the kettle had begun its climb toward whistle. She moved with deliberate focus, selecting mugs, measuring loose tea into strainers, arranging everything on a tray with the careful precision of someone needing small tasks to occupy trembling hands. The ceremony of preparation offered momentary distraction from the day's events – her father's desecrated grave, Rodriguez's concerned face, the cemetery workers scrubbing at paint that seemed to have stained her memory as thoroughly as it had the granite.

The phone rang – a sudden electronic intrusion that sent Casey's heart racing, tea leaves scattering across the counter in a dark constellation of her startled response. Through the doorway, she saw Kirk reach for his phone, his movements cautious as if expecting the device itself might wound him.

"Manning," he answered, voice pitched low but carrying clearly in the quiet house.

Casey turned back to the kettle as it began to whistle, pouring steaming water over the tea strainers, the fragrant steam rising to fog her glasses briefly. Behind her, Kirk's voice continued, too quiet now to distinguish words but carrying a tone that raised goosebumps along her arms despite the kitchen's warmth.

When she returned to the living room, tea tray balanced carefully between uncertain hands, the transformation in Kirk's posture stopped her at the threshold. He sat perfectly still on the edge of the sofa, phone pressed to his ear, his normally warm complexion drained to the color of old paper. Something cold and heavy settled in Casey's stomach at the sight, anchoring her in place as Kirk finished his call with short, clipped responses.

"Yes. I understand. Tomorrow morning. Thank you for calling."

The phone lowered from his ear in slow motion, his gaze fixed on some middle distance between him and the opposite wall, seeing something Casey couldn't access. She set the tray on the coffee table, the gentle clink of porcelain against wood impossibly loud in the room's dense silence.

"What is it?" she asked, the question emerging soft with dread.

Kirk's eyes finally found hers, their amber depths darkened by something that went beyond anger or fear into territories without adequate names. "Charlotte's grave," he said, each word carefully formed as if speaking a foreign language. "Same message. Same red paint."

The world tilted briefly beneath Casey's feet, understanding arriving with nauseating clarity. Not random vandalism or generalized intimidation but a calculated assault on the graves of those Kirk had loved and lost – his sister, Casey's father. A methodical desecration of memory and sanctity designed to wound beyond physical boundaries.

"That was the cemetery caretaker in San Diego," Kirk continued, his voice hollow with controlled emotion. "A groundskeeper found it during evening rounds. They called me because I'm listed as next of kin."

Casey sank onto the couch beside him, close enough that their shoulders touched, offering silent solidarity through physical connection. She knew about Charlotte's death – the sister Kirk had failed to protect from an abusive relationship, her life ended in what had been disguised as a car accident but was something far more deliberate. Another loss, another grief that had shaped Kirk as thoroughly as her father's decline had shaped Casey.

"How could she know where Charlotte is buried?" Casey asked, the question emerging before she could consider its implications.

Kirk's jaw tightened, a muscle jumping beneath stubbled skin. "She would have researched. Layla is nothing if not thorough when planning an attack." His hands clasped between his knees, knuckles whitening with pressure. "She's sending a message. About who's vulnerable. Who she can reach."

The tea sat untouched on the table before them, steam rising in diminishing curls as the water gradually surrendered its heat to the room's still air. Casey watched it dissipate, transfixed by this small visible evidence of entropy while her mind worked through the implications of this coordinated assault on memory and sacred ground.

"She's not going to stop." Kirk's voice had transformed, the hollow shock replaced by something hard-edged and resolute. "We need to do more than just wait for the police to catch her."

Casey turned toward him, studying the new determination etched in lines around his eyes, the set of his jaw that spoke of decisions already crystallizing. "What are you thinking?"

Kirk shifted on the couch, angling his body toward hers, eyes intent with focused energy that contrasted sharply with his earlier shock. "Rodriguez is doing what he can within the system, but that system moves too slowly. Restraining orders are just paper. Patrols can't be everywhere."

He reached for his phone again, opening a notes app where he began typing with quick, decisive movements. "We need to hire a private investigator – someone who can track Layla's movements, gather evidence the police can actually use." His fingers moved rapidly across the screen, cataloging action items with military precision. "Install higher-grade security cameras with facial recognition. Consider relocation, at least temporarily, to somewhere she can't find easily."

The list grew as he spoke, each item a brick in a defensive wall he was constructing around them with words and determination. Casey watched his face, noting how purpose had restored color to his features, how the shock had been channeled into methodical planning – Kirk's natural response to threat, to transform fear into actionable steps.

"I have a friend from my service days who works in private security now," he continued, scrolling through his contacts. "He can recommend someone discreet, someone who understands threats like Layla."

Casey's hand covered his, stilling his rapid cataloging of defensive measures. Their fingers interlaced, the contact sending a current of warmth through her palm and up her arm – not passion but connection, an affirmation more powerful than words. Kirk's eyes met hers, the amber depths still haunted but now anchored by resolve rather than adrift in shock.

"We'll do whatever we need to do," she said, each word weighted with promise. "But we do it together."

Outside, the rain continued its steady percussion against glass and roof, a liquid veil separating their illuminated interior from the darkened world beyond. Somewhere in that darkness, Casey knew, Layla moved with methodical malice, planning her next violation. But here, in this pool of lamplight with Kirk's hand warm against hers, determination began to crystallize into something that might eventually resemble hope.

The tea grew cold on the table before them, forgotten

as they leaned into each other, shoulders touching, breath gradually synchronizing as they faced this new reality together. Two graves desecrated with the same threatening message. Two beloved dead whose memory Layla had tried to tarnish with her hatred. Two survivors, side by side, refusing surrender even as the battlefield expanded beyond what they'd imagined possible.

"Living in constant fear gives her exactly what she wants," Casey said, breaking the contemplative silence that had settled between them. The realization had been building inside her through their conversation, crystallizing into clarity that felt like the first ray of sunlight after endless storm. "That's Layla's real objective – not just to frighten us, but to remake our lives around that fear. To make us into people who jump at shadows, who see threats in ordinary sounds, who can't exist without looking over our shoulders."

Kirk looked up from his phone, his fingers pausing mid-text. Something shifted in his expression – a subtle softening around eyes that had been hard with strategic focus. "You're right," he said, the admission carrying weight beyond its simple syllables. "Fear changes who we are. Rewires our responses. Narrows our world."

He set the phone down deliberately, screen darkening as if recognizing its dismissal from their attention. "We take precautions, gather evidence, protect ourselves – but we don't let her remake us." His gaze held Casey's, something like wonder dawning across features that had been rigidly controlled since the cemetery. "How do you do that? Find clarity in the middle of all this chaos?"

Casey felt heat rise to her cheeks at the naked admiration in his voice. "I've had practice," she said, thinking of her father's long decline, the endless adjustments to each new diminishment, the determined preservation of his dignity amid deterioration. "Finding the person beneath the fear. Remembering who we are beyond the crisis."

Kirk's hand reached for hers, fingers intertwining with gentle pressure that sent warmth spreading up her arm. "You are remarkable, Casey Preston," he said, voice dropping to a register that vibrated along her skin like tactile music. "Your strength. Your resilience. The way you refuse to be diminished by circumstances that would break most people."

The praise settled warm and unexpected in her chest, a counterweight to the day's horrors. Casey studied Kirk's face – the stubble darkening his jaw, the exhaustion shadowing his eyes, the tenderness that transformed his features when he looked at her. Despite everything – the desecrated graves, Layla's escalating threats, the constant vigilance – he remained her sanctuary, her partner in both crisis and connection.

Without conscious thought, Casey moved toward him, sliding onto his lap with a fluid grace that surprised even her. Kirk's arms circled her waist automatically, steadying her against him, his eyes widening slightly at this unexpected shift from strategy to intimacy. Their faces hovered inches apart, breath mingling in the narrow space between them, a different kind of tension replacing the day's anxious hypervigilance.

"Casey," Kirk whispered, her name an entire question contained in two syllables.

She answered by closing the distance between them, her lips meeting his with gentle pressure that rapidly transformed into something hungrier, more urgent. His hands tightened at her waist, drawing her closer until she felt the solid heat of his body against her, through her, awakening parts of herself that had been dormant beneath layers of fear and vigilance.

Kirk responded with equal fervor, one hand rising to

tangle in her hair, angling her head to deepen the kiss. Their tongues met in velvet exploration, tasting, testing, rediscovering territory that had been temporarily abandoned during weeks of crisis. Casey felt something uncoil inside her chest – a tightly wound spring of tension gradually releasing with each point of contact between their bodies.

Her fingers found the buttons of his shirt, working them free with trembling urgency. Kirk pulled back slightly, studying her face with careful attention. "Are you sure?" he asked, voice husky with desire but eyes serious with consideration. "After today, everything that's happened—"

Casey silenced him with another kiss, fiercer than before, her answer unmistakable in the press of her body against his. "I need this," she whispered against his mouth. "I need you. Something real, something ours that she can't touch or taint or take away."

Understanding darkened Kirk's eyes to amber flame. His hands slid beneath the hem of her sweater, palms warm against the sensitive skin of her back, raising goosebumps in their gentle wake. Casey lifted her arms, allowing him to draw the garment over her head, leaving her in a simple cotton bra that suddenly felt inadequate against his appreciative gaze.

"Beautiful," he murmured, his eyes traveling the landscape of her exposed skin with reverence that made her flush with renewed heat. His fingers traced the delicate lace edging, following the curve where fabric met flesh with exquisite patience. "So beautiful."

Casey worked the last buttons of his shirt free, pushing the fabric from his shoulders to reveal the terrain of muscle and scars she'd come to know as intimately as her own body. Her fingers traced the white line across his ribs – evidence of military service he rarely discussed – then moved lower to the waistband of his jeans where the hard ridge of his arousal pressed against denim constraint.

Kirk's breath hitched as her hand brushed against him, his eyes closing briefly before reopening with intensified focus. In a fluid movement that revealed his physical strength, he shifted their positions, laying Casey back against the couch cushions, his body a warm weight above hers. His mouth traced a path from her lips to her jaw, then lower to the sensitive hollow of her throat where he lingered, learning her pulse with his tongue.

"Kirk," she gasped, her fingers threading through his short hair, guiding him lower to where her breasts strained against cotton confinement.

He understood her wordless plea, deft fingers unhooking her bra to expose flesh that pebbled instantly in the room's cool air. His mouth closed around one nipple, drawing it to taut attention while his thumb circled its twin with gentle insistence. Casey arched into the dual sensation, a soft moan escaping her throat as pleasure radiated outward from these twin points of contact.

Kirk's attention was methodical yet spontaneous, thorough yet surprising – moving from one breast to the other, varying pressure and rhythm to map her responses with attentive precision. His free hand worked the button of her jeans, sliding beneath denim to cup her through cotton underwear already damp with evidence of her desire.

"I want to taste you," he murmured against her breast, the words vibrating through sensitive flesh. "Every inch of you."

Casey could only nod, words temporarily beyond her capability as he slid lower, removing her jeans with careful efficiency that still managed to feel like seduction. Cool air met newly exposed skin, raising goosebumps instantly banished by the heat of Kirk's mouth tracing patterns along her inner thigh. His hands splayed across her hips, thumbs tracing the elastic of her underwear with teasing patience.

Kirk's eyes met hers as he hooked his fingers beneath the thin fabric, seeking permission she granted with eager nod and lifted hips. The garment joined her jeans on the floor, leaving her exposed to his appreciative gaze, vulnerability transformed to power by the naked desire in his expression.

His lips returned to her inner thigh, tracing an ascending path of kisses that ignited nerve endings she'd forgotten existed. Each press of his mouth against her skin sent cascading waves of sensation through her body, anticipation building with each inch he climbed toward her center. Casey's fingers tangled in his hair, not guiding but connecting, anchoring herself to him as pleasure threatened to sweep her beyond herself.

When his mouth finally reached her most sensitive flesh, the contact drew a gasp that seemed pulled from the deepest part of her chest. Kirk's tongue moved with deliberate skill, mapping her contours, learning her responses with the same methodical attention he brought to everything important. His hands slid beneath her, lifting her slightly to improve his access, his appreciative hum vibrating against sensitive tissue in a feedback loop of pleasure.

"Your taste," he murmured against her, the words themselves a caress. "So perfect."

Casey felt herself climbing toward release, each stroke of his tongue bringing her closer to an edge she suddenly, desperately needed to cross. Her body tensed beneath his ministrations, thighs trembling on either side of his head, breath coming in shortened gasps that carried his name in increasingly urgent repetition.

When release claimed her, it was total − a cascading surrender that arched her back and drew a cry from her throat before collapsing her boneless against the cushions. Kirk continued, gentler now, easing her through aftershocks that rippled outward with decreasing intensity, until sensitivity made her pull away with gentle hands against his shoulders.

"Come here," she whispered, voice husky with aftermath.

Kirk complied, moving up her body to claim her mouth in a kiss that carried her own taste, the intimacy of it sending renewed heat spiraling through her sensitized body. With newfound strength, Casey pushed against his shoulders, reversing their positions until he lay beneath her, eyes darkened to nearly black with desire.

"My turn," she said, making quick work of his remaining clothing, revealing the full extent of his arousal – hard and straining against his abdomen, evidence of his own need that had been temporarily set aside for hers.

Casey's hands explored familiar territory with fresh appreciation – the firm planes of his chest, the ridged muscle of his abdomen, the sensitive skin where hip met thigh. Kirk watched her with heavy-lidded eyes, control evident in every taut line of his body, patience warring with obvious desire.

That patience shattered when Casey lowered her head, taking him into her mouth with deliberate slowness that drew a strangled sound from his throat. Her tongue traced patterns against sensitive skin, learning his responses with the same attention he'd shown her, varying pressure and pace to build his pleasure with methodical precision.

"Casey," Kirk gasped, his hand tangling gently in her hair, not directing but connecting as she'd done earlier. "God, your mouth..."

She hummed appreciation against him, the vibration drawing another broken sound from his throat. His body tensed beneath her ministrations, muscles cording with the effort of restraint. When his breathing shortened to staccato gasps, Casey felt herself claimed by renewed urgency, need rising again despite her recent release.

She pulled away, meeting his questioning gaze with heat that required no verbal explanation. In one fluid movement that spoke of military strength never fully abandoned, Kirk rose from the couch, lifting her against him. Casey's legs circled his waist, her arms around his neck as he carried her toward the stairs, their naked bodies pressed together in perfect alignment.

They made it halfway up before the urgency overtook them both. Kirk pressed Casey against the wall, the cool surface a shocking counterpoint to the heat of his body against her front. His eyes held hers, seeking final confirmation she gave with a single nod and a subtle shift of her hips that aligned them perfectly.

He entered her with a single powerful thrust that drew synchronized gasps from both their throats. Casey's fingers dug into his shoulders, legs tightening around his waist as he established a rhythm that spoke of restraint rapidly unraveling. Each movement pressed her back against the wall, the slight discomfort only enhancing the pleasure building again low in her abdomen.

"Kirk," she moaned, her head falling back against the wall, exposing her throat to his hungry mouth. "Please, don't stop, I want you to really fuck me!"

His pace increased at her urging, each thrust deeper, more urgent than the last. One hand supported her weight while the other found her breast, thumb circling sensitive flesh in counterpoint to his movements below. Casey felt herself climbing again toward that precipice, the dual sensations building toward something that promised to eclipse her earlier release.

Kirk's rhythm faltered as his own control began to fragment, his breathing harsh against her neck, muscles trembling with exertion and approaching climax. "Casey," he gasped, the word both warning and prayer. "Together. Come with me."

His hand slid between their joined bodies, finding the sensitive bundle of nerves that sent her instantly over the edge. Casey's cry echoed in the stairwell as pleasure claimed her completely, walls pulsing around Kirk and drawing his own release in powerful waves she felt deep inside.

For long moments they remained joined, supported by the wall and Kirk's trembling legs, breath gradually slowing from desperate pants to even rhythm. Kirk's forehead rested against hers, eyes closed as if memorizing the sensation of their bodies still connected, still humming with aftermath of shared pleasure.

"I am not done with you yet," he whispered as his hands squeezed her ass cheeks pulling her closer than either thought possible.

"Oh really?" she said breathlessly

"Really, you want to really be fucked do you?" he murmured while kissing her neck

The only response Casey had left was a moan in agreement

He walked them the rest of the way into the bedroom taking them passed the bed and straight into the shower in the ajoining ensuite, never putting her down he turned on the water and stepped them in, once the temperature was right. He slowly lowered her until she was standing before him, soaping up his hands and washing her all over, the intimacy of it all made her speechless and just thrumming with pleasure, her body still throbbing from the previous encounter every touch sending her into overdrive. Slowly he turned her pushing her gently against the glass so her breasts get the sudden bite of the cool material against her skin. His erection pushing against her as he cups her breasts in his hands and runs his mouth down the length of her body.

When he appears satisfied they are clean he switches off the water, no drying leading them out of the shower and lifting her onto the counter kneeling down he throws both her legs over his shoulders and burys his face hard and grinding into her most sensitive flesh, he waits for the wetness to fill his mouth with the arrival of pleasure, then picks her up and carries her to the bed, kissing and giggling enjoying every sensation, everything except them and this moment long forgotten, standing up near the foot of the bed kissing her body passionately. "So are you ready to be really fucked?" he asks seductively. "Please" unsure if its a response to a question or she is now begging.

He turns her around and gently presses her down onto the bed, raising Casey's hips and spreading her legs with his knee. His fingers trace along the slick wetness and around her rear entry as he kneels behind, pushing his tongue into her while holding the hips firmly in place. Casey grips the sheets, overwhelmed by the exquisite plea- sure, as he transitions from his tongue to his fingers. "You are so incredibly wet and taste amazing," he murmurs, emphasising each word with a thrust of his hand. He then teases around her rear entry, making it contract at the unfamiliar yet thrilling sensation.

Face down in the mattress with her hips elevated, Kirk ignites every nerve in her body. Just when she thinks she can't possibly feel more, his tongue laps around the edges of the forbidden zone, an alien yet intoxicating feeling. In one swift motion, he withdraws his fingers, stands, and thrusts his hard length into her awaiting wetness, fulfilling every desire they each have. Each thrust gains momentum and force until they feel as if they are going to shatter. Casey's muscles tighten around him as he slams into her, praising how incredible she feels. She can only scream out in pleasure as he explores every part of her, some she didn't know existed. His hands, which had been gripping my waist, suddenly disappear, and She feels a finger entering her forbidden passage. It undoes her completely; crying out in shuddering waves as her orgasm rips through her, leaving her breathless Kirk roll his hips, grinding into her as his erection pulses and he finds his own release.

They collapse onto the bed, and Casey wraps herself around Kirk as they try to steady their breathing, listening to the rain fall outside. "Wow," I whisper into his chest. Kirk lets out a small chuckle, "Did I achieve my objective then?" he asks. "When I say I want to be fucked, that is exactly what I mean," I reply, surprised by my own boldness.

Outside, rain continued its gentle percussion against glass, but the sound had transformed again – no longer threat or lullaby but simply weather, ordinary and benign. Casey felt sleep approaching with unusual speed, the day's emotional and physical demands finally claiming their toll. Kirk's breathing had already deepened, his arm a heavy, comforting weight across her waist.

In these last moments before consciousness slipped away, Casey recognized the victory they'd claimed – not through security systems or police reports or private investigators, but through this: the ability to find peace in each other's arms despite all Layla had done to steal it from them. Tomorrow would bring new challenges, new strategies, new defenses. But tonight, in this moment of perfect connection, they had reclaimed something essential that no external threat could diminish.

Chapter 31

The gravel road wound deeper into the forest, narrow and twisting as it climbed into hills that seemed increasingly removed from civilization. Kirk guided his truck through the gathering dusk with steady hands, glancing occasionally at Casey beside him. Her profile was limned in the fading light, her posture still carrying the rigid vigilance that had become second nature over these past weeks. The cabin had been Kirk's idea – a desperate gambit to give them both space to breathe after the suffocating pressure of Layla's campaign against them.

"Almost there," Kirk said, his voice soft against the rhythmic crunch of tires on gravel and the whisper of wind through pine needles. "Just around this next bend."

Casey nodded, her attention divided between the dark shapes of trees pressing close against the road and her phone's screen, which she checked compulsively every few minutes. The device had remained mercifully silent during their two-hour drive, but absence of threat didn't translate to security – not anymore. Her finger traced the edge of the screen, hovering over the security app that would alert them to any breaches at the house they'd left behind.

The cabin materialized from the forest like a conjurer's trick – one moment hidden, the next revealed in a small clearing as Kirk steered the truck into a dirt driveway. It was smaller than Casey had imagined, its log exterior weathered to a silvery patina that caught the day's last light. A covered porch wrapped around two sides, its railing adorned with carved wooden figures worn smooth by weather and time. Smoke curled from a stone chimney, evidence that Kirk had arranged for the cabin to be prepared before their arrival.

"You like it?" Kirk asked, killing the engine but making no immediate move to exit the truck. His eyes watched her face closely, tracking her response with the careful attention that had characterized their relationship since Layla's intrusions began.

"It's beautiful," Casey said, meaning it despite the tension that had settled between her shoulder blades during the drive into increasingly remote territory. Beautiful but exposed – the thought formed before she could suppress it, her eyes automatically scanning the tree line that encircled their temporary sanctuary.

As if reading her thoughts, Kirk reached across the console to squeeze her hand gently. "The nearest neighbor is two miles away. The road we came in on is the only vehicle access. And I've arranged for a security service to drive by twice daily." His thumb traced circles on her palm, a grounding technique they'd developed when her anxiety spiked. "We're safe here, Casey."

Safety had become a relative concept, measured in degrees rather than absolutes. But Casey nodded, feeling some of the rigidity leave her spine as she took in the sturdy walls of the cabin, the warm glow of lights visible through curtained windows, the sheer isolation that made unexpected visitors nearly impossible.

They gathered their bags from the truck bed, the cool

evening air carrying scents of pine resin and woodsmoke as they approached the cabin's front door. Kirk produced an old-fashioned iron key, turning it in the lock with a solid click that suggested security more substantial than modern electronic alternatives.

Inside, the cabin enveloped them in rustic warmth – wooden walls burnished to a honey glow by time and care, a stone fireplace dominating one wall with flames already dancing across seasoned logs. The furnishings were simple but comfortable: a worn leather couch positioned to capture the fireplace's heat, a dining table crafted from a single massive slab of wood, reading lamps placed strategically to create pools of light against the gathering darkness.

"The owner is an old family friend," Kirk explained, setting their bags beside the staircase that led to a loft bedroom. "I called in a favor. Asked her caretaker to stock the fridge and start the fire before we arrived."

Casey nodded, barely hearing his words as she moved to the nearest window, peering through a gap in the curtains at the darkening forest beyond. Her fingers rose unconsciously to the fading bruise at her temple – a souvenir from three days ago when a startled response to an unexpected sound had sent her crashing into a doorframe. The injury itself had been minor, but its existence represented something more significant: physical evidence of how deeply Layla's campaign had affected them.

Kirk moved methodically through the cabin, checking locks on doors and windows, testing the landline phone, confirming cell reception. Casey watched his practiced movements, the military precision that became more pronounced in unfamiliar surroundings. He'd brought his handgun, she knew – had seen him secure it in the glove compartment before they left home. Another adaptation to their new reality, like the security system app on their phones, the chain locks they'd installed on every door, the habit of texting each other when arriving at or leaving any location.

"Everything's secure," Kirk announced, returning to where Casey stood still half-hidden by curtains. His hand settled gently on her shoulder, warm and steadying. "Hungry?"

The simple question served as anchor, pulling her attention from vigilance to more immediate, manageable concerns. Casey realized with mild surprise that she was, in fact, hungry – an ordinary sensation that had become rare in recent weeks as anxiety suppressed appetite.

"Starving, actually," she admitted, allowing Kirk to guide her toward the kitchen area at the cabin's rear.

The kitchen, like the rest of the cabin, balanced rustic charm with practicality – stone countertops, a deep farmhouse sink, cabinets handcrafted from local wood. Kirk had indeed arranged for the refrigerator to be stocked, its contents organized with the same attention to detail he brought to everything. They moved around each other in the small space with growing ease, falling into a rhythm they'd developed during months of working on her father's house together – passing ingredients without needing to ask, anticipating each other's movements in a domestic dance that required no instruction.

Casey felt her shoulders gradually descending from their permanent position near her ears, the constant tension in her neck easing fractionally as they assembled a simple meal – pasta with fresh herbs, crusty bread, a salad of greens and sliced pears. Kirk opened a bottle of red wine, pouring two glasses with a steadiness that belied the vigilance still evident in his occasional glances toward windows and doors.

They ate at the heavy wooden table, conversation flowing more freely than it had in days. The cabin's isolation provided a buffer against the constant anticipation of threat that had characterized their lives at home, allowing space for discussions unrelated to security measures and legal proceedings. Kirk described a client whose renovation plans kept expanding, Casey shared an amusing email from a former colleague. Ordinary conversation, the kind they'd once taken for granted.

Later, with dishes washed and put away, they settled on the leather couch before the fire. The warmth radiated against Casey's skin, firelight casting their shadows in elongated patterns across wooden floors and log walls. Kirk handed her a second glass of wine, the rich liquid catching ruby highlights from the flames.

"I have a proposal," Kirk said, his arm sliding around her shoulders as she nestled against his side. "For the next two days, let's pretend Layla doesn't exist."

The suggestion hung in the air between them, audacious in its simplicity. Casey's fingers rose again to the fading bruise at her temple, the discoloration now barely visible but still tender to the touch – a physical reminder of what they were trying to escape. The fire popped and hissed as a log settled, sending a shower of sparks up the chimney.

"Just two days," Kirk continued, his thumb tracing gentle circles on her shoulder. "No checking the security app every ten minutes. No scanning rooms for threats. No looking over our shoulders." He pressed a kiss against her hair, his voice softening. "Just us, Casey. The way it should be."

Casey turned to look at him directly, studying the face that had become her sanctuary in a world gone suddenly hostile. The firelight caught the amber flecks in his eyes, illuminated the strong line of his jaw, the slight crease between his brows that spoke of concern never fully banished despite his attempt at lightheartedness.

"Yes," she said simply, allowing herself to yield to the promise of temporary peace. "Just us."

She leaned into his embrace, the wine warm in her belly, the fire warm against her skin, Kirk's body warm and solid beside her. Outside, darkness had claimed the forest completely, but for once, the shadows beyond the windows didn't seem to harbor threats. For the next two days, at least, they would reclaim what Layla had tried so hard to steal from them − not just safety, but the simple pleasure of existing together without fear shadowing every moment.

The cabin had surrendered to darkness outside its windows, the forest beyond reduced to abstract shapes against a moonless sky. Inside, they created their own small universe of light and warmth—the fire had burned down to glowing embers that painted the room in amber tones, complemented by a single lamp whose light pooled softly on the worn leather couch where they sat. Casey tucked her feet beneath her, wine glass balanced on the armrest, her body angled toward Kirk with the new ease that had gradually claimed her since their arrival hours earlier.

Kirk studied her face in the gentle light, noting how the furrow between her brows had softened, how her shoulders had finally dropped from their perpetual position near her ears. She looked almost peaceful—still vigilant, but no longer carrying the brittle tension that had characterized her movements at home. The change solidified his resolve for what came next.

"There's something I need to show you," he said, setting his wine glass on the rough-hewn coffee table. He rose, moving to retrieve his duffel bag from where it rested near the stairs. "I've been wanting to tell you for days, but home didn't feel... safe enough."

Casey watched him, body tensing slightly in uncon-scious preparation for unpleasant news. The past weeks had conditioned her to expect the worst from unexpected announcements. "What is it?"

Kirk returned to the couch with a manila folder, worn at the edges from handling. He sat beside her, close enough that their thighs touched, and placed the folder on his lap. His fingers traced the edge of it, a rare gesture of uncertainty from a man who typically moved with decisive confidence.

"I hired someone," he said finally. "A private investigator named Malone. Ex-law enforcement with specialized experience in stalking cases."

Casey's breath caught, eyes widening as she processed this information. "How long?"

"Two weeks. Since the cemetery." Kirk opened the folder, revealing neatly organized documents inside— photographs, printed emails, handwritten notes in cramped, precise handwriting. "He's been gathering evidence, building a case against Layla where the police couldn't or wouldn't."

I know we said she didn't exist right now, but I don't want secrets, he handed the folder to Casey, their fingers brushing in the exchange. The contact lingered, Kirk's thumb tracing a gentle arc across her knuckles before releasing the documents into her care. "Malone works differently than standard PIs. More thorough. More... determined."

Casey spread the contents across her lap, the firelight catching on glossy photographs and highlighting typed text. The first document detailed Layla's movements over the past ten days—a clinical accounting of places visited, people contacted, patterns established. Casey recognized several locations near their home, confirmation of their suspicions about Layla's continued surveillance.

"He's been tracking her?" Casey asked, fingers trembling slightly as she sifted through the evidence of Layla's obsession with their lives.

Kirk nodded, leaning closer to indicate specific notations on the documents. "Not just tracking. Building a comprehensive profile. Establishing patterns that demonstrate intent rather than coincidence." His finger tapped a typewritten page listing dates and times. "These are all instances where she violated the temporary restraining order—most too subtle for conventional law enforcement to pursue, but real violations nonetheless."

Casey turned to a series of photographs—Layla entering a hardware store, emerging with a bag whose contents couldn't be identified. Another showed her car parked three blocks from Casey's house, well outside the exclusion zone specified in the restraining order but positioned for optimal surveillance. The methodical documentation transformed abstract threat into concrete evidence, Layla's campaign of terror reduced to dates, times, and locations that could be presented in court.

As Casey sorted through the materials, a separate folder emerged from beneath the photographs—older documents with different formatting, some yellowed slightly with age. "What are these?" she asked, opening the secondary file.

"Malone's background research," Kirk explained, his voice dropping lower. "Previous restraining orders against Layla. Complaints filed by other men she dated after our divorce. A pattern of escalating behavior that spans years, not just our situation."

Casey's hands stilled as she absorbed this new information. "Other restraining orders? How many?"

"Three," Kirk said, the single word weighted with significance. "All filed after our divorce. All granted, but ultimately dropped when the men moved away or gave up fighting her. Malone found them by digging deeper than the standard background checks the police ran."

The documents blurred slightly as tears gathered in Casey's eyes, not from fear but from something more complex—the realization that Kirk had been working to protect them even as the situation seemed hopeless, that he'd been fighting when official channels had failed them. One particular page caught her attention—a handwritten statement from a man named David, describing behavior eerily similar to what they had experienced. The parallels were chilling in their precision.

"This is why you've seemed less... resigned lately," Casey said, understanding dawning. "You've had someone gathering evidence while we were dealing with the immediate threats."

Kirk nodded, reaching to brush a strand of hair behind her ear, his fingers lingering against her cheek. "Malone believes we have enough now for a permanent restraining order with actual enforcement provisions. And if she violates it—when she violates it—enough documentation to support criminal charges." His eyes held hers, fierce with determination. "He's building a case the district attorney can't ignore, Casey. One that doesn't rely solely on our testimony."

Casey gathered the documents with trembling hands, carefully returning them to the folder. The weight of it felt substantial—physical evidence of their path forward, proof that their nightmare might eventually end through legal means rather than endless vigilance. She set the folder aside, placing it carefully on the coffee table, giving it the respect something so potentially life-changing deserved.

When she turned back to Kirk, her vision was blurred with tears that transformed the firelight into fractured stars. "You did this," she whispered, voice unsteady with emotion. "While dealing with everything else—the security systems, the police reports, taking care of me when I couldn't..." Her hands rose to frame his face, palms warm against the stubble that shadowed his jaw. "You never stopped fighting."

Kirk leaned into her touch, his eyes revealing vulnerability he rarely allowed to surface. "I couldn't," he said simply. "Not with you at stake."

The moment stretched between them, laden with unspoken emotion. Casey's thumbs traced the contours of his cheekbones, memorizing the geography of his face through touch. In his features she read exhaustion, determination, and something deeper that had sustained them both through weeks of terror—a commitment that transcended ordinary devotion.

"I love you," she said, the words emerging with quiet certainty, as if they had always existed and were simply finding voice at last. "I should have told you sooner. Before all this started. Before Layla ever appeared at my door." Her fingers trembled against his skin. "I think I've loved you since you showed up with that casserole after Dad's funeral. Since you sat with me on the porch and didn't try to fix my grief with empty words."

Kirk's hands rose to cover hers where they framed his face, his palms warm and slightly calloused against her fingers. The gesture mirrored their first real reconciliation after Layla's initial appearance, but now held deeper significance—not forgiveness or understanding but absolute certainty.

"I've loved you through all of it," he said, voice rough with emotion. "Through rebuilding your house. Through your father's death. Through Layla's worst. I'll love you through whatever comes next."

He drew her toward him then, his mouth finding hers with a tenderness that gradually transformed into something more urgent. Casey melted into him, her body curving against his as if designed specifically for this connection. The kiss deepened, his hands tangling in her hair as he pulled her closer, her arms encircling his neck as the space between them dissolved completely.

Outside, the forest night enveloped their cabin in darkness punctuated only by distant stars. Inside, the fire popped and hissed, sparks ascending the chimney like ephemeral messengers. On the coffee table, the folder containing evidence against Layla lay temporarily forgotten—not abandoned but simply set aside for this moment where nothing existed beyond the two of them, their bodies pressed together, hearts beating in gradually synchronizing rhythm as the kiss continued, deepened, promised more.

Chapter 32

The kiss deepened, transforming from tender confession to something more urgent, need crackling between them like the embers shifting in the fireplace. Casey's fingers found the buttons of Kirk's shirt, working them free with growing impatience. His skin was warm beneath her palms as she slid the fabric from his shoulders, revealing the landscape of muscle and scars she'd come to know intimately yet never tired of exploring. Kirk's breath hitched as her fingers traced the thin white line across his ribs—evidence of military service he rarely discussed but which had shaped him into the protector who now gathered her closer, as if trying to eliminate any remaining space between them.

"Casey," he murmured against her mouth, the two syllables carrying layers of meaning—desire, reverence, invitation. His hands slid beneath her sweater, palms warm against the sensitive skin of her back, raising goosebumps in their wake.

She raised her arms, allowing him to pull the garment over her head, the cool cabin air a brief shock against newly exposed skin. Firelight painted her in amber and

gold, shadows gathering in the hollows of her collar-
bones, the gentle curve where neck met shoulder. Kirk's
eyes traveled her body with visible appreciation, his gaze
a tangible caress that sent heat pooling low in her
abdomen.

"You are so beautiful," he whispered, fingertips tracing
the delicate lace edge of her bra, following the boundary
where fabric met flesh with exquisite patience.

Casey leaned into his touch, her hands unfastening his
belt with practiced efficiency that still managed to feel like
discovery. Each layer removed revealed more of them to
each other—not just physically but emotionally, barriers
dissolving under the honesty of skin against skin. Kirk's
jeans joined her sweater on the cabin floor, their discarded
clothing creating an impromptu trail from couch toward
stairs as they moved in wordless agreement toward the loft
bedroom.

They paused halfway up, Kirk pressing Casey gently
against the wall, his mouth finding the sensitive spot
beneath her ear that invariably drew soft sounds from her
throat. Her head fell back, offering more access as his lips
traced a path down her neck to the hollow of her throat.
His fingers worked the clasp of her bra, the garment falling
away to reveal breasts that immediately pebbled in the
cabin's cool air.

"So perfect," Kirk murmured, his hands cupping her
with reverent appreciation before his mouth replaced his
fingers, drawing a gasp from Casey that echoed in the
cabin's quiet interior.

They navigated the remaining stairs in a tangle of
limbs and half-removed clothing, stumbling slightly in their
urgency, catching each other with laughter that quickly
dissolved into renewed kisses. The loft bedroom welcomed
them with moonlight streaming through uncurtained
windows, transforming the simple space into something

ethereal—the pine bed frame silvered, the white sheets gleaming like fresh snow.

Their remaining clothes fell away, barriers abandoned completely as they tumbled onto the bed, cool sheets a counterpoint to heated skin. Kirk positioned himself above Casey, his weight supported on forearms planted beside her head, eyes seeking hers in the moonlight that painted them both in monochrome clarity.

"I love you," he said again, the words carrying new weight in this moment of absolute vulnerability.

Casey's hands framed his face, thumbs tracing the strong line of his jaw, memorizing him through touch. "Show me," she whispered, the simple request carrying all her need, her trust, her conviction that what they created together transcended the fear that had shadowed them for weeks.

Kirk's response was to lower his body to hers, skin meeting skin in a constellation of contact points that sent currents of pleasure radiating outward. Their mouths found each other again in a kiss that spoke of patience suspended, restraint abandoned. Casey's legs circled his waist, drawing him closer, alignment creating exquisite friction that drew synchronized gasps from both their throats.

When he finally entered her, the connection felt like homecoming—familiar yet never ordinary, intimate yet still carrying the thrill of discovery. They moved together with the synchronicity of partners who had learned each other's rhythms, each other's responses. Kirk's hands mapped her body with deliberate attention, finding the places that drew sighs, gasps, soft moans that seemed loud in the cabin's stillness.

Casey matched his pace, her fingers tracing patterns across his shoulders, down the strong planes of his back, learning him again through touch as their bodies conversed in the oldest language. The moonlight caught the sheen of perspiration on their skin, transforming ordinary evidence of exertion into something luminous, almost otherworldly.

Release built slowly, intensely, a gathering wave that finally crested in shared surrender. Casey's body arched beneath Kirk's, her soft cry mingling with his deeper sound as they fell together into perfect, temporary oblivion. For precious moments, nothing existed beyond their joined bodies, their synchronized heartbeats, their breath gradually slowing from desperate to measured.

Later, tangled in sheets dampened slightly by their exertions, they lay facing each other in the moonlight that streamed unimpeded through the loft windows. Kirk's finger traced the contours of Casey's face—the arch of her eyebrow, the curve of her cheekbone, the fullness of her lower lip—as if committing her to memory through touch alone. His eyes held a tenderness that made her heart constrict with emotion too complex for simple naming.

"What are you thinking?" he asked, voice low in deference to the night's quiet sanctity.

Casey captured his hand, pressing a kiss against his palm before interlacing their fingers. "About the future," she admitted. "For the first time in weeks, I can actually imagine one beyond just surviving day to day."

Kirk nodded, understanding illuminating his features. "Tell me about it. This future you're imagining."

Casey shifted to rest her head on his chest, ear pressed against his heart where its steady rhythm provided counterpoint to their conversation. "I want to reopen my studio," she said, the admission carrying the weight of dreams long deferred. "Before Dad got sick, photography was everything to me. Weddings, portraits, some commercial work—but my real passion was landscape photography."

Kirk's hand moved in gentle patterns across her bare shoulder, encouraging her to continue.

"I closed it when he needed full-time care. Couldn't balance both." Her fingers traced abstract patterns on his chest as she spoke. "After he died, there was the house to deal with, and then..." She didn't need to finish the sentence. Then Layla had arrived, transforming grief into terror, recovery into survival.

"You never told me about your photography," Kirk said, no accusation in his tone, merely observation.

Casey nodded against his chest. "Another piece of myself that got... misplaced during everything. But being here, seeing this landscape—I found myself thinking about apertures and light values again for the first time in forever." Her voice strengthened with conviction. "I want that back. My eye, my camera, my studio space on Maple Street with the north-facing windows."

Kirk's arms tightened around her, his approval evident in the gesture. "You'll have it," he said, the simple declaration carrying absolute certainty. "Once we've dealt with Layla permanently, you'll reopen. I'll help you renovate the space."

The confidence in his voice warmed something inside Casey that had been cold for too long. "What about you?" she asked, tilting her head to study his profile in the moonlight. "Beyond resolving the situation with Layla, what do you want?"

Kirk was silent for a moment, his free hand moving to stroke her hair with gentle, rhythmic motions. "I've been thinking about starting my own security consulting business," he said finally. "Using my military experience plus what I've learned from our situation to help others protect themselves more effectively than conventional systems allow."

Casey nodded, understanding the motivation behind this path. "You'd be amazing at that. You already think ten steps ahead of most people when it comes to security."

"The contracting business is satisfying in its way," Kirk continued, warming to the subject. "There's something rewarding about physical labor, about creating something tangible. But this situation with Layla—" His voice hardened slightly at her name, the only acknowledgment they'd made of her existence since arriving at the cabin. "It's shown me how vulnerable most people are, how inadequate standard protections can be against someone truly determined to cause harm."

His fingers continued their gentle exploration of her hair, the touch grounding them both in the present moment despite discussion of future plans. "I could help people avoid what we've experienced. Create customized protection based on specific threats rather than one-size-fits-all solutions."

Casey raised herself on one elbow, looking directly into his eyes. "You should do it," she said, conviction strengthening her voice. "You have insight most security professionals lack—you understand that safety isn't just about cameras and alarm systems. It's about patterns, psychology, specific vulnerabilities."

Kirk smiled, the expression transforming his features with boyish pleasure at her endorsement. "Partners, then," he said, pulling her back down to rest against his chest. "You with your photography studio, me with my security consulting. Building something new together."

"Partners," Casey agreed, the word carrying weight beyond its immediate context.

They talked further as moonlight tracked its slow path across the bedroom floor—details of business plans, potential locations, timelines that extended months and years into a future they now allowed themselves to envision. Their voices gradually softened, sentences occasionally interrupted by gentle kisses, until conversation gave way to comfortable silence and finally to sleep.

Casey drifted off with her head pillowed on Kirk's chest, his arm a secure weight across her waist, their legs tangled beneath sheets now warmed by shared body heat. Outside, the first hints of dawn began to lighten the eastern sky, but neither witnessed this transition. For the first time in weeks, Casey slept without starting awake at small sounds, without the hypervigilance that had transformed normal rest into fitful dozing. Instead, she surrendered completely to sleep's embrace, secure in Kirk's arms, their shared plans for the future a shield against present fears.

Morning light poured through the cabin's eastern windows, transforming the simple space with golden illumination that caught dust motes dancing in its beams. Casey folded the last blanket with precise motions, smoothing its surface before adding it to the neat stack on the bed they'd stripped earlier. The night's intimacies lingered in the air between them, not as memory but as foundation—something solid upon which they now built with quiet efficiency, preparing for the return journey with movements that seemed choreographed in their synchronicity.

Kirk moved through the small kitchen, wiping counters and returning borrowed space to pristine condition. His methodical approach remained unchanged, but the tension that had characterized his vigilance upon arrival had transformed into something more purposeful—less hyperawareness of potential threat, more dedication to task at hand. Occasionally his eyes sought Casey across the cabin's open layout, his gaze carrying warmth that transcended the morning sunlight angling through pine-framed windows.

Casey descended from the loft, overnight bag balanced against her hip, hair gathered in a loose ponytail that exposed the graceful line of her neck. The fading bruise at her temple had softened to a yellowish shadow, barely visible unless you knew to look for it. More noticeable was the change in her movement—the cautious hypervigilance replaced by deliberate grace, shoulders relaxed rather than braced against expected impact. She hummed softly, an unconscious melody that filled the cabin's morning quiet.

"You're different this morning," Kirk observed, pausing in his methodical gathering of their possessions. He leaned against the rough-hewn kitchen counter, studying her with the careful attention that characterized all his observations. "Something's changed."

Casey set her bag near the door before crossing to where he stood. Her fingers traced the strong line of his jaw, a gesture of casual intimacy that would have been unthinkable in the preceding weeks of constant alertness. "I feel different," she acknowledged, the simple statement carrying layers of meaning. "Like I've been underwater for weeks, everything muffled and distorted, and suddenly I can breathe again."

Kirk caught her hand, pressing a kiss against her palm before interlacing their fingers. "The cabin was a good idea, then."

"The cabin was an excellent idea," Casey corrected, leaning into his solid warmth. "But it wasn't just this place." Her free hand rose to rest against his chest, feeling the steady rhythm of his heart beneath her palm. "It was having space to remember who we are together—not just two people in crisis mode, but us. Kirk and Casey."

Something shifted in Kirk's expression—a softening around eyes that had maintained vigilant assessment for so long they'd developed permanent creases at the corners. "I've missed you," he said simply. "Not just physically, but the you beneath all the fear and hypervigilance."

Casey nodded, understanding precisely what he meant. The constant state of alertness had transformed them both, narrowing their existence to threat assessment and defensive positioning. Even their most intimate moments had carried undertones of vigilance—doors double-checked, phones positioned for quick access, sleep interrupted by the smallest sounds. This weekend had provided not escape but reclamation—of themselves as individuals, as partners, as something more than Layla's targets.

"I feel stronger," Casey said, stepping back to resume packing with renewed purpose. "Not because the threat is any less real, but because I'm more than just someone being hunted. I'm still me—the photographer who loves early morning light, the woman who rebuilt her father's house, the person who loves you."

Kirk smiled, the expression transforming his features with boyish charm that made her heart skip. "The person who loves me," he repeated, satisfaction evident in his tone. "I could listen to that all day."

They finished packing with efficient coordination, moving around each other in the small space with the ease of partners attuned to each other's rhythms. Casey swept the wooden floors while Kirk closed the fireplace damper and secured windows. They stripped the bed together, laundered sheets folded with hospital corners that betrayed Kirk's military background. Their movements formed a domestic ballet—passing items without needing to ask, anticipating each other's next task, occasionally pausing for brief touches that carried both affection and affirmation.

Standing in the cabin's main room, surveying their completed preparations, Casey felt a momentary pang at leaving this sanctuary. The simple space had provided more than physical distance from threats—it had created emotional space for recovery, for reconnection, for remembering what they were fighting to preserve.

"We don't have to leave for another hour if you want to stay longer," Kirk offered, reading her expression with characteristic perception.

Casey shook her head, resolution firming her posture. "No, it's time. We've reclaimed ourselves here. Now we need to carry that strength back with us."

Kirk nodded, understanding implicit in the gesture. He loaded their bags into the truck while Casey completed a final walkthrough, checking that lights were off, water taps fully closed, everything returned to the order in which they'd found it. Outside, sunshine filtered through pine boughs, casting dappled patterns across the dirt driveway where Kirk's truck waited, loaded for departure.

They stood together on the cabin's porch, Kirk's arm draped casually across Casey's shoulders, her body leaning slightly into his side. The forest surrounded them in verdant tranquility—pine needles rustling in the gentle morning breeze, distant birdsong punctuating the otherwise profound quiet. Casey breathed deeply, filling her lungs with air scented by resin and earth and subtle wildflowers, committing the sensation to memory as thoroughly as she might compose a photograph.

"What are you thinking?" Kirk asked, his voice pitched low in deference to the forest's hushed atmosphere.

Casey considered the question, organizing her thoughts with the same care she'd once applied to arranging photographic compositions. "That I'm not the same person who arrived here yesterday," she said finally. "That woman was... fractured. Holding herself together through sheer force of will, but cracking beneath the pressure."

Kirk nodded, his arm tightening slightly around her shoulders. "And now?"

"Now I remember who I am. What I'm capable of." Casey turned to face him fully, her eyes meeting his with clear determination. "Layla is still out there. The threat hasn't diminished. But my response to it has changed. I'm not just enduring anymore—I'm fighting back."

Something like pride illuminated Kirk's features, amber

eyes warming to gold in the morning light. He pulled her into a proper embrace then, arms encircling her completely, his strength offered not as protection but as partnership. Casey melted against him, face pressed to the solid plane of his chest where his heartbeat provided steady percussion beneath her ear.

For long moments they remained thus entwined, absorbing the forest's tranquility, each other's presence, the simple miracle of standing together in sunlight rather than shadows. When they finally separated, Kirk's hands remained on Casey's shoulders, his gaze intent as he studied her face with careful attention.

"Whatever she throws at us," he said, each word weighted with resolve, "we face it together. Not just surviving, but fighting for the future we want—your photography studio, my security business, our life together."

Casey nodded firmly, jaw set with fresh determination, eyes clear and focused. "Together," she affirmed, the single word carrying the strength of covenant.

They descended the porch steps hand in hand, moving toward the truck with synchronized purpose. Kirk held her door, an ordinary courtesy transformed by context into something more significant—not protection based on perceived weakness but respect grounded in acknowledged strength. Casey slid into the passenger seat, her gaze traveling one last time over the cabin that had provided sanctuary and restoration.

As Kirk guided the truck down the gravel road, tires crunching against stone in rhythmic counterpoint to the engine's steady hum, Casey felt a curious lightness despite their journey back toward conflict. They were returning to face Layla's continued threats, to engage with legal proceedings, to maintain vigilance against unpredictable malice. Yet they carried with them something Layla couldn't touch—the renewed certainty of who they were together, the shared vision of a future beyond present crisis, the unshakable knowledge that whatever came next, they would face it not as victims but as partners whose bond had been tested by fire and emerged stronger.

The forest gradually thinned around them, sunlight replacing dappled shadows as they descended toward civilization. Casey watched the transition with clear eyes, her mind already mapping strategy rather than escape. The weekend had served its purpose—not as retreat from reality but as preparation for more effective engagement with it. Two days of pretending Layla didn't exist had paradoxically strengthened their capacity to face her continued existence, to counter her threats with unified response rather than fractured fear.

Kirk reached across the console, his hand finding Casey's with unerring accuracy. Their fingers interlaced in silent affirmation as the truck carried them homeward, back toward the battlefield they now approached not with dread but with determined purpose.

Chapter 33

The truck rounded the final bend toward Casey's street, tires humming against familiar asphalt. Afternoon sunlight filtered through neighborhood trees, casting dappled patterns across the dashboard and Kirk's steady hands on the wheel. Something had shifted between them during their weekend away—a reclaiming of themselves beyond Layla's reach, a remembering of who they were together. Casey's hand rested lightly on Kirk's thigh, her fingers relaxed in a way they hadn't been for weeks, the weekend's peace still lingering in her loosened shoulders and softened expression.

"Almost home," Kirk said, his voice carrying none of the tension that had characterized their departure two days earlier. He glanced briefly at Casey, the corner of his mouth lifting in a half-smile that carried more meaning than mere expression—acknowledgment of the strength they'd rediscovered, the plans they'd made for a future beyond present threats.

Casey nodded, her gaze drifting through the passenger window to the familiar landmarks of her neighborhood— Mrs. Abernathy's meticulously pruned hydrangeas, the

Thompson kids' bicycles abandoned on their front lawn, the corner stop sign perpetually tilted five degrees counter-clockwise. Home, with all its ordinary imperfections, its comforting rhythms that had been disrupted but not destroyed by Layla's intrusions.

The distant wail of sirens registered first as background noise, unremarkable until their frequency increased—a harmonizing chorus of emergency vehicles that seemed to be converging rather than passing through. Casey sat straighter, a frown creasing her forehead as she noticed an unusual glow through the trees ahead—not sunset's amber warmth but something more volatile, flickering with unnatural rhythm.

"Kirk," she said, her hand tightening involuntarily on his thigh. "Something's wrong."

He had already noticed, his posture shifting from relaxed to alert, hands repositioning on the wheel as he increased their speed slightly. The peaceful suburban scene transformed with each yard of asphalt they covered—neighbors standing in clusters on lawns, faces turned toward some unseen calamity ahead; children hoisted onto shoulders for better views; phones raised to capture whatever spectacle had interrupted the street's normal afternoon quiet.

As they crested the small rise that marked the entrance to Casey's block, the source of commmotion came into full, horrifying view. Casey's renovated house—the structure she had painstakingly restored after her father's death, the space where she and Kirk had found each other—stood transformed into a roaring inferno. Flames consumed the roof entirely, reaching hungry fingers toward the darkening sky, while black smoke billowed in thick columns visible for blocks.

"No," Casey whispered, the single syllable containing disbelief, denial, devastation.

Kirk pulled the truck sharply to the curb, tires scraping against concrete as he brought them to an abrupt stop. Three fire engines were already positioned around the property, their red emergency lights pulsing against neighboring houses in rhythmic warning. Firefighters in heavy gear maneuvered massive hoses directing powerful jets of water that seemed pitifully inadequate against the conflagration's ferocity.

Casey didn't remember opening the truck door, didn't recall the physical act of exiting the vehicle. She simply found herself standing on the street, her body rigid with shock as she watched her home—her sanctuary, her inheritance, her connection to her father—disintegrate before her eyes. The roof's central portion collapsed inward with a thunderous crash that sent a fresh eruption of sparks spiraling skyward like malevolent fireflies.

The heat reached them even at this distance, rolling outward in tangible waves that forced onlookers to step back, hands raised instinctively to shield their faces. The air carried acrid chemical notes beneath the primary scent of burning wood—paint vaporizing, synthetic materials melting, the accumulated possessions of a lifetime transforming to ash and memory.

Kirk's arm circled Casey's waist, both support and anchorage as her legs threatened to fold beneath her. His face reflected a complex interplay of emotions—anger hardening the line of his jaw, concern softening his eyes as they moved between the burning structure and Casey's pale features.

"My father's things," Casey said, her voice sounding distant and unfamiliar to her own ears. "His records. His books. The photographs." Each item represented not just material loss but the severance of tangible connections to what had been—evidence of lives lived, moments captured, history preserved. "The quilt my grandmother made. Dad's military medals. The box of letters Mom wrote before she died."

A firefighter shouted commands to his team as the eastern wall began to bow outward, structural integrity compromised by the inferno's relentless consumption. Water hissed as it met superheated surfaces, creating a ghostly steam that mingled with smoke to form a hellish atmosphere. The crackling sound of wood surrendering to flame provided constant accompaniment to human voices —orders shouted, questions called, the murmured commentary of gathered neighbors.

"Everything I own," Casey continued, her voice hollow with shock. "Everything I am. My cameras. My portfolios. The negatives from all those years." Her photography equipment—the tools of the career she'd planned to revive, the artistic expression she'd only just reclaimed the courage to pursue—would be melted beyond recognition, digital memory cards warped and useless, irreplaceable images lost.

Kirk's arm tightened around her waist, his body a solid presence against the world that seemed to be dissolving in flame before them. "You're safe," he said, the words emerging rough with emotion. "That's what matters. You weren't in there. We weren't in there."

Casey recognized the truth in his statement even as fresh grief washed through her—gratitude for their absence competing with devastation at what that absence had cost. If they had returned earlier, could they have prevented this? If they hadn't gone away at all, would the house still be standing? Questions without answers swirled like the smoke that continued to pour from broken windows and the collapsed section of roof.

A firefighter approached them, his reflective gear gleaming wetly in the firelight, face partially obscured by protective equipment but posture communicating official purpose. "You the homeowner?" he asked, voice raised to carry over the cacophony of destruction.

Casey nodded mechanically, unable to formulate words that could adequately encompass her relationship to the burning structure. More than owner—caretaker, inheritor, preserver of her father's legacy. All roles now rendered hollow by the flames that continued to consume what she had sought to protect.

"I'm sorry, ma'am," the firefighter said, the sympathy in his voice suggesting he understood something of what this loss represented. "We're doing everything possible, but the fire had too much of a head start. Structure was fully involved before the first call came in."

Casey nodded again, acknowledging his words without fully processing their meaning. The implications would come later—insurance forms, temporary housing, the mechanics of rebuilding a life from literal ashes. For now, there was only the hypnotic horror of watching flames devour the physical manifestation of her history.

"Everything," she whispered as another section of roof gave way with a sound like distant thunder. Her fingers clutched at Kirk's shirt, anchoring herself to his solid presence as the world she'd known transformed before her eyes. "Everything's gone."

Kirk's arms encircled her completely then, turning her gently away from the spectacle of destruction, his body forming a bulwark between Casey and the consuming flames. He made no promise that things would be alright, offered no platitudes about possessions being replaceable. Instead, he simply held her, his heartbeat steady against her ear, his presence the one constant in a world suddenly reduced to ash and uncertainty.

The firefighters' efforts continued with grim determination, their silhouettes dark against the flickering orange backdrop as they battled what was clearly becoming a losing fight. Water arced in powerful streams that disappeared into the roaring flames, creating momentary dark patches that reignited almost immediately. Casey stood motionless in the circle of Kirk's arms, her eyes reflecting twin images of her home's destruction, her body occasionally shuddering with quiet sobs that seemed wrenched from somewhere beyond conscious control.

The crowd of onlookers had grown, neighbors emerging from surrounding homes drawn by the spectacle of destruction and the human instinct toward witnessing calamity. They gathered in small clusters, voices lowered in respectful murmurs, occasional phrases carrying to where Casey and Kirk stood—"such a shame," "just finished renovating," "poor thing, after everything with her father."

Casey barely registered their presence, her focus consumed by the disintegration of her life's physical evidence—photo albums curling in the heat, furniture reduced to glowing frameworks, walls that had sheltered generations of her family now collapsing inward with succession of thunderous crashes. Each new surrender of structure to flame seemed to remove another piece of herself, as if her identity were burning alongside the house.

Her gaze drifted across the gathered spectators—familiar faces from the neighborhood, some strangers drawn by the commotion, all illuminated in the unnatural flickering light that painted their features in amber and shadow. And then, across the street partially obscured by a cluster of maple trees, a figure that sent ice through Casey's veins despite the fire's radiating heat.

Layla.

She stood alone, separated from the other onlookers by several yards of empty sidewalk, as if even strangers sensed something dangerous in her presence. The flames reflected in her eyes, transforming ordinary green to something feral and hungry. Her lips curved in a smile that contained neither humor nor warmth—satisfaction distilled to its purest form, pleasure derived from destruction rendered visible in human expression.

"Kirk," Casey gasped, fingers digging into his forearm with sudden desperate strength. "Look. It's her."

Kirk's body tensed beneath her touch, head turning sharply in the direction she indicated. His posture shifted subtly—weight redistributing, muscles coiling with potential energy, the marine's readiness for immediate action emerging through the contractor's everyday exterior.

As if sensing their attention, Layla's gaze shifted from the burning house to meet Casey's directly across the intervening space. No shame colored her features, no attempt to hide her presence or disguise her satisfaction. Instead, she offered a small, mocking wave—a parody of neighborly greeting transformed by context into something obscene.

Kirk was already moving, disentangling himself from Casey with careful efficiency. "Stay here," he instructed, voice tight with controlled fury. "I'm going to—"

But even as he spoke, Layla stepped backward into deeper shadows. A fire truck repositioned with a hydraulic whine and blaring horn, momentarily blocking their view. When the vehicle settled into its new position, the space where Layla had stood was empty, as if she had been a hallucination conjured by stress and firelight.

"She was there," Casey insisted, scanning the dispersing crowd as neighbors shifted to accommodate the firefighters' movements. "I saw her watching. She was smiling, Kirk."

Kirk's expression hardened further, jaw muscles visibly working beneath stubbled skin. "I believe you," he said, eyes still tracking the area where Layla had disappeared. "We'll tell Rodriguez when he—"

"Ms. Preston. Mr. Manning."

The familiar voice carried easily through the chaos of

firefighting operations. Officer Rodriguez approached from the direction of newly arrived police cruisers, his uniform neat despite the hour, notepad already in hand. Where previous encounters had been characterized by professional detachment, his expression now carried genuine concern as he surveyed the destruction before them.

"I came as soon as dispatch confirmed this address," he said, removing his cap briefly to run a hand through close-cropped hair—a gesture that seemed less professional protocol than human response to the devastation. "I'm deeply sorry about your home."

Casey nodded mechanically, acknowledgment without meaning as her eyes continued to scan the crowd for Layla's distinctive blonde hair and calculated smile.

"She was here," Kirk said, explaining Casey's distraction. "Layla. Standing across the street watching. She disappeared into the crowd just before you arrived."

Rodriguez's expression shifted from sympathy to sharp focus, eyes narrowing as he made rapid notes. "Did she approach you? Say anything?"

"No," Casey answered, finding her voice despite the ash that seemed to have settled in her throat. "Just watched. Smiled. Waved at me when she realized we'd spotted her."

Rodriguez nodded grimly, continuing his notation before looking back toward the burning structure. "This wasn't an accident," he said, confirming what they had already intuited but dreaded hearing officially stated. "Fire investigator found clear evidence of accelerant use at multiple ignition points. Forced entry through the back door. Classic arson pattern."

The words struck Casey with physical force, her knees buckling as the last fragile hope that this might somehow be random misfortune—faulty wiring, a gas leak, any explanation that didn't involve deliberate malice—disintegrated. Kirk caught her before she could fall, his arm once again circling her waist with supportive strength.

"You're sure?" Kirk asked, though his tone suggested he'd expected nothing else.

Rodriguez pointed toward the eastern side of the property where a figure in specialized gear was photographing something near what remained of the back porch. "Multiple pour patterns. Professional accelerant. Someone knew what they were doing—wanted to ensure the fire would be well-established before anyone noticed."

Casey felt a curious doubling in her perception—part of her standing on the street absorbing this information with clinical detachment while another part screamed from some unreachable distance. The house that had sheltered her through childhood, that had been her father's pride, that she had lovingly restored with Kirk's help—deliberately destroyed not by accident or fate but by calculated human malice.

"We have officers searching the area," Rodriguez continued, his voice gentling as he observed Casey's pallor. "If Layla is still nearby, we'll find her. With the arson evidence and your confirmation of her presence at the scene, we have grounds for immediate arrest."

Chapter 34

An older woman approached, her bathrobe hastily belted over nightclothes despite the early evening hour, a stack of blankets clutched in arthritis-gnarled hands. "You'll be needing these, dear," she said, pressing the offering into Casey's numb fingers. "Shock sets in quick, even with the heat. You come over to my place when you're ready—spare bedroom's all made up."

Others followed—a mug of tea appearing from some-where, a neighbor offering use of his phone, another promising to contact Casey's insurance company first thing tomorrow. The community's response materialized as if conjured, practical assistance and human comfort arriving in equal measure amidst the continuing sounds of destruction.

Casey accepted their kindnesses with automatic thanks, her body operating on social autopilot while her mind remained trapped in loops of disbelief and horror. The air tasted of metal and chemicals, ash particles coating her tongue with each breath, embedding themselves in her hair and clothing like microscopic brands of what had occurred. The heat continued to pulse against her skin in rhythmic waves, the fire's heartbeat strong despite the fire-fighters' relentless assault.

"Casey?" Kirk's voice seemed to reach her from great distance, though his face hovered just inches from hers, concern etched in lines around his eyes. "Casey, can you hear me?"

She nodded, struggling to focus on his features rather than the devastation beyond. Something wet struck her cheek—not tears, which seemed trapped behind some internal dam, but water from the fire hoses catching the shifting wind and carrying to where they stood.

"I'd like to get a preliminary statement," Rodriguez was saying, though Casey couldn't remember when he had started speaking again. "Just the basics for now—when you left town, what you saw when you returned, confirmation of Ms. Manning's presence."

Casey stared past him toward what remained of her home—a skeletal framework of charred beams outlined against the darkening sky, occasional flames still licking at what little combustible material remained. The structure that had contained her life now rendered down to its most basic elements: carbon, ash, memory. Her gaze remained fixed on the ruins as she answered Rodriguez's questions, voice flat and distant, the words emerging without conscious thought or emotion.

Around them, neighbors continued to offer support, firefighters shouted technical instructions to each other, police established a wider perimeter with yellow tape and stern warnings. Through it all, Casey existed in a curious suspended state—physically present but emotionally removed, as if some essential connection had been temporarily severed to protect her from the full impact of what had occurred.

Only Kirk's hand, warm and solid against the small of her back, provided any tether to immediate reality—a reminder that while everything else had been reduced to ash, this one fundamental truth remained: they faced this together, just as they had promised at the cabin that now seemed to exist in some other lifetime, before fire had redrawn the boundaries of their world.

The fluorescent lights in the motel corridor flickered with an irregular rhythm that sent shadows dancing across worn carpet. Casey followed Kirk down the hallway, her body moving with the mechanical precision of someone operating on instinct rather than conscious direction. The events of the day—their hopeful return from the cabin, the discovery of her burning home, the hours of questions and statements and terrible, irrefutable reality—had stripped her capacity for anything beyond the most basic functions. One foot in front of the other. Breathe in. Breathe out. Survive until tomorrow.

Kirk paused at room 214, swiping the plastic keycard with practiced efficiency. The lock's green light blinked approval, accompanied by a metallic click that echoed in the midnight quiet. He pushed the door open, holding it as Casey moved past him into the room—a space simultaneously familiar in its generic design and jarringly foreign in its sterility.

Twin beds dominated the center, their thin beige comforters pulled taut across mattresses that promised minimal comfort. A particleboard dresser supported a television that might have been state-of-the-art a decade earlier. Generic landscape paintings hung at precisely measured intervals—mountain vistas and autumn forests that bore no resemblance to any real place, chosen for their inoffensive blandness. The distant hum of ice machines and occasional door closings filtered through walls thin enough to suggest privacy was more theoretical than actual.

Casey stood motionless just inside the doorway, her

brain struggling to process this new environment through layers of shock that muffled perception like cotton wool wrapped around fragile objects. Nothing here connected to the life that had existed twelve hours earlier—no photographs, no familiar furnishings, no objects imbued with memory or meaning. Just beige walls and industrial carpet designed to hide stains rather than please the eye.

Kirk moved past her to deposit their meager possessions on the dresser—her purse retrieved from the truck before the fire, his wallet and keys, the emergency overnight bag they'd fortunately left in the truck after their weekend away. The sum total of their material existence now fit in a space smaller than her father's toolbox. The day's final hours had been consumed by practicalities—Rodriguez arranging emergency credit cards through victim services, a stop at a discount store for basic toiletries and sleepwear, this motel chosen for its proximity and vacancy rather than any comfort it might offer.

Casey crossed to the nearest bed and sat on its edge, the mattress yielding reluctantly beneath her weight. She was still wearing the same clothes she'd had on when they discovered the fire, fabric permeated with smoke that assaulted her nostrils with each movement. The acrid scent had become so constant she'd stopped consciously registering it, but now in this closed space, it reasserted itself—chemical and sharp, a persistent reminder of what had been lost.

"You should shower," Kirk suggested gently, removing toiletries from their plastic shopping bag and arranging them on the bathroom counter with careful attention. "It might help you sleep."

Casey nodded, the simple movement requiring concentration as fatigue dragged at muscles and thoughts alike. She rose, accepting the clean t-shirt and sweatpants Kirk handed her, generic garments in approximate sizes chosen hastily from limited options. The bathroom's fluorescent brightness assaulted her eyes after the dimmer main room, white tiles and chrome fixtures reflecting light with merciless efficiency.

The water took long moments to warm, pipes rattling protest at her midnight demand. Casey stood before the spotted mirror, finally confronting her appearance—hair dulled with ash, face smudged with soot in abstract patterns, eyes haunted by shadows that had nothing to do with physical exhaustion. A stranger gazed back at her, someone fundamentally altered by the day's events in ways that transcended the visible grime of destruction.

When she finally stepped under the shower's spray, the water ran dark with evidence of what she'd witnessed —soot and ash swirling in hypnotic patterns before disappearing down the drain. Casey watched, transfixed by this tangible representation of loss—her home, her possessions, her connection to her father, all reduced to this darkness flowing away into sewage systems and treatment plants, physical evidence diluted until no trace remained.

She scrubbed methodically, watching her skin emerge from beneath layers of contamination. The hotel's complimentary soap smelled aggressively of artificial flowers, a synthetic brightness that seemed to mock the day's devastation with its manufactured cheer. Still, she worked it into a lather, cleansing what surfaces she could reach while understanding that some stains had settled deeper than soap could penetrate.

When she emerged from the bathroom, skin pink from heat and friction, Kirk had transformed the room's configuration. The twin beds now stood pushed together at their center, creating a makeshift double that eliminated the separation the room's designers had intended. He had turned off the overhead lights, leaving only a single bedside lamp whose glow created a small island of warmth in the otherwise institutional space.

"I hope that's okay," he said, gesturing toward the joined beds. "I thought—"

"Yes," Casey interrupted, the single syllable carrying gratitude she couldn't fully articulate. The thought of physical separation, even by the narrow gap between twin beds, felt unbearable after a day when everything solid had been revealed as terrifyingly vulnerable to destruction.

Kirk disappeared into the bathroom for his own shower while Casey slid between sheets that carried the faint chemical scent of industrial laundry facilities. The mattress proved as uncompromising as its appearance suggested, with springs that pressed against her hip and shoulder regardless of position. She lay still anyway, listening to the water running behind the bathroom door and trying not to think of flames consuming the handmade quilt that had covered her bed since childhood.

When Kirk returned, hair damp and skin scrubbed to military cleanliness, he switched off the remaining lamp before joining her between the rough sheets. Darkness pressed around them, broken only by thin strips of light that filtered through gaps in the poorly fitted curtains. In silent agreement, they shifted toward the center of their improvised bed, bodies aligning with practiced ease until they lay face to face, close enough that Casey could feel Kirk's breath warm against her cheek.

His hand found hers in the darkness, fingers interlacing in that space between their bodies—a bridge connecting islands of shared devastation. Outside, a passing car sent headlights sweeping across the ceiling in momentary illumination before returning them to shadows and silhouettes.

"She won't win," Kirk whispered into the darkness, his voice low but threaded with steel determination that seemed to vibrate between them. "We won't let her destroy what we have."

Casey's fingers tightened around his, drawing strength from the solid reality of his presence when everything else had proven so terrifyingly fragile. The unfamiliar room creaked and settled around them, water pipes knocking in the walls, the air conditioning unit humming with mechanical persistence.

"Promise me," she said, the words emerging ragged with emotion that had been held at bay by shock throughout the endless day. "Promise we'll get through this."

Kirk's free hand rose to cup her face, thumb gently tracing the curve of her cheekbone still warm from the shower's heat. No hesitation preceded his response, no calculation or consideration—just immediate, absolute certainty.

"I promise."

The simple declaration hung in the darkness between them, more substantial than the flimsy walls that surrounded them, more enduring than the house that had been reduced to ash and memory. Casey shifted closer until their foreheads touched, her breath synchronizing with his in unconscious harmony.

Whatever Layla had hoped to accomplish with fire and deliberate destruction, she had failed in this essential way: the connection between them remained unburned, unbroken—tempered by crisis rather than consumed by it. Casey felt tears finally breaking free, tracking silently across her temple to dampen the polyester pillowcase beneath her head. Kirk's arms encircled her completely, drawing her against the solid warmth of his chest where his heartbeat provided steady counterpoint to her quiet weeping.

They held each other through the night's deepest hours, finding in human connection what material possessions could never provide—comfort drawn not from things but from presence, strength borrowed and lent in equal measure. Occasional headlights swept across the ceiling, illuminating them briefly before returning the room to darkness. The building creaked and murmured around them, other travelers shifting behind thin walls in their own private dramas of travel or transition.

Through it all, Casey and Kirk remained entwined—her head tucked beneath his chin, his arms maintaining gentle pressure around her shoulders, their legs tangled beneath scratchy synthetic blankets. Not sleeping, not yet, but resting in the quiet certainty that whatever came next, whatever Layla might still attempt, they would face it as they lay now: together, connected, unbowed by the day's devastating losses.

Chapter 35

The keys gleamed in the afternoon sunlight, ordinary metal transformed into symbols of possibility as the real estate agent placed them in Casey's palm. Three weeks had passed since fire had consumed her family home, three weeks of hotel rooms with thin walls and thinner mattresses, of insurance forms and police reports and nights when sleep came only in broken fragments. Now she stood on the porch of a modest craftsman, its blue-gray siding and white trim promising something she'd almost forgotten existed: normalcy.

Casey's fingers trembled slightly as they closed around the keys, the metal warm from the agent's hand. Beside her, Kirk's attention divided between the paperwork being passed across clipboards and the street beyond, his eyes performing the automatic assessment that had become second nature since Layla entered their lives.

"Congratulations," the agent said, her smile professional but genuine beneath stylish glasses. "The expedited closing was unusual, but given your circumstances..." She left the sentence unfinished, everyone present aware of the fire that had made front-page news, the insurance company's rare efficiency motivated by the arson determination.

"Thank you for everything," Casey replied, the words inadequate against the weeks of frantic house-hunting, the agent's dedication to finding something that could be purchased quickly with the insurance advance. "This means more than I can express."

The craftsman sat on a quiet street lined with mature oaks, their branches creating dappled patterns across the front yard. Two stories of solid construction, with deep-set windows and a covered porch that wrapped around one side of the house. It lacked the character of her family home, the generations of memories soaked into floorboards and embedded in walls, but perhaps that absence was itself a kind of blessing—a clean slate unmarked by either cherished history or recent trauma.

Kirk signed the final document with deliberate strokes, his handwriting precise and controlled like everything else about him these days. His eyes continued their regular sweeps—porch to yard to street to neighboring houses—cataloging potential approaches, lines of sight, vulnerability points. The house had appealed to him immediately for reasons entirely separate from its architectural charm: corner lot with clear visibility in multiple directions, sturdy construction, limited blind spots, manageable perimeter.

"The security system is already activated," the agent said, correctly reading Kirk's assessment. "Previous owners installed it last year—top of the line, cellular backup, the works. Code's in the welcome packet."

Kirk nodded his appreciation, the tension in his shoulders easing fractionally at this confirmation. Casey felt a familiar pang watching him—guilt that his life had narrowed to these considerations of threat and protection, mingled with gratitude for the unwavering strength he continued to provide.

The agent departed with final congratulations, her car pulling away from the curb with a gentle purr that seemed at odds with the silence that followed. Casey and Kirk stood for a moment on their new porch—their porch—the weight of ownership settling around them with the afternoon light filtering through nearby trees.

"Shall we?" Kirk asked, his hand finding the small of her back with practiced ease.

The front door opened with a satisfying solidity, revealing a modest entryway that led to an open-concept living area. Their footsteps echoed against hardwood floors as they moved through empty rooms, the space somehow both smaller and larger than it had appeared during previous viewings—smaller without furniture to define its purpose, larger with possibility stretching before them.

The house smelled of fresh carpet in the bedrooms and newly applied paint throughout, the previous owners having prepared it meticulously for sale. Casey could detect lemon-scented cleaning products beneath these dominant notes, and beneath that, the indefinable scent of a place waiting to become a home—dust and sunshine and wood warmed by afternoon light.

Kirk moved with methodical attention through each room, noting features with quiet approval. "Solid core doors. Good sight lines to the street from here and here. These windows have proper locks, not just latches." His finger traced the metal mechanism with professional assessment. "Easy to add security film if we want extra protection against breaking."

Casey wandered to the living room windows, where sunlight created geometric patterns on the hardwood floor, warm honey-colored rectangles that shifted almost imperceptibly with the movement of branches outside. Through the glass, she could see children riding bicycles at the far end of the block, their high voices carrying faintly through closed windows—ordinary suburban sounds that seemed to belong to some other lifetime before surveillance photos and desecrated graves and flames consuming generations of memories.

"I was thinking sage green for this room," she said, running her hand along a wall currently painted inoffensive beige. The smooth surface held no history, no layer upon layer of her father's chosen colors, no pencil marks tracking her childhood height. "With cream trim. And maybe built-in bookshelves along that wall."

Kirk crossed to stand behind her, arms encircling her waist, chin resting lightly on the top of her head. She leaned back against the solid warmth of him, his heartbeat steady against her spine, his breath stirring her hair.

"No more hotel rooms," she said softly, the words carrying layers of meaning beyond their simple syllables—no more temporary existence, no more living in suspended animation while waiting for their real lives to resume.

"This is our fresh start," Kirk promised, his arms tightening fractionally around her waist. His body remained relaxed against hers, but she felt the slight shift in his attention as his eyes continued their practiced survey of the room, checking corners and entrances with the automatic vigilance that had become as natural to him as breathing.

Casey covered his hands with hers where they rested against her abdomen, her fingers tracing the veins that stood in relief along his forearms. Outside, a child's delighted shriek pierced the quiet, followed by laughter and the rhythmic squeak of bicycle wheels needing oil. Inside, sunlight continued its slow migration across empty floors ready to hold furniture, to absorb conversation, to witness the unfolding of days both ordinary and profound.

"Our fresh start," Casey echoed, testing the phrase against the hollow spaces of the house, the words seeming to absorb into bare walls that would soon hold photographs and memories yet to be created. For the first time since fire had consumed her past, she allowed herself to truly consider the future—not just surviving day to day but building something new, reclaiming pieces of herself long buried beneath grief and fear.

Behind her, Kirk pressed a kiss to her temple, his vigilance momentarily suspended as he too embraced the possibility contained in empty rooms and fresh paint. Tomorrow would bring moving trucks and security installations, locks to reinforce and blinds to hang. But today, in this moment, they stood together in sunlight, keys warm in Casey's palm, the house around them waiting to become home.

The living room had transformed into an obstacle course of cardboard boxes and bubble wrap, furniture in various states of assembly creating an archipelago of domestic intent. Afternoon had faded into evening, the windows now reflecting their interior activities rather than revealing the darkening street outside. Kirk knelt by the front window, screwdriver gripped in one hand as he secured a motion sensor to the frame, his movements precise and methodical. Across the room, Casey unpacked glassware wrapped in newspaper, each piece emerging like an archaeological find from layers of protective covering.

"That's the third sensor on this window alone," Casey observed, placing a wineglass on the half-assembled bookshelf beside her. The shelf stood as an island of order amid the chaos of their moving process, its surface already bearing the few framed photographs that had been with them at the cabin that weekend, spared from the fire by mere coincidence of timing.

Kirk tested the sensor's connection to his phone app before answering. "Different trigger thresholds," he explained, eyes fixed on the device as he calibrated its settings. "This one detects glass breakage. The one above is motion. The one on the sill is contact." He didn't add what they both knew—that redundancy had become their watchword, each backup system a thin additional layer of protection against Layla's determined intrusions.

Casey nodded, unwilling to challenge the necessity of these measures despite the fortress-like atmosphere they created. The insurance settlement had been generous, the arson determination expediting their claim, providing funds for both replacing necessities and installing security far beyond what most homes required. She crossed to the bookshelf, carefully placing a frame containing a photograph of her father—one of the few that had been with her at work that day, preserved in her desk drawer while every other family image burned.

"He would have liked this house," she said softly, arranging the photograph so her father's gentle smile seemed directed toward the room rather than the camera. "Solid craftsmanship. Good bones, as he would say."

Kirk glanced up, his expression softening as he watched her small ritual of placement. "He'd approve of the neighborhood too. Established. Quiet."

Their eyes met briefly across the room, mutual recognition passing between them—this shared act of imagining approval from a man now gone, this attempt to carry forward his memory into spaces he would never see. Casey felt the familiar constriction in her throat, the grief that still ambushed her at unexpected moments despite the months since his passing.

Her attention turned to a medium-sized box positioned carefully apart from the others, its sides unmarked by moving company logos or hastily scrawled content descriptions. Instead, a single word had been written in careful block letters across its top: "SALVAGED." She approached it with unconscious reverence, her movements slowing as if the box contained something volatile rather than the few remnants of her previous life.

Kirk continued his installation work, but she felt his awareness shift toward her, his peripheral vision tracking her progress toward the box that had remained sealed since the fire department had delivered it to them three days after the blaze. The firefighters had recovered what little they could from the ruins once the embers had cooled enough for safe entry—a gesture of kindness from men who had witnessed too many such losses to harbor illusions about what mattered most.

Casey's fingers trembled slightly as she broke the tape seal, the sound unnaturally loud in the quiet room. The box's cardboard sides fell open to reveal contents nestled in protective padding provided by the fire department's victim services unit. She lifted out the items one by one, each a miracle of partial preservation amid total destruction.

Her father's pocket watch emerged first, its gold case blackened along one edge but the glass face somehow intact, hands frozen at 2:17—the likely moment when heat had finally overwhelmed its ancient mechanism. Next came a charred photo album, its edges crisped to carbon but its center pages paradoxically preserved, held tight enough in the album's embrace that oxygen hadn't reached them to feed the flames. A small jewelry box yielded her mother's wedding ring and a silver locket, both tarnished by smoke but structurally whole.

"They found these in the ruins of my bedroom," Casey said, her voice barely above a whisper as she laid each item on the coffee table with ceremonial care. "The watch was in the nightstand drawer. The album and jewelry box must have fallen between the wall and dresser." Such arbitrary salvation—objects preserved by chance positioning, by quirks of airflow and structural collapse, while irreplaceable photographs and letters had vanished completely into ash.

The final item emerged from the deepest layer of padding: a ceramic mug, white with blue hand-painted flowers, miraculously unbroken though smoke-stained along its rim. Casey's hands began to shake in earnest as she cradled it, memories flooding back with physical force. Her father had painted it in occupational therapy after his first significant cognitive decline, the flowers childlike in execution but created with fierce concentration over several sessions, his gift to her on her last birthday before his death.

"I can't believe this survived," she whispered, fingers tracing the irregular blue petals with their uneven edges. "Everything else from that cabinet was shattered. The investigators found melted glass everywhere. But somehow this..."

Her voice broke, the sentence left unfinished as emotion overtook her capacity for speech. The mug blurred before her eyes, tears distorting its simple design into wavering impressions of her father's final creative effort. The trembling in her hands intensified until she feared she might drop this one preserved treasure, this single tangible connection to the man she had lost twice—first to dementia's slow erosion, then to death's finality.

Kirk crossed the room in four long strides, security installation temporarily abandoned. He knelt beside her, his larger hands enveloping hers around the mug, steadying her grip with gentle pressure.

"We're going to be okay," he said, voice low and certain against her ear. Not empty reassurance but statement of intent, of determination that had carried them through loss and threat and rebuilding. His thumbs traced small circles against her wrists, finding the rapid pulse and working to calm it through touch alone.

The doorbell's electronic chime shattered their moment of connection, its cheerful three-note sequence incongruously bright against the emotional weight that had settled over them. Both froze in instinctive response, bodies tensing as if the sound carried physical threat. Kirk's hands tightened fractionally around Casey's before releasing, rising from his crouch in a single fluid movement that placed his body between her and the entranceway.

"Stay here," he murmured, the transition from comforting partner to protective sentinel occurring in the space of a heartbeat. His hand moved unconsciously toward his waistband where his concealed weapon rested —a recent addition he'd obtained after extensive discussion and licensing processes, another adaptation to their altered reality.

Casey set the mug carefully on the table beside the other salvaged items, her body coiled with tension as she watched Kirk approach the door with measured steps. He moved along the wall rather than directly to the entrance, positioning himself to see through the sidelight window without being immediately visible from outside. His posture had changed completely—civilian ease replaced by the marine's calculated readiness, shoulders squared, weight balanced for immediate response.

Through the window, a delivery truck became visible at the curb, its logo matching the appliance company they'd ordered from the previous week. Kirk's shoulders relaxed incrementally, though his approach to the door remained cautious. He checked the security app on his phone, confirming the front camera's view before finally opening the door to reveal two uniformed delivery men with clipboards.

"Manning residence? We've got your refrigerator," the older man said, consulting his paperwork with bored efficiency.

Relief washed through Casey in a physical wave, her knees weakening slightly as tension released its grip. Such an ordinary moment—a delivery, a new appliance, the mundane mechanics of establishing a household—transformed into heightened drama by what they had endured. She watched as Kirk signed for the delivery, his conversation with the men perfectly normal despite the hand that had been ready to draw a weapon moments earlier.

The evening continued with similar contrasts—boxes unpacked with domestic efficiency while Kirk checked each lock three times before bedtime; curtains hung with aesthetic consideration for how they'd look from inside while also ensuring they revealed nothing to potential observers outside; Casey flinching at the sound of a car backfiring down the street while arranging books alphabetically on newly assembled shelves.

Small rituals of normalcy performed against a backdrop of hypervigilance—their new normal, their continuing adaptation to a world where threat had once materialized in flame and might again wear Layla's calculating smile. Yet amid these necessary precautions, Casey found unexpected moments of peace—Kirk's hand brushing hers as they arranged kitchen utensils in drawers, the satisfaction of seeing her father's photograph on a shelf that would soon hold new books, the promise contained in empty spaces gradually filling with evidence of their shared life.

The flames reached for her through darkness, hungry fingers of orange and gold stretching across what had once been her bedroom ceiling. Casey couldn't move, her limbs leaden as fire consumed photographs, books, the quilt her grandmother had made—each item disappearing in a bright burst of impossible heat. Smoke filled her lungs despite her desperate attempts to hold her breath, and somewhere beyond the crackling destruction, she heard laughter—high, feminine, satisfied. She tried to scream but produced only a strangled gasp as she jerked upright in bed, the nightmare shattering around her like glass.

For several disorienting seconds, Casey couldn't place herself in time or space. The unfamiliar shadows of the new bedroom offered no immediate reassurance, the month they'd spent in this house not yet sufficient to make its contours familiar in darkness. Her nightshirt clung to her back, damp with sweat that chilled rapidly in the air-conditioned room. Her heart hammered against her ribs with such force she imagined it visible through skin and fabric, a frantic morse code of lingering terror.

"Casey." Kirk's voice came from beside her, quiet but instantly grounding. Not a question, just her name, an anchor thrown into her storm of panic.

She fumbled for the bedside lamp, fingers trembling so violently that the simple task became a challenge. Light finally spilled across rumpled sheets, illuminating their bedroom with its half-unpacked moving boxes still stacked in one corner, the framed photographs they'd positioned carefully on the dresser, the security panel glowing green beside the door. Reality reasserted itself in these concrete details, pushing back the vivid imagery of her dream.

Kirk was already sitting up beside her, his back against the headboard, eyes shadowed with concern. He wore only boxers, his chest bare in the lamp's glow, muscles defined by the angled light. His hair stood in sleep-mussed spikes, but his eyes carried the alert awareness that told her he hadn't been sleeping when her nightmare woke her.

"The fire again?" he asked, voice gentle with understanding.

Casey nodded, still struggling to regulate her breathing. Her lungs seemed unable to draw sufficient oxygen, each inhalation shallow and unsatisfying, as if smoke still filled them. She pressed her palms against her thighs, focusing on the solid feel of muscle and bone beneath her hands, the tactile reality of her own living body.

"Wait here," Kirk said, sliding from bed in a single fluid movement.

He returned moments later with a glass of water, condensation beading on its surface in the room's cool air. Casey accepted it with both hands, still trembling slightly as she raised it to her lips. The water was cold enough to track its progress down her throat and into her stomach, the sensation helping to further distance her from the dream's lingering heat.

Kirk sat on the edge of the bed, the mattress dipping slightly beneath his weight. In the month since they'd moved in, they'd established new routines, created fresh patterns of shared existence—but these nighttime inter-ruptions remained a constant, her subconscious refusing to release the trauma it had witnessed.

"I'm sorry," Kirk said, the words emerging with obvious difficulty, his jaw tightening around them as if they carried physical weight. "This is all because of me."

He stared at his hands, palms up on his thighs, as if reading some indictment written there in invisible ink. His shoulders curved forward slightly, the only concession to the guilt he carried but rarely verbalized. In the lamp's gentle illumination, Casey could see the weariness etched around his eyes, the vigilance that never fully abated even in their most intimate moments.

"No," Casey said, setting the water glass on the night-stand with deliberate care. "This is because of Layla."

She reached for his hand, drawing it into her lap where her fingers traced the calluses that mapped his work—rough patches along his palm, thickened skin at the base of each finger. Hands that built things, that protected, that held her through nightmares and celebrated small victories. Hands that had nothing to do with Layla's calculated malice.

"You didn't create her," Casey continued, her voice stronger now as conviction pushed aside the remnants of terror. "You didn't make her obsessive or dangerous. You didn't set fire to our home."

Kirk's fingers curled around hers, the gentle pressure at odds with the capability for violence these same hands possessed. "I brought her into your orbit," he countered, the familiar argument they'd had in various forms since Layla first appeared. "If we hadn't met, if I hadn't fallen in love with you, she would never have targeted you. Your home would still be standing. You wouldn't wake up screaming three nights a week."

The guilt in his voice scraped against Casey's heart, its rawness exposing the depth of responsibility he shouldered. She shifted closer, her knee pressing against his thigh, physical contact reinforcing emotional connection.

"If we hadn't met," she said carefully, each word weighted with consideration, "I would still be drowning in grief. Alone in that house with nothing but memories and regrets." Her free hand rose to his face, fingers tracing the stubble along his jaw, the slight crease between his brows, the tension held in his temples. "I don't regret us. Not for a second."

His eyes finally met hers, amber depths troubled beneath the surface calm he maintained for her benefit. "You've lost so much because of me."

"I've gained more," Casey insisted, her palm settling against his cheek. "I've gained you. Us. A future beyond just surviving day to day."

She leaned forward to press her forehead against his, their breath mingling in the narrow space between them. Outside, a distant siren wailed briefly before fading into night sounds—

a dog barking several houses away, the soft mechanical hum of the security system, wind stirring tree branches against the bedroom window. Inside, the lamp cast their shadows against the wall, merged into a single silhouette of connection.

"I don't regret us," she repeated, the words a covenant between them. "Not the joy, not the pain, not even the fear. All of it has been worth finding you."

Kirk's arms encircled her, drawing her against his chest where she could feel his heartbeat, steadier than her own but quickened by emotion. His chin rested atop her head, his breath stirring her hair with warm regularity. For long moments they remained thus entwined, the nightmare's grip loosening in the face of this more immediate reality.

"Try to sleep," Kirk murmured eventually, easing her back against the pillows with gentle hands. He reached to switch off the lamp, returning the room to darkness relieved only by the soft green glow of security monitors and the faint illumination filtering through curtains from streetlights outside.

Casey settled against him, her body curving to fit the spaces of his, her head finding its accustomed place on his shoulder. Kirk's hand moved in slow, soothing circles across her back, touch communicating what words sometimes couldn't—protection, care, commitment beyond circumstance.

She knew without asking that he would remain awake long after sleep reclaimed her, his body a sentinel beside hers, eyes open in darkness as he listened for sounds that didn't belong, maintained vigilance against threats both real and imagined. This was the price of their shared life now—his hypervigilance, her nightmares, the security measures that transformed home into fortress. But beneath these adaptations to threat, beyond the precautions and protocols, remained the essential truth: they had chosen each other, would continue choosing each other through whatever came next.

Sleep approached gradually, her body surrendering by increments to exhaustion as Kirk's rhythmic breathing provided counterpoint to the night's ambient sounds. His arms remained around her, a bulwark against both physical harm and the darker threats that lurked in her subconscious, ready to emerge in dreams. Her last conscious thought before drifting off was simple gratitude—not for safety, which remained uncertain, but for his presence beside her in darkness, constant despite everything they had endured.

Chapter 36

Malone's hands moved with practiced efficiency, spreading photographs and documents across the kitchen table in a precise arrangement that suggested both methodical thinking and frequent repetition. He was a compact man in his late fifties, with close-cropped salt-and-pepper hair and the watchful eyes of someone who had spent decades observing human behavior at its worst. His clothing—khaki pants and a navy button-down rolled at the sleeves—seemed deliberately forgettable, the uniform of a man whose profession required him to blend into backgrounds rather than stand out in foregrounds.

"I've organized everything chronologically," he explained, his voice carrying the slight rasp of a former smoker. "Starting with the initial harassment at your previous residence, through the cemetery desecrations, culminating in the arson." His finger tapped each section as he named it, the timeline stretching across their kitchen table like a roadmap of escalating malice.

Casey leaned forward, eyes tracking the evidence of what they'd lived through these past months. Seeing it laid out with such clinical precision felt surreal—their personal nightmare transformed into exhibits and evidence markers, their terror reduced to timestamps and documentation codes. Kirk stood behind her chair, one hand resting on her shoulder, the other curled into a fist at his side. She could feel the tension radiating from him, controlled but potent, like heat from banked coals.

"The restraining order petition includes forty-seven documented violations of the temporary order," Malone continued, sliding forward a thick sheaf of paperwork bound with metal clips. "Incidents where she approached within the prohibited distance, attempts at contact, surveillance confirmed through photographic evidence." He tapped a sequence of images showing Layla's distinctive blonde hair and calculated movements near locations Casey and Kirk frequented—their former neighborhood, Casey's workplace, the community center where they'd attended support group meetings.

"Most of these incidents weren't actionable individually," Malone acknowledged, his tone suggesting professional frustration with legal limitations. "But collectively, they establish a pattern that no judge can reasonably ignore. Particularly when combined with the arson evidence."

He pulled forward another document, this one bearing official letterhead from the fire investigation unit. "The accelerant analysis matched traces found at the scene to purchases Layla made at a hardware store in Riverdale." A security camera image showed Layla at a checkout counter, her expression neutral as she paid for what appeared to be ordinary household items.

"She used cash, wore a hat, but the facial recognition is definitive. This alone would be enough for criminal charges, if the district attorney's office would move on it."

Kirk's hand tightened on Casey's shoulder, his frustration with the legal system's pace palpable in that small gesture. Casey reached up to cover his hand with hers, a silent acknowledgment of shared impatience.

"What's the timeline on the permanent restraining order?" Kirk asked, his voice controlled but edged with the urgency they both felt.

Malone consulted a calendar on his tablet. "The hearing is scheduled for Thursday morning. Given the evidence package we've submitted and the fire marshal's testimony, approval is virtually guaranteed. Once issued, violation would mean immediate arrest."

"And until then?" The question hung between them, weighted with the reality of four more days of uncertainty, of watching shadows and flinching at unexpected sounds.

"Be vigilant. Document everything." Malone's advice was familiar, the same counsel they'd been following for months, but his eyes carried additional meaning as they briefly met Kirk's. An unspoken conversation seemed to pass between the two men—former military recognizing each other through bearing and approach, acknowledging realities beyond what civilian language could comfortably express.

Casey's attention drifted to a particular photograph in the array spread before them. Unlike the others, which had been taken by Malone during his investigation, this image had been captured by a neighborhood security camera the night of the fire.

Layla stood across the street from Casey's burning home, flames reflected in the lenses of oversized sunglasses despite the late hour, her blonde hair distinctive even in the grainy surveillance footage.

The image captured exactly what Casey remembered from that night—not panic or shock but satisfaction, a small smile playing at the corners of Layla's mouth as she watched destruction consume what Casey had loved.

"She enjoyed it," Casey said softly, one finger hovering above the photograph without touching its surface. "Not just the damage, but knowing what it would do to us. Knowing what I'd lost."

Malone nodded, his expression suggesting this observation aligned with his professional assessment. "The profile fits classic obsessive behavior with narcissistic features. The destruction wasn't just about harming you—it was about asserting control, proving her power."

He gathered several documents into a discrete pile. "Which is why the restraining order alone won't resolve this. It's a necessary legal step, but not a guaranteed end to the situation."

Kirk moved from behind Casey's chair to pace the kitchen's perimeter, his body too charged with tension to remain stationary. "We've upgraded security at every access point," he said, gesturing toward the reinforced door frames, the sensors visible above windows, the cameras discreetly positioned at strategic angles. "Motion detection, glass break sensors, facial recognition alerts."

Malone nodded approval. "Good. Keep your routines unpredictable. Vary your routes, arrival times, regular activities. She's watching for patterns she can exploit."

Casey studied the timeline Malone had constructed, noting how Layla's actions had escalated in both frequency and severity over time. From the dead birds and surveillance to property damage, from desecrated graves to arson—each escalation followed periods of apparent inactivity. "She's patient," Casey observed. "She plans carefully, waits for opportunities."

"Precisely why your own vigilance can't lapse," Malone confirmed, beginning to gather the materials with the same efficiency with which he'd arranged them. "The restraining order will help, but your awareness remains your best protection." He slid the compiled evidence into a leather portfolio, the action closing their informal briefing with understated finality.

As he prepared to leave, Malone paused at the door, his usual professional detachment softening slightly. "You've done everything right so far," he said, eyes moving between them. "The security measures, the documentation, maintaining your routines while taking precautions. Keep it that way."

The implicit message beneath his words was clear enough —don't give Layla any advantage through carelessness or complacency, don't provide any opening she could exploit either physically or legally.

The door closed behind him with a solid thunk, followed by the multiple locks engaging automatically in their programmed sequence—deadbolt, security bar, electronic confirmation chime from the alarm panel.

Kirk returned to the table, standing beside Casey's chair as they both stared at the empty space where evidence of their ordeal had been spread moments before. His hand came to rest on her shoulder again, thumb tracing small circles against the tense muscle at the base of her neck.

"Thursday," he said, the single word carrying layers of meaning—anticipation, determination, the promise of one more tool in their ongoing battle for safety and normalcy.

Casey nodded, rising from her chair to move into the living room where security measures had been integrated into what otherwise appeared as ordinary domestic space.

Cameras disguised as smoke detectors, sensors concealed within decorative moldings, reinforced windows behind stylish curtains—their home transformed into fortress without sacrificing the appearance of normalcy they both craved.

The baseball bat propped discreetly beside the front door caught her attention—a simple wooden Louisville Slugger that had been Kirk's in high school, now positioned for quick access rather than nostalgia. Beside it stood an umbrella stand containing not just rain protection but a heavy tactical flashlight, its weight and construction making it an effective defensive tool if necessary.

"We're going to get through this," Casey said, turning to find Kirk watching her from the kitchen doorway, his posture still carrying the tension of their meeting with Malone. She crossed to him, hands rising to frame his face, thumbs smoothing the worry lines that had deepened around his eyes in recent months. "Thursday is just four days away."

Kirk's hands settled at her waist, drawing her closer until their foreheads touched, breath mingling in the narrow space between them. "Four days," he echoed, the words both commitment and countdown.

Outside, a car door slammed somewhere down the street, and Casey felt the momentary tensing of Kirk's body, the instinctive alertness that never fully abated even in their most intimate moments.

Their world had narrowed to this constant vigilance, this perpetual readiness for threat—but as Casey's arms encircled Kirk's waist, she reminded herself that even this heightened state wasn't permanent. Thursday would come. The restraining order would be issued. One step at a time, they would reclaim normal life from the shadow Layla had cast across it.

Chapter 37

Laughter rippled through the living room, the sound remarkable not for its volume but for its very existence in a space that had known primarily tension since they'd moved in six weeks ago. Warm light from strategically placed lamps created pools of amber illumination, transforming their once-sparse furniture arrangement into an inviting gathering place now filled with friends and neighbors. Wine glasses clinked, conversation flowed in comfortable currents, and Casey moved through it all with a lightness in her step that felt both foreign and familiar—a remembered sensation from before Layla had entered their lives.

The housewarming party had been Jen's idea—"Claim the space, make it yours with witnesses," she'd insisted with the gentle forcefulness that characterized her approach to both friendship and her role as Casey's former grief support group facilitator. Now Jen sat on the newly acquired sectional sofa, gesturing animatedly as she described her daughter's latest school project to Kirk's contracting client, the two finding unexpected common ground in children's science fair experiences.

Officer Rodriguez stood near the fireplace, his uniform

exchanged for dark jeans and a charcoal button-down that softened his usual official presence. He held a glass of the non-alcoholic cider Casey had thoughtfully provided, his conversation with Kirk punctuated by occasional surveying glances around the room—a habit Casey recognized from Kirk's own vigilant behavior, the unconscious assessment of environment that came with their respective professions.

Mrs. Winters, their seventy-something neighbor from two doors down, had arrived first and would undoubtedly leave last, her social enthusiasm matched only by her generosity. The massive casserole dish she'd contributed to the evening's spread had been placed in the center of the dining table, its contents already half-consumed and enthusiastically praised. She moved between conversation groups with grandmotherly ease, her gray curls bobbing as she ensured no one's plate or glass remained empty for long.

Casey paused in the kitchen doorway, momentarily overwhelmed by the scene before her. Just two months earlier, she had stood among the ashes of her family home, everything she owned reduced to cinders and memory. Now she surveyed a space transformed from empty rooms to realized vision—sage green walls with cream trim, built-in bookshelves Kirk had constructed with meticulous care, framed photographs depicting not just past memories but new ones they'd created in this house.

Flowers brightened every surface—arrangements from friends who couldn't attend, potted plants as house-warming gifts, a particularly spectacular orchid from her former workplace. Their fragrance mingled with the savory notes from the dining table's spread, creating an atmosphere of domestic celebration that felt almost defiant against the background knowledge that Layla's threat, while legally restrained, had not disappeared entirely.

"Earth to Casey," Jen teased, suddenly beside her with

an empty wine glass extended for refilling. "You went somewhere else for a minute there."

Casey smiled, accepting the glass. "Just taking it all in. It feels..."

"Normal?" Jen suggested, her expression knowing beneath stylishly asymmetrical bangs.

"Yes," Casey acknowledged, the simple word carrying layers of significance. Normal—the state they'd been fighting to reclaim through security systems and legal proceedings, through nightmares and hypervigilance and deliberately placing furniture to allow clear sightlines to exits.

Jen's gaze softened as she studied her friend's face. "Tell me a completely ridiculous story about one of these guests," she challenged, nodding toward the living room. "Something that has nothing to do with restraining orders or security cameras or anything serious."

Casey's eyes swept the gathering, landing on Mrs. Winters who was enthusiastically describing something to Rodriguez's increasingly wide-eyed expression. "Mrs. Winters used to be a competitive ballroom dancer," she offered, the random fact emerging from a welcome conversation they'd had over the fence last week. "She and her husband won regional championships three years running in the seventies. She still has all her costumes in vacuum-sealed bags in her attic."

"Perfect," Jen nodded approval. "Now imagine her in sequins doing the tango."

The mental image struck Casey with unexpected force —dignified Mrs. Winters with her sensible shoes and cardigan sweaters transformed into a whirling, glittering figure on a dance floor. Laughter bubbled up from some long-dormant place inside her, emerging in a bright sound that momentarily paused conversation in the living room.

Kirk looked up from across the room, his eyes finding

hers with unerring accuracy despite the gathered bodies between them. Something passed between them in that glance—recognition, wonder, gratitude for this moment of unguarded joy. His smile transformed his features, erasing the vigilant furrows that had become so familiar Casey sometimes forgot they hadn't always been there.

The evening progressed with the comfortable rhythm of successful gatherings everywhere—conversation groups forming and dissolving, plates being refilled, compliments exchanged about the home's transformation. As the hour grew later, guests began the gradual process of departure —gathering purses and jackets, exchanging final comments and thanks, promising future get-togethers with varying degrees of sincerity.

As Mrs. Winters collected her now-empty casserole dish with obvious satisfaction at its popular reception, Officer Rodriguez approached Casey and Kirk near the front door, his expression shifting to something more professional despite his casual attire.

"I wanted to update you before heading out," he said, voice lowered slightly though most remaining guests were engaged in goodbye conversations across the room. "The restraining order is being properly monitored. We have patrol cars making regular passes by her residence, and she appears to be complying with the terms."

Casey nodded, relief mingling with the persistent undercurrent of caution that colored all discussions of Layla. The permanent restraining order had been granted ten days ago, its terms even more comprehensive than the temporary version—increased exclusion zones, explicit prohibitions against any form of contact, monitoring requirements that included regular check-ins with a court-appointed officer.

"We're keeping an eye out," Rodriguez continued, his gaze steady and reassuring. "The arson investigation is still active, and the DA is reviewing the case. There's still a strong possibility of criminal charges."

Kirk's hand found the small of Casey's back, a gesture both protective and grounding. "We appreciate everything you've done," he said, extending his other hand to Rodriguez in a handshake that carried more meaning than the simple social ritual would suggest.

After the final guest departed and the door closed behind Mrs. Winters' cheerful promise of cinnamon rolls tomorrow morning, Casey and Kirk stood in momentary silence amid the evidence of sociability—empty glasses on side tables, napkins crumpled beside plates, the pleasant disorder of a space that had been thoroughly enjoyed.

"Come outside with me?" Casey suggested, already moving toward the back door, retrieving two clean wine glasses from the kitchen as she passed.

The back porch extended from the kitchen door, its wooden planks still carrying the scent of the sealant Kirk had applied last weekend. They had strung fairy lights along the railings and overhead beams, creating a gentle illumination that defined their small outdoor sanctuary without penetrating the darkness of the yard beyond. The night air carried a hint of autumn's approach, cool enough to raise goosebumps on Casey's bare arms but not uncomfortable.

Kirk followed with an open bottle of red wine, filling both glasses as they settled into the Adirondack chairs positioned to face their small backyard. Beyond the porch's golden glow, the yard stretched in deepening shadows to the fence line where additional security lights stood ready to activate at any unexpected movement.

"This felt good," Casey admitted, swirling the wine in her glass, watching how it caught the light from above. "Having people here. Laughing. Acting like normal people with a normal house."

Kirk nodded, his free hand reaching across the space between their chairs to find hers. Their fingers interlaced with practiced ease, the contact both casual and essential—a connection maintained through nightmare and crisis, through rebuilding and recovery.

"Like we're taking our lives back," he said, giving voice to the sensation that had been building throughout the evening. Not just occupying space or going through motions, but actively reclaiming territory that fear had annexed—emotional, physical, psychological real estate they were determined to inhabit fully again.

Casey leaned her head back, looking up at the fairy lights strung in gentle arcs above them, their warm glow creating a ceiling of soft illumination between their porch and the night sky beyond. "I forgot I could laugh like that," she said softly. "It surprised me."

"It was beautiful," Kirk replied, his voice carrying a reverence usually reserved for natural wonders or artistic masterpieces. His thumb traced gentle arcs across her knuckles, the simple contact grounding them both in this moment of shared peace.

They sat in comfortable silence, sipping wine and listening to the night sounds beyond their illuminated sanctuary—distant traffic, an occasional dog barking, the subtle symphony of insect life undisturbed by human drama. Ordinary sounds, unremarkable except in contrast to the hypervigilant state that had characterized so many of their evenings.

"The restraining order is helping," Casey acknowledged after several minutes of quiet communion. "I don't jump at every sound anymore. I'm not constantly looking over my shoulder."

Kirk nodded, though his posture suggested he hadn't yet granted himself the same latitude. Even now, in this moment of relative relaxation, his eyes continued their periodic assessment of the yard's perimeter, tracking the motion of branches in the gentle breeze, noting the precise location of security lights positioned at strategic intervals.

"One day at a time," he said, raising his glass in a small toast that encompassed their journey so far and the uncertain path still ahead. "One moment of normal at a time."

Casey clinked her glass against his, the crystalline sound bright against the night's soft background murmur. Beyond their circle of light, the yard remained dark, the world beyond their fence unknown and unpredictable. But here, in this small illuminated space they had created together, existed proof of what they were reclaiming step by step—not just a house but a home, not just survival but living, not just caution but occasional, precious joy.

Kirk's eyes continued their vigilant survey of shadows beyond their porch light, his body relaxed but alert, the marine's readiness never fully abandoned. But his hand remained warm in Casey's grasp, his presence beside her as steady as his heartbeat, as reliable as his promise that they would face whatever came next together. The fairy lights reflected in their wine glasses, transforming ordinary merlot into something that sparkled with possibility, with future rather than just present—a small miracle of light against darkness that seemed, in this moment, entirely sufficient.

Chapter 38

Morning light streamed through the kitchen windows, painting golden rectangles across the new tile backsplash. Casey moved with practiced ease between refrigerator and stove, the rhythm of their shared breakfast routine now familiar after six weeks in the new house. Kirk watched her from the doorway, coffee mug cradled in his palms, struck by how ordinary—how wonderfully, blessedly ordinary— their mornings had become in the absence of new threats from Layla.

"Pancakes are almost ready," Casey said without turning, somehow sensing his presence behind her. Her hair was gathered in a loose ponytail, exposing the nape of her neck where a single freckle had become a particular fascination of Kirk's in recent weeks. "There's more coffee in the pot."

Kirk crossed to her, pressing a kiss against that perfect freckle before refilling his mug. The kitchen smelled of coffee and maple syrup, of normalcy reclaimed inch by precious inch over the past month. No new photographs had appeared in their mailbox, no dead animals on their doorstep, no mysterious cars idling at the street corner.

The restraining order had held firm, its legal boundaries apparently respected—for now, at least.

"I need to meet with a client this morning," Kirk said, the practiced lie sliding past his lips with only the slightest prickle of guilt at its edges. "Shouldn't take more than a couple hours. Renovation consultation for a kitchen remodel on Maple Street."

Casey nodded, sliding a perfectly browned pancake onto a waiting plate. "Mrs. Winters asked if we'd join her for dinner tomorrow," she said, moving on to pour another circle of batter into the sizzling pan. "I told her probably, but I'd confirm with you first."

Kirk nodded, sipping his coffee to hide the edge of excitement that had been building in his chest for weeks now. With each day of peace, with each night undisturbed by security alarms or nightmares, the plan forming in his mind had gained substance and certainty. Today was merely the next step—transforming intention into tangible reality.

After breakfast, Kirk locked the house with practiced attention to security protocols that had become automatic rather than anxious. Three weeks without incident had softened their vigilance only marginally—habits of survival now integrated into their daily existence rather than existing as constant, conscious burden. He checked his phone once more before sliding it into his pocket, ensuring the ringer was silenced to prevent Casey calling while he was at the jeweler's.

His truck carried him through neighborhoods just beginning to show autumn's first tentative claims—scattered yellow leaves on still-green lawns, pumpkins appearing on porches, school buses making their morning rounds. Ordinary scenes that now registered as precious after months when every shadow had contained potential threat, every unexpected sound a possible herald of Layla's return.

The jewelry store occupied a corner in the town's historic district, its modest exterior belying the expertise Kirk had researched exhaustively online. Bell chimes announced his entrance, the sound startlingly bright in the hushed interior where glass cases gleamed beneath carefully positioned lighting. The space smelled faintly of leather and metal polish, an atmosphere of understated luxury that made Kirk acutely conscious of his work boots and casual clothing.

"Mr. Manning?" A man emerged from the back room, his white hair immaculately styled, his hands bearing the subtle calluses of decades working with delicate tools. "I'm Howard. We spoke on the phone. You brought family pieces to incorporate?"

Kirk nodded, reaching into his jacket pocket where a small velvet pouch had rested against his heart during the drive. His hands, usually so steady when framing houses or installing cabinetry, trembled slightly as he placed the pouch on the glass countertop.

"My grandmother's ring and earrings," he explained, watching as Howard carefully emptied the pouch's contents onto a black velvet display pad. The jewelry was modest by contemporary standards—a small diamond solitaire engagement ring and matching stud earrings that had adorned his grandmother for fifty-seven years of marriage. "And this—" He produced a second, smaller pouch from his other pocket. "This belonged to Casey's mother. Her Aunt gave it to me after her father's funeral. Said Casey never wore it, but she thought she might want it someday."

The jeweler's experienced fingers extracted a delicate pendant from the second pouch, a small sapphire surrounded by seed pearls on a fragile gold chain. "Beautiful piece," Howard murmured, examining the stone under a jeweler's loupe that materialized from his pocket. "Early 1900s, I'd guess. The sapphire has excellent color, and these pearls are natural, not cultured."

Kirk felt a warmth in his chest, an uncomfortable heat that he recognized as the culmination of months of planning. "I want to combine them," he said, indicating the gathered stones. "Her mother's sapphire as the center, my grandmother's diamonds surrounding it. Something that brings our families together."

Howard nodded, his expression softening beneath professional reserve. "A beautiful sentiment," he said, arranging the pieces side by side on the velvet. "We could create a halo design with the diamonds around the sapphire. The proportions would work well together." His fingers sketched possibilities in the air above the stones. "The gold from all pieces could be melted down for the new setting, maintaining the material connection to both families."

For the next hour, Kirk examined ring designs spread before him in leather-bound portfolios, discussing settings and band widths and practical considerations for a woman whose hands worked with cameras and darkroom chemicals. Howard sketched preliminary designs, erasing and refining as Kirk described Casey's preferences and style— simple but not plain, distinctive without being flashy, something that would look as right paired with her practical overalls as with a dress for rare formal occasions.

"You're combining more than just jewelry," Howard observed, his hands carefully returning the family stones to their protective pouches. "You're creating a physical representation of families united." He paused, eyes moving to the calendar displayed discreetly on the wall. "If we begin work immediately, we could have this ready within three weeks. Would that align with your plans?"

Kirk nodded, the timeline perfect for what he had in

mind. "There's a spot near the lake where we had our first real conversation," he explained, surprising himself with the personal detail offered to this near-stranger. "I thought, end of October, when the leaves have turned..."

He trailed off, suddenly self-conscious, but Howard merely nodded with the understanding of someone who had witnessed countless similar plans. "A perfect setting for a new beginning," the jeweler said, indicating where Kirk should sign the work order. "We'll call when it's ready for your approval."

The design consultation had taken longer than anticipated, and as Kirk climbed back into his truck, he realized he'd left his phone silenced for nearly two hours. His hand fumbled in his pocket, anxiety spiking as he imagined Casey trying to reach him during his absence, suspicion aroused by his uncharacteristic unavailability.

The screen revealed three missed calls and a text message that simply read: *Where are you? Everything ok? *

Kirk's thumb hovered over the call button, but he hesitated, aware that his voice might betray the nervous excitement coursing through him. Instead, he typed a response —*Sorry, consultation running long. Client talking my ear off. Heading home now.*—and hoped the simple explanation would suffice.

Traffic seemed deliberately designed to delay him, each red light an eternity as he calculated how to explain his extended absence without revealing his true purpose. The receipt from the jeweler had been carefully tucked into his wallet's most secure pocket, safely hidden alongside the preliminary sketch of Casey's ring. His mind raced ahead, imagining the moment when he would slide that ring onto her finger, when symbol would transform to covenant between them.

The house came into view at last, its sage green exterior and white trim a welcome sight after the morning's nervous errand. As Kirk pulled into the driveway, he noticed Casey's silhouette through the front window, moving about the living room with the graceful efficiency that characterized all her movements. He took a deep breath, composing his features into casual normalcy, tucking away the secret that now had form and substance and a timeline measuring the distance between intention and realization.

Casey stepped back from the newly hung curtains, assessing how the fabric's subtle pattern caught the afternoon light. The living room was gradually taking shape under her careful attention, each addition transforming generic space into something that felt uniquely theirs. After weeks of living with bare essentials and temporary solutions, the pleasure of deliberate design choices felt almost rebellious—a statement that they were here to stay, that they intended to build a life in this house regardless of what shadows might still lurk at its edges.

She moved to the collection of framed photographs spread across the coffee table, each one representing a piece of their combined histories rescued from time or fire or deliberate destruction. Her fingers traced the edge of a silver frame containing one of the few surviving pictures of her father—taken three years before his diagnosis, his face unlined by illness, eyes bright with the sharp intelligence dementia would later claim. He stood beside the porch swing he'd built, one hand resting on its chain, expression caught between pride and his characteristic humility.

Beside it lay a photograph of Kirk and Charlotte, their arms slung around each other's shoulders at what appeared to be a Fourth of July celebration. Charlotte's blonde hair was gathered in a messy bun atop her head, her smile radiating the warmth Kirk had described when speaking of his sister. The image had survived because Kirk kept it in his wallet, folded and creased but intact, carrying his sister with him long after her death. Casey had discovered it while doing laundry one day, had it professionally restored and framed as a gift that had left Kirk speechless with emotion.

Another photograph showed Casey's parents on their wedding day, her mother's delicate features suggesting where Casey had inherited her own. The image had been rescued from her father's military footlocker, which had been stored in the garage rather than the house proper—one of the few items that had survived the fire. The collection felt like a family altar of sorts, memory preserved in image, connection maintained across time and loss.

Casey arranged the frames on the built-in shelves Kirk had constructed along one wall, creating a visual narrative of their separate and now combined histories. The smell of fresh paint still lingered in the air, mingling with the scent of lemon oil she'd used on the wooden surfaces and the faint, pleasant smell of the fabric swatches spread across the floor where she'd been contemplating upholstery options for the window seat.

She hummed softly as she worked, an unconscious melody that rose and fell with her movements around the room. It was her mother's favorite song, though Casey only realized this when her father had mentioned it during one of his increasingly rare moments of clarity before his death. Now she found herself humming it often, especially when engaged in domestic tasks that connected her to the women in her family who had created homes before her.

The fabric swatches formed a palette of possibilities across the hardwood floor—deep blues and subtle greys, warm creams and occasional hints of the sage green that had become a signature color throughout their home. Casey knelt among them, arranging and rearranging combinations, imagining how each might transform the window seat from architectural feature to inviting nook. She had spent so many years focused solely on her father's care, then on mere survival, that this act of creation felt like reclaiming some essential part of herself long set aside.

The sound of Kirk's truck in the driveway interrupted her contemplation. Her fingers reached automatically for her phone, checking the time—nearly an hour since his vague text about a client consultation running long. Not unusually late for his line of work, yet something about his silence had triggered old watchfulness, habits of vigilance not fully abandoned despite weeks without incident.

Kirk entered through the front door, his practiced gaze sweeping the room in the automatic assessment they both still performed. His expression shifted from vigilant to appreciative as he took in the changes Casey had made during his absence.

"This looks amazing," he said, crossing to where she knelt among fabric swatches. His hand settled briefly on her shoulder, a casual intimacy that still sent warmth through her despite its familiarity. "You've been busy."

Casey rose to her feet, the anxious edge that had accompanied his absence dissolving in the solid reality of his presence. "Tour?" she offered, her hand finding his with unconscious ease.

She led him through the living room, pointing out the newly arranged photographs, the curtains she'd hung herself, the throw pillows she'd selected for the sofa. "I was thinking indigo for the window seat cushion," she explained, indicating the fabric swatches. "With these cream pillows as accents. It would pick up the blue in the landscape painting you liked."

Kirk's attention moved between the options she indicated, his expression suggesting genuine interest tinged with something she couldn't quite identify—a distraction that flickered at the edges of his focus. His fingers played absently with the edge of his wallet in his back pocket, a nervous gesture she'd never observed before.

"The blue would be perfect," he agreed, his other hand squeezing hers with reassuring pressure. "Makes me think of the lake in autumn."

Casey led him toward the dining room, where she'd arranged a collection of mismatched china on the hutch they'd found at an estate sale three weeks prior. "I thought we could use these for special occasions," she explained, running her finger along the edge of a blue-patterned plate. "Nothing too formal, but something that feels more intentional than everyday dishes."

Kirk nodded, his face softening in that particular way that told her he was thinking beyond the immediate moment, imagining future gatherings around their table. "Charlotte would have loved this," he said quietly, his finger tracing the pattern on a smaller dessert plate. "She was always collecting odd pieces of china at thrift stores. Said every plate had a story."

The mention of Charlotte created a moment of shared remembrance, the bittersweet acknowledgment of absence amid their creating of home. Casey leaned into his side, her head resting briefly against his shoulder in silent understanding.

"Oh, I almost forgot," she said, straightening to lead him toward the small room they'd designated as a shared office space. "The desk we ordered arrived while you were out. The delivery guys set it up, but I wanted your opinion on the placement before I arranged all the drawers."

As Casey moved ahead of him into the office, Kirk seized the moment of separation to extract the jeweler's receipt from his wallet, folding it into a tiny square before slipping it into the pocket of his jeans. The paper seemed to burn against his thigh, tangible evidence of his secret mission, of the future he was planning while Casey worked to anchor them in the present.

The desk sat positioned beneath the room's north-facing window, its dark wood gleaming in the natural light. "I was thinking your drafting supplies along this side," Casey was saying, her hands indicating various compartments. "And maybe the file organizer here. What do you think?"

Kirk crossed to stand beside her, one arm circling her waist as they contemplated the newest addition to their shared space. "It's perfect," he said, meaning far more than the furniture or its placement—meaning this woman who had survived fire and threat and loss, who still found joy in creating beauty, who hummed her mother's songs while selecting fabric for a home they were building together in defiance of all attempts to separate them.

Casey leaned into his embrace, her attention still fixed on the practical considerations of desk organization, completely unaware of the small square of paper in his pocket or the plans it represented. Kirk pressed a kiss to her temple, inhaling the scent of her hair mingled with fresh paint and lemon oil and possibility, his secret a warmth between them, a promise not yet spoken but already taking shape in silver and sapphire and diamond, in past and present and future combined.

Chapter 39

Candlelight caught the deep ruby tones of the wine as Casey poured two glasses, the liquid flowing in a graceful arc that reflected floating points of flame. The dining room table—rescued from an antique store and lovingly refinished by Kirk's hands—gleamed beneath a proper tablecloth, white linen that contrasted with the dark wood. Steam rose in delicate spirals from the pasta Casey had prepared, the scent of garlic and fresh herbs filling the space they had transformed from empty house to sanctuary over these past months.

Kirk had positioned the speakers discreetly in the corner of the room, the plaintive notes of Ella Fitzgerald emerging at a volume that enveloped without overwhelming conversation. The music and candlelight transformed their ordinary Wednesday evening into something elevated—a celebration not of any particular occasion but of normalcy itself, of the quiet victory contained in an uninterrupted dinner.

"This is incredible," Kirk said after his first bite, the appreciation in his eyes genuine and immediate. The pasta was a new recipe Casey had been wanting to try, delicate handmade noodles tossed with roasted vegetables and a light cream sauce that carried hints of white wine and thyme.

Casey smiled, pleasure warming her cheeks. "Mrs. Winters lent me her pasta roller," she explained, twirling noodles around her fork with deliberate enjoyment. "It was my mother's favorite dish, according to my father. I found her recipe card in that box we salvaged from the garage."

Kirk reached across the table to squeeze her hand briefly, understanding the significance of this small reclamation of family history. His thumb traced gentle arcs across her knuckles, a gesture that had become their private language of connection through crisis and recovery.

"I've been thinking about the back garden," Casey said, releasing his hand to reach for her wine. "Spring is months away, but I'd like to plan a proper vegetable plot where that empty space is now. Maybe some raised beds that you could build?" She paused, a soft smile playing across her lips. "My father always grew tomatoes. Said store-bought ones were an insult to the entire concept of produce."

Kirk laughed, the sound warm and relaxed in a way that still struck Casey as miraculous after months when tension had been their constant companion. "We could put in an irrigation system," he suggested, his mind already mapping possibilities in the space she'd described. "Make it low-maintenance but productive. Tomatoes, peppers, maybe some herbs right outside the kitchen door."

The conversation flowed between them with comfortable ease, future plans unspooling like the gentle Fitzgerald melodies filling the room. They discussed the spring garden, a bathroom renovation Kirk had been sketching in his spare time, Casey's tentative steps toward reopening her photography business. Ordinary plans that felt extraordinary in their very mundanity—evidence of a life extending beyond mere survival.

"I've been contacted about a possible commission," Casey admitted, her eyes dropping to her plate as if the acknowledgment might somehow jinx the opportunity. "A local magazine wants regional landscape photography for their spring issue. Nothing huge, but it would be a starting point."

Kirk's expression brightened with genuine pleasure. "Casey, that's fantastic. Your landscapes were always your strongest work." His hand reached for hers again across the table, fingers interlacing with practiced familiarity. "Have you thought about when you might set up a darkroom here? The storage space off the laundry room would work with some ventilation adjustments."

Their fingers brushed, and they felt a spark – static from the dry air, but it jolted them nonetheless. The physical connection seemed to intensify as Kirk's thumb traced her wrist where her pulse beat steady beneath delicate skin. His eyes held hers across the candlelit space, something unspoken but significant passing between them.

"Actually," he began, voice dropping to a register that sent pleasant shivers along Casey's spine, "I was thinking we might take a weekend away soon. The lake house where my family used to go is available for rental, and the fall colors should be at their peak next weekend. It would be the perfect place for you to capture some landscapes for your portfolio."

Casey felt her heart quicken at the invitation—not from fear but from its opposite, the expanding sense of possibility that had been growing between them these past weeks of peace. Her lips parted to respond, eyes locked with Kirk's across the intimate space between them—

The lights went out.

Darkness descended with startling completeness, interrupted only by the gentle glow of candles they'd placed on the table and sideboard. The music cut off mid-note, leaving a sudden silence that seemed to press against Casey's eardrums with physical weight. Outside the dining room windows, the neighborhood had gone equally dark— no porch lights, no neighboring windows gleaming, just absolute blackness beyond the glass.

Casey's fork clattered against her plate, the sound unnaturally loud in the silence that followed the power failure. Her body tensed immediately, muscles coiling with the habitual readiness that weeks of apparent safety had dulled but not erased. Her eyes darted to the windows, suddenly transformed from architectural features to potential vulnerabilities, their glass surfaces now reflecting only candlelight and offering no visibility into what—or who—might be standing just beyond.

"It's okay," Kirk said immediately, his voice calm and steady, a counterpoint to the rapid acceleration of Casey's heartbeat. "Probably just a blown transformer or a fuse. The whole street is dark, by the look." His hand squeezed hers once more, the pressure deliberate and grounding. "I'll check the electrical panel in the basement, but I'm guessing this is neighborhood-wide."

Casey nodded, attempting to match his rational response, to suppress the immediate surge of adrenaline that flooded her system at this sudden disruption. "Of course," she said, her voice emerging higher than intended. "The candles give us plenty of light for now."

Kirk rose from his chair, moving around the table to press a kiss against her temple before retrieving his phone from the sideboard. He activated its flashlight feature, the beam cutting through darkness with reassuring technological effectiveness. "I'll be right back," he promised, his free hand squeezing her shoulder. "Just going to check the panel and look out the front window to see if other houses are affected."

Casey watched the beam of his flashlight recede through the dining room doorway, listened to his footsteps moving confidently across the darkened living room toward the basement door. The sound of the door opening carried clearly through the silent house, followed by his descending footsteps gradually fading as he moved down the stairs.

Alone in the dining room, Casey wrapped her arms around herself, fighting the irrational fear that threatened to climb her spine vertebra by vertebra. The candlelight that had seemed romantic minutes earlier now cast ominous shadows across the walls, the flames' gentle move-ment creating an illusion of shifting presences at the periphery of her vision. Outside, the darkness seemed to press against the windows like something tangible, some-thing with weight and intention.

It's just a power outage, she told herself firmly, reaching for her wineglass with fingers that trembled slightly. *Nothing to do with Layla. Nothing to do with anything except ordinary electrical problems.*

Yet even as she formed these rational thoughts, some deeper instinct raised the fine hairs along her arms, sent a prickling sensation across the back of her neck. The windows behind her—Kirk had installed security film on the glass, had ensured the locks were top quality, had positioned cameras at strategic angles—suddenly felt thin and insufficient. The sensation of being observed grew with each passing second, as if the darkness outside contained watching eyes, as if the very absence of light had somehow transformed into presence.

Casey turned slowly in her chair, peering into the dark-ness beyond the dining room windows. Candlelight reflected against the glass created ghostly duplicates of the flames, floating disembodied in the blackness outside.

Between these spectral lights, was that movement? A shifting shadow darker than the surrounding night? The suggestion of a face, pale and watching, framed by hair that caught what little ambient light penetrated the darkness?

Her hand reached automatically for her phone beside her plate, fingers fumbling to unlock the screen, to call Kirk's number despite knowing he was merely rooms away in the basement. The screen illuminated with painful brightness, momentarily blinding her to whatever might or might not be visible through the window beyond. As her vision adjusted to the sudden light, Casey found herself staring at the reflection of her own frightened face in the darkened glass, eyes wide with a fear she had believed—hoped—they were finally leaving behind.

Chapter 40

Casey lowered her phone slightly, the screen's harsh glow illuminating only her own reflection in the window glass. The dining room had become a cave of shadows beyond the candlelight's reach, the familiar corners of their home transformed into unknown territory. She strained to hear Kirk's movements in the basement, seeking reassurance in the ordinary sounds of his investigation, but the house had gone unnaturally silent—as if it were holding its breath, waiting.

Just a power outage, she repeated to herself, the mantra wearing thin with each passing second. Outside, rain had begun to fall, its gentle patter against the windows providing a rhythm that should have been soothing but instead heightened her unease. The candles flickered as if disturbed by a draft, their small flames bending in unison toward the dining room doorway.

Casey's fingers hovered over Kirk's contact on her phone screen. Calling him when he was just downstairs seemed ridiculous, the action of someone unable to manage normal household disruptions. Yet the prickling sensation along her spine refused to subside, a primitive warning system triggering without clear cause.

A soft creak sounded from the hallway—wood settling, perhaps, or the natural contraction of an old house as temperature dropped with the failing heat. Casey's head turned sharply toward the sound, eyes straining to penetrate the darkness beyond the candlelight's boundary. Another sound followed, too deliberate to be dismissed: the whisper of fabric against a doorframe, the controlled exhalation of breath that wasn't Kirk's familiar rhythm.

"Kirk?" Casey called, her voice emerging as a thin thread of sound. "Is the breaker box okay?"

No answer came from the basement. Instead, the distinct sound of a footstep on hardwood—lighter than Kirk's solid tread, carefully placed to minimize noise. Casey's thumb pressed Kirk's contact, the phone beginning its connecting tone that seemed obscenely loud in the tense silence. She rose halfway from her chair, muscles tensed for flight, eyes fixed on the dining room doorway where the darkness seemed to gather and solidify.

The call connected, Kirk's phone ringing distantly from the basement. In the same moment, a figure detached itself from the shadows, silhouetted against the deeper darkness of the hallway. The candlelight caught blonde hair first—once-elegant strands now tangled around a face that had haunted Casey's nightmares for months.

Layla.

She stood in the doorway, her posture suggesting casual confidence despite the wild disarray of her appearance. Designer clothing hung from her frame, wrinkled as if she'd been wearing it for days. Her makeup, once impeccable, had smudged into dark hollows beneath eyes that gleamed with feverish intensity in the candlelight. Most terrifying was the absolute stillness of her body—a predator's patience—contradicted by the slight tremor in the hand that emerged from shadow to reveal the gun's dull metal surface.

"Hang up," Layla said, her voice carrying the brittle edge of someone maintaining control through sheer force of will. "Now."

Casey's phone slipped from suddenly numb fingers, clattering against the table's surface. The call disconnected, cutting off Kirk's distant voicemail greeting mid-sentence. In the silence that followed, the candle flames steadied, casting Layla's shadow in grotesque elongation across the dining room floor.

"You've made yourself quite at home, haven't you?" Layla's lips curved in a smile that never reached her eyes as she stepped fully into the room. "Candlelight dinner. Wine. Music. Playing house with what's mine." She moved with the deliberate precision of someone who had rehearsed this moment, each step bringing her closer to where Casey remained half-risen from her chair, frozen between fight and flight.

"Layla, please—" Casey began, her mind racing through options, calculating distance to doors, to potential weapons, to her phone now lying screen-down on the table.

"Please what?" Layla interrupted, the gun rising to point directly at Casey's chest. "Please don't interrupt your perfect little life? Please don't remind him who he really belongs with?" Her free hand gestured sharply at the care-fully arranged table, the romantic setting now transformed into evidence for her perceived betrayal. "You think this is real? What you've built with him? It's counterfeit. Stolen. He was mine first."

The gun wavered slightly, matching the tremor in Layla's voice. Casey saw the dilation of her pupils, the slight sheen of perspiration across her forehead despite the room's growing chill. Not just anger but something else—

something unbalanced and unpredictable that made the weapon in her hand infinitely more dangerous.

"You and Kirk are divorced, Layla," Casey said, forcing calm into her voice. "You're violating a restraining order right now. The police—"

"The police!" Layla laughed, the sound high and broken. "By the time they respond to a power outage in this neighborhood, we'll be long past that mattering." She advanced another step, close enough now that Casey could smell her—expensive perfume overlaid with the sharper notes of unwashed skin and something chemical that might have been alcohol or something stronger. "Do you know how easy it was to cut your power? To disable those pathetic cameras Kirk installed? I've been watching you for weeks. Learning your patterns. Your weaknesses."

Casey's gaze darted to the security panel near the kitchen doorway, its display dark and lifeless. The system Kirk had installed with such care—the redundancies, the backup batteries—all neutralized by whoever had cut power to their entire street. Had Layla engineered even that, or merely seized the opportunity when it occurred naturally?

"You've ruined everything," Layla continued, gesturing with the gun in sweeping arcs that made Casey flinch with each pass. "We were rebuilding our relationship before you came along with your sad little story and your needy eyes. He felt sorry for you—that's all it ever was. Pity. Not love."

Casey saw mud on Layla's shoes, leaf fragments clinging to the hem of her once-immaculate trousers. Her hair hung damp from the rain, suggesting she'd been outside for hours, perhaps watching through windows as they prepared dinner, as they talked and laughed and moved through their home with the comfortable synchronicity of true partners.

"He was coming back to me," Layla insisted, her voice

dropping to a confidential whisper, as if sharing a secret Casey wasn't privy to. "We were working through our issues. And then you—" The gun steadied, pointing directly at Casey's heart, Layla's finger visibly tightening on the trigger. "You inserted yourself between us. Made him think he needed to protect you. Made yourself so pathetically vulnerable that he couldn't walk away."

The candlelight caught a tear tracking down Layla's cheek, incongruous against the hatred etched in every other feature. "I tried to warn you off. The messages. The little... reminders that you weren't welcome in his life." Her lips twisted in a smile that contained no humor, only a terrible pride. "But you just wouldn't listen."

Casey's mind flashed to the dead birds on their doorstep, the slashed tires, the desecrated grave—all the torments that had haunted them for months, now claimed in Layla's casual confession. The dispassionate calculation required to inflict such prolonged psychological torture contrasted sharply with the dishevelment before her, suggesting a mind unraveling even as it executed meticulous plans.

"What do you want, Layla?" Casey asked, struggling to keep her voice steady.

"What's rightfully mine," Layla answered, the gun unwavering now, her momentary emotional display replaced by cold determination. "Kirk will understand once you're gone. He'll remember what we had. What we were building before you confused him with your neediness." Her head tilted slightly, listening. "He's coming. I can hear him on the stairs."

Casey heard it too—the distant sound of the basement door opening, Kirk's familiar tread approaching the hallway. Layla stepped closer, pressing the gun's barrel directly against Casey's ribs, her breath hot against Casey's ear as she leaned in to whisper:

"Don't make a sound. Don't try to warn him. Or I'll make sure he watches you die before I explain everything to him." Layla's free hand gripped Casey's arm with bruising force, fingernails digging into flesh through the thin fabric of her sleeve. "It's time to fix what you broke."

The beam of Kirk's flashlight swept into the dining room, illuminating the scene in stark white light that turned the intimate dinner setting into a crime scene tableau. He froze in the doorway, the light catching Layla's blonde hair in a perverse halo before settling on the gun pressed against Casey's ribs. For one suspended moment, no one moved—three figures locked in a deadly diorama, the candles still flickering with indifferent serenity on the table between them.

"Layla." Kirk's voice emerged low and controlled, the flashlight beam unwavering despite the sudden tension evident in his posture. "Put the gun down. Whatever you're thinking, this isn't the way."

The flashlight's harsh illumination carved deep shadows beneath Layla's cheekbones, transforming her once-beautiful features into something mask-like and alien. Her eyes widened at the sound of his voice—a momentary flash of something like joy crossing her face before hardening into determination.

"You weren't supposed to be down there so long," she said, the words emerging with childlike petulance. "I had it all planned. We were going to talk, and you were going to understand."

Kirk took a single step forward, his movements deliberate and non-threatening, hands visible at his sides. The flashlight remained in his left hand, beam angled to illuminate the scene without blinding anyone. Casey recognized his stance—the marine's calculated approach to an armed threat, weight balanced on the balls of his feet, eyes continuously assessing angles and distances.

"I'm here now," he said, voice gentle as if soothing a frightened animal. "Let's talk. Just you and me. Let Casey go—she doesn't need to be part of this conversation."

Casey saw the exact moment when calculation replaced fear in Layla's eyes—a subtle shift that hardened her gaze and steadied her hand. Without warning, Layla pivoted, the gun swinging away from Casey toward Kirk with terrifying speed.

"No!" Casey lunged forward, but she was too late.

The gunshot cracked through the room with deafening finality, a sound so loud in the enclosed space that it seemed to compress the air itself. The muzzle flash briefly illuminated the room in stark detail—Layla's face contorted in a grimace, Casey's outstretched hand, Kirk's eyes widening in shock rather than fear.

Kirk's body jerked backward, the flashlight tumbling from his grip as his hands instinctively reached for his left thigh where the bullet had torn through denim and flesh. He staggered against the doorframe, one hand bracing against the wood to prevent himself from falling completely as the other pressed against the wound. Blood immediately seeped between his fingers, dark and viscous in the flashlight beam that now rolled crazily across the floor, illuminating random sections of the room in chaotic sweeps.

"Kirk!" Casey's scream tore from her throat as she moved toward him, but Layla's arm snaked around her waist, yanking her backward with surprising strength.

The gun, still warm from firing, pressed hard against Casey's ribs again. This time, Casey felt the difference in Layla's grip—the previous theatrical threatening replaced by desperate purpose, the metal barrel digging painfully between her ribs with bruising force.

"Don't move," Layla hissed, her breathing rapid and shallow against Casey's ear. "Don't fucking move."

Kirk had managed to remain upright, though his weight rested heavily against the doorframe. His face had gone pale, sweat beading along his hairline, but his eyes remained clear and focused. Even as one hand maintained pressure on the bleeding wound, he had already torn a strip of fabric from his shirt with the other, preparing to create a tourniquet with the calm efficiency of someone trained for battlefield injuries.

The scent of gunpowder hung acrid and sharp in the air, mixing with the metallic tang of blood that Casey could almost taste at the back of her throat. The candles continued to burn, their light now supplemented by the fallen flashlight's beam creating grotesque, moving shadows as it rolled slightly on the uneven floor.

"You shot me," Kirk said, his voice tight with pain but remarkably steady. He tied the makeshift tourniquet around his thigh, wincing as he pulled it tight above the wound. "That wasn't part of your plan, was it, Layla?"

Layla's body trembled against Casey's back, adrenaline or shock or both causing fine tremors that transmitted through the arm locked around Casey's waist. For a moment, Casey felt the gun's pressure lessen slightly as Layla processed what she had done, as if the reality of having shot Kirk had momentarily shocked even her.

"You moved," Layla said accusingly, her voice pitched higher than normal. "You startled me. This is your fault."

Kirk's eyes never left Layla's face, though Casey could see the strain it took for him to remain standing, to appear stronger than he was. Blood continued to seep around his fingers despite the tourniquet, dripping to pool on the hardwood floor in a slowly expanding circle. The flashlight's beam caught the liquid, turning it black with occasional ruby highlights when it captured the candlelight's reflection.

"Tell her to back up," Layla ordered, her grip on Casey

tightening again as she regained her composure. "Against the wall. Now."

Kirk shifted his weight, grimacing with the movement but complying slowly, hands raised to show compliance despite the one still pressed against his bleeding thigh. The flashlight's beam now illuminated him from below, casting strange shadows across his face that emphasized the tightness around his mouth, the paleness of his skin growing more pronounced as blood continued to leak between his fingers.

Casey felt a terrible calm descend over her as she watched Kirk struggle to remain upright, to appear less wounded than he was. Terror receded, replaced by a clarity that seemed to slow time around her. She noted details with preternatural sharpness—the exact pressure of the gun barrel against her fourth rib, the slight tremor in Layla's breathing pattern, the way Kirk's right foot was positioned to brace his weight while keeping pressure off the injured leg.

Kirk met Casey's eyes across the room, a silent communication passing between them. Despite the pain evident in the tight lines around his mouth, his gaze remained steady, conveying both reassurance and warning. *I'm okay. Stay calm. We'll get through this.* His marine training was evident in every controlled breath, every calculated movement that concealed the severity of his injury from Layla's increasingly unstable perception.

"This can still end well, Layla," Kirk said, his voice dropping to a gentler register despite the strain visible in his posture. "No one has to get hurt worse than this."

"End well?" Layla laughed, the sound brittle and dangerous. "It was supposed to end with her gone and you remembering what we had." The gun pressed harder into Casey's side, emotion making Layla's movements less controlled. "This wasn't how I planned it."

Casey cataloged their options with cold precision, her mind functioning with a clarity that seemed disconnected from the terror still pulsing beneath the surface of her thoughts. The dining room offered few advantages—too open, too far from potential weapons, the table between them and any exit. Kirk was losing blood, his complexion growing paler with each passing minute despite his efforts to appear unaffected. The flashlight on the floor continued to roll slightly, its beam creating unpredictable patterns of light and shadow that might either help or hinder any sudden movement.

"You didn't think this through," Casey said, surprised by the steadiness of her own voice. "The gunshot was loud. Neighbors will have heard it. Police will be on their way."

"Shut up," Layla snapped, the gun shifting position as her attention divided between Casey and Kirk. "Just shut up. I need to think."

In that brief moment of distraction, Casey saw Kirk shift his weight, testing his injured leg's capacity for sudden movement. Their eyes met again, and Casey read his intention with the clarity of someone who had learned to communicate with him through crisis after crisis. *Not yet. Wait for my signal.*

Blood continued to spread across the hardwood floor beneath Kirk's feet, the small pool expanding in careful increments that marked the passage of time more clearly than any clock. Casey felt Layla's breathing grow more erratic against her back, the fine tremors in her arm increasing as whatever chemical courage had propelled her through the home invasion began to war with the reality of what she had done—and what she still might do.

"You're bleeding a lot," Layla said to Kirk, her voice suddenly small, almost childlike in its confusion. "I didn't mean to... You moved so suddenly." The gun wavered slightly against Casey's ribs. "This wasn't supposed to happen."

"I know," Kirk replied, his voice gentle despite the pain evident in his tightly controlled breathing. "But it did, and now we need to figure out what happens next."

Casey felt the slight shift in Layla's posture—confusion temporarily displacing rage, uncertainty weakening her grip—and began her own careful mental preparation. She measured the distance to Kirk, calculated the arc needed to break free from Layla's hold, assessed whether Kirk could move quickly enough to help despite his injury. The flashlight's beam had nearly settled now, illuminating a section of floor between them like a spotlight awaiting performers in some terrible, unscripted drama that was far from over.

Chapter 41

Kirk's breathing had settled into a controlled rhythm, the marine's discipline asserting itself despite the blood still seeping around his fingers. His eyes never left Layla's face, his voice maintaining a deliberate calm that belied the gravity of his wound. "Think about what happens next, Layla," he said, each word measured and precise. "You've crossed a line here. But there's still a way out that doesn't make things worse."

The candlelight caught the sweat beading along his hairline, evidence of the effort it took to remain standing, to appear stronger than he was. His complexion had taken on a waxy pallor that frightened Casey more than the blood pooling beneath him, but his gaze remained sharp and focused, intent on maintaining Layla's attention.

"Worse?" Layla's laugh held a hysterical edge. "What could be worse than this? Than watching you bleed on the floor while you look at her the way you used to look at me?" The gun pressed harder against Casey's ribs, emotion making Layla's movements jerky and unpredictable. "There's no going back now."

"You don't want to do this," Kirk continued, his voice

dropping lower, gentler, as if they were having a private conversation despite the gun and the blood and Casey caught between them. "This isn't who you are, Layla. Not really."

Casey felt Layla stiffen against her back, sensed the conflicting impulses warring within her—the desire to be understood fighting against the rage that had driven her to such extremes.

"You don't know who I am anymore," Layla said, bitterness threading through her words. "You stopped seeing me the minute you met her. Started protecting her instead of remembering what we built together."

"Then help me understand," Kirk urged, wincing slightly as he shifted his weight to better brace himself against the doorframe. "Tell me what you've been thinking. What you've been feeling." His eyes flicked briefly to Casey, a silent message passing between them: *Keep her talking. Keep her focused on me.*

The strategy was clear—Kirk was drawing Layla's attention deliberately, giving Casey space to think, to plan, to look for an opening. The gun against her ribs had relaxed fractionally as Layla's focus shifted to Kirk, the barrel's pressure lessening as emotion overtook calculation in her grip.

"You want to know what I've been feeling?" Layla's voice rose, indignation sharpening each syllable. "Betrayed. Abandoned. Replaced." The words tumbled out with increasing speed, as if a dam had broken inside her. "I tried to warn her off. Little reminders that she didn't belong in your life."

Casey felt Layla's grip tighten momentarily, the gun digging painfully into her side again. "The flat tires were just the beginning," Layla continued, a perverse pride entering her voice. "Did you like the messages I painted on your car, Casey? The words I chose specially for you?"

The memory of those hateful slurs, dripping in red paint across her car's hood, made Casey's stomach clench. She remained silent, understanding that any response would only redirect Layla's unstable attention from Kirk back to her.

"You didn't take the hint," Layla said, her tone shifting to something almost conversational, as if discussing a minor social faux pas rather than acts of harassment and vandalism. "So I had to be more creative. The birds were a nice touch, don't you think? Symbolic. I left them while you were sleeping. Stood on your porch in the dark, imagining you inside, oblivious."

Kirk's gaze never wavered from Layla's face, his expression careful, controlled, even as the blood beneath him spread in a widening circle on the hardwood floor. "That was you on the porch that night," he said, not a question but a confirmation. "The security camera caught a figure, but the image was too grainy to identify."

Layla's laugh held a note of genuine amusement. "Your precious security systems. So predictable, Kirk. Always the protector, never understanding that some threats can't be kept out with cameras and motion sensors."

"Why Elliot's grave?" Kirk asked, the question gentle but direct, steering the conversation deliberately. "He never did anything to you."

The question struck a nerve. Casey felt Layla's body tense, her breathing quicken with renewed agitation. "Her father," she spat, contempt dripping from each syllable. "The great tragedy in her life. The foundation of your pathetic savior complex." The gun wavered slightly as Layla gestured with increasing animation. "She used him to manipulate you, don't you see? Poor little Casey, all alone after daddy died. Needing big strong Kirk to save her."

Kirk's jaw tightened, the only sign that Layla's words

had affected him. "You desecrated a dead man's grave," he said, voice still measured but harder now. "Spray-painted vile things on his headstone. Left mutilated animals on the grave of someone who never harmed you."

"He created her," Layla hissed, the words emerging with such venom that spittle flew from her lips, catching the candlelight in tiny droplets. "His pathetic, needy daughter who couldn't stand on her own. Who needed to steal someone else's husband because she couldn't find her own."

Casey remained perfectly still, using Layla's distraction to scan the room for any advantage. Her eyes caught a small, steady red light in the corner near the ceiling—the security camera Kirk had installed, its backup battery apparently still functioning despite the power outage. Hope flared briefly in her chest at the realization that everything happening was being recorded, evidence accumulating with each passing second of Layla's confessions.

"And the fire?" Kirk prompted, his voice strained now as the pain and blood loss began to overcome even his disciplined control. "Was that you too, Layla?"

Pride radiated from Layla, her posture straightening despite the gun that remained pressed against Casey's side. "My masterpiece," she said, satisfaction evident in every syllable. "Weeks of planning. Learning the neighborhood patterns. Finding the blind spots in your precious security setup." Her voice took on a dreamy quality, disturbing in its disconnect from the horror she described. "I used accelerant at multiple points. Waited until you were both gone —that weekend at the cabin. The perfect opportunity."

Casey's blood ran cold at the casual admission of such calculated destruction. Every photograph, every keepsake, every tangible connection to her father—deliberately erased by the woman who now held her at gunpoint, who spoke of arson with the self-satisfaction of an artist describing their finest work.

"You watched it burn," Casey said, the words escaping before she could stop them, the memory of seeing Layla at the periphery of the gathered crowd too vivid to contain.

"Of course I did," Layla replied, something like tenderness entering her voice. "It was beautiful. Cleansing. Removing every trace of your life so Kirk could remember what mattered." The gun shifted slightly as she leaned closer to Casey's ear, her voice dropping to a confidential whisper. "You were supposed to give up after that. To recognize you'd lost. To leave him."

Kirk's eyes met Casey's again over Layla's shoulder, a silent communication passing between them. His gaze flicked momentarily toward the security camera, confirming what Casey had already noticed—evidence being gathered, Layla's confessions preserved for police who would inevitably arrive. His hand pressed harder against his wound, but Casey could see the blood continuing to seep between his fingers, his complexion growing paler with each passing minute.

"But you didn't leave," Layla continued, anger resurging in her voice. "You just kept clinging to him. Making him think he needed to protect you." Her arm tightened around Casey's waist, the gun grinding painfully against her ribs. "You were supposed to leave him! He was supposed to come back to me!"

The shouted words echoed in the dining room, bouncing off walls and hardwood floors, hanging in the air like physical things. Kirk winced at the volume but kept his expression carefully neutral, his attention never wavering from Layla's increasingly volatile state.

"I never left you, Layla," he said quietly, the statement simple but devastating in its impact. "You betrayed our marriage. You were unfaithful. You left me before we were even really together."

The truth landed like a physical blow. Casey felt Layla's entire body jerk as if struck, the gun momentarily wavering in her grip as decades of self-deception collided with stark reality. In that moment of shock, Casey saw Kirk shift his weight subtly, testing his injured leg's capacity to support sudden movement despite the blood loss.

"Liar!" Layla's voice cracked on the word, tears suddenly streaming down her face, cutting tracks through the makeup smudged beneath her eyes. "I made one mistake! One! And you never forgave me!" Her arm gestured wildly as she spoke, the gun barrel lifting briefly from Casey's ribs as emotion overwhelmed tactical aware-ness. "Everything I did was for us, for our future, and you threw it away for her!"

Casey felt the subtle shift in Layla's stance, saw the momentary loosening of her grip as emotion overwhelmed calculation. Her muscles tensed in preparation, weight shifting incrementally to maximize leverage when the moment came. The security camera's red light blinked steadily in the corner, documenting every word, every confession that Layla seemed no longer capable of containing.

"I did everything for you, Kirk," Layla continued, her voice rising with each word, the gun waving in increasingly erratic patterns that betrayed her fracturing control. "I protected our marriage from everyone who tried to come between us. That promotion you didn't get? The colleague who suddenly backed off? The friends who stopped call-ing? All me, keeping you safe, keeping us together."

The extent of Layla's manipulation unfolded in horri-fying detail, years of sabotage and interference revealed in a torrent of justifications and accusations. Through it all,

Kirk maintained eye contact, his expression carefully neutral despite the shock Casey could see registered in the tightening around his eyes, the slight parting of his lips. He was learning, as she was, the true scope of Layla's obsession—how far back it reached, how deep it ran, how comprehensively it had warped her perception of reality.

"And then she came along," Layla spat, the gun gesturing briefly toward Casey before returning to its threatening position. "With her sad eyes and her needy existence. And you fell for it completely." Her breathing had become erratic, her body trembling with the force of emotions too powerful to contain. "She has to go, Kirk. It's the only way we can start over. The only way you'll remember what we had."

Casey felt the exact moment when Layla's grip began to slacken, when rage and justification superseded tactical awareness. The gun barrel lifted slightly from her ribs as Layla turned more fully toward Kirk, her need to make him understand overwhelming her initial purpose. Casey caught Kirk's gaze one last time, saw the almost imperceptible nod that signaled readiness despite his injury, the slight tensing of his muscles in preparation for whatever might come next.

The security camera continued its silent witness, red light steady in the darkness, capturing Layla's every confession, every threat, every revelation of months of calculated torment. Casey drew a deep breath, muscles coiling like springs as she prepared to seize the moment that was rapidly approaching—when Layla's emotional state would finally overwhelm her tactical awareness completely, creating the opening they needed to end this nightmare once and for all.

The moment crystallized with perfect clarity—Layla's gun hand drifting slightly away from Casey's body as she gestured emphatically toward Kirk, her balance shifting forward as emotion overwhelmed calculation, her attention fixed entirely on Kirk's face rather than the hostage in her grasp. Casey felt time compress into a single point of decision, her muscles humming with readiness beneath the artificial stillness she had maintained. There would be no second chance, no opportunity to reconsider once she committed to movement.

"Layla, we have never had anything near what Casey and I have." he said deadpan

"You never understood what I sacrificed for us," Layla was saying, her voice pitched high with desperation, the gun wavering in her agitated gestures. "Everything I did was—"

Casey moved.

Her elbow drove backward with every ounce of strength she possessed, finding the soft space between Layla's ribs with unerring accuracy. The impact forced air from Layla's lungs in a surprised whoosh, her body folding instinctively around the point of impact. In the same fluid motion, Casey twisted sharply to her right, breaking the loosened grip around her waist, her body rotating away from the gun that suddenly seemed to move in slow motion as Layla's finger reflexively tightened on the trigger.

Kirk lunged forward despite his injured leg, a strangled warning caught in his throat as he saw what was about to happen. Casey felt rather than saw Layla stumble backward from the force of the strike, her balance already compromised by emotion and the unexpected counterattack. The gun, no longer pressed against Casey's body, swung in a wild arc as Layla tried to regain both her breath and her aim.

The second gunshot exploded through the room with the same deafening crack as the first, but this time accompanied by Layla's shocked cry of pain. In her stumbling retreat, the gun had turned inward, the bullet tearing through the flesh of her own left shoulder rather than finding Casey. Blood bloomed immediately across Layla's designer blouse, her face contorting in disbelief as much as agony.

The gun clattered to the hardwood floor, falling from suddenly nerveless fingers as Layla's right hand instinctively moved to cover the wound. Her eyes widened in shock, looking down at her blood-soaked fingers as if unable to comprehend what had happened, that the weapon meant for Casey had turned against its wielder through the physics of struggle and unstable footing.

Despite his own injury, Kirk dragged himself forward in a desperate crawl, leaving a smeared trail of blood across the floor as he reached for the fallen weapon. His face had gone gray with pain and blood loss, sweat standing out in beads across his forehead, but his movements remained deliberate and focused. His hand closed around the gun's grip, sliding it across the floor and well beyond Layla's reach before collapsing back against the doorframe, his breath coming in shallow, controlled gasps.

"Kirk!" Casey scrambled to his side, her hands immediately pressing against the wound on his thigh where blood continued to seep through his makeshift tourniquet. The fabric beneath her fingers felt hot and slick, saturated beyond its capacity to absorb more. "Stay with me. Stay awake."

Across the room, Layla had crumpled to her knees, her injured shoulder hunched at an awkward angle as blood spread in an ever-widening stain across her once-immaculate blouse. Her face had lost all color except for two bright spots of hectic red high on her cheekbones, shock beginning to set in as she stared at Casey and Kirk with an expression of bewildered betrayal, as if they had somehow orchestrated her injury rather than acted in desperate self-defense.

"You shot me," she whispered, the words slurred slightly at the edges. "You made me shoot myself."

"Don't move," Kirk ordered, his voice weak but carrying the unmistakable authority of someone accustomed to command. The gun rested across his lap now, his hand steady despite everything he'd endured. "The police will be here soon. It's over, Layla."

The dining room had transformed into a grotesque battlefield—blood pooled beneath both Kirk and Layla, the fallen flashlight's beam creating harsh shadows that emphasized the carnage, candles still burning with incongruous serenity on the table that had been set for a romantic dinner only an hour earlier. The acrid smell of gunpowder hung in the air, mingling with the metallic tang of blood and the sharper scent of fear-sweat that clung to all three of them.

Casey tore a clean napkin from the table, folding it into a pad to press against Kirk's wound. Her hands were steady despite the adrenaline still coursing through her system, movements efficient as she applied pressure where it was most needed. "The tourniquet helped," she said, voice low and focused. "But you've lost a lot of blood."

"I've had worse," Kirk replied, the attempt at reassurance undermined by the pallor of his skin, the shallow quality of his breathing. His eyes remained fixed on Layla, tracking her every movement despite his weakened state. "Check her wound. Make sure she's not bleeding out."

Even now, even after everything, his instinct was to ensure no one died—not even the woman who had tormented them for months, who had burned Casey's home, who had held them at gunpoint and confessed to calculated destruction of their lives. Casey felt a surge of love so powerful it momentarily overwhelmed the fear and adrenaline, a recognition of the fundamental decency that defined him even in crisis.

"She's conscious and alert," Casey said, unwilling to leave his side even to check on their tormentor. "The shoulder wound is bleeding but not arterial." She could see that much from where she knelt—Layla's blood seeping rather than pulsing, the woman's posture pained but controlled enough to indicate no immediately life-threatening damage.

"They'll arrest me," she said, the words small and frightened, like a child suddenly understanding consequences too large to process. "They'll put me in prison."

"Yes," Casey confirmed, no satisfaction in her voice despite everything Layla had done. Only exhaustion remained, the bone-deep weariness that follows terror and violence. "For arson. For assault. For attempted murder."

"I didn't mean to shoot him," Layla insisted, the denial immediate and reflexive. "He moved. He startled me."

"It's all on camera," Kirk said, nodding toward the security device still recording in the corner, its red light blinking steadily. "Every confession. Every threat. Everything that happened here tonight."

Layla's gaze followed his, fixing on the small red light with dawning horror as she realized the extent of her exposure—not just for tonight's violence but for months of calculated torment, all admitted in her own voice, recorded for police and prosecutors to review in horrifying detail.

"It's over," Kirk said again, his hand finding Casey's where it continued to apply pressure to his wound. His fingers were cool against hers, his skin clammy with shock, but his grip remained surprisingly strong. "It's finally over."

Casey leaned forward, pressing her forehead briefly against his in a moment of connection that transcended the chaos surrounding them. The metallic scent of blood filled her nostrils, mingled with the lingering gunpowder and the familiar scent of Kirk's skin beneath it all. His breath came shallow but steady against her cheek, proof of continued life despite the blood that had soaked through napkin after napkin.

Chapter 42

The dining room had transformed into a battlefield tableau—chairs overturned from Casey's desperate lunge, wine pooling like blood across the white tablecloth, candles guttering in their holders as wax dripped onto fine china. Real blood mingled with the spilled wine, creating dark abstract patterns across the hardwood floor that gleamed wetly in the flashlight's erratic beam. The metallic scent of it hung in the air, mixing with the acrid burn of gunpowder that coated the back of Casey's throat with each shallow breath.

"Stay where you are," Kirk commanded, his voice strained but authoritative as he kept the gun trained on Layla. "Casey, your phone—"

Casey scrambled across the floor, retrieving her phone from where it had skittered beneath the table during the struggle. Her fingers left smudges of Kirk's blood on the screen as she dialed, the three simple digits requiring more concentration than she would have thought possible. The dispatcher's voice sounded distant and tinny through the speaker, somehow both too loud and too soft against the ragged breathing that filled the room.

"There's been a shooting," Casey said, her voice emerging with startling steadiness despite the tremor in her hands. "Two people injured. We need ambulances and police." She recited their address with mechanical precision, adding details about Kirk's leg wound and Layla's shoulder with the detached clarity of someone operating beyond normal emotional parameters.

Across the room, Kirk had torn his belt free from his pants loops, his movements deliberate despite the pallor of his skin. He wrapped the leather twice around his thigh above the bullet wound, pulling it tight with a sharp intake of breath before securing the makeshift tourniquet. Blood still seeped around his fingers where they pressed against the entry wound, but the heavy flow had slowed to a steady ooze.

"ETA five minutes," Casey reported, ending the call and moving back to Kirk's side. She pressed another clean napkin over his wound, her hands steadier than her racing heart would suggest possible.

Layla remained kneeling on the floor, her designer blouse ruined by an expanding bloom of blood, her face contorted in a grimace that transformed gradually from pain to fury as shock gave way to comprehension. "This is your fault," she spat, eyes fixed on Casey with undiluted hatred. "Everything was fine before you came along. We were working things out."

"Don't talk," Kirk ordered, the gun unwavering despite the tremor of exhaustion beginning to show in his arms.

Layla's laugh was high and brittle, closer to a sob than genuine amusement. "Look at you, bleeding all over her nice clean floors, still protecting her." She shifted slightly, wincing as the movement jostled her wounded shoulder. "What do you think happens now, Kirk? You think they arrest me and you two live happily ever after?" Her eyes narrowed, calculation replacing pain in their depths. "You shot me. Both of you. In my own home."

"Your home?" Casey couldn't contain her disbelief. "You broke in here. You cut our power. You held us at gunpoint."

Layla's smile was terrible in its sudden calmness, a predatory expression that seemed untethered from the blood soaking her clothing. "It's going to be your word against mine."

"No," Kirk said, nodding toward the corner of the room where the security camera's red light continued its steady blinking. "It's going to be your word against video evidence of every confession you made tonight."

For the first time, uncertainty flickered across Layla's features, her gaze darting to the camera and back to Kirk. "You're bluffing. The power's out."

"Battery backup," Kirk replied, his voice weakening but his eyes remaining clear. "Everything. Every word. Every threat. The moment you pressed that gun into Casey's side."

In the distance, sirens wailed—a thin, keening sound that gradually strengthened as emergency vehicles approached. The noise seemed to crystallize something in Layla, her posture straightening despite the pain evident in the tight lines around her mouth.

"You think I didn't plan for this?" she asked, her voice dropping to a confidential whisper. "You think I don't know how to manipulate evidence? Recordings can be edited, Kirk. Systems can be hacked." She leaned forward slightly, her expression suddenly earnest. "It doesn't have to be like this. We can fix this, together. Like we always did."

Casey watched this performance with horrified fascination, witnessing the transformation happening before her eyes—the unstable, vengeful woman of moments ago receding beneath a mask of wounded vulnerability that was all the more terrifying for its calculated precision.

The sirens grew louder, then abruptly cut off as vehicles pulled up outside their home. Red and blue emergency lights strobed through the windows, painting the dining room in alternating colors that lent an unreal quality to the blood and overturned furniture. Heavy footsteps approached the front door, followed by insistent knocking and calls of "Police! Open up!"

Casey moved toward the entrance, but Kirk's voice stopped her. "Don't turn your back on her," he warned, his words slurring slightly at the edges as blood loss took its toll. "Not for a second."

The front door burst open before Casey could respond, revealing Officer Rodriguez with weapon drawn, flanked by two uniformed officers whose flashlight beams cut through the darkness of the entryway.

"In here!" Casey called, raising empty hands to show compliance. "We're in the dining room!"

Rodriguez moved with practiced efficiency through the darkness, his officers flanking him as they entered the chaotic scene. Their flashlights swept across overturned furniture, spilled wine, the blood pooling beneath both Kirk and Layla, the gun still held in Kirk's increasingly unsteady grip.

"Drop the weapon, Mr. Manning," Rodriguez ordered, his own gun trained on Kirk with professional detachment.

Kirk complied immediately, placing the gun on the floor and sliding it toward Rodriguez with his foot. "She broke in," he said, words coming with visible effort now. "Cut the power. Had a gun. It's all on camera."

Before Rodriguez could respond, Layla's demeanor transformed completely. Her body seemed to crumple in on itself, her face crumpling into an expression of terror and relief so convincing that Casey felt a chill run down her spine despite witnessing the calculation behind it.

"Oh thank God you're here," Layla sobbed, tears suddenly streaming down her face. "They kidnapped me. Brought me here at gunpoint. I thought they were going to kill me." She reached toward the nearest officer with her uninjured arm, fingers grasping at empty air in a perfect mimicry of desperate relief. "Please help me. They're dangerous. They've been stalking me for months."

Rodriguez's expression remained neutral, though his eyes narrowed slightly as he took in the scene—the elegant dining setup now in ruins, the security camera blinking steadily in the corner, the blood trail showing Kirk had dragged himself across the floor rather than moving freely as an aggressor might.

"Check the security system," Kirk said, his breathing becoming more labored as adrenaline ebbed, leaving pain in its wake. "Northwest corner of the room. Battery backup. Everything's recorded."

Rodriguez nodded to his partner, a silent instruction that sent the younger officer moving toward the camera. "We'll need statements from everyone once medical attention has been provided," he said, his tone professionally neutral despite his obvious recognition of Kirk and Casey from their previous interactions. "Ambulances are right behind us."

Paramedics appeared in the doorway, their arrival bringing a sudden flurry of efficient activity to the chaotic scene. They moved first to Kirk, whose pallor and blood loss marked him as the more critical case despite Layla's dramatic pleas. As they worked, Rodriguez stepped closer to Casey, his voice low enough that only she could hear.

"We received multiple 911 calls from neighbors who heard gunshots," he said. "Does this connect to your previous complaints about Ms. Manning?"

Casey nodded, watching as paramedics established IVs for both Kirk and Layla, preparing them for transport. "She confessed to everything. The arson. The grave desecration. All of it." Her voice remained steady, the surreal calm that had carried her through the confrontation still holding her together despite the horror of what they'd experienced. "It's all on the security footage."

Rodriguez's partner approached, holding up a small memory card retrieved from the security camera. "Got it, sir. System was running the whole time."

For the first time since the officers had arrived, Casey felt something loosen in her chest—not relief, not yet, but the first tentative acceptance that the nightmare might truly be ending. As paramedics lifted Kirk onto a stretcher, his eyes found hers across the room, pain-dulled but determined, communicating without words what they both knew: the truth would be impossible to deny this time.

The ambulance interior closed around Casey like a mechanical womb—tight, urgent, pulsing with the rhythm of emergency lights and monitor beeps. The gurney occupied most of the narrow space, paramedics working with practiced efficiency on either side of Kirk's body as the vehicle lurched through night streets. Casey sat wedged in the corner, her hand clasping Kirk's with desperate pressure, as if their physical connection might somehow stem the blood loss that had left his skin ashen beneath the harsh overhead lights.

"BP's ninety over sixty and dropping," announced the paramedic nearest to Casey, a young man whose face remained impassive as he attached sensors to Kirk's chest. "IV's wide open. Let's get another liter running."

The ambulance smelled of antiseptic and sweat, the metallic undertone of blood persistent despite the paramedics' efforts to clean and dress Kirk's wound. Every bump in the road translated into a jarring motion that sent fresh waves of pain across Kirk's features, though he betrayed it only in the momentary tightening around his eyes, the subtle clench of his jaw.

"Bullet's still lodged in the thigh," the second paramedic explained, her gloved hands expertly unwrapping Kirk's makeshift tourniquet to assess the damage. "No exit wound. Doesn't appear to have hit the femoral artery, which is the only reason you're still conscious."

Kirk nodded, his grip on Casey's hand tightening briefly as the ambulance swerved around a corner, the siren wailing overhead in a continuous banshee cry that seemed to vibrate through Casey's very bones. "Marine Corps training," he explained to the paramedic, his voice strained but steady. "Had worse in Afghanistan."

Casey watched his face as he spoke, noting how he downplayed his injury with the same matter-of-fact tone he might use to describe a minor inconvenience. Even now, pale from blood loss and clearly in significant pain, he maintained the composed exterior that had carried them through months of threats and uncertainty.

"What happened back there?" asked the male paramedic, efficiently attaching a new blood pressure cuff while his partner adjusted the IV flow.

Kirk's eyes met Casey's briefly before he answered, a world of shared history passing between them in that brief contact. "Home invasion," he said simply. "Ex-wife broke in during dinner. Cut the power. Had a gun."

"Jesus," the paramedic muttered, shaking his head as he recorded Kirk's vitals. "The other patient—that was her?"

Casey nodded, suddenly aware of the bizarre reality that Layla was likely in another ambulance somewhere behind them, receiving treatment for the wound she'd accidentally inflicted upon herself while trying to hurt them. She glanced down at her own clothes, noticing for the first time the extent of blood staining her blouse and pants—Kirk's blood on her hands and sleeves, Layla's blood splattered across her side where she'd been standing when the second shot went off.

"She's in police custody," Kirk added, his words becoming slightly slurred at the edges. "Been stalking us. Burned down Casey's house. Desecrated her father's grave."

The female paramedic's eyes flicked briefly to Casey, professional neutrality unable to completely mask her shock. "Let's hold off on the full statement until the hospital," she suggested, checking the dressing on Kirk's wound which had already begun to seep red through the white gauze. "Need to conserve energy."

Casey turned toward the small window at the back of the ambulance, watching the city lights stream past in blurred ribbons of color. Each intersection they sped through brought a momentary flash of illumination inside the vehicle, painting Kirk's face in stark relief before returning it to the blue-tinged shadows created by the ambulance's interior lighting. The familiar architecture of their neighborhood gave way to commercial districts, then the medical complex, each transition marking their physical distance from the horror they'd left behind.

"Any allergies to medications?" the male paramedic asked, preparing a syringe with practiced movements.

"None," Kirk answered, his voice growing fainter as blood loss and the beginnings of shock continued to take their toll. "Type O positive. No pre-existing conditions."

Casey watched the rhythmic blips on the heart monitor, finding strange comfort in the steady pattern that confirmed Kirk's continued presence despite his weakening state. When the ambulance hit a pothole, she saw his jaw clench, a muscle twitching along its edge as he suppressed a groan. Her thumb traced soothing arcs across his knuckles, a silent acknowledgment of his pain and his strength in enduring it.

"We're three minutes out," the female paramedic announced, pressing a fresh dressing against Kirk's wound. "Trauma team's waiting. They'll take you straight to surgery to remove that bullet and repair any vascular damage."

Kirk nodded, his eyes finding Casey's again. Despite the clinical lights and the urgent beeping of monitors, despite the blood and pain and lingering fear, something passed between them in that look—a recognition that they had survived not just tonight's violence but months of calculated torment. They had emerged wounded but alive, together rather than separated as Layla had intended.

"You okay?" Kirk asked, the question emerging as little more than a whisper, his concern for her condition somehow taking precedence over his own critical injury.

Casey attempted a smile, though she suspected it emerged as more of a grimace. "I'm not the one with a bullet in my leg."

His fingers tightened around hers with surprising strength given his weakened state. "It's over," he said, the simple statement carrying layers of meaning only they could fully comprehend—not just tonight's confrontation but the months of hypervigilance, of security cameras and reinforced doors, of checking shadows and flinching at unexpected sounds.

"Almost there," the male paramedic announced as the ambulance slowed, then turned sharply. Through the small window, Casey could see the illuminated emergency entrance growing larger, medical personnel already gathering with a gurney and equipment.

The ambulance came to a stop with a gentle lurch, its siren cutting off mid-wail to leave an almost uncomfortable silence broken only by the steady beeping of Kirk's heart monitor. As the back doors swung open, revealing the harsh fluorescent lighting of the hospital entrance, Casey felt Kirk's fingers slip from hers, their connection temporarily severed as medical staff swarmed the vehicle.

"Thirty-two-year-old male, GSW to the right thigh, bullet retained, BP eighty-five over fifty, pulse one-twenty and thready," the female paramedic reported as they transferred Kirk to the waiting hospital gurney. "Two liters normal saline wide open, type O positive, no known allergies."

Casey followed the gurney's rapid progress through automatic doors, suddenly bereft without Kirk's hand in hers, without his steady presence beside her despite his injured state. The brightness of the emergency department assaulted her eyes after the dim interior of the ambulance, the bustle and noise overwhelming after the confined space they'd shared. She hurried to keep pace with the medical team, her blood-stained clothes drawing startled glances from waiting patients and staff alike.

As they approached the trauma bay doors, a nurse stepped into her path with gentle authority. "I'm sorry, but you'll need to wait here," she said, her eyes kind but firm. "They'll take good care of him."

Casey watched through the small window as Kirk disappeared behind a curtain, immediately surrounded by a team of medical professionals whose choreographed movements suggested both urgency and routine. The doors swung shut, leaving her alone in the corridor with the lingering scent of antiseptic and the echo of Kirk's words in her mind.

It's over.

The hospital room existed in a perpetual state of twilight—neither fully bright nor truly dim, the fluorescent panels overhead diffused by plastic covers that rendered everything in the same flat, shadowless illumination. Kirk lay propped against white pillows, his skin nearly matching their pallor save for the dark circles beneath his eyes. The bullet extraction had taken just over an hour, the surgeon emerging with professional satisfaction to tell Casey that no major vessels had been damaged, that Kirk had been "remarkably lucky, all things considered." Casey had wanted to explain that luck had nothing to do with it—that survival was what they did, what they had been doing for months now in the face of Layla's escalating threats—but she had merely nodded, accepting the assessment with the same numb detachment that had carried her through the endless hours of waiting.

Now she sat beside his bed, her body a catalog of accumulated stress—shoulders knotted with tension, eyes burning from exhaustion, clothes stiff with dried blood despite the scrub top a sympathetic nurse had offered to replace her ruined blouse. Her hair hung in limp strands around her face, occasionally falling forward when she leaned to check Kirk's dressing or adjust his blanket, these small ministrations allowing her hands to remain busy while her mind processed the night's events in fragmented flashes—the gun's muzzle pressed against her ribs, the deafening crack of the first shot, Kirk's blood pooling beneath him on their dining room floor.

Kirk stirred, his eyelids fluttering before opening fully to focus on Casey's face. The pain medication rendered his usual sharp gaze slightly unfocused, but the recognition in his eyes was immediate and warming.

"Hey," he said, voice rough from the intubation during surgery.

Casey's fingers found his, interlacing with careful pressure that acknowledged his weakened state without treating him as fragile. "Hey yourself. Doctor says no major vessel damage. Clean track through the muscle. You'll need physical therapy, but full recovery expected."

Kirk nodded, wincing slightly as he shifted position to better see her face. The movement disturbed the arrangement of monitoring wires and IV lines that tethered him to various machines, their steady electronic beeping creating a persistent backdrop to their conversation.

"Layla?" he asked, the single word carrying layers of inquiry.

"Separate floor. Under guard." Casey's thumb traced small circles on the back of his hand, the simple connection anchoring her to the present rather than the horror they'd escaped. "That's all they've told me so far."

A light knock interrupted them, drawing their attention to the doorway where a woman stood observing them with professional assessment. She was tall and angular, her dark suit wrinkle-free despite the late hour, her salt-and-pepper hair cut in a practical style that required minimal maintenance. She carried herself with the unmistakable bearing of law enforcement—alert, contained, constantly evaluating.

"Mr. Manning, Ms. Preston," she said, stepping into the room with economical movements. "Detective Simmons. I'm handling your case." She displayed her credentials briefly before tucking them back into an inside pocket. "I understand this isn't ideal timing, but I wanted to provide an update as soon as possible."

Casey straightened in her chair, her hand maintaining its connection with Kirk's as they both focused on the detective's carefully neutral expression.

"We've reviewed the security footage from your home," Simmons began, her voice low and professionally modulated. "Extremely comprehensive evidence. Ms. Manning's confessions regarding the arson, the grave desecration, and the various harassment incidents are all clearly captured, along with tonight's assault and attempted murder."

Kirk's fingers tightened around Casey's, the slight pressure communicating what words couldn't—vindication, relief, the first tentative acceptance that they might finally be believed without reservation.

"Additionally," Simmons continued, "the search warrant executed at Ms. Manning's residence has yielded substantial corroborating evidence. We found materials matching the accelerant used in the fire at your previous home, Ms. Preston. Photos of both of you taken without your knowledge. Documentation of your routines and schedules dating back months." She paused, her expression suggesting professional distaste for what she'd discovered. "There were also journals detailing her plans and justifications in considerable detail."

"What charges will she face?" Kirk asked, his voice stronger now despite the medication dulling his usual sharpness.

"Attempted murder. First-degree arson. Stalking. Breaking and entering. Criminal damage to property." Simmons listed each charge with precise emphasis. "The district attorney is reviewing additional potential charges related to the desecration of Mr. Preston's grave. Given the premeditated nature of her actions and the extensive documentation we've recovered, we anticipate no issues with prosecution."

Casey felt something loosen in her chest—not a sudden release but a gradual unwinding of tension that had become so constant she'd ceased to recognize it as abnormal. The careful fortifications she'd built around her emotions began to shift, hairline fractures appearing in walls constructed to withstand Layla's sustained assault on their peace and safety.

"She'll remain in custody?" she asked, the question carrying all her remaining fear that somehow, despite everything, Layla might still find a way to reach them.

"She's under guard at the hospital now, and will be

transferred to county detention once medically cleared," Simmons confirmed. "Given the severity of the charges and the clear flight risk, bail is unlikely to be granted." Her expression softened marginally, professional detachment giving way to genuine understanding. "She won't be able to reach either of you again."

Kirk's hand found Casey's again, his grip stronger than seemed possible given his weakened state. "Thank you," he said simply.

Simmons nodded, her assessment of them suggesting she recognized the weight of what they'd endured. "I'll need formal statements from both of you, but that can wait until tomorrow. For now, focus on recovery." She placed her card on the bedside table. "Call if you remember anything else. Otherwise, I'll be in touch tomorrow morning."

After the detective departed, silence settled over the room, broken only by the rhythmic beeping of monitors and the occasional squeak of rubber-soled shoes passing in the corridor outside. Casey stared at the closed door, the detective's words playing on repeat in her mind: She won't be able to reach either of you again.

"It's over," Kirk whispered, echoing his words from the ambulance ride, only now they carried the weight of official confirmation.

Casey felt the first tear track down her cheek before she realized she was crying, the emotion finally breaking through the shock that had sustained her through the violence and its aftermath. The tears came silently at first, then in shuddering waves that bent her forward until her forehead rested against their clasped hands on the edge of the hospital bed.

Kirk's free hand came to rest on the crown of her head, fingers threading gently through her tangled hair. "We made it," he said, his voice rough with medication and emotion. "We're still here."

Casey raised her head, tears tracking unimpeded down her face, to find Kirk's eyes—clear and focused despite the medication, holding her gaze with the same steady presence that had anchored her through months of escalating terror. Without speaking, she rose from the chair and perched carefully on the edge of the bed, mindful of his injury and the medical equipment surrounding him.

"I thought I might lose you," she admitted, the fear she'd suppressed during the crisis finally emerging in her trembling voice.

Kirk's hand rose to cup her cheek, his thumb gently brushing away tears with a tenderness that seemed impossible after the violence they'd witnessed. "Not a chance," he whispered. "We fought too hard for this."

Casey leaned forward until their foreheads touched, her tears dampening both their skin as they breathed the same air in the narrow space between them. Their fingers remained intertwined on the white hospital sheet, blood—both Kirk's and Layla's—still embedded in the creases of Casey's knuckles despite her attempts to scrub it away in the hospital bathroom.

Around them, the hospital continued its night rhythm—monitors beeping, nurses murmuring at their station down the hall, the pneumatic hiss of doors opening and closing as the business of healing proceeded with institutional regularity. Within their small sphere of connection, Casey and Kirk remained forehead to forehead, breath synchronizing unconsciously as the first genuine feelings of safety began to penetrate the armor they'd constructed around themselves.

"What happens now?" Casey asked, the question encompassing far more than their immediate future—hospital discharge, physical recovery, legal proceedings.

Kirk's thumb traced the curve of her cheekbone, his touch gentle but certain. "Now we live," he said simply. "Not just survive. Live."

The fluorescent lights continued their flat illumination, the antiseptic smell hung in the air, the beeping monitors created their persistent electronic rhythm—all the clinical realities of their environment unchanged. Yet as Casey's breathing aligned with Kirk's, as their foreheads remained pressed together in this most basic form of connection, the sterile hospital room seemed transformed into something else entirely: a beginning rather than an ending, a threshold rather than a conclusion, the first moment of their lives without Layla's shadow stretching behind them.

Chapter 43

Dr. Winters' office embraced them in muted tones—soft beige walls, plush armchairs in faded blue, and abstract watercolors that suggested rather than depicted landscapes. Casey sank into the cushions beside Kirk, their shoulders not quite touching as they faced the therapist across a low wooden coffee table. The space smelled faintly of lavender and old books, a carefully cultivated atmosphere of calm that stood in stark contrast to the turbulence they carried inside.

Three sessions in, and Casey still found herself cataloging escape routes whenever they entered a new space—the door behind them, the windows to their right, the distance between furniture pieces that might become obstacles. Beside her, Kirk shifted position, extending his injured leg with a barely perceptible wince. His jeans concealed the wound, but his fingers occasionally drifted to his thigh, applying gentle pressure as if reassuring himself of the healing process beneath the denim.

"How have the nightmares been this week, Casey?" Dr. Winters asked, her voice carrying the measured cadence of someone accustomed to creating safe spaces with words alone. She was a woman in her mid-fifties with silver-streaked hair pulled back into a practical knot, her eyes kind behind tortoiseshell glasses that slipped periodically down her nose.

Casey's hands found each other in her lap, fingers twisting together as if the physical connection might steady her voice. "They've changed," she admitted, gaze fixed on the geometric pattern of the area rug beneath their feet. "Before, I mostly dreamed about the fire—flames climbing the walls, photographs curling into ash." Her hands trembled slightly, and she pressed them more firmly together to still them. "Now I dream about the dining room. The candlelight. The gun."

Dr. Winters nodded, her pen making minimal notations on the pad balanced on her knee. "That's not uncommon. As one trauma begins to process, others can surface more prominently." Her eyes moved to Kirk, including him in the conversation circle. "And you? Any changes in your sleep patterns?"

Kirk's jaw tightened almost imperceptibly, the small movement betraying his discomfort with vulnerability despite three weeks of sessions. "Less sleep overall," he answered finally. "I wake up thinking I've heard something —a door, footsteps. The security system says everything's fine, but I still have to check." He paused, his hand finding the seam of his jeans along his wounded thigh, tracing the ridge where bullet had torn through muscle. "I keep reliving the moment she pulled the trigger, but in slow motion, understanding exactly what's happening but unable to move fast enough to stop it."

Casey turned slightly toward him, recognizing the admission for what it was—trust extended not just to Dr. Winters but to her, allowing her to see past the capable exterior he maintained even during physical therapy sessions where pain clearly radiated through his entire body.

"I'd like to suggest a technique that might help both of you," Dr. Winters said, setting her notepad aside and leaning forward slightly. "The mind processes trauma differently during sleep than in waking hours. Writing down your specific fears before bed can help externalize them, make them less likely to manifest in dreams." Her gaze moved between them thoughtfully. "But I'd suggest taking it a step further—share what you've written with each other. Not just the fears themselves, but why they frighten you."

The thought of articulating her nightmares—of putting words to the sensation of smoke filling her lungs or the precise pressure of metal against her ribs—made Casey's chest tighten. Her fingers gripped each other with renewed intensity.

"The sharing creates connection," Dr. Winters continued, noting Casey's response with attentive eyes. "It prevents isolation within trauma, which can be as damaging as the trauma itself."

Kirk's hand moved to cover both of Casey's, his palm warm against her knuckles, the simple gesture communicating solidarity more effectively than words. "We can try that," he said, answering for both of them with characteristic decisiveness.

Dr. Winters smiled slightly, the expression softening the professional detachment of her features. "Good. Now, Kirk, you mentioned something last week that I'd like to revisit—the sense of responsibility you feel for what happened."

Kirk's shoulders stiffened, his posture shifting subtly from open to guarded. His hand remained on Casey's, but she felt the change in his grip, the slight increase in pressure that suggested tension rather than comfort.

"I should have warned you about Layla sooner," he said, addressing Casey directly rather than filtering the words through Dr. Winters. His voice carried a rough edge of self-recrimination that scraped against Casey's heart. "I knew what she was capable of. I recognized the patterns, the escalation. I'd seen it before, with Charlotte." His eyes were dark with memory, with the weight of two women he'd failed to protect adequately—his sister and his ex-wife, both victims of violence he hadn't managed to prevent.

Dr. Winters remained silent, creating space for the conversation to unfold between them rather than through her professional interpretation. Casey turned her hands beneath Kirk's, reversing their positions so that she now held his between her palms.

"We survived because we were together," she said, the simple truth emerging with quiet certainty. "If you hadn't been there that night, if I'd been alone when she cut the power..." She let the sentence hang incomplete, the alternative too terrible to voice aloud. "You didn't bring danger into my life, Kirk. You brought protection, preparedness. The security system you installed captured everything she did. The evidence that's going to put her away for years."

His hands were warm between hers, steady despite the pain she knew still plagued him daily. Casey's eyes held his, refusing to allow him to look away or retreat behind the walls of guilt he'd been constructing since the shooting.

"Your responsibility began and ended with your own choices," she continued, echoing words Dr. Winters had offered in their previous session. "Layla's choices were never yours to control."

Kirk's breath released in a slow exhale, not acceptance but perhaps the beginning of it—a small crack in the foundation of guilt he'd built beneath their relationship. Dr. Winters watched them with the quiet attention of someone witnessing important work happening before her, making minimal notes that didn't intrude on the moment.

"I'd like to give you one more tool before we end today," she said eventually, setting her pen down with deliberate care. "A safe word. Something either of you can use when memories become overwhelming, when you need immediate support without having to explain why." Her eyes crinkled slightly at the corners. "Something that isn't related to the trauma, that won't trigger associations."

Casey and Kirk exchanged glances, a silent communication passing between them as they considered possibilities.

"Your homework this week," Dr. Winters said, "is to decide on that word together. And to begin the writing exercise we discussed—fears articulated and shared, rather than hidden and festering."

As the session concluded and they gathered their coats, Casey felt Kirk's hand settle briefly at the small of her back —not guiding, not controlling, just connecting. His leg trouble was evident in the careful way he descended the three steps from the office building to the parking lot, but he refused the arm she offered, determined to navigate the distance himself despite the slow healing of damaged muscle and tissue. Progress happened in small, measured steps—physical and emotional wounds closing at their own pace, new patterns of safety gradually replacing hypervigilance and fear.

In the car, before turning the key, Casey reached for Kirk's hand once more, her fingers sliding between his with the familiarity of repetition. "We're going to be okay," she said, not as question but as statement, as promise they would fulfill together, one therapy session, one nightmare, one shared fear at a time.

The community center smelled of industrial cleaner and burnt coffee, its fluorescent lights casting a stark glow over folding chairs arranged in an imperfect circle. Casey adjusted the information packets on the side table for the third time, aligning their edges with mechanical precision that betrayed her nervousness more clearly than her shaking hands. The poster she'd designed herself—"Dementia Caregivers Support Group, Wednesdays 7-8:30 PM"—hung slightly crooked on the wall behind her, the simple text failing to convey what she hoped to create in this anonymous beige room: the community she'd desperately needed during her father's decline.

Six weeks after Layla's attack, three weeks after her last hospital visit to check on Kirk's wound, Casey had made this decision—to be defined by what she could give rather than what had been taken from her. The therapist had encouraged it, called it "reclaiming narrative control." Kirk had simply nodded when she'd explained her plans, his eyes reflecting understanding without need for elaborate justification.

The door opened, admitting a middle-aged woman with prematurely gray hair pulled back in a messy ponytail. She clutched her purse with white-knuckled intensity, her gaze darting around the room before settling on Casey.

"Is this the caregiver group?" she asked, voice pitched slightly too high, the tone of someone perpetually braced for bad news.

Casey nodded, summoning a smile she hoped appeared more confident than she felt. "Yes, please come in. I'm Casey—I started the group. Coffee's on the side table."

The woman—Barbara, Casey would later learn—took a Styrofoam cup with trembling hands, filling it halfway as if afraid to commit to a full portion of anything. She chose a chair near the exit, perching on its edge rather than settling into it. Casey recognized the posture of someone accustomed to sudden departures, to life interrupted by unpredictable needs.

Over the next fifteen minutes, others arrived in similar states of tentative hope—an elderly man with weathered hands and a wedding band worn thin by decades; a young woman barely out of her twenties accompanied by her teenage brother, their matching eyes suggesting they shared both genetics and an unexpected burden; a professionally dressed man in his forties who kept checking his phone as if expecting urgent messages. Each entered with the same hesitant assessment of the space, the same careful selection of seats that revealed as much about their emotional state as the dark circles beneath their eyes.

At seven-oh-five, with seven attendees clutching coffee cups and expectations in equal measure, Casey cleared her throat. The sound emerged more tentative than she'd intended, and she swallowed hard, taking a deep breath before trying again.

"Thank you all for coming," she began, fingers gripping the edge of her chair until her knuckles whitened. "My name is Casey Preston. Until eighteen months ago, I was the primary caregiver for my father, who had early-onset dementia."

Her voice wavered slightly over the numbers—eighteen months marking not just her father's death but the beginning of what she now recognized as a period of suspended grief, as if she'd been holding her breath since he died, waiting for permission to exhale. Permission that Layla's violence and its aftermath had somehow, paradoxically, finally granted.

"I started this group because—" she paused, searching for words that wouldn't sound rehearsed despite having practiced them in front of her bathroom mirror for days. "Because I wish I'd had something like this when my journey began. Somewhere to bring the questions no one else understood, to share victories too small for others to recognize as significant."

Around the circle, heads nodded in silent recognition. Casey felt something loosen in her chest, courage flowing into the space created by their tacit understanding.

"In the beginning, I didn't even know what to ask, what to prepare for. By the end, I'd become an expert in a subject I never wanted to study, caring for someone who no longer recognized me most days." Her voice grew stronger with each sentence, steadied by purpose. "I thought I was alone, but none of us should have to face this journey without support."

The elderly man shifted in his chair, his wedding band catching the fluorescent light as he adjusted his position. "My Martha started hitting last week," he said, the words emerging with the hesitant quality of a confession. "Fifty-three years married, and she never so much as raised her voice before the disease." He extended his arm, sleeve pulling back to reveal a bracelet of bruises circling his wrist in distinct finger patterns. "Doctor says it's normal at this stage, but nothing about it feels normal."

Casey's eyes fixed on those bruises, so familiar in their placement and coloration—evidence of a reflexive grab, the kind her father had inflicted countless times as his condition worsened. Without thinking, she rose from her chair and crossed to the man, kneeling before him to examine his wrist more closely.

"These happen during transitions, don't they?" she asked gently. "When you're helping her move from one place to another, or trying to assist with personal care?"

The man's eyes widened, surprise giving way to naked relief at being so precisely understood. "Every time I try to help her into the bath," he confirmed. "She grabs hold like she's drowning, then starts swinging with her other hand."

Casey nodded, rising to address the entire group but

maintaining eye contact with the elderly man. "The fear response intensifies during transitions. Their brain perceives movement as threat when they can't process what's happening." She moved to the center of the circle, her earlier nervousness forgotten in the face of expertise earned through painful experience. "I developed some techniques that helped reduce these episodes with my father."

With deliberate movements, Casey demonstrated how to approach from the side rather than head-on, how to use a calm, low voice that avoided triggering startle responses, how gentle pressure on the upper arm could provide reassurance that words alone couldn't convey. Her body moved with practiced grace through motions she'd performed hundreds of times during her father's worst periods, muscle memory translating theory into practical application.

"The most important thing I learned," she continued, returning to her seat but leaning forward to maintain connection with her audience, "is that their reality is valid to them, even when it makes no sense to us. Arguing only escalates fear. Redirecting works better than correcting."

For the next hour, the conversation flowed with increasing ease—the young siblings described their mother's sudden personality changes, the professional man detailed his struggle to balance career and caring for his partner, Barbara tearfully recounted finding her husband wandering the neighborhood in his underwear. Each story emerged in the distinctive cadence of people unused to being heard, to having their daily battles acknowledged as significant.

Casey listened, offered targeted suggestions from her own experience, but more importantly, created space for connections to form between attendees. By the time she glanced at her watch and realized they'd exceeded their scheduled ending time by twenty minutes, the atmosphere had transformed—tension replaced by the particular solidarity of those who recognize their struggles in others.

"Same time next week?" she asked, gathering the mostly untouched information packets that had proven less necessary than simple human connection.

The elderly man approached as others gathered coats and exchanged phone numbers. He held himself with the careful dignity of his generation, but his eyes shone with unshed tears. "My daughter's been after me to find help," he said, extending his bruised wrist toward Casey in a gesture that seemed almost like benediction. "First sensible suggestion she's made in months." His weathered hand clasped hers briefly. "Thank you for making an old man feel less crazy."

One by one, the others said their goodbyes—some with embraces, others with grateful nods, all with promising to return. Casey stood in the emptying room, surrounded by discarded coffee cups and crumpled napkins, feeling the first stirrings of something she'd thought Layla's fire had destroyed permanently—purpose beyond survival, identity beyond victimhood, connection beyond shared trauma.

As she stacked the chairs against the wall, Casey imagined her father watching her with the clarity that had become increasingly rare in his final years. "Good job, little bear," she could almost hear him say, using the childhood nickname that had been among the last memories to fade from his deteriorating mind. For the first time in eighteen months, the imagined words brought more warmth than pain.

Chapter 44

Evidence of violence arranged in neat stacks across their kitchen table—such was the contradiction of their Thursday evening. Black-and-white security camera stills fanned out between coffee mugs, the frozen moments of Layla's intrusion captured in grainy but unmistakable detail. Casey's finger traced the edge of one photograph where the gun was clearly visible, its metal surface reflecting the dining room candlelight they'd arranged so carefully for a romantic evening that had dissolved into nightmare. Despite the central heating's steady thrum, she felt a persistent chill whenever her gaze lingered on these images, as if Layla's presence had been somehow captured within the glossy paper itself.

Three months had passed since the attack, yet these preparations for the upcoming trial forced them to relive every moment with clinical precision. The prosecution had sent over additional disclosure documents that morning— hundreds of pages of forensic reports, witness statements, and psychological evaluations that reduced their trauma to evidence markers and exhibit numbers.

Kirk shifted in his chair, a small grimace crossing his

features as he extended his injured leg beneath the table. Though the wound had closed, the damaged muscle still protested prolonged periods of sitting, the physical discomfort an unwelcome reminder of that night. Casey had noticed how he unconsciously rubbed the spot when deep in thought, fingers pressing through denim as if to reassure himself of the healing beneath.

"You've been sitting too long," she observed, rising from her chair without waiting for confirmation. In the living room, she retrieved the special cushion his physical therapist had recommended, its contoured design alleviating pressure on the damaged tissue.

Kirk accepted it with a nod of thanks, his discomfort evident in the tightness around his eyes despite his attempt to mask it. Casey's fingers lingered on his shoulder as she returned to her seat, the brief contact communicating what words often couldn't—recognition of pain endured, solidarity in its bearing.

"The prosecutor has scheduled our final prep meeting for Tuesday," Kirk said, his finger tapping a notation in the margin of their shared calendar. "They want to run through potential cross-examination scenarios, make sure we're prepared for whatever defense tactics might arise."

Casey nodded, sorting a stack of photographs into chronological order—the security footage showing Layla cutting the power, her approach to the front door, her movement through their darkened house with the gun extended before her. Each image documented another step in Layla's methodical invasion of their sanctuary, evidence that now seemed surreal in its detached perspective, as if she were viewing someone else's nightmare rather than her own.

"Do they have any updates on her plea strategy?" she asked, her voice containing the careful neutrality they'd both developed when discussing legal matters—a tone that created distance from the emotions still roiling beneath.

Before Kirk could answer, his phone vibrated against the table's surface, Detective Simmons' name appearing on the screen. He pressed the speaker button, positioning the phone between them.

"Mr. Manning, Ms. Preston," Simmons' voice emerged crisp and professional through the speaker. "I wanted to update you before you hear it elsewhere. The judge has confirmed the trial date for the seventeenth. Jury selection will begin that Monday."

Casey's fingers stilled on the photographs, her body tensing involuntarily. Three weeks. Three weeks until she would have to sit in the same room as Layla, feel those eyes on her again, retrieve memories she'd been working so hard to process and contain.

"Any other developments we should know about?" Kirk asked, his gaze fixed on Casey's face, reading her reaction with the attentiveness that had become second nature between them.

"The defense has been making noise about insufficient evidence for the arson charge," Simmons replied, paper rustling in the background suggesting she was consulting notes. "Standard procedural maneuvering. Nothing to be concerned about with the confession captured on your security system."

Casey closed her eyes briefly, the memory of Layla's voice intrusive and immediate: *My masterpiece. Weeks of planning.* The casual pride with which she'd claimed responsibility for destroying everything Casey had loved.

"We're also getting push-back on the psychological evaluation," Simmons continued. "They'll likely argue diminished capacity, attempt to position Ms. Manning's actions as resulting from a break with reality rather than premeditated."

Kirk's jaw tightened, the only visible sign of his response to this information. "They're going to paint her as a victim," he said, not a question but a resigned conclusion.

"They'll try," Simmons confirmed. "But the journal evidence works against that narrative. The detailing of plans over months, the calculated surveillance. It's difficult to argue temporary insanity when someone documents their intentions so thoroughly." Another pause, more papers shuffling. "I'll send the updated witness schedule tomorrow. The DA wants to prep both of you again next week."

After the call ended, silence settled between them, broken only by the refrigerator's mechanical hum and the occasional creak of the house settling around them. Casey stared at the scattered evidence without really seeing it, her mind racing ahead to the courtroom, to the moment she would have to face Layla again.

"I don't know if I can do it," she whispered finally, the admission emerging with difficulty. "Sit in that courtroom, feel her watching me, hear her voice..." She trailed off, fingers unconsciously moving to her side where the gun had pressed against her ribs, the phantom sensation some-times returning in moments of stress.

Kirk reached across the table, taking both her hands in his. His palms felt warm against her suddenly cold fingers, his grip firm but gentle. "We'll face her together," he said, voice low and steady. "Just like we've faced everything else."

His thumbs traced small circles against her wrists, finding the pulse points where fear had accelerated her heartbeat. She focused on the sensation, allowing it to anchor her to the present moment rather than the antici-pated future or the traumatic past.

"She wanted to separate us," Kirk continued, his eyes holding hers with unwavering intensity. "To destroy what we've built. Going through this trial together—that's the final proof that she failed."

Casey's fingers curled around his, drawing strength from the connection between them. "I keep thinking about what Dr. Winters said about narrative control," she said, her voice steadier now. "This is our chance to tell the truth, to put our version of events on record."

Kirk nodded, understanding immediately. "Not as victims," he said, "but as survivors."

The word hung between them, its power gradually dissipating the chill that had settled in Casey's chest at the thought of the approaching trial. She released his hands with a gentle squeeze, turning her attention back to the documents spread before them with renewed purpose.

"Let's organize our testimony chronologically," she suggested, reaching for a legal pad where she'd been making notes. "The prosecutor said juries respond best to clear, linear narratives."

They worked with quiet efficiency, sorting evidence into categories, annotating photographs with specific details they remembered, cross-referencing their individual accounts to ensure consistency without rehearsed perfection. Occasionally their hands would brush as they reached for the same document, each casual contact reinforcing the connection that bound them beyond physical touch.

"Do you remember what you said to me in the hospital?" Casey asked, looking up from a photograph of their dining room taken after the struggle, chairs overturned and blood staining the hardwood floor. "When I asked what happens now?"

Kirk's eyes softened, memory smoothing the tension from his features. "'Now we live,'" he quoted himself, the words carrying the weight of promise fulfilled in the months since. "Not just survive."

"That's what I want to communicate on the stand,"

Casey said, her finger tapping the legal pad where she'd written *key themes* at the top of a page. "That she tried to destroy us, but instead..." She paused, searching for words that wouldn't sound trite or rehearsed.

"Instead, she stripped away everything except what matters," Kirk finished for her, reaching across the table once more to intertwine his fingers with hers. "Us. This. What we're building together."

Outside their window, evening had deepened into night, the kitchen's warm light transforming the glass into a mirror that reflected their image back at them—heads bent toward each other over the evidence of violence, hands joined across maps of trauma, creating something new and lasting from what was meant to destroy them completely.

Chapter 45

Autumn had transformed the park into a study in impermanence—leaves in various stages of surrender clung to branches or carpeted the paths in russet and gold, their decay somehow more beautiful than their summer vitality had been. Casey tugged her burgundy scarf higher against the evening chill, her breath forming delicate clouds that dissolved almost immediately in the cooling air. Beside her, Kirk walked with the slight limp that had become part of him since Layla's bullet tore through muscle and sinew, leaving behind both physical scars and the invisible ones they'd spent months learning to carry together.

Six months had passed since the attack, two since Layla's conviction and sentencing. Twenty-five years without possibility of parole—a number that had seemed both impossibly long and somehow insufficient when the judge had pronounced it. They'd sat in the courtroom, fingers intertwined, as the woman who had tried to destroy them was led away in handcuffs, her blonde hair now grown out to reveal dark roots, her designer clothes replaced by standard-issue attire that hung loosely on her diminished frame. Neither of them had spoken as they left the courthouse that day, but something had shifted between them—a collective exhale, a burden set down, a future no longer shadowed by fear of her return.

"You're quiet tonight," Casey observed, glancing sideways at Kirk as they followed the winding path deeper into the park. Streetlights were beginning to flicker on around the perimeter as dusk gathered beneath the trees, but this inner section remained caught between day and night, details softening in the fading light.

Kirk's response was a distracted smile, his hand reaching unconsciously to check his jacket pocket for the third time since they'd left the car. His limp seemed more pronounced than usual, whether from the day's exertions or the dropping temperature that sometimes aggravated the healing tissue. Casey had noticed other signs of unusual tension throughout the evening—his careful attention to his appearance before they left home, the slight tremor in his hands as he'd locked the door behind them, the way his eyes kept scanning the path ahead as if searching for something specific.

"Just thinking," he replied finally, his breath visible in the cooling air. "About the first time we walked here."

From somewhere nearby, the tinny sound of a radio drifted through the gathering darkness—a news broadcaster discussing the upcoming election in the same measured tones Casey remembered from that first night, when Kirk had appeared beside her father like some manifestation of exactly what they'd needed. The coincidence sent a shiver along her spine that had nothing to do with the autumn chill.

"Feels like years ago," she said, though it had been less than two. "So much has happened."

Kirk nodded, his pace slowing as they approached a familiar bench positioned beside an ancient oak tree, its surface worn smooth by countless occupants before them. "This is where I was sitting," he said, indicating the bench with a nod. "With Max. He heard you before I did—started pulling on the leash, trying to get to your dad."

Casey's memory supplied the image with perfect clarity —her father wandering away from her in the dusky park while she frantically searched, Kirk emerging from the gathering darkness with a dog straining at its leash, the careful way he'd approached as if understanding immediately that something more complex than a simple walk had been interrupted.

"You didn't ask questions," she recalled, stopping beside the bench, its wooden slats silvered with age and weather. "You just helped. Talked to him like his confusion was the most normal thing in the world."

Kirk's hands slipped into his pockets, his weight shifting more heavily to his uninjured leg as he stood before her. His restlessness was becoming more pronounced, a nervous energy that seemed at odds with his usually controlled demeanor. He checked his watch, then glanced around the park as if confirming they were in exactly the right spot at precisely the right moment.

"What's going on with you tonight?" Casey asked, her head tilting slightly as she studied his face in the fading light. "You've been checking your pocket every five minutes since we left home."

Kirk took a deep breath, his exhalation visible as a small cloud that dispersed between them. "This place changed my life," he said, his voice dropping to a register that sent warmth curling through Casey's chest despite the evening chill. "I was just walking my dog, trying to outrun my own thoughts, and suddenly there you were—this woman with tired eyes and infinite patience, treating her father with such gentle dignity that it stopped me in my tracks, I had already known how beautiful you were, but that night—that night, the playful laugh and the smile when you saw that Elliot had remembered Max from my visits, that smile it undone me."

He took a step closer, close enough that she could see the amber flecks in his eyes catching the last of the daylight. "I didn't know that night that you'd become essential to me. That your courage would inspire mine. That together we'd face things neither of us could have imagined."

Something shifted in Casey's understanding, the pieces of the evening—Kirk's careful appearance, the deliberate walk to this specific location, his growing nervousness—suddenly arranging themselves into a pattern she recognized with a clarity that took her breath away.

"Kirk," she began, but he shook his head slightly, asking for silence with the gesture.

"Let me say this," he requested, his voice steady despite the emotion evident in his eyes. "I've been practicing for weeks."

With careful movements that betrayed the lingering discomfort of his injury, Kirk lowered himself to one knee before her. The position couldn't have been comfortable, his damaged leg protesting the uneven distribution of weight, but his face showed only determination as he reached into his pocket and withdrew a small velvet box.

"You saved me as much as I saved you," he said, his voice breaking slightly on the words. "Before you, I was just existing—going through motions, using work and routine to avoid facing what I'd lost. You showed me there was still purpose, still connection worth fighting for."

The box opened with a small creak of hinges to reveal a ring nestled against dark velvet—a sapphire surrounded by smaller diamonds, the stones catching the last rays of sunset with surprising brilliance.

"The sapphire was your mother's," Kirk explained, his gaze never leaving her face. "Your aunt gave it to me after your father's funeral, said you might want it someday. The diamonds were my grandmother's—she wore them for fifty-seven years of marriage. I wanted you to have something that brings our families together, that carries their love forward into ours."

Casey stared at the ring, its beauty heightened by the meaning behind each stone, by the thoughtfulness evident in how Kirk had combined their separate histories into something new and shared. Her vision blurred with tears that gathered but didn't fall, suspended like the moment itself between what had been and what might be.

"Will you marry me?" Kirk asked, the simple question carrying the weight of everything they'd survived together, everything they hoped to build.

Casey reached down, her hands grasping his forearms to pull him carefully to his feet. His injured leg had begun to tremble slightly from the unnatural position, a detail that only intensified the emotion tightening her throat. Even in this moment, she was mindful of his pain, unwilling to allow him to endure it longer than necessary even for this milestone.

"Yes," she whispered against his neck as she drew him into an embrace. The word seemed simultaneously too small and entirely sufficient, containing within its single syllable a universe of shared understanding—of promises they'd already demonstrated through crisis and recovery, of commitment proven long before this formal acknowlededgment.

Kirk's arms encircled her, one hand still holding the open ring box as the other pressed against the small of her back, drawing her closer until she could feel the steady rhythm of his heartbeat against her chest. Around them, the park's automated lighting system activated with soft mechanical clicks, illuminating the path with a gentle glow that pushed back the gathering darkness.

With slightly trembling fingers, Kirk slid the ring onto her hand, the metal cool against her skin but quickly warming, becoming part of her just as he had—gradually, inevitably, healing something she hadn't realized was broken until it no longer hurt.

"It fits perfectly," she said with wonder, turning her hand to watch how the stones caught and reflected the path lights now glowing around them.

"I had help," Kirk admitted with a small smile. "Your ring size was in the hospital admission forms. Detective Simmons may have helped me access that information— said it was the least she could do after everything we'd been through."

Casey laughed, the sound bright and unrestrained in the evening air—a sound that would have been impossible during those dark months of hypervigilance and healing, yet now emerged naturally, evidence of how far they'd traveled from trauma toward something resembling normalcy.

As they turned to continue their walk through the park, now transformed by gentle illumination that created pools of light along the winding path, Casey felt the weight of the ring on her finger—not a burden but an anchor, connecting her to this man who had stood beside her through fire and violence and recovery, who had seen her at her most broken and still found something worthy of forever.

The park lights gleamed against fallen leaves, trans-forming decay into temporary beauty, just as time and love had transformed their shared wounds into something that no longer defined them but simply marked the path they had traveled together. Ahead, the illuminated path beckoned toward home, toward a future neither could have imagined separately but now seemed not just possible but inevitable—a life built not in spite of what they had endured, but partly because of it, strengthened by fire rather than consumed.

Chapter 46

The garden transformed under late afternoon sunlight, its ordinary beauty elevated for this extraordinary day. White chairs formed neat rows across the lawn, their simplicity offset by cascades of flowers that seemed to spill from every surface. Lanterns hung suspended on nearly invisible wires, waiting for evening to reveal their soft glow. Casey watched from the window of their bedroom, her fingers absently touching the glass as if to confirm the reality of the scene below—this celebration of love that had survived fire and bullets and courtroom battles to reach this golden afternoon.

"Ready?" A soft voice came from behind her. Mrs. Winters—no longer just their therapist but now a friend—stood holding the simple bouquet of white roses and blue forget-me-nots that Casey had chosen for their colors rather than their meanings, though Kirk had later told her that forget-me-nots symbolized true love and memories, which seemed appropriate for a couple whose history was etched in both beauty and pain.

"I think I've been ready for this longer than I realized," Casey replied, turning from the window. Her dress was elegant in its simplicity—ivory silk that skimmed her body without clinging, its only adornment a delicate pattern of beading across the bodice that caught light like scattered stars. She had rejected anything with trains or veils, anything that might restrict movement or visibility—choices the therapist in Mrs. Winters had recognized without comment.

Casey's hair was swept up in an arrangement more artful than her usual messy bun, small white flowers tucked among the brown strands that had grown longer since the trial, since they'd begun building this new life from the ashes of the old. Her father's watch—one of the few items that had survived the fire, rescued from a drawer in the garage—circled her wrist, its worn leather strap and slightly scratched face more precious than any jewelry she might have chosen.

"He's waiting," Mrs. Winters said, handing her the bouquet. "And if the look on his face when he arrived is any indication, he's as ready as you are."

Downstairs, Kirk stood beneath an arch of white roses and greenery, his weight shifted subtly to favor his stronger leg. The physical therapist had promised the limp would eventually disappear entirely, but Casey had come to see it as part of him now—evidence of survival rather than injury, strength rather than weakness. His suit fit his broad shoulders perfectly, the dark fabric emphasizing the controlled power of his frame. His hands, capable of both building and protection, were clasped loosely before him, the only sign of nervousness the occasional adjustment of his cuffs.

The string quartet began a piece they had chosen together—nothing traditional, but a melody that had been playing the first time they'd danced in their kitchen, still surrounded by unpacked boxes but already feeling the potential of home in each other's arms. Kirk's gaze swept across the gathered guests before settling on the house, waiting for Casey's appearance with the steady patience that had carried them through hospital rooms and court-rooms and therapy sessions.

On one side of the aisle sat Casey's support group members, their faces familiar from weekly meetings where shared burdens had gradually transformed into shared celebrations. Barbara with her perpetually worried eyes now shining with unshed tears of joy; the elderly man whose bruised wrists had healed as his confidence in caring for his wife had grown; the siblings who had become like family to Casey, their matching eyes now crinkled with genuine happiness. On the opposite side, Kirk's marine buddies presented a study in contrasts—some in formal uniform, others in civilian suits that seemed to constrain their military bearing. They sat with the disciplined posture of men accustomed to standing at attention, but their expressions had softened for this occasion, pride evident in their watchful gazes.

The music shifted, a subtle change in tempo that signaled Casey's moment. She appeared in the doorway, silhouetted briefly against the house's interior light before stepping into the warm embrace of late afternoon sun. The garden's fragrances intensified around her—roses and jasmine and the earthy sweetness of grass freshly cut that morning. A breeze stirred the lanterns overhead, creating a gentle sway that mimicked the rhythm of her heartbeat.

Kirk's expression transformed at the sight of her— discipline melting into wonder, patience into barely contained joy. Their eyes locked across the distance that separated them, a private communication passing between them as it had in their darkest moments, now translated into this brightest of days. Casey's steps were unhurried, each one carrying her closer to the future they had fought so hard to secure.

When she reached him, their fingers brushed, and they felt a spark – static from the dry air, but it jolted them nonetheless. Something elemental passed between them with that simple contact—recognition, certainty, home.

The officiant's words faded into background noise as they faced each other, hands joined, the outside world receding until it seemed to exist only as context for their connection. When the moment came for vows, Kirk's voice emerged steady and sure, carrying clearly to even the last row of seats.

"Casey," he began, his thumb tracing small circles on her wrist where her father's watch rested. "You know I've never been a man of many words. But today, I need to tell you what you already know in your heart—that you saved me in ways I didn't know I needed saving. When we met, I was a man defined by what I'd lost. Now I'm defined by what I've found." His voice caught slightly, emotion briefly overcoming military discipline. "I promise to build with you. To protect without controlling. To remember that the strongest foundations are the ones that bend without breaking."

Casey's response came with quiet certainty, her voice soft but unwavering. "Kirk, I spent years learning how to care for others while forgetting how to be cared for myself. You taught me that strength includes allowing yourself to be supported." Her fingers tightened around his. "I promise to stand beside you in all seasons. To face whatever comes with the same courage we've found together. To remember that home isn't a place but a person—and you have become mine."

The exchange of rings carried particular significance for them both—the physical symbol of commitment sliding onto fingers that had gripped each other through terror and testimony, through healing and hope. Casey's ring—the sapphire from her mother surrounded by Kirk's grandmother's diamonds—caught the sunlight, sending fractured patterns of blue and white across their joined hands. When she placed his band on his finger, the simple platinum circle seemed to capture the last rays of afternoon sun, gleaming with promise.

"By the power vested in me," the officiant declared, her voice carrying across the garden where lanterns had begun to glow as shadows lengthened across the lawn, "I now pronounce you husband and wife."

Their kiss was gentle yet profound, a sealing of promises already tested by circumstances few marriages would ever face. Around them, applause erupted—marines with their disciplined enthusiasm, support group members with their emotional understanding, all witnesses to this culmination of a journey that had begun with chance and continued through choice.

As they turned to face their guests, hands still intertwined, Casey felt Kirk's steady presence beside her—the reliable strength that had never wavered, even when his body had been broken and bleeding on their dining room floor. The setting sun ignited the garden in golden light, transforming ordinary flowers into extraordinary beauty, much as adversity had transformed their connection into something rare and unbreakable.

The string quartet began again, a triumphant melody that carried them back down the aisle together, past smiling faces and murmured congratulations, toward the reception that awaited—the celebration of a union forged in fire, tested by violence, and emerged undefeated.

Golden hour descended like a benediction, transforming the garden into something from a half-remembered dream. Shadows stretched long across the grass while the lowering sun gilded every surface it touched—the rims of champagne flutes, the silk of Casey's dress, the medals on the uniforms of Kirk's marine brothers. One by one, the lanterns were lit, each small flame joining the collective glow that would illuminate their celebration long after sunset stole the natural light. The transition was seamless, day into evening, ceremony into celebration, as if the world itself understood the significance of what had transpired between them.

Tables draped in simple white cloths had appeared during the brief interlude when guests were enjoying champagne by the rose garden. Now they stood arranged in a semicircle around a wooden dance floor laid specially for the occasion, its surface gleaming with subtle amber reflections from the lanterns swaying overhead. The string quartet had relocated to a small raised platform, their formal attire blending with the shadows while their instruments caught occasional flares of golden light.

"Ladies and gentlemen," announced a friend of Kirk's from his contracting business, his voice carrying across the garden with unexpected grace, "please welcome for their first dance as husband and wife, Mr. and Mrs. Manning."

Casey's hand rested in the crook of Kirk's arm as he guided her to the center of the floor, his limp nearly imperceptible except to those who knew to look for it. The quartet began a melody that seemed to rise from the gathering dusk itself—not the song they'd originally chosen but one Kirk had substituted without telling her, a piece that had often played in her father's room during his better days.

"You remembered," she whispered as recognition dawned, her eyes filling with sudden brightness.

"Of course," Kirk answered, his hand settling at the small of her back with protective tenderness as he drew her into the dance. The pressure of his palm was warm through the silk of her dress, his touch both steadying and electrifying as they began to move together.

They had practiced this dance for weeks—not because

they needed the rehearsal but because they had discovered unexpected joy in the ritual of preparation, in the simple pleasure of moving in synchronicity after months when physical contact had been fraught with painful associations. Now Casey's fingers traced the lapel of Kirk's jacket with delicate precision, feeling the solid presence of him beneath the formal attire. His hair was military-short but softened for the occasion, his expressions no longer guarded by necessity but open in a way only she was privileged to witness fully.

Around the dance floor, their guests watched with varying degrees of understanding. The support group members exchanged glances laden with shared knowledge —they had seen Casey transform from a woman hollowed by grief and trauma to someone capable of this luminous joy. Barbara dabbed at her eyes with a corner of her napkin, while the elderly man nodded with the satisfied expression of someone witnessing the culmination of a story he had helped author in some small way.

On the opposite side, Kirk's marine brothers maintained more reserved expressions, though their eyes held approval that went beyond simple friendship. They had seen too many of their number destroyed by the things they'd endured, too many who had never found their way back to normalcy, much less happiness. Their subtle nods acknowledged what they recognized in Kirk's movements —a man who had refused to be defined by damage, who had rebuilt himself not despite his scars but with them integrated into his strength.

As the song's final notes hung suspended in the evening air, Kirk bent to press his forehead gently against Casey's, the gesture more intimate than their ceremony kiss had been. "From strangers to this," he murmured, the words meant for her alone. "Sometimes I still can't believe it."

"Remember that night you crashed through my door?"

Casey asked, her voice quietly playful as they moved toward a quieter corner of the reception, fingers intertwined with the ease of long practice. "All discipline and suspicion. I thought you might arrest me for breaking into my own house."

Kirk's laugh was soft, a sound she had worked so hard to draw from him in those early days when trust was still a fragile, tentative thing between them. "I remember thinking you were either a very young wife to an old man who liked his beers too much or the most patient child in the world."

They reached a small table tucked beneath a flowering tree where champagne flutes waited, bubbles rising through golden liquid like tiny ascending stars. Casey traced the condensation on her glass, watching as the moisture collected on her fingertip, the diamond and sapphire of her ring catching lantern light in miniature constellations.

"And now here we are," she said, gesturing with her free hand at the celebration unfolding around them. "Building something new from all the broken pieces."

Their moment of quiet reflection was interrupted by Barbara, who approached with uncharacteristic confidence, her perpetually worried expression replaced by genuine warmth. "You've given us all hope," she said simply, embracing Casey with surprising strength before turning to include Kirk in her gaze. "Not just for surviving the hard parts but for finding joy afterward."

As Barbara moved away, one of Kirk's marine brothers materialized beside them—a tall man with a scar running along his jawline and eyes that had seen too much to ever be truly carefree again. He embraced Kirk with the fierce, brief hug of men accustomed to expressing emotion through action rather than words.

"Never thought I'd see this day," he said, stepping back

to include Casey in his assessment. "After Charlotte, after Layl—" He stopped himself, awareness of the unspoken agreement not to mention certain names on this day flickering across his features. "After everything. You deserve this, both of you."

The reception flowed around them in waves of conversation and laughter, plates of carefully prepared food appearing and disappearing, champagne glasses refilled by attentive servers who moved through the gathering with practiced invisibility. The garden had fully transformed now, daylight completely surrendered to the gentle illumination of lanterns that swayed in the evening breeze, creating pools of warm light separated by intimate shadows.

When the music called them back to the dance floor, Casey and Kirk moved together with the effortless coordination of partners who had learned each other's rhythms through experience. His hand at her waist, her palm against his shoulder, they navigated the wooden surface with graceful economy of movement that accommodated his healing leg without drawing attention to it.

"Look at us," Casey murmured, genuine wonder in her voice. "Dancing at our wedding when there were times I wasn't sure we'd..."

Kirk's hand tightened briefly at her waist, understanding the unfinished sentence. "We made it," he said simply. "Every step of the way, we chose each other."

As the song ended, they remained for a moment in their intimate tableau, silhouettes merged into a single form within the lanterns' golden sphere of illumination. Around them, their guests continued their own celebrations—glasses raised in toasts, heads bent in conversation, occasional laughter rising above the quartet's melodies. The night air had cooled but remained gentle, carrying the mingled scents of flowers and candle wax and the subtle perfume Casey wore only on special occasions.

In that moment, surrounded by people who had witnessed their journey from different vantage points, Casey felt the full weight of what they had accomplished— not just surviving but thriving, not just escaping darkness but creating light. Kirk's eyes found hers across the small distance between them, his gaze reflecting the same recognition, the same quiet amazement at the ordinary miracle they had managed to build together.

The lanterns continued their gentle sway overhead, casting ever-changing patterns of light and shadow across the celebration—across faces that had known fear and pain but now shone with something stronger, more enduring. Champagne flutes clinked together in distant toasts, the crystalline sound carrying across the garden like transparent bells, heralding not an ending but a continuation, a story still being written with each breath, each touch, each moment claimed from a future that had once seemed uncertain but now stretched before them, luminous with possibility.

The vintage Mustang gleamed beneath strings of rice and trailing streamers, its polished surface reflecting the last golden light of day and the first silver glow of emerging stars. Someone—likely one of Kirk's marine brothers—had painted "Just Married" across the back window in white shoe polish, the letters slightly uneven as if executed with more enthusiasm than artistic precision. Casey laughed as Kirk held the passenger door for her, the formal gesture somehow both ridiculous and perfect as her wedding dress billowed briefly before settling into the leather seat that still carried the faint scent of the restoration work he'd completed just weeks before their wedding day.

Kirk slid behind the wheel with the easy grace that

belied his injury, his hand reaching automatically for hers once they were enclosed in the private bubble of the car's interior. The engine came to life with a purr that represented countless hours of his patient attention—rebuilding, restoring, transforming something abandoned into something valued. They pulled away from the curb to a chorus of cheers and well-wishes, Barbara's voice rising above the others with unexpected volume, the elderly man from Casey's support group raising his cane in salute as they passed.

The Mustang turned onto the winding country road that would carry them away from town, toward the small coastal cottage they'd rented for a week of solitude before returning to the life they'd built together. Dusk had fully descended now, the sky a watercolor wash of indigo and fading orange, the headlights cutting a pathway through gathering mist that rose from the fields on either side like soft exhalations from the cooling earth.

Inside the car, soft music played from the restored vintage radio—Ella Fitzgerald again, her voice a gentle accompaniment to the mechanical symphony of engine and wheels against asphalt. Casey slipped off her shoes, tucking her feet beneath her on the leather seat with the comfortable familiarity of someone at home in this space, in this moment, with this man. Her head found its natural resting place against Kirk's shoulder, their bodies aligning with practiced ease despite the formal attire they still wore.

Their fingers remained intertwined on the center console, the new weight of his wedding band occasionally catching against her engagement ring when he adjusted his grip, the metals creating a soft, musical chime that seemed to echo their unspoken contentment. Casey's hair had begun to escape its careful arrangement, dark strands falling around her face in a way that reminded Kirk of their earliest days together, when her messy bun had been a practical necessity rather than an occasionally indulged comfort.

"The cottage has a widow's walk," Casey said, breaking the comfortable silence as they left the last streetlights behind, the road now illuminated only by their headlamps and scattered stars emerging in the darkening sky. "The rental listing said you can see three lighthouses from it on clear nights. I thought maybe we could keep track, see if it's true."

Kirk smiled, the expression softening the disciplined lines of his face. "Detective Casey," he teased, squeezing her hand gently. "Always verifying claims, testing evidence."

"Occupational hazard," she replied, her free hand moving to trace the line of his jaw with affectionate familiarity. "Though I'm thinking of it more as vacation research. Lighthouse counting as extreme relaxation technique."

The road curved gently to the right, revealing a valley spread beneath them—scattered farmhouses with warm lights glowing from windows, patchwork fields divided by dark lines of trees, a small river catching moonlight in silver flashes where it emerged from shadow. The landscape unfurled before them like possibilities, like future pages yet to be written.

"What do you think about the Pacific Northwest next year?" Kirk asked, his voice carrying the easy tone of someone making plans without fear of interruption. "I've always wanted to see those old-growth forests. Maybe rent a cabin for a couple weeks, do some hiking if the leg's up for it."

Casey nodded against his shoulder, the simple domesticity of vacation planning casting its own special enchantment over the moment. "I could bring my cameras. Try to capture those massive trees." Her voice held the quiet wonder of someone still growing accustomed to making plans beyond mere survival, to imagining futures without constant vigilance.

Kirk glanced at her briefly, his eyes leaving the road for just a moment, drawn to her face as if to reassure himself of her presence, her reality beside him. Even after these months together, after building a home and planning a wedding and exchanging vows, he sometimes found himself caught by unexpected amazement that they had reached this point—that the woman whose father he had helped guide home that night in the park was now his wife, his partner, his future made tangible in the warm weight of her against his side.

"What?" Casey asked, catching his glance, her lips curving into a smile that held both question and understanding.

"Just..." He paused, searching for words adequate to contain his feeling. "Sometimes I still can't believe we made it here. That we found this after everything."

Her hand tightened around his, acknowledging the depth beneath his simple statement. "We built it," she corrected gently. "Stone by stone, day by day. Every time we chose to stay, to trust, to try again."

The road narrowed as it wound through a stretch of forest where trees pressed close on either side, their branches creating lacework patterns against the night sky when viewed through the windshield. Mist gathered in the hollows between trunks, transforming ordinary woodland into something ethereal and slightly otherworldly, as if they were driving through the physical manifestation of transition itself—the space between what had been and what would be.

"Remember that park bench?" Casey asked, her voice soft with memory. "Where you proposed? I drive by it sometimes on my way to the support group meetings. It always looks so ordinary to everyone else, just a bench under an oak tree. But to us..."

"...it's where everything changed," Kirk finished, the familiar completion of each other's thoughts no less magical for its frequency. "Like that street corner where we first talked about your father. Or the hospital room where you wouldn't leave even though I told you to go home and rest."

The forest thinned, opening into rolling countryside once more. The moon had fully risen now, casting the landscape in silver light that transformed familiar terrain into something new and unexplored. A deer stood frozen at the roadside, its eyes reflecting their headlights briefly before it bounded away into protective darkness, a fleeting reminder of the wild things that existed alongside their human journey.

They drove in comfortable silence, the Mustang's engine providing a steady backbeat to their quiet breathing, to the occasional soft observations they shared about particularly beautiful views or unusual cloud formations illuminated by moonlight. The road curved and dipped, carrying them steadily toward the coast where waves would provide tomorrow's soundtrack, where salt air would fill their lungs, where they would walk barefoot along shores far removed from the places that had witnessed their hardest moments.

Behind them, the road disappeared into darkness, the string of events that had led them to this moment receding like the landscape in their rearview mirror—still visible but increasingly distant, defined now by where it had led rather than by its individual hardships. Ahead, the road continued to unfurl, revealing itself only as far as their headlights reached, the remainder a promise rather than a certainty, an invitation to continue the journey they had begun together.

Eventually, the Mustang crested a final hill before beginning its descent toward the coast, its taillights forming two ruby points against the darkness. From a distance, the car might have appeared no different from any other traveling this remote stretch of road—just another vehicle carrying people toward a destination, unremarkable in its ordinary progress through the night. But inside that moving shell of metal and glass, inside that small traveling universe of two, existed a hard-won peace that transformed the simple act of driving into something profound —movement without fear, journey without vigilance, future without limitations.

The taillights grew smaller as the car rounded a bend in the road, then disappeared completely, leaving behind only the quiet countryside with its patient fields and silent trees, its mist-filled hollows and moonlit hills. The night continued its measured progression toward dawn, stars wheeled in their ancient patterns overhead, and somewhere beyond the next curve, beyond the visible stretch of road, Casey and Kirk drove on together—two people who had emerged from darkness with an unshakable certainty in the light they had found in each other.

Epilogue

luorescent light seared the small cell with unforgiving precision, the harsh glow leaving no corner untouched, no shadow in which to hide. Concrete walls, once institutional gray, had all but disappeared beneath a meticulously arranged collage of newspaper clippings, wedding announcements, and photographs—all featuring the same two faces. Some images had been carefully preserved, while others bore the violent evidence of Layla's rage: Casey's face obliterated by furious red pen strokes, Kirk's image circled and annotated with cramped handwriting that crawled across any available space. The effect was that of a deranged investigation board, connections mapped with strings and symbols that made sense only to their creator.

Layla sat at the metal table bolted to the floor, her posture unnaturally perfect despite the surroundings. Her once-elegant blonde hair hung in uneven strands around her face, the dark roots now several inches long, creating a two-toned effect that emphasized the contrast between who she had been and what she had become. She wore the standard-issue beige uniform with the same poise she had once brought to designer suits, as if the coarse fabric were silk against her skin. Only her hands betrayed her deterioration—fingernails once professionally manicured now bitten to the quick, skin around the cuticles torn and scabbed from nervous picking, blue and black ink embedded beneath what remained of the nails.

In front of her lay the latest edition of the local newspaper, delivered by a well-meaning but naive cousin who believed Layla's insistence that she needed to "stay connected to community happenings" as part of her rehabilitation. The newspaper had been carefully folded to display a photograph of Casey and Kirk at a charity event three weeks before their wedding. Casey wore a simple blue dress, her face turned toward Kirk with an expression of uncomplicated happiness that seemed to particularly offend Layla, whose scissors hovered over the image with predatory intent.

"Mine," she whispered, the word emerging as a hiss of air between barely parted lips as she began to cut around Kirk's figure with surgical precision. The scissors made a soft, rhythmic snicking sound as they separated his image from Casey's, the blade following the exact outline of his shoulder, his jaw, the crisp edge of his suit jacket. Her movements were unhurried, deliberate, practiced—this ritual clearly performed countless times before.

The cell door's small window darkened briefly as a guard passed by on routine patrol. Layla didn't look up, but her body tensed slightly, shoulders drawing back as if preparing for inspection. The guard's footsteps continued without pausing, and the tension gradually left her frame, allowing her to resume her task with the same meticulous attention.

"Making progress on your art project, Manning?" The guard's voice carried through the door on his return pass, the false cheerfulness barely masking his unease at what he could see of her wall collage.

Layla's expression remained unchanged, though her fingers tightened almost imperceptibly around the scissors. "Rehabilitation through creative expression," she replied, her voice carrying the cultured cadence that had once charmed juries before she'd become their subject. "Highly recommended by the prison psychologist."

The guard's footsteps receded, taking with them the brief interruption of her concentration. Layla returned to her cutting, separating Kirk's figure completely from the background before turning her attention to Casey's image. Here, her technique changed dramatically—no careful preservation but jagged, violent cuts that decapitated the photographed figure before shredding the remainder into confetti-sized pieces that gathered in a small pile at the corner of the table.

When Kirk's cut-out was complete, Layla rose from the table with balletic grace that seemed at odds with the prison setting. She moved to a section of wall where similar cut-outs had been arranged in neat rows, like paper dolls waiting to be dressed or positioned. Each represented Kirk at different events, in different clothing, but always with the same expression Layla had deemed worthy of preservation. She selected a spot, applied a small dot of contraband adhesive she'd charmed from an administrative assistant, and pressed the newest addition into place with reverent care.

"Twenty-three," she counted aloud, her finger hovering over each image as she tallied her collection. "Twenty-three times you've appeared in public without me. Twenty-three betrayals."

Her attention shifted to another section of wall where wedding announcements had been gathered—some official newspaper notices, others pieced together from social media printouts smuggled in by the same well-meaning cousin. These bore the most violent alterations: Casey's name crossed out with such force that the pen had torn through the paper in places, her face in accompanying photos scratched out with hundreds of tiny, furious pen strokes that had left permanent blue and black stains on Layla's fingertips.

She returned to the table where the pile of shredded Casey-confetti waited. With methodical precision, Layla gathered the tiny pieces into her palm, carried them to the small metal toilet in the corner, and flushed them away, watching with obvious satisfaction as the fragments swirled and disappeared. The ritual complete, she washed her hands with obsessive thoroughness, though the ink stains remained embedded in her skin like a negative of the violence she had inflicted on the images.

The fluorescent light overhead flickered—a brief stutter in the harsh illumination that cast momentary shadows across Layla's face, emphasizing the hollows beneath her cheekbones and the intensity of her unblinking stare. In that instant of altered lighting, the carefully maintained facade slipped, revealing the churning rage beneath the controlled exterior. Then the light stabilized, and so did her expression, the mask of composure sliding back into place with practiced ease.

She returned to the table where another newspaper waited, this one featuring a small announcement about an upcoming charity auction that would be attended by local business owners, including Kirk Manning of Manning Renovations. There was no photograph, just a brief mention of his name among dozens of others, yet Layla had circled it repeatedly, the pen pressing so hard it had embossed the words onto several pages beneath.

"Not over," she murmured, fingers tracing the embossed indentation of Kirk's name. "Never over."

Her nail caught on the edge of the paper, tearing a small, jagged opening that immediately captured her attention. She worked at it deliberately, widening the tear with the same methodical patience she brought to all her destructive activities. When the paper had been rendered into an irregular pattern of torn edges, she arranged the fragments into a new configuration atop the table—a broken mosaic that somehow formed the letters "C-A-S-E-Y" when viewed from her seated position.

With sudden violence that contradicted her previous control, Layla swept her arm across the table, scattering the arranged fragments onto the floor. Her breathing accelerated, shoulders rising and falling with the effort of containing whatever emotion had briefly overwhelmed her careful composure. Then, just as quickly, the storm passed. She knelt on the concrete floor, gathering each torn scrap with patient attention, reorganizing them into a new pattern that pleased her more.

The fluorescent light flickered again, longer this time, casting the cell into shadow before returning with its unforgiving glare. In that moment of darkness, Layla's lips curved into a smile that never reached her eyes—an expression of private satisfaction as she surveyed her kingdom of paper and obsession, of past glories and future reckonings, all cataloged and annotated with the precision of a mind that recognized no boundaries, acknowledged no defeat, accepted no ending that didn't align with her own carefully constructed narrative.

Also by Laci Mae Wyld

I Do…Hate You

In the heart of a city ruled by crime, survival means embracing the darkness within.

Meli Vasquez, a fierce and clever young woman, has long been confined to a life of servitude within the walls of a notorious crime family's stronghold. When the ruthless and feared Corbin Argyros, known as "The Executor " for his lethal efficiency, unexpectedly claims her as his bride to fulfill an ancient family decree, Meli is thrust into a world of opulence, danger, and power beyond her wildest dreams.

To Corbin, Meli's defiance is an intriguing challenge, her sharp wit a valuable asset. But to Meli, he is nothing more than a monstrous captor with haunted eyes and hands that stoke a dangerous fire within her. Their fiery clashes soon give way to forbidden passion, blurring the lines between loathing and longing.

In Corbin's brutal world, where compassion is weakness and love is a liability, Meli and Corbin realize that their unlikely partnership may be their most potent weapon yet. As betrayals mount, they must stand together against all who seek to tear them apart.

Content Warning: Contains explicit language and sexual scenes, including light choking, oral sex, manual stimulation, sexual violence, murder, kidnapping, torture, physical and sexual abuse, and themes of parental death.

Mark Me

35-year-old Mica Greer harbors a talent for intricate designs and a shield against emotional entanglements. But when Nyah Summers, with her haunting past and hidden pain, walks into his life, the flames of change flicker to life.

In a bold stand against Nyah's abusive past, Mica's defiance sets off a spark that neither of them can ignore. Drawn together by shared scars and unspoken desires, their connection deepens as they navigate the shadows of their histories.

Offering Nyah refuge within his sanctuary and a role in his creative world, Mica finds himself unraveling the layers of his own defenses. As their bond intensifies from friendship to something more, they must confront the looming threat of Nyah's vindictive ex-lover.

Experience a tale where redemption emerges from chaos, and the brightest flames are forged from the depths of darkness.

Good Girl To Goddess: Dancing with Desire

Cast aside on her birthday for not fitting in a mold, Elara James sheds her timid skin and overnight becomes a bold enchantress. Guided by her loyal confidante, she swaps modest clothing for daring outfits and quiet behavior for a fearless, take-no-prisoners attitude.

For six months, Elara indulges in fleeting affairs and casual flings, vowing to avoid emotional entanglements to protect her heart. One golden rule guides her nights: never stay until dawn.

Then enters Ryker Davis—confident, commanding, and undeniably captivating. In the heat of passion, he awakens her submission to his every whim. But beyond the bedroom, he reveals a tenderness that challenges the barriers guarding her heart.

As her former lover seeks reconciliation and her closest friend leaves town, Elara faces her deepest fears alone. Will she embrace the vulnerability that comes with true desire, or retreat into the safety of emotional distance?

Buried With You

A decade since the night they buried a dark secret in the shadows of the woods, Harper Lane is thrust back into the chilling embrace of Ash Pines, her reluctant return shrouded in impending doom. With her father's life waning and her past haunting her every step, she must face not only the memories she fled but also the man she once abandoned.

Eric Ransom harbours a festering wound from that fateful night —a wound reopened when Harper arrives at his garage, her presence reigniting a dangerous flame long thought extinguished. Amidst whispered threats in the dead of night and ominous messages left at the desolate grave site, they find themselves ensnared in a sinister game of retribution.

As they unravel a sinister web of deceit and betrayal, they realise their victim was no ordinary stranger. With allegiances crumbling and shadows closing in, Harper and Eric must unite to unmask their relentless stalker before they become mere pawns in a deadly chess match.

In a town where alliances shift like whispers in the wind and buried secrets claw their way to the surface, Harper and Eric are faced with an impossible choice—embrace the flames of passion reigniting between them as a beacon of hope or succumb to the darkness that threatens to consume them whole.

Amidst looming threats and betrayals lurking within familiar faces, Harper and Eric must navigate treacherous waters to uncover the truth behind their shared past. Will they emerge unscathed from the shadows of their sins, or will they be swallowed whole by the echoes of the grave that refuse to stay silent?

Vex Me: The Widow Queen

First Book in Vex Me Series: In a world teeming with danger and deceit, Kiera Moore's life takes a treacherous turn when her husband's death leaves her drowning in both grief and debt. Enter the enigmatic figure of Hudson Vex, a man shrouded in mystery and power, who offers Kiera a chilling deal she can't refuse - one night of boundless pleasure in exchange for erasing her late husband's debts and safeguarding her daughter.

As Kiera navigates the treacherous underworld of crime and betrayal, she embraces her transformation into the formidable "Widow Queen," unearthing her own strength and resilience. With Vex by her side, their twisted bond blurs the lines between love and manipulation as they build an empire fuelled by fear and respect.

But when her daughter falls prey to a ruthless cartel, Kiera must unleash her newfound ferocity to save her child, even if it means embracing the darkness within herself. As alliances shift and tensions rise, Kiera and Hudson find themselves entangled in a dangerous dance of passion and manipulation where love and vengeance blur into one.

Can Kiera navigate this treacherous path to reclaim her life, or will she succumb to the seductive allure of power and corruption? Prepare for a gripping tale of obsession, danger, and moral ambiguity in "The Widow Queen," where the line between hero and villain blurs beneath the intoxicating allure of the underworld's most dangerous game.

Fiery Fate (Vex Me: Book 2)

What began as a desperate bid for survival twists into a mesmerising metamorphosis. Immersed in Vex's clandestine world, Kiera unearths a seductive allure in the very violence that shattered her existence. Each brutal lesson and fiery encounter propels the grieving widow towards an unsettling evolution—a queen reborn amidst the chaos.

As an old nemesis resurfaces from Vex's past, Evelyn is forced to confront her escalating duality. With empires crumbling and blood staining her path, she teeters on the precipice between saviour and savage. Her daughter's fate hangs by a thread, and the boundaries between prey and predator blur into oblivion.

In this intoxicating thriller of power and fixation, Kiera will learn that certain debts demand payment in blood—and some reigns can only be forged in flames.

The Heir Will Not Turn (Vex Me: Book 3)

When Sophie is abducted by Falcom, the shadowy puppet masters steering global crime, Kiera and Hudson unleash their full power to rescue her. Their bond—fierce, primal, and unshakeable—drives a perilous chase across continents as they rally allies from the depths of their clandestine Shadow organisation. Clues lead through a web of brutal confrontations, where every victory costs blood and all threats point back to Sophie's fate.

As Falcom tightens its grip, the lovers push past fear toward a final, fortified base where extraction erupts into a desperate war. A heart-stopping gamble ends in a brutal revelation: Sophie's fate hinges on a line between loyalty and danger that could cost them everything. Love for Sophie becomes resolve as Kiera and Hudson vow to crush Falcom, harnessing every ally, every skill, every daring instinct to save the girl who has always been their guiding light—and to claim their own, hard-won happiness in the process.

Awakenings: Legacy of Shadow and Light

From the ashes of tragedy, her fate began to unfold...

Unveiled to a destiny she never fathomed, Suri Taylor emerges from the ruins of her shattered life. Taken captive by the malevolent Lyle Shawcross, she unearths a startling revelation: she is an immortal being bearing dormant powers, safeguarded to shield her from an age-old conflict.

Rescued by enigmatic saviours emanating celestial light, Suri is propelled into a clandestine realm where immortal entities coexist with mortals. As she hones her supernatural gifts under the tutelage of the guardian Drake Tudor, a rare bond sparks between them—a glimmering aura branding them as uniquely united.

Yet Lyle refuses to relinquish his coveted prize without a fight. Embracing her regal lineage and electing her allegiance in the immortal strife, adversaries encroach from every angle. With treachery lurking in the recesses and her extraordinary abilities still unfolding, Suri must discern whom to confide in while navigating her emotions for Drake and bearing the burden of her newfound legacy.

In a realm where luminescent gazes unveil true motives and everlasting existence exacts a dire toll, Suri's emergence may either reconcile ancient rifts or cast both worlds into eternal obscurity.

Content warning: Book contains scenes of sexual abuse and violence

Texting Fate

In the glittering world of Hollywood, he's the enigmatic heartthrob whose every move makes headlines. She's a refreshingly unfiltered woman who just wants to survive an epic Tinder disaster. But when a chance encounter lures them into a whirlwind of mistaken identities and electric chemistry, their lives are about to collide in the most unexpected way.

When a sassy text message meant for a Tinder date gone wrong lands in the hands of A-list actor Charlie Benton, it sparks a digital dance of wit and warmth with a mystery woman known only as Bee. Little do they know that amidst the virtual sparks lies the beginning of an uncharted romance that transcends fame and fortune.

As their playful banter deepens into a magnetic pull, Charlie and Bee find themselves entangled in a hot and steamy connection. But can they navigate the treacherous waters of stardom's spotlight without losing themselves in its glare? With paparazzi lurking and fans clamouring for every detail, their connection is put to the ultimate test.

Amidst the chaos of Hollywood whispers, Charlie and Bee search for authenticity in a world defined by illusions, and they must choose: embrace the unpredictable journey of love despite the odds or retreat to the safety of their separate worlds. Will their hearts find solace in each other's embrace, or will fame's cruel glare shatter their fairy tale dreams?

Haunted Memories of a Broken Girl

Haunted by visions of a violent crime, Kelly's melodic voice offers solace amidst the chaos of her past. Lawyer Michael Lawson is captivated by her singing, his own memories stirred by her haunting presence. When he rescues her from danger, a chilling realisation sets in - Kelly bears an uncanny resemblance to a long-lost childhood friend's deceased wife.

As their connection deepens, Kelly's fragmented past unravels.

Each revelation brings them closer to a shocking reality: Kelly is Helayna Cook, the missing daughter of arms tycoon Richard Cook.

Navigating the treacherous waters of truth and deception, their unexpected romance blossoms. But sinister forces lurk in the shadows, determined to keep buried what should never see the light of day. Threats loom and loyalties are tested as Kelly and Michael find themselves ensnared in a dangerous game of obsession and vengeance.

To survive, they must confront the ghosts of their pasts and unearth the secrets shrouding Kelly's mother's untimely demise - before a malevolent force silences them forever.

You Will See Me

When the lifeless body of Louise Mansfield is found on the bustling Chicago River Walk, seasoned detective Samuel Barron is thrust into a macabre investigation that unravels a web of dark secrets and chilling connections. Louise, daughter of the influential Senator James Mansfield, had been striving to escape her turbulent past as an exotic dancer and reconcile with her powerful father before she became the target of a sadistic killer's wrath.

As Samuel delves deeper into the case, he uncovers a sinister pattern linking Louise to five other tormented women, all tied to the charismatic senator. The discovery hints at a twisted serial killer fixated on beautiful victims associated with the prominent politician. The tension escalates when the primary suspect meets a gruesome demise in a manner mirroring the previous murders, pushing Samuel to confront a ruthless and calculating murderer with a disturbing agenda.

The investigation takes an alarming turn when someone they least expected, is driven by a volatile obsession to protect the Senator's reputation, escalating their vendetta by targeting the Mansfield family. In a heart-pounding race against time, Samuel finds himself in a deadly showdown with the killer, unearthing the depths of their malevolent rage. Their harrowing clash culminates in an intense confrontation of wits and wills, revealing a tapestry of hidden truths, envy, and intricate familial bonds.

Haunted by the specter of this chilling case and facing a new wave of brutal crimes, Samuel realises that history has a way of resurfacing when least expected. To thwart the cycle of violence and deceit, he must confront his own demons and navigate through treacherous waters to prevent further tragedy. In this riveting tale of suspense and redemption, Samuel grapples with the enduring legacy of past sins in his relentless quest for justice amid shadows that refuse to fade.

Betrayal of Blood

In a whirlwind of betrayal, Sarsha Mitchell's once-promising future implodes when she catches her fiancé, James, entangled with her very own sister. Reeling from the heartbreak, Sarsha takes flight, leaving the shards of her shattered dreams behind. With her picture-perfect life in ruins, she seeks solace on an impromptu getaway to their abandoned honeymoon destination with her loyal confidante, Jess.

From the sun-kissed shores of Perth to the dazzling allure of the Gold Coast, Sarsha attempts to outrun her anguish amidst carefree escapades and electrifying nights out. Just as the shadows of her past threaten to engulf her present, a chance encounter at a club propels Sarsha into an unexpected charade with a mysterious stranger named Riley.

As sparks ignite between Sarsha and Riley during their fabricated romance, healing begins to seep into her wounded soul. However, upon their return to Melbourne, old wounds are ripped open anew as James refuses to relinquish his hold on her heart while envious desires stir chaos within her own family.

Supported by Riley's unwavering presence and unwavering gallantry, Sarsha finds the courage to confront the toxicity suffusing her familial bonds. Yet just as hope blossoms for a brighter tomorrow, a cruel act of revenge orchestrated by James and Megan threatens to shatter everything they hold dear.

In a race against time and treachery, Sarsha stands vigil by Riley's bedside, clinging to hope amidst the turmoil. Together, they uncover the depths of deceit woven by those she once trusted most. With Riley's love paving the way towards redemption and renewal, Sarsha severs the ties that bind her to darkness and steps boldly into a future brimming with promise

From Hatred to Heat

When fate entwines two souls marked by enmity, can they rewrite their story before the darkness consumes them both?

Within the walls of Hidden Chapters Bookstore, Jetta Kinsley revels in the sanctuary she's created with her partner-in-crime, Brandi. Embracing the solitary bliss of her life, Jetta's world is upended when Brandi's heart veers off course to Owen Cooper, leading Jetta down a path she never wished to tread again. Standing before her is Ethan Cole, the ghost of her past whose cruel grip once shattered her world and scattered the pieces.

Bound by loyalty to their friends, Jetta and Ethan forge a fragile alliance. Buried beneath their animosity smolders an undeniable attraction, stirring emotions neither thought possible. When danger lurks in the shadows of a nightclub, Ethan emerges as Jetta's fierce protector, unveiling a side she never dared to imagine.

From Broken Roads to Healing Hearts

When Natalie's car breaks down on a secluded Tasmanian road, little does she know it will lead her to a ruggedly handsome stranger named Kai and his highland cow farm. Far from the city bustle, Natalie and Kai find themselves tangled in a web of past heartbreaks and hidden scars.

Amidst the picturesque countryside, they form an unexpected bond, discovering solace and passion in each other's arms under the starlit sky. But as secrets unravel and old flames flicker back to life, they must confront their demons together or risk losing everything they've found.

A Dark Descent into Chaos

Caught in the sinister grip of Sydney's underworld, at just 23, she becomes Diego's pawn, a mere facade of a girlfriend to the heartless crime lord. Imprisoned in opulence at Diego's Rose Bay mansion with no way out, Mila endures a life of torment and manipulation. Joe Sullivan is no stranger to shadows and secrets. With a steely gaze that betrays his hidden motives, he infiltrates Diego's inner circle on a covert mission for the authorities. Witnessing Diego's brutal nature firsthand, Joe risks everything to shield Mila from the savagery that lurks within their glamorous facade.

Bound by a dangerous game of deception and desire, Mila and Joe must join forces to uncover the truth amidst a battlefield of power-hungry adversaries. As their partnership deepens, forbidden attraction ignites, threatening to consume them both. With danger closing in and lives hanging in the balance, Joe is determined to protect Mila at any cost, even if it means forsaking everything he holds dear.

In a whirlwind of perilous escapades, high-stakes confrontations, Mila and Joe must navigate a treacherous path towards freedom and justice. But in a world where loyalties shift like shadows and love teeters on the edge of ruin, will they emerge unscathed from the dark empire they're entwined in?

Friend or Foe weaves a tale of passion, loyalty, and sacrifice against the backdrop of Sydney's underworld glamour and danger. In a battle where survival could mean surrendering to love's embrace, will Mila and Joe triumph over the sinister forces that seek to tear them apart?

After tragedy strands Casey and Kirk in separate worlds of longing, an unlikely encounter entwines them in a slow dance toward solace. Their love, a tender construction of two battered hearts, finds a tenuous rhythm until a specter from Kirk's past tears through the fragile façade. Obsessed and ruthless, Layla— his ex-wife—emerges from shadow with a plan to reclaim what she believes is hers. As threats mount, Casey and Kirk must fight not only for their love but for their lives, finding strength in their scars and shelter in each other.

Lucky in Love and Bullets

Kitty and Peter are madly in love. Kitty, a successful hair stylist, and Peter, a partner in a prestigious law firm, celebrate a lavish wedding in Hawaii. Their perfect day turns tragic when a gunman appears. Kitty is shot in the head. She regains consciousness in the hospital with no memory of Peter, though she recalls everything else. Kitty struggles to reconnect with Peter, who moves into a separate bedroom. Suspecting he is hiding something, she returns to work and meets Fynn, a handsome new client.

Kitty and Fynn find themselves in dangerous territory with criminals as they try to uncover the truth about why she was shot on her wedding day, with each discovery they see how involved Peter was with the wrong kind of people

Twisted Obsession

In the shadows of a seemingly perfect life, Anya Willows discovers that the past she thought she'd escaped is about to collide with her present in the most terrifying way imaginable. After years of uncertainty, Anya finally finds stability with a loving boyfriend, a loyal best friend, and a newfound relationship with the father she never knew. But when tragedy strikes and her world begins to crumble, Anya finds herself at the centre of a twisted web of obsession, deceit, and murder. As the body count rises and the lines between friend and foe blur, Anya must confront a darkness that has been stalking her since childhood. With each shocking revelation, she's forced to question everything and everyone she thought she knew. Who can she trust when the very foundations of her life prove to be built on lies? In this heart-pounding psychological thriller, love becomes a weapon, trust becomes a liability, and the truth becomes the most dangerous thing of all.